the split-

-ting storm
rene gut

teridge

Tyndale House Publishers, Inc.,
Carol Stream, Illinois

For Amy,
fellow storm chaser and weather watcher,
thanks for being my sis and my supporter.

And in memory of my good friend,
David Fox,
who faced the storms of life with dignity, courage, and faith.
The earth has lost, and heaven has gained,
an incredible man of God.

Visit Tyndale's exciting Web site at www.tyndale.com

TYNDALE is a registered trademark of Tyndale House Publishers, Inc.

Tyndale's quill logo is a trademark of Tyndale House Publishers, Inc.

The Splitting Storm

Copyright © 2004 by Rene Gutteridge. All rights reserved.

Cover face photograph copyright © Thinkstock LLC. All rights reserved.

Cover tornado photograph copyright © 2004 by A. T. Willet/Alamy. All rights reserved.

Designed by Dean H. Renninger

Edited by James H. Cain III

This novel is a work of fiction. Names, characters, places, and incidents are either the product of the author's imagination or are used fictitiously. Any resemblance to actual events, locales, organizations, or persons, living or dead, is entirely coincidental and beyond the intent of either the author or the publisher.

Library of Congress Cataloging-in-Publication Data

Gutteridge, Rene.
  The splitting storm / Rene Gutteridge.
   p. cm.
  ISBN-13: 978-0-8423-8602-9 (sc)
  ISBN-10: 0-8423-8602-5 (sc)
  I. Title.
  PS3557.U887S68 2004
  813'.6—dc22   2003028186

Printed in the United States of America

11 10 09 08 07 06 05
10   9   8   7   6   5   4

"I know there is a God. . . . I see the storm coming, and I know that His hand is in it. If He has a place and work for me—and I think He has—I believe I am ready."

Abraham Lincoln
(Joseph Gilbert Holland,
The Life of Abraham Lincoln)

prologue

baby child, come and eat. Come and eat your dinner."

His mother's sweet voice nearly drowned in the spectacular battle that played within the walls of his mind. He lifted his sword, fashioned from a paper towel roll and aluminum foil. The white light of his lamp glinted within its folds if he held it in just the right manner. Swiftly, he poked it into the dragon that stood before him. Its fiery breath poured into the tiles of the ceiling as it fell with a sickening groan onto the carpet near his bed.

"Ah-hah!" he yelled.

"Baby child, it is time to eat."

She called him again. He smiled. Now it was safe to eat. The dragon was dead. He planted his foot on top of its head, stabbing his sword into the beast one more time.

"This shall teach you a lesson!" he proclaimed. "You cannot defeat a warrior!"

The door to his room creaked open. He could hear the theme to *The Love Boat.* His mother's gentle face, round and soft, peered around the corner of the doorframe. "Baby child."

"Hi, Mama." He put his sword gently on his chest of drawers. She came to him and cupped her hands around his face.

"Aren't you hungry?"

"Yes."

Comic books cluttered the top of the tattered quilt she'd made him when he was born, before he could even sleep in a bed. He quickly tried to straighten them up. His mama never liked clutter. But she patted him on the back as she picked one up and flipped through it.

"You get your imagination from your grandmother, you know."

He nodded. She'd told him that before. He didn't understand it though. The only thing he'd ever seen his grandmother do was rock back and forth in a rocking chair. Sometimes she'd knit something. Mama said she was in an institution now, but he didn't know what that was or why she was there.

"I killed the dragon, Mama."

She dropped the comic book to the bed and looked at him. Her warm eyes dimmed slightly, but her small mouth kept a steady smile.

"You are a brave soul."

"It can't hurt us anymore. See? It's dead on the floor. Watch out. Don't step on it."

"Well, a warrior needs a good meal, then." She stepped on the dragon anyway as she went toward the door.

"Mama?"

"Yes, baby child?"

"He's not coming home for dinner tonight?"

She swallowed. Her face tightened into a grim expression. But those eyes of hers, ever kind, locked with his. He and his mama had this understanding—always had—since the first time they'd found they had a beast among them. It was six years ago, on his fourth birthday.

"No. Not tonight." She grinned at him. "I thought we'd eat by the TV, just you and me, find something good to watch. Maybe a game show." Her shadow swept across the bedroom floor as she walked away.

He carefully stepped around the dragon. This beast was dead for now. But sometimes it came back.

chapter one

the storm rotated so low to the ground it gave the impression of nearly engulfing the earth. The swirling clouds mesmerized, groaning and screaming in a way that made Mick Kline feel small. And that is why, over and over again, he found himself chasing them.

Behind him the other team, which included a meteorologist, an NOAA scientist, a cameraman, and one other storm chaser, were pointing at a map and shouting above the fierce winds, trying to locate a road nearby that would take them to the storm's south side. Meteorologist James Richards stood in front of the camera as his team reported on the location of the storm. Ryan the cameraman perfectly framed the scene, including a usually well-groomed Richards, whose hair was now flying over his head like a wind-whipped flag. It did confirm, however, that he did not wear a toupee.

The NOAA scientist shouted out wind speeds, now topping 100 miles an hour. Mick's heart thumped at an accelerated pace. This was a big one. The prime of spring had ushered in another monster.

Mick's friend and fellow storm chaser, Al, who had been standing near the NOAA van, with its fancy computers and large satellite dish, joined Mick at his truck. Mick and Al had been chasing the storm earlier, had met up with Richards' team, and had followed them to this location. Mick took his Canon 35mm camera and shot upward, capturing the sun peeking through the western edge of the storm, as if heaven were reminding those who cared that the chasm between itself and earth was delicate and mighty all at once.

"It's gonna drop," Al said. Heavy rain pelted the pavement for a few seconds, then let up.

"I'd say in about three minutes." Mick shot two more pictures, then quickly reloaded his camera.

"You okay?"

Mick glanced at Al. "What are you talking about?"

"You're usually right in the middle of the action over there." He nodded toward the truck, which sported the words National Oceanic and Atmospheric Administration on its side.

Mick shrugged. "I can only take so much of their fancy degrees and doctoral language. Sometimes I like to stand here and enjoy this for what it is."

Al looked back at the storm. The rotation had tightened, and phantomlike fingers were twirling to the earth and then disappearing. The storm teased them. But it gave its final warning: the sky was now green.

Richards called to them. "Come on! We got to get to the south. It's getting too close. Ryan found a road two miles west. Let's go!"

Mick looked at Al. "Ride with them, will you?"

"Why?" Rain splashed Al's dumbfounded face.

"I'll radio you guys, catch up with you, okay?"

"What are you doing, Mick?"

"Nothing. Just go with them, okay? I'll be fine."

When Al didn't move, Mick glanced around him to where Ryan stood staring at them. "Look, Al," he said softly. "I want to get some good pictures. Some really good ones. And you know those guys are going to freak out if you're not at the exact distance they say you should be according to their storm-chasing manual." He looked back at Ryan. "Ryan! Al's going to go with you. I'll catch up. I'm going to track the storm to the north."

"I'll stay with you," Al said, but his eyes showed fear.

"No. Go. I'll meet back up with you. *Go.*" Mick guided Al around and nudged him toward the van.

"Hurry up if you're coming!" Ryan said.

A sudden shower of hail encouraged Al to make up his mind quickly, and within seconds the others were all inside the van. The brake lights indicated something was being explained, and Mick saw Richards look out the back window with an irritated expression. But the van quickly took off over the next hill and out of sight.

Mick held up his arm, but the hail, not even the size of a penny, still bruised his skin. He'd seen it the size of softballs and had the auto insurance claim to prove it. There was no need to move his car to the side of the road; nobody would be coming. And he had learned that trees didn't do much to shield a car from rocks of ice.

Walking off the road, he picked a leafy tree to stand under, knowing it wouldn't help. Still, standing out in the open seemed even dumber. The storm crawled closer, moaning and creaking and issuing its threats with brilliant strikes of lightning. But Mick didn't budge.

Since he was a little boy he'd heard tornadoes called "the finger of God." Mick was about to find out how strong God's finger was.

Yelling into the wind was futile. His own voice would carry away so quickly it would sound like a whisper. Now was the time to match strength against fury.

The winds that would soon sweep the earth could snap his body like a twig, but he managed to hold his camera steady. He quickly wiped the lens, trying to get just one shot. Just one shot.

And now even the shelter of the tree couldn't protect him from the hail. His body stung as the hard ice sliced into him, chipping away at his dignity. He cowered, his arms over his head, unable to stand up. The entire sky roared above him, a dark hole like the open jaws of a lion. Mick's hands stung so badly the camera tumbled from them onto the ground.

And then it was quiet.

The hail stopped as if a celestial bucket had suddenly emptied. All around him, it looked as if he stood in the purest of snow.

But he knew that in the quiet of the storm lurked danger. He ran out from underneath the tree and looked up. There it was, right above him. The rotation was massive, more than a mile across. Gasping, he realized his camera was still underneath the tree.

Mick fell, then scrambled to his feet, trying to get a foothold on the ice underneath him. Any second a tornado was going to wind itself through the atmosphere and down to earth. And whatever was in its path would cease to exist. He imagined he might have the chance to get the closest picture of a tornado in history.

But he'd never stood under one before. He'd never seen up into the clouds like he was doing now. Breathlessly, he forced himself to take it all in. A supercell over a mile wide hovered above him, regarding him not in the least.

Even more awesome than the sight above him was the sound. Within the cell's walls was the ability to demolish anything on earth, yet the clouds now only whispered their power. Ghostly lights streamed through the mass. Mick fell to his knees.

And then it passed. Warm rain washed over him, melting the ice that had just moments before covered the ground. To the south and west he saw the hook. The twirling rope dipped to the ground with perfect elegance, as if it were engaged in a dance, and tore through the distant wheat fields.

Mick gasped for air. He felt the atmosphere's pressure change. He glanced over at the tree under which he had stood. His camera had settled against a dead limb.

Closing his eyes, he realized it wasn't his passion for storms and storm photography that had led him to stare down a supercell.

It had nothing to do with the storm in the sky.

Mick poured a stream of sugar into the flimsy paper cup that held six ounces of wretchedly stale coffee. His last dating casualty, Gwyn, used to complain how much he smelled like stale coffee every time they'd see each other. Of course, Gwyn had complained about a lot of things, ending what was, by his standards, a perfectly good relationship.

Stirring his coffee, he thought momentarily about calling her up, seeing what she was doing, how things had gone during the six months they'd been apart. But he disregarded the thought as quickly as he discarded his little plastic stirrer. If Gwyn had had an ounce of optimism in her, it might've worked. But in Mick's line of work, he needed something positive to come home to, and Gwyn just happened to see the whole world from the perspective of a glass half empty.

"You spent another night here."

Reggie Moore, Mick's partner, stood next to him at the watercooler, filling a jug to the rim. Everything about Reggie was round: his face, his body, his nose, his eyes, his fingers. The only thing that broke up the roundness was a killer grin that stretched from one ear to the other in a nearly straight line.

"I know these things. I am a detective after all," Reggie said and smirked. But then his eyes widened. "What happened to your face?"

"Nothing."

"And your arms!" Reggie gasped. "Did you get into a fight or something over the weekend? A church brawl?"

"Cute. Yes, I got into it with a little old lady who took my seat in the front pew."

"Looks to me like she wasn't too little," Reggie laughed.

"Actually, I was chasing a storm this weekend. Saw a good one, an F4, in east Texas. Got caught in some hail."

Reggie followed Mick to their desks and sat across from him, sipping his water and opening a plastic bagful of baby carrots.

Mick grimaced. "How can you eat those things?"

"I've lost ten pounds in ten days."

"I don't know anyone who has lost more pounds in less days than you and still weighs what they did when they started."

"I fluctuate. Middle-aged men tend to fluctuate. That's what the book says."

Mick shook his head and sipped his coffee. "So is this still part of the Slim-Fast plan?"

"That one worked for a while, but I guess you can't really drink ten of their shakes a day and expect to lose weight. If I hadn't stumbled upon the fudge flavor, I would've been okay, but that stuff was so good I just couldn't stop." He crunched on a carrot.

"So this is a new diet?"

"Guaranteed to work, too, or your money back." Reggie held up a carrot. "Eat fifty baby carrots a day, five cups of pineapple every other day. Broccoli and one bagel every morning for breakfast with a glass of orange juice, and then a sensible dinner. The great thing about this is you can have all the ice cream you want, but you have to eat it between eight and ten at night." Reggie answered Mick's skeptical expression with a shrug. "It has something to do with how all the foods interact with each other—speeds up your metabolism or something. Anyway, it seems to be working."

"How do you stomach broccoli for breakfast?"

"You get used to it after a while. The bagel helps."

"You know, you could just get out and jog a mile a day."

"I'd rather eat broccoli for breakfast." He closed his bag of carrots, but not before offering Mick one.

Mick waved it away. "I found another case last night. Out of Texas. Not far from where that sheriff was murdered. I'd say about two hundred miles."

"Where do you sleep, anyway? In your chair? On Tom's sofa? In the lounge?"

"Are you listening to me?"

"Just curious."

"I sleep on your desk."

Reggie chuckled.

"Anyway, this guy was a police officer. Leaves a party, gets killed in a parking garage. Pretty random, wouldn't you say? Happened almost two years ago."

Mick watched Reggie's gleeful eyes focus and turn serious. "Okay, yeah, it's random."

"I'm just connecting the dots. One by one." Mick leaned back in his chair, clasped his arms around the back of his head, and rocked back and forth, staring at the folder on his desk. "I think I may have enough to go talk to Tom again."

Reggie leaned forward. "Do you think that's a good idea?"

"Why wouldn't it be?"

"What'd he say last time?"

Mick paused, rocking in silence.

"I'll tell you what he said." Reggie stared hard at Mick. "He said he wasn't seeing a connection. He was worried you were putting evidence together to *prove* your theory, not collecting evidence to *form* a theory. He thought you might be acting on emotion rather than instinct. Oh yeah, and something about being obsessive. And that's your watered-down version. Who knows what he really said."

Mick blew a sigh through tense lips. "All right, fine. Tom's not yet on board with my theory. But I know I have something here." He grabbed a piece of paper out of the folder and held it up. "Look at this. Eight murders of men in law enforcement over the past two years. Five unsolved. And all within a radius of about 300 miles, in four states."

Reggie took the paper from him and looked it over skeptically.

"They were all murdered in different ways, and I know that doesn't fit into the profile of a serial killer necessarily, but the link here is that they're all law enforcement. And they were all killed for no apparent reason. You see where I'm coming from?"

Reggie handed the paper back to Mick. "When are you going to talk to Tom?"

"Maybe today."

Reggie's fingernails found their way to his mouth. "I don't think it's a good idea."

"Reggie, we've worked together enough years for me to know that when you start slurping on your fingers, you're hiding something. Now spit it out . . . and I'm not talking about that fingernail on your tongue."

"Okay, fine. There's talk."

"Talk. About what?"

"You." A worried expression flickered across Reggie's

face. "I'm not the only one worried, okay? Tom's saying things like 'losing it.' Not in a bad way."

"Is there a good way?"

"He means it in a . . . sympathetic way."

"I don't need sympathy."

"We're all a little worried, all right? It's only been three weeks, and when you should be with your parents and *Jenny,* for crying out loud, you're here combing the computers, sleeping on desks, putting together theories that don't have a lot of . . . credibility."

"If he hadn't been my brother, none of you would be thinking twice."

"If he hadn't been your brother, you'd be thinking twice about your theory. I'm not saying you're wrong. I'm just saying you don't have enough proof, definitely not enough to give us jurisdiction." Reggie looked at Mick carefully. "Or to start the hunt for a serial killer."

"I'm not a fool. I know what this means."

"I know," Reggie said softly.

A relieving silence settled between them, and Mick tried to let his anger go. He knew Reggie cared. His emotions were getting the best of him these days.

"Jenny needs you right now," Reggie said. "Your mom and dad need you. An entire police department is working this case. Your brother was one of their own. You don't think they're working this case like crazy?"

Mick lowered his gaze to the small pink piece of paper that held a handwritten message: *Please call Jenny. Calling to check on you. 11:46 a.m.* He slid the message underneath a folder, out of his sight. "They're looking at people who might've held a grudge against Aaron."

"And that's a good place to look. It makes sense." Reggie sipped his water. "What made you think the killer didn't know Aaron? I mean, in the beginning?"

9

"There were just a few things I could deduce." Mick studied the brown liquid in his cup. "Aaron was asleep in his bed. Shot in the head." Mick looked up. "If someone had had a grudge against him, they'd want him to know who was taking his life and why, if it is someone who knew Aaron. There would have been multiple shots fired, not one bullet in his head, execution-style. And you know as well as I do that this doesn't have the signature of a mob killing, which would be execution-style: two or more deliberate shots into his head. And as far as I know Aaron was not involved in the arrest of any gangsters anyway. It's not a robbery gone wrong. What idiot would break into a house with a police car sitting in the driveway? No, whoever it was staked out the house, maybe for as long as a month. He knew their schedules, knew Jenny would be leaving for work, knew Aaron would be asleep." Mick took a breath. "So I just started doing research, and I came across these other cases."

Reggie seemed to consider Mick's speculation while staring at his own desk, and Mick knew something was registering. Reggie then said, "You're doing okay, right? I mean, with Aaron's death?"

Mick studied the paper. "I think with these new cases I found, Tom might be convinced. I've got more to my theory now—more links, more connections."

Without looking up, Reggie said, "Just be careful."

"That's what you say when we go on a stakeout, not when I go in and talk to the boss."

"Just take it easy with him."

Mick's eyes narrowed as he studied Reggie. There was something more Reggie knew.

"Look, Mick, don't overstep your boundaries. Let Tom make a decision and be at peace with that." Reggie picked up a pencil and nibbled at the eraser like it was a carrot.

"That's what you're always talking about, right? Peace. Peace with God, peace that He's in control." He pointed upward with the pencil.

Mick smiled a little. "You were listening all this time."

"Well, you talk about it so much I feel like I'm in Sunday school."

"If you'd get to Sunday school more often, I wouldn't have to talk about it so much."

"Try taking your own advice, eh? As you like to put it, 'Give it to God.'"

Mick glanced up at his partner, then stared at the thick folder on his desk. A dose of his own medicine. Right now it tasted awfully bitter.

chapter two

What is it going to take with you, son?"
The tone in Tom Bixby's voice made every
other enthusiastic suggestion on the tip of
Mick's tongue fall flat. He had deliberated on Reggie's
advice for fifteen minutes, but not a second longer. Reggie
had excused himself from their area to take a bathroom
break, which, thanks to the eighty ounces of water he was
drinking, occurred every quarter of an hour. Mick had
walked to Tom's office, and it was one of those rare occa-
sions when Tom wasn't on the phone or chewing some
first-office agent to pieces behind a door that might as well
have been made of cardboard.

The word *son* made him cringe too. Tom was certainly
older than Mick—by nearly twenty years—but the reference
made Mick feel inferior, and there were times when Tom
could make him feel very much like an equal.

Tom seemed to sense Mick's anguish. The severity of
his brow line softened a bit, and after a few awkward
seconds he said, "Look, I talked to Brady from homicide
last night. I swear the guy hasn't slept in three weeks. He's
working round the clock on this, Mick. And I don't have to
tell you it's nothing short of a miracle that a state agency is
willingly giving us any information at all."

Mick clenched the folder in his hands. "But I'm telling

you, they're looking in the wrong places. It's not who they think it is."

"They don't know who it is, Mick, and neither do you. They're working up the forensics angle. They're talking to witnesses. They're making their suspect lists." Tom leaned forward on his desk, folding his long, lean fingers together with professionalism. He met Mick's eyes. "And what are you doing? You're naming your suspect and finding clues to match."

Mick wished he could name his suspect, but he knew what Tom meant. He didn't have a name, but he had a profile. He had a theory. And he had enough evidence, in his opinion, to start looking for—

"A serial killer's not impossible in this case, Mick. You and I know they aren't as rare as people think. You studied it some at the academy. But every moviegoer in America thinks there's a serial killer around every corner. You know better." He emphasized the last statement by raising his eyebrows high. Then he said, "I want you to know that I'm not under the impression you're caught up in some fantastical theory about who killed your brother."

Mick felt his chest tighten. "Then why are you sitting there with that smug expression on your face, as if I'm some bright-eyed, bushy-tailed rookie ready to snag my very own Hannibal Lecter? For crying out loud, Tom, do you think I'm just out for a little more excitement in my life?"

"Mick—"

"Don't *Mick* me, Tom! Don't cock your head to the side and narrow your eyes like you're concerned. And stop talking to Reggie! What, are you asking him to keep an eye on me? Make sure I haven't lost it?"

Tom's lips formed a straight line.

Mick stood, throwing the folder on the floor. The papers coasted across the tile.

The first sign of emotion from Tom was a careful swallow. "I asked Reggie to make sure you were doing okay. Out of concern. Nothing more, nothing less. Your brother was murdered in cold blood, and you barely tore yourself away from here to make it to the funeral."

Mick turned his back to Tom, and he felt an uncontrollable grimace seize his features. "You've always trusted me."

"I still trust you."

Mick turned. "You don't dig around for back-channel reports on someone you trust."

Tom's nostrils flared, and Mick knew he was crossing the line, as if he hadn't already crossed it. In the quasi-military setting of the FBI, sustaining the thin line of respect others have for you is as important as the job itself.

Tension forced out every word Tom spoke. "It's not your place to investigate a local murder. This is not even close to our jurisdiction, as you are well aware. Homicide is giving you a lot of leeway because it's your brother. But the more you interfere, the more they're going to cut you off. Brady already told me you'd been out questioning their witnesses."

"So? I'm capable."

"You're out of line. Don't you think there is enough stress between the bureau and every other law enforcement organization in the world without you waving the superiority flag?"

"I'm not doing that."

"Maybe not, but that's how they're taking it. You know our reputation, and this crusade of yours isn't helping. Now back off, and let these guys—who incidentally are really good at what they do—do their job."

Tom stood suddenly, felt his jacket pocket, his pants pocket, and then pulled out a drawer in his desk. He reached in the back and emerged with a lighter and a pack of cigarettes. "I need some air," he groaned, walking past Mick, stepping on the flood of papers on the floor.

"I thought you quit."

"I thought I had too." He glanced at Mick. "No thanks to you. You're the one harping on me to quit, and now you're the one driving me back to it."

Mick was left standing alone in Tom's office. He bent down and scraped the papers off the floor. His head pounded with the despair that he'd tried so hard to disregard. But crouched down in the middle of his boss's office, combing through papers that seemed senseless to everyone but him, Mick had to admit, at least momentarily, that perhaps he *was* losing it. A heavy lump swelled in his throat as he examined his latest find, a case he had thought Tom would acknowledge at least as being more than a coincidence.

Mick sat quietly for a while in the middle of the floor of Tom's office. Thankfully, Tom had shut the door on his way out, so Mick had a few moments of peace and solitude. His knees were pulled to his chest, his arms wrapped around each leg, his chin resting on the tops of his knee-caps. He took a few deep breaths, trying to sort out his lost cause.

Everyone was losing faith in him. They thought he was on an emotional whim. Was he? His forehead now rested on his knees, and he stared down at the cold gray tile beneath him. His eyes caught the top of one of the newspaper clippings he'd pulled.

He read the victim's name: Bradley James Seacrest. From Waco.

Bradley James Seacrest, 28, an eight-year veteran of the Waco Police Department, was found dead at Lake Whitney on Saturday. Investigators declined to comment, but sources close to the investigation say Seacrest died after a single gunshot to the head. Waco police are actively seeking witnesses and information.

His mind ran down the mental list he'd made of the other victims. He couldn't shake the feeling that he was on the right track because it wasn't his mind talking to him. It was his gut.

He scooped up the rest of the papers and shoved them in his folder. Hurrying out of Tom's office, he ran right into Lois, a middle-aged, frail-looking woman whose Brooklyn accent was thicker than she was. He grabbed her elbow to keep her from hitting the ground.

"Lois, I'm sorry. I didn't see you."

A skeptical expression was a permanent accessory to Lois's face, which somehow made it easier for her to keep all the gruff law-enforcement men around her in line. She also looked very grandmotherly, which didn't help one's defenses against her. It was hard not to obey someone's grandma.

"Mick, this is the third note I've written down from this poor young woman." She handed it to him. Every word was doubly underlined, as if Mick had somehow failed to get it before. *Jenny, 4:30. Please call.*

"Thank you," Mick said with a slight smile. But Lois didn't budge an inch. "I'll call her."

"Are you sure about that?" Lois said. Mick could smell the tobacco on her breath. He'd nagged Tom about quitting, but he was sure Lois was better off as a human being with this particular vice. Imagining her edgy was, well, terrifying. "I think I've left you one note today and a note yesterday. I can look up the number for you if you'd like."

"I know the phone number at my brother's house, Lois."

"Listen, kiddo, I know this has been tough on you. Did you get my card? I sent you a card."

"I did. Thank you."

"Good. And I say this because I care: Get back to your desk, get your ear to the receiver, get those long fingers of yours on that number pad, and ring-a-ling your sister-in-law, will ya? I can hear it in the poor girl's voice. She's worried about you, and for heaven's sake, she doesn't need another thing to worry about."

Lois's lingering smell, a combination of cigarette smoke and drugstore perfume, hovered in the air with the good dose of guilt Mick threw into the mixture. He wasn't trying to make Jenny worry. But he couldn't make things right in her life, and that's all he wanted to do. The pink note with Lois's cat-scratch handwriting was now crumpled in the palm of his hand.

He couldn't make things right. But if he ever found out who killed Aaron, he could certainly make things even.

chapter three

Seven varieties of Hungry-Man TV dinners lined the shelves of the freezer. Mick stared into the icebox, his eyes scanning each box, but his mind seeing nothing but his brother's coffin being lowered into the grave. Before he knew time had passed, his face was suddenly very cold, and the refrigerator motor had kicked into high gear, rumbling to try to keep up with all the air escaping. Mick snatched two dinners and shut the door.

He opened the microwave, popped in the trays, and set the timer for two dinners. Then he sat down at his kitchen table, his legs weary, his mind bubbling with uncontrollable images.

"Mick, it's Jenny—" was followed by hysterical screams.
"Jenny! Jenny?"

"Mick! Aaron, Aaron—" She wasn't able to finish the sentence. He heard voices in the background, and the next thing he knew he was in his car, driving ninety miles an hour through Dallas toward Irving.

Police cars swarmed his brother's house; he counted more than twenty. He pushed officers aside, then stopped cold when he saw the yellow crime-scene tape.

His brother's supervisor, Chief Perry, met him in the middle of the front lawn. "Mick . . ."

Mick glanced through the front bay window of Aaron and Jenny's home. Jenny was standing near the couch, crying, the

19

phone still in her hand. A female officer was touching her shoulder.

"Mick? Hello?"

Mick blinked and realized someone was pounding at the front door of his apartment. The muffled voice called out his name again.

He opened the door. "Jenny?"

She smiled at him, but her eyes were tired, and her delicate and radiant skin was dulled by what had surely been gallons of tears. "Hi," she said simply, sticking her hands in the back pockets of her jeans. "Is this a good time?"

"Um, yeah, sure, of course. Come in." He opened the door wider, then hustled around his small living room, picking up shirts, shoes, magazines—anything he could grab quickly. He hurried off to the hallway and quickly dumped his armload in the bathroom. He reemerged sheepishly. "Sorry. Haven't cleaned in . . . a while."

She laughed and wandered around the living room a moment, staring at the few framed pictures he had, grazing her hand over his old leather couch.

"And, um, sorry I haven't called you back. I've been really busy, and every time I'd pick up the phone to call you, someone would interrupt. I'm working this big RICO case. I was going to call you tonight."

Jenny shot him a look. "Give me a break, Mick. I know you've been avoiding me." She picked up a small picture he had of himself, Aaron, and Aaron's favorite baseball player, Tug McGraw, taken fifteen years ago. "But I understand."

"I wasn't avoiding you." But the words fell flat as his gaze dropped to the carpet. "Anyway, why are you here?"

She set the picture down. "Because I want to know how you're doing. I'm worried about you."

The microwave gave off one long beep, and the tension

in Mick's chest released ever so slightly as he had an excuse to turn his back to her.

She followed him to the kitchen. "What's on the menu for the bachelor tonight?"

He smiled as he took the dinners out. "Turkey and gravy with dressing and carrots. And let's see here, looks like Salisbury steak, mashed potatoes, and some vegetable— green beans maybe?"

"You could come over and I'd cook you a good meal, you know. Give me something to do."

"Maybe I'll take you up on that," he said while he removed the film from the dinners and waved away the steam. "You want one of these?"

"Already ate. But thank you."

"There are drinks in the fridge."

"Thanks." She opened the refrigerator door and laughed as she grabbed a Coke. "You don't have to refriger- ate peanut butter, you know." She looked deeper into the fridge. "Or honey. Or . . . is that a can of peas?"

Mick shut the door for her. "I don't take chances with food poisoning. I'm sure you remember that night."

"Who could forget?"

"Yeah, well, I refrigerate everything and never, ever eat at the church potluck."

She laughed and popped open her Coke can. "Sit down, eat. Don't let me stop you." She joined him at his small table. "I hope it's okay that I stopped by."

"Of course. You can stop by anytime, you know that."

"So, what've you been doing?"

Mick smiled a little. "Wrestled with a storm."

Jenny's eyebrows shot up. "Sounds . . . interesting. Who won?"

"I'm not sure, but I got really wet." He laughed.

"I forget—spring is your season, isn't it?" She glanced

over to the large framed photograph of a tornado that hung on the living-room wall. He'd shot it May 3, 1999, in Oklahoma City. The F5 had ripped open the city. Some even believed it was an F6, though technically there is no such thing. On his coffee table he had a scrapbook containing nearly a hundred different photographs he'd taken since he started storm chasing as a hobby.

Mick nodded. "How're Mom and Dad doing?"

"Your mom has called me every day, bless her heart. She's hurting. Devastated, really. They're coming down this weekend, I think. They wanted to make sure they got the headstone right. Have you talked to them?"

"Not really. I mean, a couple of times. Dad is pretty quiet about his emotions."

"Yeah." She drew lines in the sweat on the drink can. "So are you. Guess that's where you get it from."

"You should've seen me today," Mick said with a half laugh. "I did some healthy emoting with my supervisor."

"What about?"

"Oh, nothing, really. Just a disagreement about a case I'm working on. Nothing big. Tom's trying to quit smoking, so he's a little on edge, I guess."

"Oh." She stared at him. "I haven't heard anything. About any suspects, I mean. Detective Stewart calls me every day, giving me this and that, but it all boils down to the fact that they have nothing." Her eyes teared, and she covered her mouth with her hand.

Mick's heart ached. He started to reach across the table to her, but then she said, "I'm moving."

Mick looked up.

"I can't stay there, Mick. I've tried. I wanted to try and stay there and remember all our happy memories, but I can't sleep in the bedroom, and I just keep seeing . . ."

Tears dropped heavily from her big brown eyes. She shook her head. "I feel like my life is destroyed."

Mick swallowed. "I know."

"I'm sorry. I didn't want to come over here and cry. I wanted to come over and talk. See how you were doing. Just . . . talk."

"It's okay." Mick shoved the TV dinners away and moved one seat closer to Jenny. He took her hand, but she pulled him near and buried her face in his shoulder.

"I can't believe this has happened." Her sobs vibrated against his chest, and he knew he couldn't hold back the tears any longer. They dripped into her blonde hair. "I can't believe he's gone."

Mick willed himself to stop crying, and after a few moments, long before Jenny regained control, his tears stopped. But his rage had not. He saw no face, but nevertheless Mick was trying to strangle it. It was just a wisp of an existence, a mere shadow of evil, but Mick could see it dying in his hands. He felt rage that he never knew existed in him.

He tore himself away from Jenny and stood, walking into the living room, his back turned.

"I'm sorry," she said.

"No, don't apologize. Please." He turned back to her. "I wish I could make it better for you, Jenny. I wish I could bring him back." His words choked at the back of his throat.

"I know." She wiped her tears, glancing away with embarrassment at her own emotions. "He's gone from here, but he's not gone. He's living on. He's safe with God."

"He should be here with you. It's where he belongs."

"I talk to him at night. I don't know if he can hear me. I just tell him how much I miss him, and I tell him how sorry

I am." She took a deep breath and her voice strengthened. "I'm going back to work next week."

"Really?"

"Yeah. I'm going to try to find a new house, work, just keep myself busy. I'm going to get another dog too. I still feel . . . I feel unsafe. Whoever did this, maybe he could come back."

"He won't." Mick walked back to the table. "He wasn't after you. He was after Aaron. He watched the house. He knew you wouldn't be there. It was all planned out."

She stared up at him. "Who, Mick? Who would do such a thing?"

"I will find him." Mick engaged her eyes. "Do you hear what I'm saying? I will find who did this."

Relief softened her expression. "I pray for that every night."

"Me too."

Mick's eyes caught the folder on the kitchen counter, the one that contained the initial case reports and newspaper articles on the other murders. Tom's dusty footprint was still on the edge of it. Mick almost reached for it. He could show her. Explain what he suspected. Draw out the map and the time line he had. Jenny would believe him. She would trust him.

He heard her get out of her chair. He lowered his hand and put it in his pocket before turning around.

"God knows," she said.

Mick nodded.

"I'm praying for you." Then she grabbed her purse off the couch. "We'll get through this. My heart is torn into a thousand pieces, but God knows how to put it all back together again. I'm sorry to have ruined your dinner."

Mick laughed. "Well, that's the great thing about TV dinners. They're pretty bad from the start."

She smiled and touched his arm as he escorted her to the door. "Are you okay?"

"I am."

"You're sure?"

He nodded and opened the door for her. "Thanks for coming by. It was good to see you. And I'm sorry I haven't called. I'll be better at that, I promise."

"Okay. Call your mom too, okay?"

"I will."

"All right. I'll talk to you soon. Let me know, okay? Anything? Any small detail. I want to know. They're not telling me anything."

"Be safe going home."

He watched her walk down the apartment stairs and to her Toyota Camry, and then she drove off after a short wave. In the dusk of the evening, that perfect warmth that accompanies a setting sun encircled him, and he stood in his doorway, letting it bathe him. It was matched by a sweet southern wind, just enough to tickle the skin and refresh the lungs. It had been a hot spring day, but now the temperature was nearly perfect. He stared out to the horizon, the purples, oranges, and reds of the ending day stretching out from the earth like a hand reaching toward him.

"Jenny found him. . . ."

"He's dead?"

"I'm sorry, Mick."

"How?"

"Um . . . shot once in the head. He died instantly. We don't have anyone in custody yet."

Mick had stared through the bay window for what seemed like hours, watching Jenny cry hysterically. He was frozen on the front lawn, unable to collapse, unable to walk, unable to breathe. He heard her screaming, saw her clutching the female officer and shaking her head. And all he could do was stare. Blink. And then throw up.

His phone rang, and Mick stepped back inside his apartment, the setting sun no longer warm enough to push away the cold memories. The caller ID announced the number, and then the answering machine kicked on.

"This is Mick. Leave a message." *Beep.*

He hadn't checked his messages in days. Was there still room on the tape? He'd had voice mail once but could never remember his access code. Answering machines were much better—he could just push play. Plus, guests always stared at the machine like it was a lost artifact.

"Mick, it's Gwyn. Honey, are you doing okay? I've left a couple of messages. I tried to talk to you at the funeral, but you were gone pretty quickly. I'm just worried about you. I know it's over for us, but if you need someone to talk to, I'm here. I want you to know that. I know you must be devastated. I'm so sorry this has happened. Please call me if you need anything. Just to talk. Or . . . or to cry . . . or whatever. I'm here for you."

Mick snatched up the receiver. "Gwyn?"

The line was silent, then was replaced by the robotic voice of the operator, which he cut off by slamming down the phone. His hands ripped through his hair. A lifetime of bad timing.

God, please don't let me lose it. I feel like I'm losing it. Control. He walked to the kitchen counter, grabbed the folder, and fell onto his leather couch, plopping the folder down on the glass coffee table. He clicked on the TV. ESPN's chattering heads filled the silence of the room. March Madness. That was the understatement of the year.

This was his favorite time of year, but not even the Final Four could numb the pain. He couldn't care less who filled the brackets. And watching basketball reminded him of his brother, anyway. They'd always place bets on who would make it to the Big Dance. He laughed to himself. Aaron was always a sucker for Texas Tech—even when they didn't have a chance. Mick had had his eye on Syracuse taking all. Whoever lost had to buy dinner at Cattlemen's. He lowered the volume on the TV and picked up the folder.

Spreading the paperwork out across the table, he organized it so he could see each case, and then he put the pages in chronological order. The first one was a police officer murdered in Pauls Valley, Oklahoma, two and a half years ago. The next, a sheriff's deputy in Lubbock, Texas, four months later. Two months after that, a DEA agent found dead in his backyard in Houston. Another police officer in Hobbs, New Mexico, three months later. Two weeks after that, a police officer was shot while leaving a party, once again in Houston. Then, within the span of only a month, three more law enforcement officers died—one in Arkansas, two more in Texas. Then the deaths seemed to stop.

Out of the eight cases, only three had suspects. One had been convicted of the deputy's murder, but court records showed the conviction was based on eyewitness testimony only. The other two, in New Mexico and Oklahoma, were awaiting trial. Every other murder was unsolved.

Mick read through each bit of information, studying every detail. He drew out charts and diagrams and maps. Law enforcers were murdered every day in this country. What made these different? Why was he so convinced there was a connection to Aaron's murder?

In Aaron's case, the dog had been killed with a single shot, possibly over the fence. No one had heard the shot, so the killer probably used a silencer. The back sliding door was open slightly, but Jenny said Aaron sometimes left it open while he slept so the dog could go in and out as he pleased.

Mick had followed the chief into the house. Two dozen men and women milled about, dusting for fingerprints, combing the carpet for hair and fibers, jotting notes, talking. Eyes shifted and averted as Mick walked through the back door. But Jenny just stared at him, a stare that spoke complete horror. From where he stood he could see her trembling.

"You want to go talk to Jenny?" the chief asked.

"I want to see him first."

"You don't want to see this, Mick."

"I said take me to him. . . ."

"Mick, you there? Pick up, buddy. Mick!"

"What?" Mick opened one eye. Why was he on the couch? He sat straight up, and Reggie's voice rang in his ear.

"Dude, where are you?"

Mick opened the other eye. Bright light made him blink them both. The answering machine. Mick lunged for the phone. "Reg?"

"Mick! What are you doing? Where are you?"

"I'm at home."

"No, I mean *where are you?* You're supposed to be at the station. We're going to interview Markowitz this morning, remember?"

Mick tried to open his eyes again. "It's morning?"

"Yes. Hello? Almost nine. Brother, are you okay?"

"I'm . . . I'm . . . I just overslept. My alarm didn't go off." Mick slumped. His back screamed with pain from falling asleep slouched over on the armrest of the couch. "Well, I can probably buy us an extra ten minutes, but get yourself down here, man."

"I'm on my way."

Mick scrambled off the couch and tripped over a shoe he'd kicked off sometime during the night. He hit the floor with a thud, but he managed to grab the edge of the coffee table to pull himself into a kneeling position.

His eyes focused on the mess of papers in front of him. The cases. He'd fallen asleep while working on them. And then he remembered. He hopped up and almost laughed.

Last night he'd found another connection.

chapter four

f there had been any trepidation in Ellen Tucker's
expression, Mick would've backed off. But the young
investigative assistant answered without hesitation.

"Do I make a request through the National Law
Enforcement Telecommunications System?" she asked.
Mick chuckled. He liked her eagerness to show him what
she knew.

"Only use the NLETS if you have to. Why don't you try
to call first? Tell them we only need one picture of the head.
Maybe we'll get lucky and they'll give 'em up with a phone
call. If not, send an admin message through NLETS
confirming the phone request. We probably won't get a yes
on every request. But I've got to try anyway."

Ellen grabbed a pen and a piece of paper, jotting the
notes down.

Mick bit his lip. "Ellen, listen, this is . . . not related to
an official bureau case."

"I know."

"You do?"

"Sure. But I want to help any way I can. Your brother's
death hit us all hard."

Mick nodded. "The thing is, you might catch some
flack if, well, if a certain somebody knows you're doing this
for me." He glanced in the direction of Tom's office. So did
Ellen.

"Nobody's going to find out. Besides, if they do, you'll cover my back, right?"

Mick smiled at her. She was going to make a great agent someday, once she got out from underneath all the grunt work. "Sure. I just wanted to warn you. You don't have to do this. I'd do it myself except I have to go interview a guy on that Fargo bank robbery."

"Hopefully I'll know something soon."

"Thank you," Mick said, rushing away from her desk and over to Reggie, who was waiting impatiently on the other side of the room.

"Dude, come on, will you?"

"Sorry, sorry," Mick said, snagging the paperwork he needed and securing his gun on his hip before accompanying Reggie down the stairwell.

Reggie shot him a look. "Thank goodness this isn't an important stakeout."

"My life could only be that exciting," Mick said with a short laugh.

Reggie pulled the car up the gravel road of the trailer park as Mick squinted, trying to read the tiny numbers on each of the homes, which all looked exactly alike except for a potted plant here and a barking dog there.

"It's 435?"

"Yep." Reggie slowed the car down a little.

"There," Mick said, pointing to the next trailer on the left. Reggie pulled the car up to the front. "Now who is this guy?"

"You didn't read the lead sheet?"

Mick shrugged. "I figured you did."

Reggie sighed. "The second cousin to Dale Markowitz, who supposedly robbed a bank up in Fargo yesterday."

"Texas?"

"North Dakota. If it were Texas, don't you think we'd be investigating the bank robbery?"

"What's he supposed to know?"

"That's what we're here to figure out. They wanted this interview immediately."

Reggie stepped out of the car and so did Mick. A few lone souls milling about the park property stole glances but went back to their business. "You look like you didn't sleep well last night."

Mick shut his car door and joined Reggie on the other side. "And you look like you've gained a few pounds."

Reggie's eyes cut sideways. "I'm serious."

"I slept at the house, so that's a start."

"True. But from the looks of it, it was upside down with your head resting against the fireplace."

They walked up the short sidewalk toward the trailer. "I found another connection last night."

Reggie sighed. "Uh-huh."

"Don't sound so enthusiastic."

"I could've predicted that's why you didn't sleep."

"I did sleep. You called me this morning and I was asleep. Don't you remember?"

"What, three hours?" Reggie knocked on the man's door.

"Is this man supposed to be dangerous?"

"I don't think so."

"Don't you want to know the connection I found?"

Reggie stared at the door, knocking again.

"You think I've lost it too, don't you?"

"Don't put words in my mouth."

"But you don't believe me."

Reggie glanced at him. "Brother, it's not that. I don't know enough to believe or disbelieve you. I'm just worried that—"

The door opened suddenly, and a tired-looking man in pajama bottoms and a sleeveless undershirt stood there blinking at them.

"Merle Markowitz?" Reggie asked.

"Yeah. Who are you?"

"FBI." Reggie pulled out his identification.

"Huh?"

"You're in no trouble, sir. We just need to ask you a few questions about your cousin Dale Markowitz. May we come in?"

"Uh, yeah, okay."

Mick and Reggie followed the man into the small living quarters, where the dining-room table sat right next to the couch.

The man offered them the couch and sat at the table. He rubbed his stubble. "Sorry. I was asleep."

"What do you do, sir?" Mick asked.

"Work the night shift at the post office." He eyed both of them. "This is about Dale?"

Reggie pulled out a pad of paper. "He's a suspect in a bank robbery up in Fargo."

"Doesn't surprise me."

"Oh?"

"Been in and out of jail since he was fifteen."

Reggie continued the questioning. "Have you seen or spoken with him lately?"

"About ten years ago."

"Know where he lives?"

"Nope."

"Heard what he's been doing or where he's been working?"

"No idea."

"Know anybody acquainted with him?"

"Didn't even know he was in Fargo. Last I heard he was in prison in Oklahoma."

Reggie and Mick stood, and Reggie said, "Well, thank you for your time."

"Did he kill anybody?"

"Yes, sir. Two tellers. He should be considered armed and dangerous, and if you do hear from him, please contact the FBI."

"Won't, but will do."

Mick shook his hand. "Thank you."

Walking down the wooden steps of the trailer, Reggie was laughing. "Well, that was worth our time."

"Who's the case agent on this?" Mick asked with a growl in his voice.

"Hanson or Branson. Something."

"Well, he did a fine job of researching."

Mick and Reggie noticed at the same time a tall, thin man walking out of the trailer opposite Mr. Markowitz's. He looked up, made eye contact with them, and then took off running. Mick also saw him drawing a gun from inside his jacket.

"Gun! Call for backup!" Mick yelled at Reggie as he started chasing the guy. The man was young and fast. But Mick knew the fence ahead would buy him three or four extra seconds.

"Federal agent! Stop!"

The man fired a shot, still trying to run.

Mick ducked but kept pursuit. He didn't have any protection other than his Smith & Wesson and a quick prayer to God. He glanced back and saw Reggie running up behind him, still several yards back.

The man reached the fence, but instead of hopping it like Mick had expected, he turned and pointed his gun, quite unsteadily, at Mick, who dove behind a large clay pot filled with brightly colored flowers. Mick could hear Reggie screaming at an old woman across from him to get inside.

Another shot rang out, and he figured it was intended for Reggie, whom he couldn't immediately locate.

By the way the man was waving his gun around, though, Mick could tell he was on drugs and probably too high to attempt to climb a large chain-link fence. He was hoping the man was seeing double and triple and had no aim. But one could never be certain about druggies. They can barely roll off a couch but can somehow get a bullet into whatever they're aiming at.

Another shot ricocheted off the top of the trailer that the flowerpot belonged to. Mick rolled, this time seeking better cover behind some cement blocks supporting the stairs. He cocked his head and could see Reggie across the small road, behind another trailer. He was signaling that there was no way out other than to climb the fence. Mick nodded. Somebody was going down, and God willing, it wasn't going to be him or Reggie.

He peeked up and saw the man making his way along the fence, his back against it, his gun pointing at everything the wind blew. Mick aimed his own weapon. All the training he'd had at the academy flooded his mind with two words: *center mass*. Which meant a chest shot. He was never taught to shoot to kill, but he was taught to stop a particular behavior. And a gunshot to center mass is the fastest way to do that. Another bullet whizzed by Mick's head, and he fired back. His bullet missed by only inches, hitting the metal fence behind the man and causing sparks to fly.

The man stumbled around, and he suddenly disappeared from view behind another trailer.

Mick made his move forward, ducking in between anything that would give him good cover. Reggie followed on the other side.

Finally Mick made it close to the fence. He took cover

across the street, on Reggie's side, behind the last trailer.
He was breathing hard and tried to steady himself to listen
for any movement or sound. But it was useless. All he could
hear were wailing sirens behind him.

He took a deep breath, then signaled to Reggie that
he was going around the corner. He looked back and saw
officers approaching. Luckily Mick could see Markowitz
signaling to the officers who the agents were so there
would be no confusion. Mick pointed his gun straight
out in front of him, cushioned between two determined
hands, and turned the corner. Immediately he located the
man.

Reggie was right behind him, gun drawn, adrenaline
lighting up his eyes.

Mick motioned for him to lower his gun. "He's down,"
he said, approaching slowly. The man lay on the grass,
facedown, his gun a foot away from his fingers.

Reggie walked up to the guy and kicked the gun away.
"Passed out."

A horde of police officers were now on the scene, and
everyone just stood around looking at the guy sleeping
comfortably in a bed of grass. Finally someone decided to
cuff him.

Mick laughed and shook his head at Reggie. "Well, that
was something."

Reggie was laughing too. "You can't ask for a better
ending than that."

"Yeah, but the guys are going to give us you know what
back at the office."

Reggie grabbed Mick around the neck while they
walked back to their car. "You know it. But I'd rather get
razzed any day of the week than have a limb shot off."

"True," Mick said.

They walked the gravel road, trying to smile and reassure the residents who were peeking out of their doors, mostly elderly people. One lady was giving them a particularly harsh look, as if they were more of a nuisance than her neighborhood drug dealer.

Captain Trent Doyle greeted the men with a handshake. "Gentlemen, good work," he said heartily. "Apparently the DEA has been looking for this guy for months."

"Who is he?"

"Steve Prowser. Just glancing in the windows, we can already see there's a meth lab set up. A search warrant's on the way."

Mick looked at Reggie and chuckled. "Well, just so everyone knows and the DEA doesn't freak out, we were actually here interviewing the guy across the street about his cousin. This Prowser guy came out as we did, took one look at us, and ran."

"That will defuse a lot of worried egos," Doyle said, winking.

"And," Reggie added, "the guy passed out before we could even get a bullet in him, so not only can we take no credit for good detective work, but we're not even heroes."

Doyle laughed. "Oh, come on, boys. Don't be so humble. The guy tried to shoot you both." He looked at Mick. "How are you doin'?"

Tension cinched the muscles in Mick's shoulder blades, but he tried to smile and receive the concern. "Fine. Thanks for asking."

Doyle nodded sharply. "We're gonna catch him, and when we do—" he glanced at Reggie—"you get the idea."

"Thanks, Captain." Mick shook his hand one more time and followed Reggie to the car. They gave a quick wave to Mr. Markowitz, who, still in his pajamas, was looking like the day's excitement might have just added ten years to his life.

Mick gave Reggie "that look" and Reggie groaned. "Please don't tell me you need a donut."

"You know sugar calms me down."

"You are so cruel."

"Maybe you could just get a donut hole."

"If I die of heart disease I'm writing you out of my will." Mick grinned. His cell phone rang. "Agent Kline."

"It's Ellen."

"Uh, hi . . ." He glanced at Reggie, who was busy trying to back the car between all the newly arrived police cars.

"You coming back soon?"

"Yeah."

"I've got some good news for you."

"Terrific."

"Oh, and just to forewarn you, the story about the guy who passed out while you were pursuing him has already made it back to the office."

"Great . . . ," Mick said, punching his cell phone off. He looked at Reggie. "I'm gonna need more than one donut."

mick and Reggie arrived back at the office to find a crowd of Tylenol PM bottles stacked on each of their desks.

"This is just the beginning," Reggie mumbled, pulling out a sack of carrots.

Nate Lentz, a field agent the spitting image of Keanu Reeves in *The Matrix*, sauntered up, his $300 pair of Ray-Ban sunglasses parked high on his forehead. "Well, well, if it isn't Cagney and Lacey."

"Lentz, give me a break," Reggie growled. "It could've happened to anybody."

Tom approached, smiling at the medicine bottles. "Boys, good work. It might not have been the showdown of the century, but you sure had the DEA shaking in their shiny boots, and you know that puts a smile on my face."

Mick rolled his eyes.

"So what'd you find out from the Markowitz guy?" Tom asked.

"Nothing," Reggie sighed. "He didn't know a thing."

"All right. I'll call up north and tell 'em what we know. Wrap it up, will you?"

"Can you leave out the part about Prowser?" Reggie moaned.

Tom cracked up. "Sure. If the money's right." He walked off, still laughing.

Lentz flipped his sunglasses down and pulled his jacket over his huge muscles and harnessed gun. "Well, boys, gotta run. Try to get some sleep, will ya? You look beat." He smirked and walked away.

Reggie gnawed on a carrot. "I hear he lifts double his body weight."

"So what." Mick groaned, eyeing the Tylenol PM and thinking it might actually come in handy. "You know, I prayed that God would protect us and He did. Nowhere in the Bible does He promise we'll come out looking like studs."

"Yeah, well, what god is Lentz praying to?"

Mick smiled, then noticed Ellen standing a few cubicles away, trying to get his attention. "Um, listen, Reg, can you finish up the paperwork here?"

"Yeah, sure. I'll have you sign off on it when I'm done."

"Thanks."

Ellen Tucker handed Mick seven autopsy photos and smiled proudly.

He stared in astonishment. "Seven out of eight. Well done, Tucker."

"Thanks." She stuck her hands deep in the pockets of her khakis.

Mick sifted through the photos, which Ellen had printed using the color printer. The images were a little fuzzy on most of them, but he got what he wanted.

"What are you looking for?" Ellen asked. She glanced shyly at him. "If it's not too personal."

Mick studied her for a moment, then looked back at the photographs. "All but one of these victims have brown hair. But I couldn't tell that from the black-and-white photos I had."

Ellen nodded, but he knew she didn't comprehend. She didn't have enough information.

"I can't believe you got this many. I figured we'd have a hard time getting any information at all. What'd you tell them?"

"The truth. That your brother was murdered and you were looking into a connection."

Mick swallowed. "Oh. The truth." He chuckled. "Good idea."

"Yeah." She moved some papers around her desk. "The only one that denied the request was this one." She pointed to the newspaper article on the police officer who was killed in front of his wife while leaving a party. "And it was a stiff *no*. I noticed you already had his photo from the newspaper, but it doesn't show his hair color well."

"All right. Well, seven out of eight isn't bad. I'll work around it."

"Mick!"

Both Mick and Ellen jumped at the shrill sound of his name. Tom was standing at his office door, looking around.

"Kline!"

"Over here," Mick said, standing straighter as he took a few steps away from Ellen's desk.

"Get in here *now!*"

Ellen swallowed. "I've never seen you before in my life."

Mick managed a weak smile.

The glass rattled and the blinds shook for fifteen minutes in Tom's office as he hollered, turned red in the face, introduced Mick to a few new ways to use a cussword, and then hollered some more.

Mick didn't have to turn around to know that everyone was on their tiptoes and peeking out the top of their cubicles to see the commotion. Mick's and Reggie's desks were positioned where they normally didn't have a good view of such things. Well, he had a front-row seat now.

Mick couldn't help but wonder about Tom's blood pressure. Maybe he *was* obsessed about his brother's death, but Tom, he thought, could certainly use some anger-management skills.

" . . . what did you think would happen, and didn't you think through that maybe these guys have these cases flagged on the UCR and that maybe they gave you the info you wanted in return for information? Mick, haven't you been in this business long enough to understand that the bureau can't ask for anything without the whole world making a federal case out of it? Now I've got twenty guys calling me and asking questions and wondering what kind of thing we're running here and making it out to be some sort of conspiracy because you and I both know that the FBI is *always* in some sort of conspiracy. And it didn't help that it took me off guard so I sounded like I was hiding something when the last thing I expected was for you to go behind my back digging around in these cases when I specifically told you to lay off and let Homicide do their job!" He had to take a breath. *"Answer me!"*

Mick jumped a little. Was there a question? "Tom, I'm sorry. I wasn't thinking. I just thought I found a connection. . . . I *did* find a connection—"

"You have got to be kidding me!" Tom nearly screamed. "Do you know that this . . . this—" he had to glance down at his notes—"this Ira Owen from New Mexico has called me five times in the last hour? I don't have time for this!"

"I know. Again, I'm sorry."

Tom managed to gain control of himself after glancing out his office window and apparently noticing a few stares.

He rounded his desk and closed the blinds, then leaned against his office door. "Mick, you're stirring up trouble. I sympathize with you. You gotta know that. But you're a federal agent, and there are policies and procedures and ways things are done. And they're there for a reason. I didn't make them. I don't agree with a lot of them. It's my place to make sure they're followed, and you are walking a very fine line here."

"Yes, sir."

"Now, I know you're not going to like this . . ." Tom walked back behind his desk and sat down, looking Mick in the eye.

Mick held his breath. "Like what, sir?"

"I want you to go see Dr. Grenard."

"What? No, please. Tom, please."

"Don't argue with me, Mick. I don't want to hear it. It's an order."

"Give me a break." Mick stood. "You don't seriously think I've lost it, do you?"

"That's why I'm sending you to see her, Mick. So you don't lose it. So you can get yourself together and think rationally, because right now you're not thinking rationally. Right now you're ordering naive investigative assistants to get crime-scene photos of dead law enforcement officers. I can't say I have a great deal of confidence in your state of mind."

Tom stood too. "You've always been one of my most dependable agents. A little religious for my taste, but dependable and good at what you do. I could always count on you. Now, I'm sorry your brother died. I know you want to get whoever did this. But I will not have you jeopardize this agency. Hear me once and for all." He touched his finger to his desk with every word, and his eyes gleamed with superiority. "I will not seek jurisdiction on your brother's case. I think your theory on some killer moving around the Southwest murdering law enforcement personnel is full of holes."

Mick could do nothing but stare at the ground, rubbing his brow furiously. "I can't believe you're making me go see the shrink."

"Well, believe it. Your appointment is in half an hour."

"Agent Kline, come in."

Mick lumbered forward into Dr. Grenard's office, a fresh, steaming cup of coffee in his grip. The best thing about the next hour was going to be a really bad cup of coffee.

Dr. Abigail Grenard was a striking Texas redhead. Though she looked like a runway model from New York City, she was the last person anybody wanted to see in the bureau. At a restaurant, sure, but not at the bureau.

Psychologists hadn't always been bureau staff. Before, if you needed to see a shrink, you'd have to go out of the office to do it. But years of neglecting the fragile minds of inflated egomaniacs, as some would call them, led to drug and alcohol abuse at levels the bureau had never seen before. What once was swept under the rug turned into one gigantic dust bunny that no one could ignore. Staff psychologists were still controversial. And it was certain, whether on-site or not, that going to the shrink was never good for an agent's career.

"Hello, Doctor."

"Please, call me Abigail." On any other occasion her drawl would have been enchanting.

"You don't go by Abby?"

She shook her head, offering him a seat across from her. "No. I always thought it sounded too Catholic. And I'm a good Southern Baptist."

Mick smiled. "Well, as long as we're being casual, you can call me Don't-Want-to-Be-Here."

She pulled out her notepad. "How original. You know, I've been doing this for three years and have yet to work with anyone who said they were glad to be in my office."

Mick shrugged and sipped the liquid, a little thick today. Tom had probably made it.

"So, are you Baptist too?" Abigail said, pulling the cap off her pen.

Mick looked up. "Why do you ask?"

"You have a reputation around here—a good one, I might add—of being religious."

"Hmm."

"Is your faith helping you through your brother's death?"

"Yep."

Abigail sighed and laid the notebook on her lap. "Look, Mick, I'm going to be up front with you. I know you don't want to be here. I know you don't want to talk about your feelings. And I know the last thing you want to do is see a shrink."

"Wow. Are you sure you're not a psychic?"

Her lips pressed together with determination. "But if you're not willing to have the courage to open up and share what's going on, then I don't expect you'll have the courage for too many other conflicts and difficulties that come up in life either."

Mick studied her dark eyes, the same color, he noticed, as his coffee. Her smile reminded him a little of Gwyn's.

"All right." He set his coffee down. "My brother was murdered with a single shot to the back of his head, killed in his sleep, in his own home, by a coward. Am I upset about it? Yes. Do I want to talk about it? No. Am I shutting out people who love me? Probably, though those are few and far between anyway. Am I feeling angry, bitter, and resentful? You betcha. Have I lost my mind? Unless you're not a redhead with a pen in your hand, I don't think I've lost it. Does that pretty much cover it? I could raise your pay real quick here, and instead of $175 an hour, you could make that much in fifteen minutes if I could be done with this and get outta here."

Her head cocked slightly to the side, as if nothing he said fazed her. "Uh-huh. For one, I'm on a salary. A nice one, by the way, but thanks for the offer. Two, what you just said there pretty much confirms that you're going to be in that wingback for at least an hour."

chapter six

here, let me help you." Dixie Abernathy's voice was kind, but Faith Kemper shook her head. She grew so tired of that phrase.

"Sissy, here, is all I need, Mrs. Abernathy."

"Dixie, please. I'm not old enough or wise enough for 'Mrs. Abernathy.' Um—" the woman rustled some papers— "I guess, well, let me show you around. I mean, tell you where you are. Silly me, of course you know where you are. Just orient you, I guess is what I'm trying to say. Do you want me to hold your hand?"

Faith forced a smile. There were days the routine was maddening. "If you could just tell me, I'll find my way around."

"Really?" Shock filled the woman's voice. Dixie had probably counted on watching Faith fumble around the room, arms outstretched, guiding herself along the walls in the stereotypical blind-person fashion.

"Just need to get my bearings."

"Okay. Well, straight in front of you, which is north, is the back door, leads out to a beautiful fenced-in backyard with a stream that runs a few yards away. Sissy'll love it. To your left is the kitchen. A little small, but it does have a dishwasher and gas stove, plus a microwave up top. We remodeled it back in '98. And you also have your dining area. Oh, and a small breakfast bar. Across the room is a hallway that goes to a bathroom and a laundry area. And then also on the northeast corner are the stairs that lead up to the bedrooms. The master is on the left, has its own bathroom. Another smaller room is on the right. That's pretty much it. Oh, and of course it's completely furnished."

"Good. Thank you."

"Any questions?"

"No."

"If you need anything, well, my number is on the fridge. Oh . . ." Dixie's voice trailed off.

Faith smiled a little. At least the woman was genuine and warm. "That's okay. Just tell it to me. I'll remember it."

"Really?"

"Yes, that's how I have to do it."

Dixie spoke her number slowly and repeated it twice.

"Thank you," Faith said, cutting off what sounded like a potential third round.

"Faith," Dixie said after a moment, "do you have anybody to help you? Family? Friends?"

"Just Sissy," Faith said, scratching the dog on the back.

"Well, my goodness, what a young, brave soul you are."

Faith's fingers tightened around Sissy's harness handle. Dixie did not know how wrong she was. "All right. Well, Dixie, thank you again."

But there were no footsteps toward the door. "By the way, I belong to the First Presbyterian down the street. Walking distance for you, as a matter of fact. And we have services every Sunday at ten and Wednesday nights at six, when we always have this big potluck, which is a lot of fun. You're welcome to come. I'll introduce you as my new friend."

"How kind. Thank you, Dixie."

"You know, this house, I used to share it with my husband, Harold. He died of an aneurysm a couple of years ago. Ripe old age of fifty-six."

"I am so sorry."

"I rent it out now, moved into something a little smaller. But I'm glad you're the new occupant. Welcome to Baker-ville."

Faith smiled, and Dixie took her free hand, shaking it firmly.

"You know, most days I sit up in my old apartment feeling sorry for myself and lonely, and I just realized that you, young lady, are going to need a lot of help orienting yourself to your new town. It's not going to be hard. It's small and organized in a real nice way. And I suppose you'll need help doing things like grocery shopping. How do you do that, anyway?"

Faith swallowed and was thinking of how to answer it and what to do with Mrs. Dixie Abernathy, when she continued with barely any hesitation. "Listen to me, being all nosy. I'm sorry. I'm just so curious. I've never known anyone blind before. You sure picked a good street to settle into. There's a small grocery store on the corner, opposite the church. Going the other way, there's a diner. Nik's. So, tell you what. I'll let you get settled, and I'll come by tomorrow afternoon We'll go grocery shopping, and I'll get you acquainted with the area."

"Dixie, I don't . . ."

"Please. I want to help."

Faith bit her lip. "Um, okay. Sure. Thank you. I could use a few groceries, I guess."

"All right, well, you're probably exhausted. I'll let you go." Dixie went to the door. "Please, Faith, call me if you need anything at all. Day or night."

"You are so thoughtful—"

"And you are so pretty! I've never seen hair color like that, outside of a bottle anyway. It's like golden sunshine. How long have you been blind? There are some real nice bachelors in this town, Faith. Handsome, good Christian boys."

Sissy whined a little, as if tired of Dixie's rambling too. Faith subtly combed her bangs down on her forehead, hoping Dixie wouldn't ask about her scar next. Luckily for Faith, she realized Dixie was one for a lot of questions but not patient enough to wait for most answers.

"And think about coming with me tomorrow night to church. It's a great way to meet people."

Faith stroked Sissy's fur. "I'll pass. I don't get out much, and I'm not great at meeting people. Not too social, I guess you could say."

A long pause was followed by, "Well, I won't hold that against you, but I can't say I understand it. I've been social my whole life, even as a baby. When my mother was alive, she loved to tell the story of how I'd beg to be passed from lap to lap at just a year old!"

"Couch." Sissy accompanied her a few feet forward and to the left. Faith sat down and released her grip on Sissy's harness. "Dixie, you say you don't work?"

"Nope."

"How'd you like a job working for me?"

A pause. "What, uh, would I be doing?"

Faith smiled. "Well, for starters, being discreet."

"And then I came across this one in Houston," Mick said. "I realize how this must look. I know how it looks to Tom. Tom thinks I'm scouring the Southwest looking for my phantom menace. But I'm telling you there is a connection here. And I'm sure any good profiler would agree that part of the connection is how absolutely random these killings were."

Abigail crossed and uncrossed her legs three times before speaking. "Okay, you're off the subject again, but let me ask you this. There must be random killings of people every day. Even law enforcement officers. You say you have this radius of 300 miles, but how did you get from your brother being killed to these eight murders being related? Seems there is a missing link. Why not 450 miles out? Or why not a murder of a cop up in Washington?"

Mick's voice was laced with urgency. This was his chance to prove his theory to someone who seemed to want to listen. "Because the other murders don't fit. I've looked at every law enforcement murder case in the last three years, and these eight have the random element to them, whereas others do not. For example, there was a sheriff killed up in the Seattle area eight months ago. But they've already arrested his ex-brother-in-law for the murder. Another one: highway patrol officer killed after pulling a car over. Already we know that he was shot by one of the occupants in the car. But these eight, like my brother, are completely and utterly random. Even though some arrests have been made, the cases depend on eyewitnesses or have other weaknesses."

"I'm not forgetting about the subject we're supposed to be on, and we'll return to it in a second, but I'm curious. Your brother was shot, as you said, sleeping in his bed. What made you jump from that murder, even as random as it was, to a serial killer? Obviously the worry here is the lack of hard evidence."

Mick nodded. Indeed. There were so many little things, but Abigail wanted a smoking gun. That he didn't have. In fact, he had only two guns in these murders. And two *different* guns. The others were killed with blunt objects or knives or other weapons. It was as if the killer knew to never kill the same way twice. Mick knew no one was going to buy that theory. It was as if randomness was the murderer's biggest mask.

Abigail's pen scratched across the page of her notebook. He could tell by how she first gave him her full attention and then jotted down her notes that he was chipping away at the doubt that she'd shown at the beginning of their session.

Mick answered the best he could. "There is a missing link. I'll admit that."

"Okay. Good enough." She finished writing and then said, "Now my turn."

Mick sighed. He could only oblige or find himself sitting here for another hour. "Fine."

"What steps are you taking to begin to process the grieving stage of this tragedy in your life?"

Mick laughed. "You sound like you're reading from a college textbook."

A subtle scowl appeared in the form of a small line that creased between her eyebrows. "Are you going to cooperate or not?"

"I *am* cooperating."

"You're being combative."

"I'm being real."

"Okay, so be real with me." She leaned forward. "Are you praying?"

"Yep. I pray every night that I'll find the killer who did this."

Abigail's face registered no certain expression. "Uh-huh." She opened her notebook, wrote something down, then said, "You said *I*. 'I'll find the killer.'" By the look on Abigail's face, that particular word was apparently very meaningful in the world of psychology. "Mick, I want to hear you say that you might be wrong about this."

Clasping his hands together, Mick let the silence do the talking.

"You can't admit that you might be wrong? That your theory might be tainted?"

Mick stood, surprising Abigail enough that she leaned back in her chair, apparently unsure of what he was about to do. But he just walked to the window. Outside, the sun was high in the sky, and the grass was thick and green from the spring rains. He turned back to her. She was watching him carefully, her pen between her teeth, her legs uncrossed.

"What are your instincts about me?" Mick asked her.

Abigail released the pen from her mouth. "What do you mean?"

"I mean, I haven't given you much to go on now, have I? You know I'm religious. You know I'm angry. Generalizations really. Give it your best shot."

Abigail shook her head, almost laughing. "You're used to running things, aren't you? Having your own way? Doing your own thing?"

Mick smiled. "Well, there you go. That's a start."

A sigh escaped her lips. "I wasn't starting, but okay, fine. What are my instincts about you." She laid her pad and pen on the table next to her and clasped her hands together. "I think you're hurting more than you're letting on; you're burying your feelings in your work. Somehow you think that your purpose in life is to find Aaron's killer. You loved your brother, but something in your past makes you indebted to him. Maybe it's religion. Maybe it's something else. I also think there's this pain from sometime before, maybe childhood or later. Probably later. Something happened to you that doesn't allow you to feel grief as you should. You have no idea how to deal with grief. Or your feelings. In fact, I believe that whatever it was has probably affected most relationships in your life, and you've had trouble keeping a steady, long-term relationship. You push people away, which is why you're unable to allow me—or anyone else—to help you. You're going to deal with the death of your brother on your own terms, in your own way, and that way is by hunting down who did this and making him pay."

The words stung. Mick could do nothing more than stare at the carpet, but when he finally looked up, he studied Abigail, wondering if he could trust her. She was good—good enough to hide any agenda behind her brown eyes. "Are you finished?"

Thoughtfulness softened her expression. "No. Your religion is deep and genuine. You're a man of faith and conviction. You have high morals, high standards for everything in your life." She opened the top of her bottled water and took a sip. "Oh, and you love basketball."

Mick laughed openly at that last statement. "How did you know that?"

"Well, you did say use my instincts." She shrugged. "It's why I get paid the big bucks."

Mick let the electricity of the moment diffuse a little. He'd turned away, but he knew Abigail was anticipating a rebuttal.

"You're right," he finally said, turning back in time to see her guard drop just enough to show astonishment.

She quickly recovered, screwing the cap back on her bottle for an excuse to avert her eyes. "Am I?"

"Yes. You are. You're right about everything you said." Abigail smiled.

"They don't teach that in books, do they?" Mick said.

"I guess not." Abigail crossed her arms. "So, if I'm right about all this stuff, are you going to let me help you deal with your brother's death?"

"No," Mick said, making direct eye contact for the first time since they'd begun. "Help me solve my brother's death."

"What does that mean?"

"It means you just proved my point."

"How's that?" she asked, her fingers nervously fidgeting with her water bottle.

Mick smiled. "Instinct." He leaned against the wall and gestured. "Another *I* word. Sometimes you have to go with your gut. You have to throw out everything they teach you and rely on your instinct."

The way Abigail was gnawing on her bottom lip, Mick knew she was consenting, whether she would admit it or not. He walked toward her. "So, Doctor, my question to you is, what are you going to go back and tell Tom?"

mick trotted down the cement steps of the small church he had attended for years. Reverend Peter Swain greeted him outside with a handshake. "Hey, brother."

"Hi, Pete."

"Any news on Aaron?"

"Working on it."

"And how are you doing? You look tired."

"Just working a lot at the office."

"Hey, you want to come over for dinner tonight? Julia's making tacos, I think."

"Oh, thanks. But I'm behind at the office. Got a ton to catch up on."

Pete squeezed his shoulder. "Mick, you're doing okay, though, right?"

"I am."

Pete patted him on the back, smiled, and then continued to greet other church members.

Mick continued down the sidewalk and realized this was the perfect spring day. Even before noon, the sun was warm—not hot—the humidity was low, the wind just a tickle. He stuck his car keys back into his pocket and kept walking. Half a mile north was a wonderful park where he and Aaron used to throw the football. On a park bench he watched the people, frisky and spirited, throw Frisbees and

balls, jog, ride bikes. Teens were on their skateboards or
scooters. Children rolled in the grass. A small utopia, if
even for a few moments.

Mick focused on a handsome couple near a tree. The
man was tall, tanned, his cotton shirt untucked and moving
slightly in the wind. His companion, a petite, blonde
woman, had her arm wrapped around his waist. They
watched a young boy and girl chase each other with delight,
screaming with excitement as they rounded a nearby tree.

He'd wanted a family. All his life. Many people
assumed he was a bachelor by choice, but it wasn't true.
He'd wanted a wife and children. He'd always hoped Aaron
and Jenny would have children, but they had tried without
success.

He cleared his mind of wistful thoughts and focused on
what he needed to do. Last night he'd decided to eliminate
one of the cases, where the victim had blond hair. He kept it
in the back of his mind, but at this point he needed some sort
of consistency to make any theory work. In his mind's eye he
methodically went through the crime-scene photos of the five
unsolved cases. There was still the one case in Houston that
wouldn't release the photos. But of the five, he still couldn't
find any connection other than that all the victims had brown
hair and were under the age of thirty-five.

He knew serial killers in general left more of a pattern,
like leaving the body in a certain position or placing an
object on the body. There was nothing like that in these
cases that he could tell.

Also, last night he'd noticed that of the eight cases, the
first four were single men. Starting with the officer in Houston, there was a wife. And after eliminating the man with
blond hair, who was not married, all the others had wives
also. Perhaps a coincidence, but he could take nothing for
granted at this point.

He also knew he was not going to find his brother's killer while sitting at a pretty park on a Sunday, watching the world play and pretending that life did not have a dark side. Life did have a dark side, but he knew one truth. And it caused him to stand up from the park bench and focus.

The world and all its darkness had been conquered by the Light.

Faith had little to unpack. Just a few clothes. Dusty pictures. Books she used to enjoy reading. She kept a lot of the CDs they had listened to, especially their favorite, *Fleetwood Mac: Greatest Hits*. Some U2. A few Chicago. But she hadn't listened to any of them since he had died.

She oriented Sissy to the house—or rather Sissy oriented herself—which seemed well planned and spacious. On the back porch she released Sissy to go explore the yard while she sat on the porch swing, taking in the fragrant smells of spring. Two things had amazed her when she became blind. Her sense of hearing had become more acute as had her sense of smell. She could tell who walked into a room by the sound of their footsteps. And what had once been vivid pictures in front of her had been replaced by vivid smells, some so overwhelming they sickened her. But she had learned to use these senses as guides. And they had never disappeared.

In the swing, she kicked back and forth like a little girl, braiding her long hair to keep it out of her face. She smelled wildflowers and thick grass and the distant reminder that rain might fall in a few hours. A certain mugginess in the air foreshadowed that perhaps it would be more than a light spring shower.

Bakerville was a new town, but there was nothing new about her life. And she wouldn't be here long, maybe a year. Then she would move on again, until possibly she faded from the memory of all who used to know her, and she could become new. But never safe. She would never be safe.

The skin of her cheeks dampened. Was it raining already? No. Tears. They came without notice sometimes. She wiped them away and thought about something other than her wretched life, which was nearly impossible. But Dixie would be coming by later. That would break up the monotony of the day.

There were things she would have to be careful of. Precautions she would have to take. It was a risk to have Dixie in her life, but it could also end up being very beneficial. She hoped she could trust this woman. She seemed nice enough, and hopefully Faith had established the fact that she expected Dixie to be prudent when it came to her tendency to talk more than she should.

Faith had tried hard not to raise even more suspicions by requesting that Dixie be heedful of her mouth, but she felt she had explained it well enough by insisting on how private a person she was. She even noticed Dixie's endless questions had seemed to taper off a bit.

Dixie had expressed concerns when Faith had asked if she knew a handyman who could install a dead bolt on the front door, plus a safety bar on the back sliding-glass door. She also wanted all the window locks checked. Dixie had told her they virtually had no crime, other than teenagers vandalizing a bridge here or there.

"When you're blind, Dixie," Faith had told her, "that's a small step in protecting yourself."

Dixie seemed to understand that and said she'd call her cousin Johnny to come over and do it right away.

From inside the house, the grandfather clock chimed two in the afternoon. Faith realized she had not yet eaten.

"Sissy!" she called, and the dog was by her side immediately. "Let's go get something to eat."

Dixie had mentioned that there was a diner just three blocks to the east of her house. Faith took Sissy by her harness and went out the front door. Apprehension bullied her effort to leave. She stood at the top of the porch steps. Only three cement steps stood in the way of a little freedom in her life.

Someone was watching her. The way her skin climbed up and down her muscles, she knew. It was the same feeling she had had just moments before . . .

She tightened her grip around the harness handle. She could tell by the strain on it that Sissy was sensing her fear. Or maybe something else.

Was there someone out there? Or was it just her emotions playing tricks on her?

Five seconds later she was back inside, the door locked, and she was hungry for something more than cheese crackers.

"Mick?"

"Um, hi. Sorry to drop by unannounced. Hope I didn't catch you at dinner."

Brady Gerber stepped out onto the front porch of his home, closing the door behind him. "What are you doing here?"

"I thought maybe I could just talk to you about your investigation."

Brady walked past Mick and stood at the edge of the porch, gazing out at his neighborhood, his hands stuffed in his pockets. Mick joined him.

"Mick, this isn't a good idea. Does Tom know you're here?"

"Of course not." Mick sighed. "Tom's furious with me. And I know you're not too happy yourself."

"It doesn't help when I've got a bureau agent going behind my back to get evidence, question witnesses. It causes a lot of confusion."

"I know. I know," Mick said. "I crossed the line. I'm sorry."

Brady seemed to let some of his frustration go with the apology. "I understand, you know," he said, glancing sideways at Mick. "I have a sister, and if she were killed, I couldn't just stand back and do nothing."

"Maybe I am consumed with it," Mick said, watching a teenager on a bike race by on the street. "But I don't know what else to be."

"Aaron was a good man. I know you know that. He was decent. Always doing the right thing. That's hard to find."

"Yeah." Mick glanced back over his shoulder.

Brady's wife was looking out the window to see where he'd gone. He gave her a little wave, and she closed the curtains. "So why are you here? I can tell you right now I don't know anything new. I want to say I have a lead, but I don't, Mick. I know that's frustrating. It is to me too."

Mick bit his lip and stared at his shoes. He was at a desperate point now. Time was going to eat up the evidence if there was any. "I have a theory."

Brady stared at his own shoes. "Tom told me."

"Did Tom tell you all of it?"

"Just that you think it's a serial killer."

"Killing law enforcement officers."

"I know, Mick," Brady said with exhaustion in his voice. "But it's just a theory. You have no hard evidence to prove any of this. And right now the better lead is that it was someone Aaron knew." Mick started to retort, but Brady cut him off. "I've looked at your supposed other cases. I don't see the connection. They weren't killed in the same way. They're not all with the same agency. They're in four different states. Two of them, I'm sure you're aware, have suspects behind bars."

"Three, actually."

Brady finally turned to Mick. "You do what you have to do. I'm not saying to stop searching. You just can't get in the middle of my investigation."

Mick closed his eyes to try to thwart the frustration building inside him. When he opened them, Brady had moved to his front door. Mick took that as a sign he should leave. He started down the porch steps.

"Mick," Brady said. Mick stopped and turned. "This is not a bureau thing. This is not an ego thing. I wouldn't let that get in the way of finding Aaron's killer."

"Okay."

"And one more thing." Brady swallowed, as if deciding whether or not he should continue to say what he was about to. "There is one thing you don't know."

"What?"

"We found a flyer in the trash can. It was a half sheet advertising cheap lawn service. Typed. No phone number. No one else in the neighborhood got anything like this."

Mick walked back up the porch steps. "Prints?"

"No. And no one saw anybody out of the ordinary in the neighborhood."

"So somebody could've knocked on the door, pretending to be offering lawn service."

"Yes."

"He could've seen the back door open and seen Aaron was asleep. Maybe he knocked one more time, as a follow-up or something, and confirmed the back sliding door was open. Or asked to see the backyard to give a quote."

"Maybe. Or maybe some idiot just forgot to put his phone number on there. Jenny said Aaron always did their yard work anyway. She said he hated it, though. And was terrible at it." Brady offered a small smile. "That's all I have."

Adrenaline surged through Mick. "Thank you."

"I'm hoping this will keep you out of my way." Brady disappeared inside his house.

Mick slowly walked to his car, his mind reeling. His theory differed from Brady's, but one thing Mick knew for sure: Whoever killed Aaron, whatever his motive, he'd been to their house at least once before. Probably twice. And offered lawn service.

chapter eight

that night, after spending hours poring over the information he had on the cases, Mick spent another hour deciding whether or not to take two sleeping pills. His nightmares had become more consistent and now were haunting him with the possibility that he would never find Aaron's killer. They taunted him in the darkness, where his sleep was never deep enough, where his conscience would not rest. Yet he could not awaken and leave it. They chained him to his bed and tortured him with fear and unrest.

But taking sleeping pills would not be a good option. He didn't trust himself at this point not to take more than two. And he did not believe that two would put him out of his nightly misery. So he had tossed them in the wastebasket and slept on the couch, turning up ESPN in hopes of drowning out the more ominous voices of the night.

It had worked in a weird way. He had dreamed he was on ESPN, with Dick Vitale doing the commentary on his abilities as an investigator while Jay Bilas gave a detailed, point-by-point description of all the evidence he had and had not found. And oddly, Mick was dressed in a basketball uniform and was six inches taller.

The early-morning sunlight caused him to open his eyes with much relief. A rerun of *SportsCenter* filled the TV screen. After making a pot of coffee and showering, he decided to take some time to look at the cases again. The lawn-service angle was interesting in his brother's case but not helpful in tying it to the others, as those victims had been killed in various ways and in various locations.

The cop in Houston was murdered in a parking garage while leaving a party with his wife. Mick thumbed through what little information he had on that case. He held up a newspaper article about it and remembered that last night he thought it odd how little information was in the story, considering it was a cop killing. In fact, all it said about the actual killing was that it happened in a parking garage at 9:47 p.m.

Mick checked the clock as he towel dried his hair. The writer's name on the article was Susan Bryant. The newspaper was the *Houston Chronicle*. He made a mental note as he dressed. It would be good to step away from this for a few hours, come back to it with a fresh set of eyes. But he would call the woman this morning, just to see what he could find out.

He sipped his coffee. Leaning back into the couch, closing his eyes, and resting the coffee cup on his knee, Mick prayed for clarity and direction. And he prayed that God would help him find Aaron's killer.

What he couldn't bring himself to pray for was restraint, if God ever did answer the other prayer.

Mick arrived at the office at 7:15 a.m., much earlier than he was accustomed to. He even beat Reggie, who tended to rise earlier than the roosters. The usual hectic pace of the office was replaced by a peaceful environment, and Mick decided to use the time to catch up on some of his work, in particular an investment-banker scam they'd been working for a month now. It would pass the time, he figured, until 8 a.m., when perhaps Ms. Bryant might be in the office.

But his mind wandered. And before he knew it, forty-five minutes had disappeared. The window he had been staring out of was brighter with the rising sun, and he hadn't even noticed the change. The only other thing that had changed was his pen, now a mess of plastic, shredded at the end. He threw it aside and decided to try to get ahold of Ms. Bryant.

After going through the switchboard, Mick heard the mature, deep voice of an older woman answer the phone. "This is Susan Bryant."

"Ms. Bryant, my name is Mick Kline. I'm in Dallas. I was wondering if you might have the time to discuss an article you wrote awhile back."

An irritated laugh prefaced her words: "Well, sir, I write a lot of articles, so you'll have to be more specific. And also more specific about why you're calling. I am an investigative reporter. I'm naturally curious."

Mick picked up his mangled pen and poked it between his molars. He had to make a decision—and quickly. Play the FBI card, make it an investigation, and stir up curiosity and trouble? Or just tell her about his brother, see if she would be willing to provide any details without wanting details in exchange?

"Hello?"

"Yes, um, I'm sorry. The article is about a man named Paul Kemper, a police officer killed almost two years ago."

"Yes, I'm familiar with that. Still unsolved.".

"I was wondering if you have any more information about the case?"

"Why?"

He squeezed the pen between his thumb and forefinger. "My brother was killed. A cop here in the Dallas area. I was just curious about it. I ran across the article you wrote and thought that it lacked a lot of details." Mick hurriedly explained. "Not on your part, I'm sure. But it seemed that the authorities weren't saying much about it."

A pause from Ms. Bryant allowed Mick to continue tormenting the pen with his teeth. But then she said, "Yes, well, you're right. It wasn't due to a lack of trying. Everyone was very tight-lipped about this incident. I suppose because it involved a cop. I don't know. My sources wouldn't talk to me at all about it. I suspect . . ."

"Yes?"

"What did you say your name was again?"

"Mick Kline."

"And you're looking for a connection?"

"Possibly."

"You're a cop?"

"No."

"What are you?"

"A brother out to find this killer. You were saying . . . ?"

"I suspected at the time there was something gruesome about the killing, or something else. I don't really know. But there was definitely more to the case than met the eye. I tried to speak with the widow, but she disappeared soon after the murder. And that's pretty much all I know."

"The wife is a suspect?"

"No. They did make that clear. She was with him when the attack happened, and she was hurt. Poor lady was blinded, by a head injury I believe. She never returned to the house they lived in together, I know that. And then she moved, but I don't know where."

"Ms. Bryant, tell me your gut feeling about this case. I mean, it was obviously a big story down in Houston when you covered it."

"I suspected the police weren't telling us everything, but

I never knew why. And I swear it was like the whole department was sealed up with superglue. Nobody would say a thing."

"So, you never got more information?"

"There were some tabloid reports, but things could never be confirmed, and we refused to print it if we couldn't verify it."

"What did the tabloids report?"

"Oh, just crazy things, like the killer left a message. And I think there was one about the wife plotting to kill the husband. Oh, and that it was a mob hit or something. I mean, the rumors were fierce. I told the chief of police that if he would tell us what actually happened, the rumors would probably stop."

"What about the wife? Did she give any details?"

"None. She was in the hospital for a while, maybe a couple of weeks or more. And I'm not sure what happened to her after that. Her friends wouldn't talk. Nobody would talk."

"All right. Well, thank you for your time."

"You say your brother was killed? How?"

Mick glanced up and realized Reggie was standing at his desk, eating a PowerBar and cocking one eyebrow. "Um, thank you for the information. You've been very helpful. Good-bye." He hung up and watched as Reggie pulled out his chair and sat down.

"You're in early," he said. "Who were you talking to?"

Mick didn't answer. He couldn't. He wasn't sure whose side Reggie was on anymore.

"It was about Aaron's case?"

"Just checking some things out, Reg. No big deal. I got in early so I could get some work done. I'm behind."

Reggie glanced down at Mick's desk, noticed the bureau file and seemed satisfied as he stuffed the rest of the rectangular cluster of protein into his mouth. Without hesitation he pulled out another one and opened it. "Tom called me at home last night," he whispered.

"What?"

"I'm not kidding. He wanted to talk to me 'out of the office.' I guess he wanted me to feel free to discuss what's going on with you."

"That's *great*," Mick growled.

"I told him I thought you were cool, brother. I said you were as concerned as any guy would be. I told him that I thought he was overreacting a bit about you."

"You did?"

"Yeah. I mean, nobody here knows what it's like to have a brother murdered in cold blood with no suspect. I told him that you hadn't lost your mind and that this was just your way of dealing with it."

Relief swelled in Mick's chest. "Thank you, Reg."

He smiled. "Dude, you'd do the same for me."

"So did he ask you about my theory?"

Reggie's attention lowered to the crumpled foil wrapper on Mick's desk. "Uh, yeah, he mentioned it."

"What'd you say about that?"

"Well, you know, we didn't really . . . it wasn't something we discussed at length. . . ."

"So what'd he say? What'd you say?"

"Look, Mick, what's important here is—"

Mick and Reggie both noticed at the same time Dr. Abigail Grenard enter Tom's office. She was dressed in a sharp blue suit, her hair tight against her head in a French twist. She was carrying a file in her hands. Tom stood, greeted her with a handshake, and then she gently closed the door behind her.

"How's that been going?"

Mick glanced at Reggie. "What?"

"The good doctor. Never been to her. Hope I never have to go."

Mick tried not to focus on Tom's office. He turned his chair a little and looked at Reggie. "It was fine."

"Hmm."

"This isn't a good sign."

"She's probably just giving a report. It might not even be about you, you know."

"Right." Mick picked up his pen again.

Reggie eyed it. "I have another PowerBar, dude, if you're, um, hungry." He pointed to the pen.

Mick rolled his eyes and threw the pen down again. "First he calls you at home, now Dr. Grenard is in his office." His fingers tap-danced their way across the folder on his desk.

"Look, everything's going to be fine. Tom is looking out for your best interests. You have to believe that. You and Tom are friends, and that's not going to change. He believes in you as an agent, and he cares that your brother was killed. Look, dude, as long as you didn't do anything as foolish as getting involved with Homicide again after he's asked you to stay out of it, I think you're fine." Reggie's eyes widened. "Mick?"

"Yeah?"

"I've been in law enforcement a long time, and I'm fairly sure I just saw guilt park itself right smack-dab in the middle of your expression."

Mick folded his hands together and rocked back and forth in his chair, glancing back at Tom's office. The blinds were now shut. He cupped his forehead with his hand and ran his thumb along his brow line.

"You didn't get involved, did you? Did you call Brady or something?"

"No." Mick couldn't even look up. "I went and saw him in person. At his home."

"Mick!" Reggie moaned. "Are you crazy? I just told Tom last night you weren't crazy. And then you go and do some crazy thing like this, brother. What is the matter with you?"

"I went there peacefully, just to see if Brady would give me some information. Share any new details. Which he did, by the way." Mick sat up straighter. "Did you know that someone came by the house claiming to be offering lawn service before Aaron was killed? There was an ad for it found in a trash can inside the house. But there was no phone number."

"Tom told you to stay away from Homicide."

"I didn't do anything to jeopardize their case. I just went to talk to Brady. No big deal. I doubt Brady thought anything about it."

"Excuse me, Agent Kline?"

Mick looked up. Lois was standing next to him, barely taller than he was sitting down. She was smacking her chewing gum as if her life depended on it. "Good morning, Lois."

"Agent Bixby needs to see you in his office."

Mick glanced at Reggie. "He couldn't just holler out the door like he usually does?"

Lois didn't seem to have an answer to that, and after depositing her gum in his wastebasket, she patted him on the shoulder and walked off.

Reggie was unfolding a piece of his own gum and cramming it in his mouth. His eyes blinked at the same rate he chewed his gum.

"This ain't good." Mick sighed.

Reggie's nostrils flared in agreement. "Gum?"

chapter nine

i can't believe this!"

"Mick, I suggest you get yourself under control."

"I am under control. At least I was—doing fine—until this! I swear I've entered the twilight zone. What kind of craziness is this?"

Tom blinked slowly, as if expecting the tantrum. Mick could only stand with his arms crossed.

"I have to make judgment calls, and sometimes they're not easy. This is one time that it's not black and white. I don't think you've lost your mind. I just think you need some time to deal with your brother's death. And I think if you're here working, you're not going to take the time you need to grieve."

"That sounds like Abigail Grenard talking."

"Well, it can sound like whoever you want, but I'm the one that makes the decisions, and I'm telling you that this is mandatory, and it's effective immediately."

Mick's arms flew into the air and then dropped to his side. He turned his back to Tom, staring at the blinds Tom had closed. "What am I supposed to do for a month?"

"I'd suggest going to Cancun. Sit on the beach, my friend. Just relax. When's the last time you relaxed?"

Mick whirled around. "Are you trying to tell me that I need to go sit on the beach while my brother's killer is roaming around, a free man?"

This time Tom closed his eyes completely for several seconds. "What I'm saying to you, Mick, is that you need time off. You need to get away from this scene. You are *obsessed.*"

Obsessed. Exhausted. But not hopeless. God knew who killed Aaron. God knew.

Tom left the protection of his desk and came to its front, leaning back against it with his arms folded in front of his chest. "You get full pay. Just get outta here for a while, okay? I'm doing this for your own good. You'll thank me for this someday."

Mick stared at his shoes. "You called Reg last night."

"Perhaps at the same time you were paying Brady a visit."

"And what'd Abigail say to you?"

"What Dr. Grenard said is privileged."

Mick smirked. "So it's about me, but it's privileged information for you. That's something."

"I made my own decision. Sometimes you just gotta go with your gut."

Mick studied Tom's intense eyes. "Yeah. I guess sometimes you do."

Mick left Tom's office, swept past Reggie, and entered the stairwell, an internal heat flushing his cheeks and dampening his skin. He rounded the corner of the fourth-floor landing when he stumbled to the side to keep from hitting the person coming up.

"I'm sorry. . . . " He looked up.

Abigail Grenard caught her breath in obvious surprise. "Agent Kline."

"Excuse me," he said, trying to get around her. But she stepped in his way.

"Wait. Tom told me he was putting you on thirty-day leave."

"No thanks to you."

"You don't know what I said in there."

"I don't need to know the details. All that matters is that I'm on mandatory leave, and that always looks real good in the old profile. Add that to my session with a shrink and you can count on the fact that if I'm ever involved in some controversial shooting or something, I'm going down."

Abigail lowered her head and shook it. She finally met his eyes. "Thirty days is extreme. I think Tom's more angry about you going to Homicide again."

"Brady called him?"

"I guess so."

"Figures."

"Look, Mick . . . " She licked her lips and chewed on the lower one. "Look, what I'm concerned about here is what you're doing to deal with Aaron's death. I couldn't care less about your theory."

"And I couldn't care less about your *concern*."

Abigail nodded. "Fair enough."

Anger exploded in Mick unexpectedly, and he hit his fist against the cement wall.

Abigail jumped, her eyes lighting up in surprise. She stepped aside and Mick started down the stairs.

"He kills quickly," she called after him. "This isn't a power trip. It's something different. He kills them before they ever know what happened. He has a conscience. A moral sense of some sort. He knows that killing is wrong, so he does it quickly, gets out fast. Or maybe, for some odd reason, he doesn't want them to suffer. Yet he uses weapons that normally do not kill instantly."

Mick turned and eyed her carefully. "And that's the sort of thing that gets you put away for a month."

Abigail chuckled. "You're not being put away, Mick. You're being told to take some time off."

"It's one and the same at the bureau, and you know it."

Abigail stood poised for something, but Mick didn't know what. She was tall, dressed professionally, gripping her briefcase like it was a limb about to fall off. But what Mick noticed most was that she did not look guilty. What was happening to him wasn't on her shoulders.

"I can't go sit on a beach and read Steinbeck and soak up the sun when my brother won't see the light of day again."

"You brother is in a better place."

"Try telling that to his widow."

She adjusted her jacket by pulling at its bottom so it tightened across the tops of her shoulders. "If you're going to go, then do it for the right reason."

Going to go? Was she reading him that well? "The right reason? Other than getting the guy that killed him?"

"Yeah." She moved up a step. "You track this guy down so he won't kill another cop. Not for revenge, Mick. It can't be for revenge. Get him so another wife doesn't have to be widowed."

Mick pressed his back against the wall, willing himself not to look her in the eyes but doing it anyway. She believed him. She actually believed his theory.

She took another step, looked once more at him, then continued up the stairwell. But before she turned the corner, she looked back and said, "And just for the record, I told Tom I thought you were doing just fine."

She was out of sight, and soon the clicking of her heels on the cement steps faded. He descended the rest of the stairs slowly, with each step reminding himself of the consequences of revenge as well as the consequences of never tracking this killer down.

Heat returned to his skin.

"I like this place, Jen."

Mick sat on a kitchen barstool while Jenny shuffled through boxes, trying to find a bottle opener to pop the lid off the root beer she'd served him.

"Ah, here it is." She straightened up with it and gave it to Mick. She stared out the sliding-glass door that led to a nice balcony, already decorated with several ferns and a couple of deck chairs. "Apartment living isn't cheap, that's for sure. Eleven hundred square feet for more than I was paying on my mortgage." She smiled a little. "I feel safe here, though. I guess because there are people around." She opened the sliding-glass door and a cool breeze came into the kitchen. "Nice view, don't you think?"

A sparkling duck pond with a fountain in the middle was right below, and nearby shimmered one of three pools the complex had. "Yeah. Real nice. I wish you would've let me help."

"I had plenty of help. You're busy." She laughed and joined him at the kitchen bar. "Never thought I'd be doing apartment life again."

"There are perks. You're not responsible when the plumbing stops up or the ceiling falls in."

Though sadness lingered in her eyes, a smile big enough to show her dimples refreshed her features. "I figure I'll be unpacked by this weekend." She opened her own root beer. "Have you talked to your parents?"

"Last night." It was good to talk to them. He told himself he needed to call more, that he *would* call more. Last night he had also spent two hours walking at a nearby park. Two long hours. He had contemplated the day's events. Was he obsessed, as Tom had said? Was he jeopardizing homicide's case? He tried his best to step outside himself, to look at it objectively. He wasn't sure if that was even possible.

"Mick?"

"What? I'm sorry. . . . "

"I asked if you wanted something to eat?"

"I got put on leave."

"What?"

"Thirty days."

Jenny's mouth hung open. "Why?"

"Tom thinks I'm obsessed with Aaron's murder. I've been interfering, they say, with the investigation."

"Interfering?"

"Just asking questions, that's all. Jen, I think . . . "

"Yes? What?"

"I've got this theory, you see. About Aaron's killer."

She frowned. "Why haven't you said something before?"

"Because everyone thinks I'm nuts." He sipped his root beer. "Homicide is doing a good job—I don't want to mislead you. They are working so hard."

"But you think they're misguided?"

"No, just . . . I have my own theory."

"What is it?" Her brown eyes focused in on him.

"There have been other killings, in three other states, and also in Texas. All the victims were law enforcement. In the last two, three years. I think they may be connected."

Her gaze intensified. "Are you saying a . . . a serial killer?"

"Maybe. It's just a theory, but I think it has some merit. And listen to me: I think that Homicide needs to continue with their investigation as it is. I thought about this a lot last night. There's no reason they shouldn't be investigating this their way."

"Why isn't Homicide onto this theory?"

"Because admittedly it has some holes. A lot of holes." He looked at her. "So I'm going to go and investigate, check some things out. I've got thirty days. There's this woman in the Houston area whose husband was killed right in front of her. It's the one case that has a witness."

Jenny was staring at her root beer. "A serial killer. Watching our house." She covered her mouth as tears trickled down her cheeks and over her fingers.

"I'm sorry. I shouldn't have said anything."

"That's not true." She glanced at him. "I want to know." She swiped the tears away, slid off the stool, and went around the bar into the kitchen, presumably to find a tissue somewhere in one of her many moving boxes. "Why didn't you tell me sooner?"

"I wasn't sure. I'm still not," he added quickly. "That's why I have to check it out." He swallowed a swig of root beer. "If there is a serial killer out there, I have to stop him before he hurts someone else."

The sparkle of worry in her eyes diminished to peace. "Yeah."

He tossed the bottle in the trash and went to the front door. "You okay? Need any help getting unpacked? I can stay. Here, let me help."

She shook her head. "Sara from work is coming over in a little while."

"Okay. Well, I'll be in touch. Jenny, make sure to lock your doors. Keep your alarm system on."

Panic froze her features. "Do you think I'm in danger?"

"No, no. You have more of a chance of being murdered by a neighbor than a serial killer."

"That's comforting."

"No, I meant—"

"I know what you meant. It sounded like something Aaron would have said."

Mick tried to recover anyway. "Just take everyday precautions, okay?"

She laughed. "This coming from a guy who decided to

try storm chasing because the FBI wasn't giving him enough of a thrill in his life."

Mick grinned and shook his head. "Well, you have to see what I do from day to day to understand that. Though," he said, holding up a finger, "I did have quite an adventure the other day with a guy who had a meth lab set up in his trailer."

"I don't have a gun." She walked to the front door where he was standing. "Aaron never wanted me to have my own gun. Wouldn't even take me to the firing range. You know why, of course." She shoved her hands in the back pockets of her jeans. "Should I get one?"

"No. You're safe." Mick knew Aaron had always refused to let Jenny keep a gun, and he agreed with the decision. They'd seen too many cases where a gun bought for "safety" ended up killing a kid or some other innocent victim.

"You can't guarantee that." Bitterness steadied her quivering voice. "You're supposed to be safe sleeping in your own bed too."

"I know," he said, hugging her. Her arms wrapped around him tightly. He let go of her and looked her in the eyes. "You're safe, Jenny. You have an alarm system. Keep it activated. But I'm telling you, the killer's not coming back."

She stared at the carpet. "If you say so."

"I'll call you if I find out anything, okay?"

Nodding, she opened the door for him and waved as he took the steps down the three flights. Then he headed back to work.

"What are you doing here?" Reggie asked, standing as Mick approached their desks.

"Just finishing up," Mick said, sliding into his chair and

turning on his computer. "I've got a couple of things to do before I leave."

Mick looked around the office. It was lunchtime, and most people were gone, including Tom, he noticed with relief.

"Wasn't it mandatory leave . . . um . . . effective immediately?"

Mick tried not to glare at Reggie. He knew it wasn't his fault. "I'm going away soon enough," Mick said, logging on to his computer. He logged in to the NLETS and typed in "Faith Kemper." A Houston address appeared, with her husband's name, Paul. But according to Susan Bryant, Faith Kemper had moved. So Mick logged in to Faces of the Nation, a locator service that relied on a person's credit card or ATM usage or a driver's license.

Reggie's unrelenting stare made Mick look up.

"The case is growing cold. It's been four weeks. I've got to go do this and you know it."

Reggie nodded. "I know." He took something out of his desk and tossed it at Mick. Mick caught it with one hand. "Drivin' music, baby."

Mick held it up. The Eagles' *Greatest Hits*. He laughed, nodded to Reggie in appreciation, then looked back at his computer. First he had to find out where Mrs. Kemper was hiding. Then he had to find out why.

chapter ten

the knock was faint. Almost a whisper. And she wasn't sure if it was a knock or a male voice. It sounded like both. Was someone calling her name? No, it was a knock. She rose, unsure whether it was night or day.

"Sissy?"

There was nothing but silence now. Not even a knock.

"Sissy! Sissy? Where are you? Come, girl."

Then it came again. A knock? Was it a knock? She stood, gripping the end of the couch. "I'm coming," she whispered. "Sissy?"

Knock.

She reached the door, but there was now a cool breeze on her face. She gasped. The door was already open. Trying to orient herself, she reached out, but all she felt was air. "Sissy? Sissy!"

A white light scorched her eyes, and then she stumbled backward. A tall, dark figure, silhouetted against the light, hovered over her, calling her name. She could see, but only a shadow. It was real and transparent all at once.

"Sissy!" she called.

"Faith?"

Faith sat up, her chest heaving, Sissy whining quietly next to her. "Faith? Hello? It's Dixie. You in there?" *Knock, knock.*

"Coming," Faith called weakly. She stumbled off the

couch, making her way to the door on quivering legs. Her fingers slid around the doorknob. "Sissy, here." The dog was at her side when she opened the door.

"My goodness," Dixie exclaimed. "Are you all right? You're white as a ghost. And look at your hands! You're shaking!"

Faith forced a smile. "I'm fine. I dozed off. Your arrival just caught me off guard, that's all."

"Okay. Well, I brought your groceries, everything you requested." Dixie moved past her, the sacks she carried rustling in her arms. "Lots of fresh fruit. They had the most beautiful Fuji apples I've ever seen. I'm a Golden Delicious fan myself. And good-looking grapes too. I'm guessing you eat healthy, my friend, since you always have me get fruit." Dixie was in the kitchen, putting everything in the refrigerator. "Looks like I arrived just in time! You're down to the bare bones. Hate for you to have to eat mayo on crackers!"

Faith smiled and joined Dixie. Sissy roamed the kitchen for a bit then went to the living room. "Thank you, Dixie. Don't forget; just log your hours, okay?"

"No problem. So, how are you doing here? Finding your way around all right?"

"I am. It's a well-designed house."

"Good."

"I was thinking of going down to that restaurant you were talking about. Nik's. Would you help me walk there, join me for lunch?"

"I'd love to! It's a nice walk. Clean, perfectly paved sidewalks. Lots of birds chirping. And lucky for us, they seem to like to take their bathroom breaks over in the park."

"Let me get my purse." Faith made her way to the counter. She opened the cabinet where she left it. Her husband had taught her to hide her purse, even at home. Some habits were hard to break. She found her keys and called for Sissy, who was at her side instantly. After securing her harness, they followed Dixie out the front door. Faith locked it before heading down the steps to the sidewalk.

Dixie's immediate chattering cut what would've been awkward silence. And luckily for Faith, Dixie enjoyed doing the talking. Between listening to Dixie chirp away about the tedious details of her shoe-shopping disaster and listening to the high-pitched melody coming from the treetops, Faith wondered how long she would be in this town, dragging her feet against perfectly paved sidewalks. She adjusted her sunglasses, hoping her eyes were completely covered along with her thoughts.

Her life was meaningless drudgery now. She had no purpose other than survival, and day by day her desire to live lessened. Dixie walked slowly beside her, and Faith knew she was probably not used to walking at this pace. But Faith did not have enough in her to walk any faster. Finally, Dixie was done recanting the saga of her shoes, and for a few moments there was silence. But it was not the kind Faith minded. Cars passed by. In the far-off distance, children laughed. A playground. The wind swished the treetops and tickled her hair. Maybe it was enough to keep her going for a day.

"Faith, have you been blind all your life?"

"No."

"Can I ask what happened?"

Faith pushed her sunglasses up her nose. "It was a car accident. Brain injury. My husband was killed."

"Oh, Faith, I am so sorry. Was that a long time ago?"

"Almost two years."

Dixie's hand squeezed Faith's shoulder as they continued to walk. "I will be praying for you."

Faith bit her lip. She hated that phrase: *I'll be praying for you.* How many times had she heard *that.* It meant about as much as *call me if you need anything.* Faith tucked the hair behind her ears and kept walking. Dixie was silent too, for a while anyway.

"I'm just so glad I can help you, Faith," she said. "It gives me purpose. We both know what it's like to lose a husband, and maybe we can find solace in that."

Faith blinked heavily. "I guess so." Dixie could never understand what it was like to lose a husband the way she did, though. And to live in a prison of fear, dark even in daylight. Faith sighed away the dreary thoughts and tilted her head upward, soaking in the warmth of the sun.

"Just a little bit to go. We're going to round the corner up here, and it will be on your left. Just across from the post office, which is across the street, two shops down from the little grocery store."

They rounded the corner and Dixie took Faith's arm, she supposed out of instinct, and led her into the restaurant, where the air was immediately cooler and the sounds turned from the natural beauty of birds and wind to the low hum of a cash register, a soda fountain, a hot grill, and indistinct murmuring.

"We're indoors now," Dixie said.

Faith reminded herself that Dixie was just trying to be helpful. But it was also a good reminder of why she didn't leave the house much and didn't get to know too many people. At least one reminder.

"Just so you know," Faith said, "I keep my sunglasses on when I'm out in public. It helps people understand I'm blind."

"Oh, good. Okay. Well the sign says to seat yourself. So how 'bout a window seat?"

"Sure."

Dixie guided Faith through the crowded restaurant and pulled a chair out for her. Faith sat and ordered Sissy down.

The dog had been relishing the attention from the restaurant patrons. Now she grunted and curled up next to Faith's feet. "Good girl," she told Sissy. Faith said to Dixie, "Don't let me forget to have them fry up a couple pieces of bacon for her. That's her treat for taking me out to eat."

Dixie laughed. "Well, it's a girls' day out, I guess."

"I guess so." Faith smiled. "So, what kind of food do they serve here?"

"All-American. Hamburgers. Hot dogs. Chicken. They have nice salads. And pretty much any deli sandwich you can imagine. Fountain drinks galore. Desserts to die for."

"Hi, there. I'm Sandy, your waitress. What can I get you to drink?"

"I'm gonna have a Coke, half diet. Mix it up real good, okay? I know all that sugar's bad for me, which is why I mix it. But I can't stand to drink that diet stuff. It tastes like dirt. So half and half, okay? Maybe a little less of the diet."

"Sure thing," Sandy said. "And for . . . um . . . you?"

"Water is fine." Faith was used to hesitation. Even the most well-meaning people were sometimes unsure of how to handle her.

"I like your dog," said Sandy.

"Me too." Faith smiled.

Sandy walked off as Dixie was explaining the decor of the restaurant. "They have old-time signs up: Coca-Cola, Route 66. Things like that. There's a jukebox in the corner. Usually there's a song playing. They have a separate room for people to drag on their cigarettes, and it's got a pool table in it, some TVs to watch sports and such."

"What do you usually get here?"

"California Club. Nearly every time. Now, I'm not too hip on California. You know those people spend a million dollars on those little shacks they call homes just to see the Pacific? I mean, if I want to see the ocean, I'll turn on the

Discovery Channel or something. And they got their bodies pierced so many places, you'd think they were trying to be holy. 'Course, Californians probably think we're just a bunch of dumb hicks."

Dixie snorted a little when she laughed, and Faith had to admit the company was good. She'd lived her life virtually alone the last two years, and since moving to Bakerville, she had decided to hire help in order to make that easier. The less she had to get out and do errands, the better. Instead of bumping into the whole town, she just had to deal with one person most of the time. And Dixie seemed to be the right person for that. She liked to chatter, but Faith figured that was probably good for her. She needed a bit of liveliness every now and then or she might just rot away in her own home.

Sandy returned with drinks and asked for their orders. "The California Club," Dixie said. Then she asked Faith if she wanted her to read the menu.

"No, I'll have the same," Faith said, and Sandy was gone again.

Lunch went by fairly quickly. Faith explained a little more about what kinds of things she might ask Dixie to do. Dixie's enthusiasm for being helpful relaxed Faith in an odd way. It was nice to have help, and she had to admit, a new friend.

Sandy cleared the plates when they were finished and brought one bill. "I'm buying," Faith insisted.

Dixie held the receipt and argued about it, but Faith finally won.

"It's twelve and fifty-two cents," Dixie said reluctantly.

Faith took her purse, got out her wallet, and put the money on the table.

Dixie gasped. "That's amazing!"

"What?"

"How did you know which bills to use? I can see change being pretty easy because coins are different sizes. But what about the bills?"

Faith closed her billfold and put it back in her purse. "I separate my money in my wallet," she explained. "That way I know where my fives and tens and twenties are."

"Sounds like it would be easier to use a credit card," Dixie said. "But that's just me, and I'm not the blind one, so I should probably shut my trap." Dixie paused while Faith told Sandy to keep the change. Then she said, "Oh, and speaking of credit cards, I have something for you to sign."

"To sign?"

"Yes, it's just some legal mumbo jumbo concerning the renting of the house."

"But I've already signed the lease."

"Yeah, but this just came back to me and I gotta have it signed. Don't ask me why. All the paperwork in this world is going to leave us treeless, just like those Californians keep saying." Dixie laughed. "I'm hard on Californians. I shouldn't be. I could be just as hard on New Yorkers, I guess. It's just a whole nother world over there, you know? Movie stars. Mansions. Money. Fame. They're all gonna wish they had moved to Texas when California drops off into the ocean."

"Back to the papers—what exactly am I signing again?"

"Oh, I'm sorry. Here." She slid the paper close to Faith. "Just anywhere on the page. It's just acknowledging that I ran a credit check on you."

Dread squeezed the air out of Faith's lungs. "What did you say?"

"It's a credit history thing I have to run. Just standard. You passed with flying colors, of course. Anyway, here's a pen. Just sign anywhere."

"You checked my credit?" Faith could not hide the tension in her voice.

Dixie paused. "Yes. Don't you remember? You gave me your credit card, then your Social Security—"

"That was just to hold the house. I told you I'd pay in cash and said not to run anything on my credit card."

A pause from Dixie made it evident that she was shocked. "I—I didn't. I didn't put anything on your card, Faith."

"But you said it was just procedure. That I could pay you in cash. And I did!"

"I know, I know. Honey, settle down. Nothing went on your card. It was just a credit check. No big deal."

"You didn't say anything about that!" Faith's voice rose an octave and cracked. "You ran my Social Security number?"

"What is wrong? Your credit is fine."

"How could you do that? without telling me? I specifically told you . . . " Faith knew she was losing control of her emotions. Rage simmered under the surface of her skin. Things were already being inferred here that Faith regretted. She stood, ordered Sissy up, and headed for the door.

"Honey, my goodness, wait! Please, let me help you! Faith?"

"Dixie, leave me alone. I can find my way home."

"Faith, what did I do?"

"Please," Faith said harshly, "don't make it worse. Just let me go." With Sissy out in front, Faith left the restaurant and headed home, tears bulging at the rims of her eyes. She quickly unlocked her door, then bolted it when she was inside. She made her way around the whole house, shutting the blinds and curtains.

Then she collapsed on her couch, sobs filling the air. Sissy nuzzled her nose against Faith's neck and whimpered her concern. But there was no comfort.

chapter eleven

a few dirt clods Mick kicked around on the top of his brother's grave begrimed his tennis shoes a little, but his toe continued to find them. He'd loved to do that since he was a kid. He'd start with one big clod, kick it down the street, and see how many times he could give it a soft tumble before it crumbled into dust.

It was early morning, when diffused light reached the sky but the sun still slept lazily behind the earth, making it cool but not cold. In the quietness the world seemed to heed the reverence he felt for his brother.

It was the first time he had visited Resurrection Cemetery since Aaron's funeral. He knew Jenny came here a lot. But he had not been able to.

Until today. To make a vow. And he didn't need to speak it. Aaron knew Mick could do nothing less than this. And he knew Aaron would have done the same for him if he were in his grave.

Mick's jaw tightened at the thought. Guilt for simply being alive beckoned him into deeper sorrow. Aaron had always been the good son. The son of integrity. The man whom everyone looked up to. Including Mick, though it took years for Mick to admit it. Mick owed so much to his brother, and now the most he could do for him was find out who took his life. It would do nothing but provide justice, which was obsolete to a man who no longer breathed.

Maybe four or five decades from now, if Aaron had died from old age, Mick could find solace. But solace was elusive now. Peace was a distant memory. And joy . . . Mick laughed, but it came from the poignant realization of how much his life had changed, and how quickly.

It wasn't as if he didn't know life could change. He saw crime and destruction and murder every day in his job. He knew evil and the havoc it wreaked on the innocent. But never in a million years could he have predicted that his brother would die like this. Mick and Aaron both knew the risks in their line of work, but to die in your own home, in your own bed . . .

"So, I'm going to get him, whoever he is." It took Mick a second to realize he'd said that out loud, talking as if they were in their mom's living room at Christmas, conversing about the new chief of police or the new line of cruisers, who would be the first seed in college hoops, or the previous tornado season. Mick and Aaron had spoken easily together in the last few years, had grown close like brothers are supposed to be. Mick had changed his life, given it to God, and the rift that had kept the brothers apart for so long had been bridged by that common bond, among many others. "I'm not sure which cards to play. Where to go first. But I know what I gotta do, and I don't care how long it takes me—I'm going to do it."

Mick's toe found another dirt clod, and he smashed it. "And I'll take care of Jenny, okay? I'll take care of her for you. I'm not going to let anything happen to her." He chuckled a little. "And I told her not to get a gun, of course. We both know women and guns make a bad combination." They'd always had a little joke about that, but they kept it to themselves for fear of looking sexist. They weren't sexist. Just practical.

Something out of the corner of his eye caught Mick's

attention. He hadn't even seen the car drive up, but it was now across the cemetery, about fifty yards away. It was a Lincoln Town Car, shiny and maroon. Mick glanced at his watch. It was already 8 a.m.

An elderly woman slowly got out of the car. He wondered about her. Probably visiting her husband. Maybe she had lost him ten, fifteen, even twenty years ago. Maybe he'd died when they were just married, and she'd never married again. Mick swallowed the emotion that came with his secret wish of finding a love that strong.

Then another movement on the other side of the car. A little boy. Maybe six or seven. Five balloons, each a bright color, floated above him and he held them carefully by their strings. Luckily the wind was not swift today.

Mick watched with amusement as these two made their way through the cemetery, holding hands and talking about something he couldn't hear. He didn't want to hear. He only wanted to watch. And wonder. Whom did they love that they could no longer hug? or talk to? Only dream about.

They stopped at a grave, and the elderly woman pointed and then hugged the little boy. Was it his mom or dad buried there? Or both? The thought sickened him. Life was cruel, but children were resilient. They knew the same evils that adults knew. They knew great loss and terrible fear. Why could they smile again, long before adults ever could? What did they know differently?

Mick watched the little boy try to untangle his balloons and wondered why he brought balloons to a grave site. Balloons were for parties and celebrations and birthdays. It was an odd choice, but then again, children knew things . . . believed things. . . .

He also wondered how this little boy intended to secure those balloons to the grave. Would he find a rock, perhaps?

The balloons suddenly lifted high, floating into the

slight wind that carried them higher and higher toward the clouds. Mick's attention darted to the little boy, sure he would hear wailing and disappointed cries. But instead, the boy was laughing and waving, and the grandmother was smiling too.

Tears streamed without warning. Mick suddenly understood—the boy let the balloons go intentionally, for the child believed in his heart what Mick perhaps could only acknowledge in his head. Whomever he loved, whomever he missed, wasn't dead in the ground but alive somewhere in a glorious place called heaven.

Mick laughed, wiped his tears away quickly, and turned back to Aaron's grave. But instead of looking down at the mound of dirt, Mick looked up at the sky. The hue of the morning's glory sent chills through him and a swelling of emotion that allowed him to miss his brother, to grieve his passing, but to smile, knowing he would see him again.

When he turned back around, to his surprise, the boy and his grandmother were gone. Mick saw that the balloons were still floating upward. He watched until he could no longer find them.

Then he slowly walked back to his car, his eyes gazing at a hundred names etched into stone, passing over life lost tragically one way or another. Was it often that there was a death that was celebrated for its fairness?

Inside his car, Mick gathered himself, then made a mental checklist to make sure he had packed everything. He'd backpacked across Europe once, and his needs were minimal. He opened his glove compartment and reached inside, feeling for a single sheet of paper. His hand emerged with it, and he unfolded it.

It was Faith Kemper's current address, where he hoped to be in just a few hours. Luckily for him, Mrs. Kemper was not too good at covering her tracks. She'd let someone run a credit check on her.

Faith sat on her couch, rubbing Sissy's fur back and forth in what was sure to be a rather aggravating manner for a dog. But Sissy didn't seem to mind, and it gave Faith something to do with her agitated hands while she listened to Dixie's stream of remorseful apologies followed by poorly disguised inquiries into why checking a credit history would be so upsetting.

Faith had dreaded this conversation long into the night and early into the morning. It worried her almost as much as what Dixie had done in the first place. Anger had quickly been replaced by that burdensome fear that infested her sense of security nearly every moment of the day. It had been many months, but Faith still did not feel safe, and she knew beyond a shadow of a doubt that she never would.

Even grief had been superseded by this fear. She often thought of Paul, but never without horrible memories, or at the very least, angst over a future that seemed hopeless and dreary and dangerous.

"Faith?"

Faith shivered as that horrible picture—the one that seemed burned into her soul—flashed through her mind's eye with such definition it seemed all at once real and nightmarish.

"Faith?"

"What?" Faith's tone was heavy with impatience. She didn't mean it to be, but she had little energy left for social pleasantries.

"I'm sorry. You seemed to be distant, and I just wanted to make sure you knew how sorry I am to have done this. I really am so sorry. I didn't understand what you meant when you told me that, and if I had, of course I wouldn't have done it."

Faith's nostrils flared with an exhausted sigh. She was trying to decide the best way to tell Dixie she was fired when Dixie said, "I know something horrible must have happened."

"What do you mean?" It was nearly the first words out of Faith's mouth since Dixie had arrived this afternoon.

"You don't have to tell me, Faith. But something bad happened to you. There's a scar on your forehead and fear in those gorgeous eyes of yours. You fear what you can't see. Maybe you were in a car accident, maybe you weren't. But whatever the case, you are one scared little girl."

"Dixie, please leave."

"No."

Faith stood, causing Sissy to as well. "I said *leave.*"

"I won't."

A heavy and angry pulse throbbed in Faith's neck. "What are you doing?"

"I'm gonna protect you."

"Dixie, what are you talking about? I'm firing you. Don't you get that?"

"Fine, you can fire me. I don't have to get paid. But I'm still not going to leave—at least not until you understand that I'm going to protect you, your privacy, and your sense of security."

Faith folded her arms against her chest. "And how exactly are you going to do that?"

"For one, I'm going to pray. I'm going to pray that a thousand angels guide you and guard you and keep you safe."

"Dixie, just stop it. Stop with this religious fervor. I don't need your God or your angels or your compassion or pity. You've already done enough damage. Don't you get that? He can find—"

Faith turned away, stomping her foot. She'd said too much! She covered her face and cried. A hand cupped her shoulder but she shook it away. "You can never understand."

"I can try," Dixie said softly.

"God was not there for my husband, and God will not be here for me. I don't trust Him to keep me safe. I have to keep myself safe."

"From what, Faith?"

Faith did not answer. But in her head, she saw the face of the devil. Black eyes of coal.

"My friend, you do not have to believe. I will believe for you. I know that right now you can't believe."

Faith's walls of secrecy, what little security she had, tumbled before her. She hated herself for being gullible enough to trust someone to help her. It had backfired. What was she to do? She had already lost her confidence in Dixie. Could she ever trust her again? Something told her this stubborn Texan wasn't about to go away quietly, though, and that was a risk in itself.

"Dixie," she finally said, "please promise me you will not utter a word of this to anyone. Promise me."

"I promise." Dixie's words were spoken with a conviction Faith couldn't deny.

Faith stepped backward and fell into the cushions of her couch, exhausted beyond the point of return. "You remind me a lot of my husband, Paul," she said quietly.

"Oh?"

"Your faith. He was always so . . . I don't know," Faith said with a small laugh, "so confident in God. He really believed what the Bible said, you know? Never questioned it. Just believed." Faith sighed. "I think I'll sleep now,

Dixie. There is a list of things to do on the counter. You can come by tomorrow around the same time if you want. Okay?"

"Okay," Dixie said. "Thank you, Faith. I won't disappoint you again."

Dixie went to the door and opened it, but Faith's conscience couldn't let this good woman leave on those terms. "Dixie, you didn't disappoint me. It was just a mistake." But Faith hoped it wasn't a mistake that would cost her her life.

chapter twelve

faith spent another restless night contemplating her next move. The more rational side of her said her fear needed to be squelched. It drove her to do things that she knew were extreme. The fear was so alive, like a consort that shadowed her every move.

Far and deep inside her, there was a remnant of who she once was. She kept it buried most of the time because it tended to speak things she would rather not hear. But every once in a while it managed to whisper. And those very small whispers caused her to stare into the darkness and contemplate what seemed to be unthinkable.

But then the whisper would fade. And the monster would growl in the form of unspeakable grief and terror, haunting her, tickling her memory, touching her skin to remind her how delicate a breath of life can be.

The next morning Faith poured two cups of orange juice into her system and spent an hour on the phone researching how she might go about legally changing her name. When she was a child, she hated the name Faith. No one else had that name, and it seemed so dumb. But she had grown into it and realized as a teen that it was quite elegant. When she'd met Paul, he told her it was one of the first things he loved about her, that every time he said her name he felt closer to God.

Susan. That was a nice, familiar name. Susan Jones.

Yes. Or Linda Smith. Something that would drown in the sea of names in the phone book.

She finished the last of her orange juice and rubbed her temples. Her shoulder muscles ached with the torment of the night. Nothing new. Nights were torture. Days were long and tiresome.

Below her, Sissy whined, apparently growing bored watching Faith absently sip a beverage Sissy was not allowed to have. Faith scratched the dog's fur with about as much enthusiasm as she was using to sip her orange juice. But another whine reminded Faith that Sissy's strong personality was not about to let this go.

A rumble from her stomach reminded her she had not eaten breakfast, and she'd thought more than once last night she might try to go to Nik's again. By herself. Like a normal human being. Which she wasn't, by a long shot.

It was just a few blocks, a straight shot, and there were plenty of people around. Plus she had Sissy. She went to her safe, opened it with the key hidden in a shoe nearby, took some money out, then closed it. She wired herself money from her Swiss bank account every two months. "Okay, Sis, let's go."

She opened her front door with Sissy by her side, and she stood there. That horrible feeling of being watched wasn't there. Maybe it was the sound of traffic or the time of day. She didn't know. All she knew was that she felt . . . okay.

She locked the door and took the steps, then turned left and walked briskly. Sissy stayed right by her side and seemed to enjoy stepping up the pace. Within only a few short minutes, they had made their way to Nik's.

Inside, the smell of strong coffee, the sizzle of frying sausage, eggs, and bacon mixed with morning busyness. She adjusted her sunglasses over her eyes and waited impatiently for someone to help her. This was the worst part. Waiting for "help."

But it wasn't long. "Hi there. It's Sandy, from the other day."

"Hi," Faith said, smiling.

"I saw you over here. Let me help you to a table."

"Just walk ahead of me and my dog will follow," Faith said.

"Great."

"Can I have a window seat?"

"My whole section is window seats. How about here?"

"Fine," Faith said. She slid her hand along the side of the table, then took her seat. "I think I'll sit in your section every time I come. What days do you work?"

Sandy laughed. "What days don't I? Off on Sundays. Here for breakfast and lunch. Don't usually do the dinner crowd."

Faith smiled. "Okay. I'll have milk, two eggs over easy, four pieces of bacon, and a side of toast, white bread."

"Gotcha. Thanks."

Sandy was back quickly with her milk, asked what flavor of jam she liked, then was gone. Faith drank the milk and waited for her breakfast, her mind churning over what steps she needed to take. Dixie's mistake was probably not as tragic as Faith imagined it, and doing things like changing her name would probably only draw more attention to herself in this small town, plus pique Dixie's interest even more. She could just imagine saying, "Say, Dixie, from now on could you call me Susan?"

The food arrived. She knew by the way her pants couldn't be worn without a belt that she'd lost too much weight over the past few months.

She finished her meal and pushed the plate away, sneaking a couple of pieces of bacon down to Sissy.

"I like your dog."

The voice came from behind Faith, and she instinctively turned around.

"Her name's Sissy."

"I like dogs a lot," the man said.

"Me too."

"I had one, got hit by a car when I was a kid. Right after my mom died. Never had one since."

"You're a waiter here?"

"Busboy. Always make sure the table is nice and neat and very clean." He was a soft-spoken man. "Name's Wallace. Don't call me Wally. I really like to go by Wallace."

"That's a nice name."

Sissy relished the attention and then sniffed Faith's hand for more bacon.

"I'll take your plate for you. I try to help Sandy out. She's got a lot of customers. Everyone likes Sandy a lot."

"I can see why. She's nice."

When the plate and Wallace were gone, Faith sighed. It was a short and sweet conversation, but at least it was something. She scolded herself for believing for a moment that her life was normal enough to enjoy everyday conversations. Sandy and Wallace were normal people. This restaurant was a normal place. Bakerville was a normal town.

But Faith Kemper could never be normal again.

She didn't wait for her bill. She just laid money down on the table and walked out of the restaurant. She headed toward home, then stopped. Beneath her dark sunglasses, tears were forming. *Why* couldn't she be normal? Why couldn't she convince her heart that one day she would lose this thorn in her side?

She was a strong woman. Courageous. She'd stared the devil in the face and lived to tell about it. And she knew very well that she was making a conscious decision to live this way.

Faith's shoulders slumped with the heaviness of defeat. She knew what she had seen would threaten her life forever. She squeezed her eyes shut, enveloped in enraging thoughts.

It was her eyes that had put fear in her life and now endangered her life indefinitely. Her eyes had trapped her in a dark prison. And they had betrayed her, because what her eyes once saw, she could never forget. She'd prayed for her mind to forget. But it had not. Sight or no sight, she could still see.

And *he* knew that.

So she dwelt in the caves of obscurity as much as possible and tried to survive. Tried to hide. Tried to free herself from this bondage of fear.

It was futile and maddening.

Faith turned the corner toward her house and found enough self-discipline to stop the chaos in her head and focus on the tranquil morning. It was indeed beautiful and serene and calming.

And it was over in the next moment. Sissy scratched at the front door, and Faith found her key and inserted it into the lock.

"Faith Kemper?"

She could not turn around. A sharp and stunning panic sent pain through her body, paralyzing her—everything except her chin, which quivered uncontrollably.

ma'am? Are you Faith Kemper?" Mick stood at the bottom of the porch steps. He'd nearly given up finding her today. He'd knocked at the house a couple of times, and there was no answer. He decided to wait across the street in his car, in case she showed up. He'd been engrossed in some files when he happened to glance up and see a woman heading up to the house and unlocking the door.

Now she stood, seemingly paralyzed, with her back to him.

"I'm, um, Special Agent Mick Kline. I'm with the FBI."

She still did not turn around. This sent an urgent tingle through Mick. People who did not turn around when the FBI identified themselves were usually trouble. But then she turned, with a deliberateness that marked her as confident and self-assured.

She wore dark sunglasses, but even with them on, he could tell she was beautiful. Her hair was golden. Her lips curved delicately. Her skin shimmered. She was statuesque, though a little thin for her height.

"As I'm sure you can tell, sir, I am blind, so your credentials will do me no good."

Mick assumed she meant a badge that he wasn't flashing at the moment. Now he was in a bit of a bind. There was an 800 number he could give her to call to verify he worked for the FBI, but of course he wasn't supposed to be working for the FBI at the moment.

His first challenge.

Before he could think further, something heavy hit his body and threw him to the ground, his head knocking against the cement. The dog barked and Mrs. Kemper screamed with surprise, so he knew she hadn't tackled him. But whoever had wasn't hard to overcome, because with one swift jerk of his left arm, he had the person beneath him, arms pinned to their lower back.

It was a her. Middle-aged. Shrieking and kicking with the might of a three-hundred-pound man.

"Who are you?" Mick demanded.

"Faith, run! Run, Faith! Now!" the woman was yelling. Mick glanced up at Mrs. Kemper, whose mouth hung open in startled awe.

"Dixie, what are you doing?"

"Saving you! Hurry, run! Just run!"

"Ma'am," Mick said over all the hollering, "calm down! I'm with the FBI."

The woman stretched her neck to try to see him better. "You are?"

"Who are you?"

"Her bodyguard."

Mick looked at Mrs. Kemper. A small, amused smile spread across her lips, followed by a laugh. Mick crawled off Dixie and sat on the grass next to the sidewalk, rubbing his pounding head.

"Are you okay?" Mrs. Kemper asked.

"Yes," Dixie and Mick said simultaneously, then glanced at one another with a scowl.

Dixie stood up and brushed herself off. "You know, you shouldn't sneak up on a blind woman like that. She can't see who you are or what you want, you know."

Mick stared up at Dixie, an average-sized woman with black curly hair that was ratted to perfection. She had black eyes to match, small but intense. And a mouth that right now was painted red and puckered up like she'd just eaten a lemon. The face said it all . . . she already disapproved of him. But the hands on the hips, he guessed, were there for extra emphasis.

"First of all," Mick said, "I didn't sneak up on her. I approached her, and from a good distance back, I called out her name." Mick glanced at Faith, who was simply standing by the door, nearly expressionless. "Secondly, ma'am, I'd advise you that before you go and tackle someone like that, you might want to consider why they are there. For all you know, I could've been with Publishers Clearing House."

Dixie huffed. "Well, judging from the balloons you weren't carrying and the cardboard check you weren't handing her, I'd say my bet was safer."

Mick rolled his eyes. "Fine. Well, if we're done with the wrestling match here, I was hoping I could speak with you, Mrs. Kemper."

Faith Kemper's expressionless face now turned unsettled. The way her lips pressed together with tension marked an uncertainty that already intrigued Mick.

"Mrs. Kemper?"

"Look, first of all, I'm going to need to see some credentials," Dixie said.

Mick handed them over. She checked them carefully. "He's the real deal, Faith."

Faith recovered quickly, because the next time he looked at her, she was poised again.

"Thank you, Dixie. Listen, why don't you stop by in a couple of hours, if that's okay. I have quite a list today."

"You don't want me to stay?" she asked, still giving Mick the evil eye.

"No, I'll be fine," Faith replied, then turned to open the door and enter her house. Mick assumed he was supposed to follow, so he did. When he glanced at Dixie on his way past, he almost felt like sticking his tongue out at her.

Inside the house, Mick closed the door. It was a small house, but simple and well kept. There wasn't much decor other than a nice grandfather clock. Light streamed from the large window and sliding-glass door that led to the back porch and yard.

"Can I get you something to drink?"

"No thank you." Mick was a little thirsty, but he couldn't imagine troubling a blind woman for a drink.

"Please, sit."

"Uh . . . thanks," Mick said, already seated on the couch.

She set her things down and walked to the chair across from the couch and catty-corner to the TV. She sat down, keeping her sunglasses on.

"Um, Mrs. Kemper, you're probably wondering why I'm here."

She smiled a little. "It's not every day an FBI agent comes calling. Please, call me Faith."

"Okay. Faith. I'll just get right to the point. It's about your husband's murder."

He figured she must have expected something like that because she didn't flinch, nor did her expression change. She was deliberately gathered.

"What do you want to know?"

"I'm just curious about the case."

"Why? Are you investigating it?"

Mick could not read her, not without looking at her eyes, making it hard to decide whether he should tell her the real reason he was here. What would make a bigger difference? The heart or the head? He studied her openly.

"I think there may be a connection between your

husband's murder and a couple others around the state. I just wanted to talk to you about it, if that's okay."

Her back was straight, in perfect posture, her hands resting on the armrests. "Why would that be okay?"

Mick couldn't help but look surprised, though he supposed that didn't matter much. "Well, ma'am, this may help to find your husband's killer. Don't you want that?"

"And how would it help do that?"

Mick swallowed. Tough customer. "I understand this is painful for you. But I need to ask you a few questions, all right? There's a real chance we could find whoever did this to Paul."

"You say his name like you know him."

Mick shrugged. "Obviously I don't, but I have read a great deal about his case. I feel like I know him a little. And you." Mick scratched his nose nervously, trying to find the right angle with this woman. "Look, I'll be honest here. I'm working on a lead that your husband might have been a victim of a serial killer."

The skin that had glowed earlier now paled to a light ash color. "A serial killer."

"Yes. I don't mean to frighten you here, but I'm just trying to connect the dots between several murders, and your husband's is the one I have the least information about."

"Oh?"

"That's why I'm here. To learn everything I can so I can catch whoever did this to your husband."

A half laugh escaped her lips. "You make it sound so personal."

Mick leaned into the couch, closing his eyes and trying to decide where to go from here. The woman wasn't wanting to cooperate, he presumed, because recounting the incident was too painful. He pulled two pieces of paper out of his pocket.

"Here's what I know. You and your husband were leaving a party almost two years ago when you were both attacked by someone." Mick paused. She gave no reaction. "You thought you'd dropped an earring in the stairwell. You went back to get it, your husband continued on. You came out to find him by your car, injured. You turned around to go get help, and you were attacked."

"Not injured. Dead. He was dead." Faith's demeanor remained steady. "Where did you say you're from again?"

"Dallas."

"Well, you came an awfully long way to recite that, sir."

He cleared his throat. "Can you tell me anything else you might remember? Even if it seems small and insignificant."

"I'm not sure what you want. Haven't you read the police report? I told them everything I know."

Mick squeezed his hands together. No, he had not. That's why he was here. "Maybe more detail about the man you saw."

"I didn't see him. Didn't you read that?"

"Yes, of course," Mick stumbled. "I just meant, any detail that you might've remembered since."

There was a long pause, as if Faith were studying him through the silence. Even studying the silence. "Why aren't you talking with the police about this?"

"I intend to. I'm just beginning my investigation. But I can tell you from experience I always get my best information from witnesses."

"And your best witness is blind. I don't understand how I can be of any help to you. I'm trying to forget what happened. I'm trying to move on with my life."

"I respect that. But can you really go on, knowing your husband's killer is still out there?"

Her arms crossed tensely. "Sounds accusatory to me."

"It's not meant to be. But it seems like you don't want to cooperate with me, and I can't imagine why."

"No, I imagine you can't." She swallowed back some of the terseness in her voice and said, "Look, it was a horrible time. My husband, as you know, was a police officer. The force did everything they could to try to solve this, but they couldn't. Pardon me for not being overly enthusiastic about your being here. I'm sure your intentions are good, but I can't help you. It's not that I don't want to. But I can't. Nothing has changed since it happened. My husband is still dead. And I don't remember anything about being attacked."

Mick nodded, then remembered to say, "Okay."

"You can show yourself to the door faster than I can." She smiled a little, gesturing in that direction.

"Right." He took out a card and laid it on the coffee table. "If you have any more information, please call my cell phone. Your bodyguard can read off the number." He went to the door, then turned back to her. She sat perfectly still. "Why do you need a bodyguard, anyway?"

"She's not my bodyguard. Just my assistant. She likes to think she can protect me."

"Protect you from what?"

He couldn't see her eyes, but he knew she blinked—that steady blink of acknowledgment that tells a profiler when someone knows more than they're saying.

"From a seeing world."

"Ah." He opened the door. "Call me if you want to discuss this further." He closed the door behind her, took a quick look around to make sure Dixie was nowhere in sight, then walked to his car.

Faith Kemper was hiding something. She was also a very scared woman. Now Mick had to find out why.

chapter fourteen

mick looked over the menu at the small diner that apparently had no name other than Diner. "I'll take the turkey sandwich. Absolutely no egg-based condiment on it. And I want it heated."

"You want it what?"

"Heated."

"It comes with lettuce and tomato. You want it heated? A cold deli sandwich?"

"For at least one minute on high in the microwave."

The waitress laughed and looked around, as if wondering if anyone else was hearing this. "Why?"

"To kill the germs."

"Listen," she hissed, "we all wash our hands around here, you got that? It says so on the bathroom mirror. Go in there and read it if you like."

Mick tried to smile. "Not your germs. Meat germs. Bacteria."

"Our meat ain't germy either, mister."

"Can you just heat it up?"

"Fine. Sure. Whatever. The customer's always right." She scratched it down on her notepad. "We got soup, you know. It's hot already."

"And tea."

"You want that boiling?"

Mick supposed in this small sub shop, the waitresses

weren't accustomed to special orders. It might be a risk to even ask for it with lemon. "On ice, please."

The waitress turned and rushed to the counter, eager to tell the other waitresses, who were ignoring their customers to stare at the new guy in town. He wasn't sure what the problem was, but thirty minutes later, a sandwich that should have taken only two minutes to assemble and one minute to heat arrived. Steaming. He let it cool for a while, then took a bite.

Mick chewed slowly, writing some thoughts down on a steno pad. Before leaving Bakerville, he'd checked into a hotel. He had a feeling Bakerville and Faith Kemper were going to give him a lot more information . . . and plenty of reasons to return.

He was now waiting for the police chief of Allana, a small and poor suburb outside Houston, to return from lunch, so he'd decided to grab lunch himself at a small sandwich shop that apparently wasn't used to strangers.

Mick tried to look inconspicuous, but even the waitress who served his turkey sub eyed him as if he might just know what she did last summer.

From the sandwich shop, he had a good view of the police department, small like in most towns of this size. It had taken him a couple of hours to drive from Bakerville, giving him time to appreciate the Eagles' CD and survey his thoughts on Faith Kemper. He would return to talk to her, but first he needed information and leverage. Apparently, offering to find her husband's killer wasn't enough.

According to the information he'd gleaned from the newspaper articles, there had been a man the police first considered a suspect, then later considered an eyewitness. Mick wanted to find out more about him and why he was still free.

Mick's appetite waned a little, and he pushed the other

half of his sandwich away. He stared out the window and watched the front door of the police station.

"You that federal agent?"

Mick looked up to find a husky uniformed officer with pinched eyes and a thick mustache staring down at him, one hand on his holster, the other holding a pair of military-issue sunglasses.

"Well, I don't know. You'll have to be more specific. There's a lot of us federal agents around."

The chief's eyes flashed. "Too many, if you ask me. Too many, if you ask the folks around here. We don't much like the federal government. And I can't imagine, boy, why you'd be poking your nose around here."

"Mick Kline." He held out his hand, and the chief took it begrudgingly, introducing himself as Chief Underwood. Mick felt like he was talking to John Wayne, the way the chief's legs bowed slightly, his hat cocked downward just a nudge. "I want some information on a man named Miguel Juarez. Does he still live around here?"

"Yeah." The chief's tightly drawn face slid into an expression of disgust. He sat down across from Mick and took off his hat, revealing nothing but baby fuzz, and not much of that. "What'd you want to know about that loser?"

"Well, he was a witness to the murder of a police officer two years ago. Paul Kemper."

"A witness." Disdain thickened his drawl.

"He claims not to have seen whoever committed the murder, right?"

"Who wants to know? The FBI?"

"We think there may be a connection between Kemper's murder and several others around Texas, Oklahoma, and New Mexico."

This obviously intrigued Underwood, and he pulled at

117

the hair in his mustache. "You think Juarez might be connected to the murder?"

Mick studied the chief. "You think Juarez did it?"

"Juarez is a good-for-nothing Mexican immigrant. Probably killed the man for his cash."

"Was there cash taken from the scene?"

"No. Probably got scared off by the wife."

"Who was also attacked."

"Yes. Poor lady." The chief's narrow eyes did not, however, glint with compassion.

"So you think it was Juarez who did it."

"There was a lot of information pointing in that direction. Juarez's story had holes in it. And it changed here and there."

"But not enough evidence to arrest him."

"That's right."

Mick realized he better back off some. Whatever the reason, this was sensitive territory. Had the police department botched the investigation? "So he still lives around here?" Mick asked.

"Out west of town. I want to know more about why you're here. What makes you think Juarez is connected to these other cases?"

"I don't know. That's why I'm here."

"You think you got yourself a serial killer, don't you?"

"Chief Underwood, with all due respect, I don't know what I have yet. Except a lot of dead law enforcement officers."

"I don't like you pokin' your nose around here, but I'd like nothing better than to see Juarez get what's coming to him."

"You're sure he did it."

"I know it."

Mick slid his card over to Underwood. "Here's my cell

number. If you think of anything else that might . . . put Juarez where he belongs."

Underwood flipped the card between his fingers, then stuck it between his two front teeth, picking at what must have been lunch. "You think you can do what we couldn't?"

"I'm just here to try to find the truth, Chief. Nothing more, nothing less."

The chief stood and plopped his hat back onto his round head. "The truth." He laughed, sliding the makeshift toothpick into his front pocket. "It's never as simple as that, Agent Kline. And I've learned from experience things aren't always what they seem now, are they?"

Mick watched the chief turn and walk out of the restaurant. The customers stared blatantly, then went back to their business. He signaled to the waitress that he needed the check. You would've thought he'd asked for a soy burger with sprouts.

"Your dog likes me," Wallace said. He didn't make eye contact with Faith, only with the dog. Animals had always liked him better than people did. But he marveled at how he was even able to speak to the woman, to come up with that kind of courage. He noticed in his life that courage would come and go, and he never quite knew when or why. "Here, you want to sit in Sandy's area, don't you?" Wallace pointed over to Sandy's section.

"Yes. It's nice to have the same waitress when possible." She paused. "I never know when to seat myself or when to wait."

"Sign hasn't changed since I been here."

"How long is that?" she asked.

Wallace was careful to seat her at the same table as before. People liked to have their own tables at a restaurant.

He didn't know why. "Here you go." Wallace moved out of her way, watching the dog curl herself under the table and stare up at him like he hadn't just taken the time to pet her. Ungrateful.

"Not long." Wallace glanced at her and then looked around the restaurant. He'd probably be in trouble if they saw him talking to a customer. "Just moved here."

She grinned. "Me, too. I just live around the corner. This is an easy walk for me."

"I'll get Sandy." He looked back once at the dog. But she had closed her eyes.

Wallace's social awkwardness did not bother Faith. He was probably a lonely soul like herself. How many were there in the world? Millions whose best friends were a TV set and takeout. What drives a lonely soul to a place like Bakerville? Unless you were born here, she couldn't imagine.

"Hi. It's Sandy."

"Hi, Sandy. Um, I'm not sure I introduced myself the other day. Faith."

"What a wonderful name. Feel free to sit in my section anytime, okay?"

"Thanks."

"Now, will it be iced tea today?"

"Yes. With lemon. And I'll take a Caesar salad."

"Our soup of the day is vegetable beef."

"Sounds wonderful. I'll have a cup."

"Good!" Sandy was gone, and without the conversation of another human being, her mind would only think of one thing: the FBI agent. Mick Kline from Dallas.

"He's from Dallas."

"Huh?"

"Hey. Figured you might be here since I went by your

120

house and nobody was home." Dixie patted her on the shoulder.

Faith realized how deep in thought she tended to be lately, even in public. She shook her head. "I'm so sorry. I forgot you were coming. I had to get out of the house for a while." That was an understatement. She'd walked in circles for over an hour, trying to get a grip.

"I understand." Dixie sat across from her and acknowledged Sissy with a pat to the head. "Hey, girl." She then spoke to Faith. "I checked him out."

"Who?"

"The FBI fellow. I mean, I guess anyone can flash credentials, you know? But I called the Dallas office."

"And they said he worked there?"

"Well, didn't get anybody to answer. Just asked the operator for him, and a voice mail picked up saying he was going to be out of the office for four weeks or something. But anyway, it was definitely his voice mail."

Sandy delivered Faith's drink and asked for Dixie's order. "Honey, I'll just take a cola. Mixed half and half just like before. That's half diet, not half vodka."

Sandy laughed. "I remember. No problem."

"So, was he here about your husband's accident?"

Faith fingered the scar on her forehead. How she wished it had been from a car accident. Now Dixie knew more than she should, and Faith also knew she wasn't buying the accident story.

"Dixie, I guess you realize that I haven't been completely forthright with you."

"It's okay. You don't have to tell me anything you don't want to."

"It's for your own protection."

"Faith, are you in trouble? in danger?" At least Dixie had enough sense to whisper about it.

"I don't want to drag you into this, okay? Please, just do what I said from the beginning, all right? Keep quiet about me as much as you can. This is a small town, but it's not tiny. I can come eat here, live at my house, and go unnoticed for the most part. You're going to have to help me do that, though. By just being quiet about me. That's all you have to do. Just be quiet."

Dixie was silent for a long time. Then she said, "Whatever you want, I will do."

"Good."

"Whatever it is you're running from, it must be terrible."

"No questions, okay? Fair enough?"

"Fair enough," Dixie said disappointedly. But then she perked up. "Listen, we're having a spring fling at the church. The ladies bring quilts and crafts they've made, and we sell them and use the money for missions."

Faith pulled money from her purse and slid it across the table to Dixie. "Here."

"What's this?"

"A twenty."

"Yes, but I mean, what's this for?"

"For your mission trip. I always believed in helping the poor."

Dixie paused again. "I meant for you to come to meet some people, Faith. There are good people in this church."

Faith shook her head. "Dixie, didn't you understand what I just said to you? I'm not here to meet people. I'm here to hide." Faith squeezed her eyes shut and wanted to curse. *Hide.* Why did she have to say that?

"You're so afraid. I won't ask of what. But I know you are."

"I'm fine, Dixie. I'm not hiding. That's too strong a word, okay? Wrong word. I'm just here to enjoy a quiet, peaceful life. I want my solitude. I meant, hiding from life, I guess. My husband's dead, and I need solitude."

"You need God. I won't push Him on you, because I know that's a turnoff for people. I could sit here and preach at you till I was blue in the face, but until you're ready in your own heart, you're not going to do anything about it."

"Dixie, I do not want to discuss God with you. I will not."

"Okay, okay. I won't push it. But think about the neighborhood picnic a couple of weeks down the road."

Faith bit her lip to keep from screaming. Was this woman deaf? Dixie slurped her soda mix through her straw, filling up the awkward silence. Sandy brought out her salad, and Faith cut the lettuce into bite-sized pieces. Well, at least Dixie could tackle a man and throw him to the ground with no problem. That might come in handy.

chapter fifteen

mick discovered that west of Allana was the poor side. Mechanic shops, tire stores, and a run-down, hole-in-the-wall diner lined the dusty streets. Latinos sat against storefronts, staring down whoever passed.

Mick managed to get a woman to tell him she thought Juarez might be working at a church "two streets down and one over."

Amazingly, Mick found it without much trouble. It was a small, wood-frame Baptist church. Slightly isolated, thankfully, so Mick didn't have to worry about what the "townsfolk" thought. He parked his car and got out. The front doors of the church were wide open, probably due to the heat already descending on southern Texas, even though it was only spring.

"Hello?"

His call went unanswered.

"Hello? Anyone here?"

The sanctuary had no stained glass, just two plain windows on either side. Mick thought the place seated about a hundred and fifty. He walked down the center aisle, figuring somebody had to be around.

Then he heard hammering coming from outside behind the church. Behind the baptistry, he found a small door

125

leading down a hallway and to the backyard of the church. He followed it, and it led him to a man on a ladder.

"Miguel Juarez?"

The man looked down at him, apparently trying to decide whether this meant he needed to come off the ladder or not. He studied Mick and then climbed down.

"Who wants to know?"

"I just wanted to ask you a few questions." Mick offered a hand. "Mick Kline. I'm with the FBI."

This drew a disgusted snort from the man. Then he took off, running toward a wooded area thick enough that if Mick didn't keep up, he could lose him. He had no backup. No partner. Mick was simply going to have to catch him.

And he did, within a matter of a few yards. He pushed the man to the ground, leapt on top of him, and pulled his hands behind his back. Mick didn't draw his gun, though his fingers were not far from pulling it out at a moment's notice.

"Who are you?" Mick demanded. "Are you Juarez?"

"Yes," he replied, his teeth clenched together, his lips pulled back like a snarling dog's. "Did Underwood send you out here? Are you arresting me? What evidence do you have? I want a lawyer! I know my rights!" His thick Spanish accent did not make his English too hard to understood.

"I'm going to get off you, but if you decide to run again, you're going to regret it." Mick slowly backed off the man and stood. Juarez rolled over and wiped dirt off his face, which Mick had planted firmly into the ground. "You're not under arrest. I meant it when I said I wanted to ask you a few questions. You obviously know about what or you wouldn't have run."

Juarez looked down, shaking his head. He stood up slowly, Mick hoped to show he wasn't going anywhere. Juarez leaned against a nearby tree, catching his breath and licking sweat off his lips. "You're FBI."

"I'm here to ask you about what you saw when Paul Kemper was killed. That's all." Mick stared at his eyes.

Skepticism drew a half smile onto Juarez's face. "Yeah, right. You're here because of Underwood, aren't you?"

"No. I'm here because—" Mick chose his words carefully—"you're a witness." *A witness who likes to run from law enforcement for no particular reason, but nevertheless, I'll give you the benefit of the doubt,* Mick thought.

Juarez was still catching his breath, his eyes blinking slowly, as if he'd been through this a thousand times. Dirt and sweat covered his white tank top, and his jeans were ripped in so many places they were barely holding together. "You're not here to arrest me?"

"No." Mick said the word with feigned conviction. If Juarez was his lead suspect, he didn't want him getting any funny ideas.

"I'm not going to talk to you," Juarez said. Mick noticed his fingernails clawing into the bark of the tree he was leaning against. A gold watch he wore glinted in the bright sun. "You've been talking to Underwood, I can tell. And it doesn't matter what I say, you will not believe it."

"That's not true." Mick stood firm, his eyes boring into Juarez's. "Don't judge me according to Chief Underwood. I am not him."

"You are trying to tell me you are here because you think I might have seen something in that murder."

"That's what I'm saying."

"I have told the police everything, but they do not believe me. Why should you?"

"I like to give people the benefit of the doubt." Mick studied Juarez. It wasn't an easy task reading him. His startled eyes told a different story than his determined mouth. Juarez's lips pressed together; his nostrils flared with a hint of knowing injustice. But those eyes . . . they betrayed him. There was something not right.

"Miguel, if you did nothing wrong, then you can trust me," Mick said. "But if you killed Paul Kemper, then you should watch your back."

"I cannot trust you. This is the land of justice, but there is no justice."

"There is justice for Paul Kemper. I will make sure of that." Mick tried to get Juarez to look at him, but he wouldn't. "You can trust me if you tell me the truth."

"Does it matter what the truth is?" Miguel said slowly. "No compass, no one way, no meaning to truth anymore. Don't you know that? You, seeing the evils of this world working for the FBI, must see how many times evil can justify itself, can tell you it is working for good."

"Miguel," Mick tried again, "you must tell me what you know."

"Yes, so you can scrutinize me, terrorize my family."

"No. So I can clear your name."

Miguel laughed with a sardonic tone that put Mick on guard. But then the tone faded, and the cynical laugh grew tired and weary. Miguel stared at the dirt and grass under his feet. "I did not kill that man."

"Then tell me."

"Tell you what?" The rage in Miguel's eyes had a certain helplessness. "I was there. I was in the parking garage, parking cars. My job. And all I saw was someone running to go get help. That's all I saw. I heard a woman screaming for someone to go get help."

"Did you get help?"

"No, someone else did. I didn't know what was going on, so I just went back to my business. It seemed handled. I have no medical expertise, so I could not do anything."

"Then why does Underwood have you under the microscope?"

"Because he's a racist! He hates Latinos. The man should move somewhere else, you know, somewhere not in south Texas. But I was the only Latino around that night. And he targeted me."

Mick's mind raced. Things were missing. Details. Facts. The dots were beginning to connect, but there were many things missing.

"He harasses my family. He is always making sure I know he is around. He is a dirty cop, you know. A dirty cop. I should leave here, but that would only make me look guilty, would it not? And so I cannot stay, I cannot leave. I have nothing to do but work and go home and try to keep my wife from . . . " His words trailed off, belying his contentiousness. "This is hard on her."

Mick nodded. "I understand. So that's all. You just happened to be in the wrong place at the wrong time."

Miguel said, "A lot like Señor Kemper."

Sweat dripped from the hollow of Faith's neck and down her chest as she sat up. "Sissy?"

Sissy's whine came from the back door, where she was scratching and obviously interested in something going on outside. With the back of her hand, Faith wiped the sweat from her forehead and tried to gather herself. She had been dreaming. Of Paul. She hated waking up from those dreams. They always seemed so real.

Her damp skin indicated she probably needed to turn on the air-conditioning. The ceiling fan wasn't doing its job. The temperature had risen from the sixties to the seventies. Summer was around the corner, but it made no difference to her what the season was. For her the change of seasons brought only changes in the weather.

Sissy whined again, and Faith joined her at the back door. "You want to go out, girl?" When she opened the door, Sissy scrambled out. Closing it again, she went to the kitchen for a glass of water.

But then a chill went down her spine. And another one. Someone was watching her. She knew it. She dropped the glass to the counter and scurried toward the back door, fumbling to get the safety bar down. Where was Sissy? Should she open the back door and call for her?

Faith returned to the kitchen and grabbed her cordless phone. If she had to, she could dial 911. But she didn't want to if it was nothing. In a small town like this, having the police surround your house was just asking to be noticed . . . for all the wrong reasons. Her fingers glided over the numbers, rehearsing the keypad so she could dial in an instant.

She opened the door and called for Sissy, but the dog was not around. "Sissy!" Her voice betrayed her feigned calm. "Come! Now!"

Suddenly she was there, her fur soft against Faith's leg. Faith shut the door quickly, put the safety bar down, and pulled the curtains. But Sissy was still whimpering. "What is it, girl?" Faith stroked her head, then went to the front door to make sure it was locked. She pulled all the blinds in the house.

She could feel being watched. She knew it, even if she couldn't see who was watching her. She prayed it was that agent. Or maybe Dixie. But someone was out there.

chapter sixteen

the meaning to the lyrics of "Hotel California" was as much of a mystery to Mick as Miguel Juarez was. As he drove toward Houston, managing the insane traffic that suffocated the city, he found himself reminiscing about a time when the lyrics to that song didn't matter. Everyone just sat around listening to it, assuming it meant that all the Eagles were addicted to cocaine or alcohol or something else. Or maybe it was their fascination with the occult. Or maybe the whole song was about Stevie Nicks. Who knew. Whatever the case, it meant a lot more back before he knew God than it did now. He laughed and punched to the next song on the CD.

Miguel Juarez, he had decided, was hiding something. Faith Kemper, he knew for certain, was also hiding something. What was the connection? Did they know each other? Whatever it was, there was a lot more to Paul Kemper's murder than met the eye.

Mick sighed at the traffic, his tendons aching from the slow pace and awkward way his foot was keeping the accelerator at fifteen miles an hour. He'd apparently hit the five-o'clock traffic, which in any big city starts at three-thirty and ends at seven. He tilted his seat back and upped the air-conditioning. Then he dialed Reggie.

"Hey, dude!"

"Hi, Reg. How's everything going?"

"It's all right, it's all right. I'm just out here going through some evidence in that Patterson case. I mean, there's like a billion file folders in this warehouse."

"Fun. Listen, can I ask a favor?"

Reggie paused. "You're in Houston, aren't you?"

"Yeah. Um, I need you to do some checking on a Miguel Juarez." Mick spelled the name for him.

"What do you need to know?"

"Just the basics, man. Just check NICS, LESC—" Mick paused. Hesitation from Reggie seeped through his earpiece. "Listen, Reg, I'm not going to ask you to do anything that compromises your morals, okay? Only do whatever you feel comfortable with. And only if you . . . if you believe in what I'm doing down here. If not, I understand. And I won't push it, okay?"

Reggie said, "I'll get back to you." Then he hung up.

Mick stuck his phone back in his pocket and looked at his map. According to his printout, St. Luke's Episcopal Hospital, where the article said Faith had been treated, looked to be just a couple miles away. He was looking for Bertner Avenue.

But he realized he didn't really need to find the street—the huge medical complex loomed on the horizon.

─────────

Mick had hoped he might catch the emergency room on a less busy day, but that was not the case. Chatter was only superseded by beeping monitors and urgent pages over the intercom system. A half-empty waiting room looked to be keeping the staff busy. A young boy holding his arm whimpered in his mother's lap. An old lady with the cough of a barking seal slumped in her wheelchair. And then there was the couple in the corner, crying, obviously waiting for news of a loved one.

Mick looked away and headed for the nurses' desk. A tired-looking woman and a thin, middle-aged man were in discussion when Mick approached. "Hi."

"Sir, if you've already registered, take a seat and we'll call your name when we can." The woman had only glanced up at him.

The male nurse said, "You don't look sick."

Mick smiled. "I'm not. I'm Special Agent Mick Kline. I'm with the FBI."

The woman looked up, then said, "Well, if you're here to question the guy who got shot this morning, he died during surgery. The police were here just a little bit ago."

"Actually, I wanted to see if I could speak with a Dr. Ramsey Mahada? Does he still work here?"

The two looked at each other. "Yes. Dr. Mahada is chief resident of Emergency Medicine."

"Good. Is he here? I just need to speak with him briefly about a patient he treated."

"Okay . . . " The female nurse left the desk and motioned for Mick to follow her. She shouted out a few orders here and there as she passed curtains and moaning patients. Mick's stomach turned. He was not one for blood, vomit, or anything else that caused the need to be in the hospital. He'd been in the hospital once, for food poisoning, and that was quite enough for him.

"Stay here," the nurse said and went behind a curtain. She emerged shortly. "Stay. He'll be out in a moment." Then she was gone.

A man behind the curtain was screaming like a woman and complaining about something or someone. The doctor came out with another nurse, saying, "Get Dr. Yates down here now. That thing's about to rupture, and he needs to be in surgery immediately." The patient screamed again.

Mick felt light-headed.

"You're the guy?" Dr. Mahada's attention was on him suddenly.

"Special Agent Mick Kline."

The doctor scribbled something down on the clipboard he was carrying. "Uh-huh. As you can see, we have our hands full today. Things are crazier than usual." The man screamed again. Mick swallowed. "Do you think you could make an appointment?"

"Dr. Mahada!" a nurse shouted. "Broken leg in two!"

Dr. Mahada glanced over his shoulder, nodded, and then looked back at Mick. "Can you?"

"It's about a patient you saw almost two years ago."

The doctor laughed. "Two years ago? Do you know how many patients I see in a day here?"

Mick nodded. "Maybe you'll recall. Faith Kemper."

The doctor's laugh vanished. And the nurse beside him, a woman in her mid to late thirties, lowered her head. The doctor looked at the nurse, handed her the clipboard, and said, "Kerri, go page Dr. Yates, okay?"

Glancing at Mick, she rushed away. Mick looked back at the doctor, who was quickly scanning the room to see what was presenting itself. Things seemed to quiet a little.

"Of course I remember Mrs. Kemper. I was on duty the night she was brought in."

"I'm investigating the murder in conjunction with a theory that it may have been serial in nature."

Dr. Mahada's eyes widened. "Oh?"

"Just wondering what you can tell me about that night."

"I told the police everything I know."

"I understand, but sometimes an insignificant detail can make all the difference when attached to another theory."

The doctor nodded as another nurse was flagging him down. He acknowledged her with a polite lift of his finger. "Okay, but it's going to have to be fast."

"Thank you." Mick took out his notepad.

"Mrs. Kemper was brought in with trauma to her head, looked like someone hit her with some sort of blunt, heavy, thin object. Like a crowbar. Anyway, she had a gash across her forehead. She had also been hit in the back of the head, but we were never sure with what. Her brain swelled, and she was in a coma for, I believe, two days. She was diagnosed with Purtscher retinopathy. Multiple cotton-wool spots were located around the optic nerve. She also suffered slight motor-skill problems due to the brain swelling."

"Purtscher retinopathy? Plain English, please."

"She's blind." The doctor shook his head. "We're guarded on the prognosis of Purtscher retinopathy. It's never cut and dry, and many times patients do not regain their eyesight. Unfortunately, that was true for Mrs. Kemper."

Mick nodded, writing notes down. "Did she ever speak about the incident, say anyone's name? Do you remember her talking about a Miguel Juarez?"

"No, she didn't say much after the coma. She was traumatized, very upset about her husband's death. Very shaken up, as I recall. I didn't take care of her, of course, after she was admitted, but I did go up to check on her one or two times." Another nurse called out to him, and he nodded at her. "Look, that's really all I know. Her husband was brought in DOA, and the police were buzzing around here, trying to get a description of the suspect. But Mrs. Kemper was in a coma, and when she awoke, she was blind. It was just a mess."

Mick held out his hand to the doctor. "I guess you see a lot of messes in here, don't you?"

The doctor smiled. "And every once in a while a miracle or two."

"Thank you for your time."

Dr. Mahada reached into his coat pocket and pulled out

a business card. "Call me if you need anything else. I sure would like to see whoever did this get caught."

"Thanks." Mick closed his notepad and watched the doctor hurry off to another patient. He tucked the doctor's card into his shirt pocket and headed out of the emergency room, trying to find free coffee. In a small corridor he found coffee service, complete with real cream on melted ice and what looked to be fairly fresh, hot coffee. He poured a cup, choosing to stir powdered creamer instead of the potentially hazardous milk product into his coffee.

As his plastic stirrer scraped around and around the sides of the cup, Mick's mind wandered. There were so many unanswered questions, so many loose ends on this case. Connecting them might be possible, but it seemed an eternity away.

"Excuse me."

Mick turned to find the nurse who had been by Dr. Mahada's side before. "Yes?"

"You were wanting information about Faith Kemper."

"Yes. Do you know anything?" Mick set down his coffee and pulled out his notepad.

"I know too much," she said, her eyes glassy with emotion. "She was my best friend."

Mick lowered his pen and pad and gave his full attention to this woman. "What's your name?"

"Kerri Pratt."

"You said Faith *was* your best friend."

"Yes. What happened to Faith was so terrible, and she never got over it. Then she moved away, moved again. I don't know. She just separated herself from everyone and everything that used to be in her former life. She was scared to death, and nothing any of us said could help her. Sometimes I think she literally went insane."

"What was she scared of?"

136

Kerri's eyes widened. "What do you mean?"

"I don't understand what Faith was scared of. Scared of whoever did this to her?" Mick was jotting down notes again. "Was someone out to get both of them or something?"

Kerri stared at Mick. "You don't know about the . . . "

Mick swallowed. This was information he was going to need. "I'm working on another case that I think may be linked, so I, uh, haven't read all the details of this case."

"She was scared because of the note."

"The note?"

Kerri looked away. "The killer left a note."

Mick's heart thumped in anticipation.

"My husband, Greg, is a police officer," Kerri continued. "He had to go in and tell Faith about the note. They went back and forth for a long time on whether or not to tell her, but in the end, they felt like she had to know. It wasn't fair for her not to know. I think that's what sent her over the edge."

"Are you telling me that the killer left a piece of paper with a note to Faith at the scene of the crime?"

Kerri shook her head. "No. It wasn't on a piece of paper." Her voice quivered. "He wrote it on the back passenger-side window of her car with lipstick he got out of her purse."

"What did the note say?"

The nurse looked around, her eyes moist with the emotion attached to whatever she was about to say. " 'If you see my face again, you will die.' "

chapter seventeen

kerri slowly peeled a banana as they sat in the hospital cafeteria. The conversation they were engaged in dimmed what Mick perceived as usually bright and cheerful eyes. He knew she did not have an appetite, but she ate anyway because it would probably be hours before she could eat again.

"It amazes me that none of this leaked to the press," Mick said. "I mean, this is a detail that I can't imagine people staying quiet about."

"Yeah, I guess." Kerri shrugged. "But it was an officer, you know? And his wife. And no one in the department wanted to jeopardize the case for any reason. Details never leaked out. To an extent, nobody wanted to talk about it anyway. As the weeks went on and there was no arrest, it just became a terrible burden on the guys. A lot of them turned to alcohol. A few had to get counseling—things like that." She bit her lip and glanced at Mick. "Our marriage even had some problems. Greg became obsessed with finding who killed Paul."

"I understand."

"That note," Kerri said with a disgusted half laugh, "it became so ironic, you know? I mean, she would never see again. . . ." She gathered herself. "The investigators thought it was probably just a scare tactic, but whatever it was, it worked. Faith was never the same again." Tears streamed down Kerri's cheeks. "She didn't want anything to do with us after that. She's been running, you know? Just running in darkness."

Kerri took a napkin and blotted her eyes. "Probably the only person she kept in some contact with, at least initially, was her grandmother. But Faith stopped visiting her when she moved and stopped writing her shortly after that. I think Faith felt that if she kept in contact with her grandmother, her life might be in danger too. I don't know. So much never made sense. It still doesn't. Senseless violence." She took a bite of her banana, chewing without delight. "I see it every day here, you know. But then it became personal. It made it hard for me to do my job from that day forward."

Mick nodded. He understood that too. He let silence clear the air for a little bit as he went over his notes. Kerri studied her banana. "Let me ask you about Miguel Juarez," Mick said finally.

"The witness."

"Yes. What do you know about him?"

"Not much. Just that he was parking cars that night."

"It's not clear whether or not he was a suspect. The police chief out in Allana thinks so."

"I don't know. Greg never talked much about the details of the case."

"But he told you about the note."

She nodded, closing the peel to the rest of the banana. She put it on the tray on the table next to theirs. "Yeah. That part he just couldn't deal with alone." Kerri watched him take notes and then said, "So, why do you think this case is linked to another one? What's the other case?"

"I can't talk about it," Mick said somberly. "I'm sorry. I wish I could. But I can say that I am working on a theory that whoever killed Paul Kemper didn't stop there."

"Greg hasn't said anything about any new leads."

"He doesn't know. This isn't something that has a whole lot of . . . merit . . . behind it. But there are possibilities, and so they're worth investigating, right?"

"Sure." Kerri checked her watch. "I'm sorry, Agent Kline. I have to get back to work."

"Please, call me Mick. Here." He handed her his card and pointed to the cell number. "I'm staying at a motel in Bakerville. Please call me if you think of anything else that might be useful."

Kerri took the card and examined it before putting it in her pocket. "I will. Good luck," she said, shaking his hand.

"Kerri, one more thing."

"Yes?"

"Where can I find Faith's grandmother?"

Mick stood outside the front doors of the nursing home, gearing himself up for what was probably going to be a very long "quick" visit. He avoided hospitals like the plague. But nursing homes were a close second for the very same reason: the plague, or at the very least, the smell and the reminder of how quickly human life can be forgotten and disregarded. He closed his eyes and gathered himself, then walked in, trying to hold his breath.

A jovial but tired-looking black woman in her fifties sat behind a reception desk, clicking away on her computer. She glanced up briefly. "Help you?"

"Here to see Bea Murtaugh."

"Uh-huh. Sign in here." She gestured toward a clipboard sitting on the counter. Mick obeyed. Then the woman said, "Down the hall, take a left, and it's the second on the right. Room 278."

"Um, thanks. Say . . . uh . . . what are the security procedures here?"

The woman, whose name tag aptly read *Bertha,* as she was large with shoulders broad enough to rival a linebacker's, cocked an eyebrow. "They don't escape, if that's what you mean."

"No, just about general security."

"Oh, I see." She stood up and put her fists on her hips. "Well, first of all, they have to get past me."

Mick chuckled. "I see. That's good enough for me."

She smiled and sat back down. "I have a sense about people, secondly; and I don't sense you're the kind of guy who's toting around a gun."

Mick headed down the hall. "Room 278, right?"

"You got it."

"Who's there?"

The old woman sat in a wheelchair pulled up to a perfectly square open window lined with fake flowers and plants on its sill. Her back was hunched, and she craned her neck around to see who might be darkening the doorway.

"My name's Mick."

She paused and then said, "Well, you sound handsome enough. Come on in."

Mick entered and watched as Bea turned her wheelchair around with some effort, then put on her glasses. "Oh my. Yes, you are."

Mick blushed and approached the woman. "You're Bea Murtaugh?"

"I am, dear. And listen, I know I look old, but in my day I looked like Grace Kelly." She grinned. Mick didn't doubt that. Her granddaughter certainly resembled the movie star. "So, what in the world do I owe this pleasure to? Are you a doctor? If so, I have been feeling a little bad lately. Probably blood pressure. Here, hold my hand and take a pulse, will you?"

Mick couldn't help but laugh. This woman was fantastic. He sat down in a chair near her bed and watched Bea make her way forward a little. "Sorry. Not a doctor."

"Drat. Then who are you?"

"My name is Mick Kline. I work for the FBI."

"The what, dear?"

"The, um, Federal Bureau of Investigation."

"Look, I paid my taxes like a saint."

Mick laughed again. "No, ma'am. Not the IRS. I'm . . . um . . . anyway, I fight crime."

"Oh . . . " Bea's eyes widened. "Listen, Bettie Broadback is trouble, and I don't care what she says, I did not take her aspirin. She misplaces things, loses her mind, you know, and then goes around blaming everyone for it. Last winter, she lost her slippers, ranted and raved about it, accused the daylights out of everyone, then come to find out she put them under her mattress. Why, is anybody's guess, but you know the kinds of people here. . . . " Bea took her index finger and made circles on the side of her head, then blew out a long whistle.

"Uh, yeah." Mick chuckled. "Actually, I fight a little more dangerous crime than aspirin thieves."

"Oh?" Bea looked excited. *"Oh!"* Mick leaned backward a little, not exactly sure what was getting Bea so excited. "Like Remington Steele?"

"Remington Steele? The TV guy?"

"The TV guy? No dear, the detective who was always getting those bad guys. The handsome one. Dark hair. That killer grin."

"Oh, yes, okay, gotcha. Yeah, like him."

Bea rubbed her hands together. "Hmm. Well, go grab that fern over there."

Mick looked over to the windowsill. A green leafy fern sat in the center. Mick swallowed, wondering if Bea was a little more like Bettie Broadback than she wanted to admit. "You want the green fern?"

"No. I want you to look at who sent it to me."

Mick rose and went over to the plant. There was a card in the center of it, and Mick took it out, then went back to sit. "You want me to read it to you?"

"I've already read it. I want you to read it."

Mick took it out and read: "'With Love, Remington Steele.'" Mick cocked an eyebrow and looked at Bea, who was glowing.

"You're getting ferns from Pierce Brosnan?"

"Who?"

"Remington Steele, I mean."

She laughed, then took the card, examining it with care. "Well, no, but wouldn't that be nice. These are actually from my granddaughter, Faith."

Mick leaned forward. "Oh?"

"Yes. She's such a kidder. A couple years ago, she started sending me these ferns and plants and letters, all signed from Remington. Now I have to admit, at first I thought it was really him. I mean, who wouldn't? But then I realized Faith was joking with me, and that she was sending them because she knows what a big fan I am. She has always been such a kidder. I don't tell anyone—it's sort of our little secret."

"Faith sounds like a wonderful girl."

Bea's eyes lit with joy. "Oh, she is. She is. Beautiful heart. Beautiful face. She's a successful businesswoman."

"Really." Mick was about to enter into some dialogue about Paul's murder but decided to just let Bea talk.

"Yes, she and her husband, Paul, they travel a lot, spend a lot of time in Europe and Asia, I think it is. Anyway, she's a doll for keeping in touch. And that husband of hers, Paul, so good to her. Just a sweetheart. They make a great couple, you know. I'm sure they're having the time of their lives traveling the world. Part of me wants to tell them to slow down, enjoy each other, have some kids. But I don't want to interfere. Nobody listens to old people anymore."

Mick sat back comfortably in his chair. "Sounds like you have an extraordinary granddaughter."

"She's a good person," Bea said, pointing her finger at Mick to indicate she was about to lecture. "Those types of people are hard to find these days. No one wants to be good. People are just out for themselves." Her eyes narrowed at Mick. "I hope you're a good person, young man."

"I try hard."

"Well, good for you. I hope you go to church."

"I do."

She smiled. "Good. So does my Faith. She's been since she was a child. She just loves the Lord. So much. Always has. And not for what He can do for her. Do you know what I mean, dear? Just because He is."

"It sounds like you were a good influence in her life."

"Yes, I did try. I had my faults. We all do. But I read the Bible to her when she was a small child, and I think that's what made her love Him so much."

Mick took a deep breath. It was refreshing to talk about God. And it was also good to try to understand who Faith had been before this tragedy. Mick could tell a lot about Faith just by this visit to Bea. Kerri thought Faith had dropped contact with Bea, but she had not. She just came up with an innovative way to stay in touch while keeping

145

Bea away from whatever danger Faith perceived. Mick knew this was a woman of the faith. He did not know where she stood now, but it had once been there, and that gave Mick an instant "in."

Mick took Bea's hand and squeezed it. "Thank you for visiting with me."

Bea squeezed back. "No, thank you. I'm always up for a visitor." She watched Mick stand and go to the door. "Young man, I guess I'm still not sure why you're here."

He winked. "Well, just don't tell Bettie Broadback. Some things have to be done undercover."

Bea gasped, then nodded somberly and whispered, "Who knows what kind of craziness she'll think up next."

Mick nodded and shut Bea's door behind him. He hurried down the hall of the nursing home to the front door, stepping out into the clean air with relief. He stood and thought about the conversation with Bea, and then his mind trailed back to his conversation with Kerri and what she'd told him about the note the killer had left: *"If you see my face again, you will die."* He started to walk to his car, then he stopped.

Again.

She'd seen him before.

chapter eighteen

a deep, lazy groan escaped from Faith's throat as she rolled to her back. She stretched her legs out and her feet touched the armrest on the other end of the couch. What time was it?

As she lay there, she tried not to focus on what she was feeling, or more truthfully, what she wasn't feeling. She was becoming numb, and she knew it. Depression was setting in. Day after day she found herself less and less active. She did not turn on the TV anymore. Or the radio. She didn't get much fresh air.

Sissy let out her own sleepy sigh, and Faith finally sat up. This is what her life had become. Sleeping all day, hardly sleeping at night. Holed up in her home, hardly any friends. The lump in her throat comforted her a little . . . at least she still had emotions.

How different it had been before. She and Paul had enjoyed such a good life. They'd had so many friends. They were always on the go, doing this and that. They had loved to travel and sometimes on Sundays would just drive until they nearly ran out of gas. Then they'd drive some more. They rode their bikes together and had been talking about training for a triathalon.

Faith jumped off the couch suddenly, stumbling over Sissy, who whimpered as she tried to get out of the way in time. Faith knocked her knee hard against the coffee table, but she did not feel pain. Only rage.

Faith dropped to her knees, with too little strength to stand and sob violently at the same time. She crumpled to the floor, lying on her side. Her cries sounded like screams, and her screams sounded like cries. She didn't care anymore. She wished she could literally cry herself to death. All she wanted was relief from the torment.

"I hate you." *You* wasn't clearly defined, but it applied to many. God, for hating her too. It was hard to be hated by God. Paul, for leaving her. Couldn't he have fought harder to live? Dixie, for making her quiet life more and more complex. Agent Kline, for prodding her like a farm animal. Sandy, for having a normal life.

She continued to mumble until she fell asleep. When she awoke, Sissy was by her side, and Faith was still on the floor. Her face was a sticky mess of tears and hair and sweat. Her fingers tore strands away from her face as she turned onto her back and sat up. Standing, she rubbed her eyes furiously. Her cheeks felt flushed, her muscles weak. She supposed it did take a lot of strength to wrestle with the God of the universe. She doubted that she'd won the match. She didn't care. She knew there was scarcely a chance she'd come out on top of anything else in her life.

Her stomach grumbled, reminding her she had not eaten all day. "Come on, Sis," she said, grabbing her purse. "Let's go eat."

The only thing that kept Faith Kemper's days and nights different was what they served at Nik's. What little comfort she had in her life now came from this new routine of walking a few blocks to the restaurant and going home again. Sandy, though she probably did not know it, had become a source of enjoyment for Faith. The small things in life, like being served a meal with a smile, were what she held on to. She whispered an apology for saying she hated Sandy. The others would have to wait for theirs.

As she walked the familiar sidewalk to the restaurant, Faith laughed a little at the idea that she'd formed a relationship with a restaurant. Oh, well. At least it was something.

The evening was warm, and Faith took her time getting to Nik's. The mugginess she didn't mind. It was a different atmosphere than her house, and any change was welcome. Sissy was particularly frisky, not wanting to stay right by her side but wanting to sniff and explore. She finally controlled herself and stayed at Faith's side obediently.

Faith was not paying too much attention to Sissy, though, because her mind had turned to Mick Kline. She wished he hadn't caught her so off guard. She had no idea there was someone new investigating Paul's murder. And the fact that it might be linked to another case intrigued her. But it was that kind of intrigue—the delusion that things could be normal only if—she knew these kinds of things could put her in danger.

Yet she had sensed something about this man. She wasn't sure what. Maybe it was the way he spoke softly, unassumingly. Or perhaps it was how he was forthright yet kind. She just did not know, but what she did know is that she could not get him off her mind.

"Come on, girl." They walked into Nik's.

By the time Faith had finished her shouting match with God and made it to the restaurant, the dinner crowd had thinned out; she preferred Nik's when it was quieter like this.

Wallace soon came to seat her.

"Thank you," she told him as she sat down.

"Sure." Wallace said in his shy manner. "Hi, Sissy." He left, saying he would get Heather, an evening waitress Faith was getting to know.

But it wasn't Heather who arrived at her table. Faith clenched her jaw. Now it was her turn to surprise. "Hello, Agent Kline."

"How did you know it was me?"

"I never forget how a person's footsteps sound. You drag your left heel a little when you walk." Faith put her trembling hands underneath the table. "Why are you back? I thought I made it clear—"

"Actually there are a lot of things you made more confusing," Mick said.

"Hi, there." Heather interrupted their conversation. "Who's your friend, Faith?"

"Hi. Mick Kline."

"Nice to meet you. I'm Heather. What can I get you to drink?"

"He's not staying," Faith said.

"Actually, I'm starving. I've had a busy day. Went out to St. Luke's Hospital—oh, and to St. Francis Nursing Home."

Surprise prickled Faith's skin, and she rubbed the back of her neck.

"So," Mick continued as he took the seat across from her, "actually, I think I'll take iced tea and a menu, please."

"What are you doing?" Faith whispered harshly as Heather walked off.

"Eating."

"You know what I mean," Faith said. "Why are you back?"

Heather returned with the menu, and Faith leaned back, hoping she didn't look too intense. But she knew her face was drawn with an impolite expression. "I didn't get all the information I need from you," Mick said.

"Don't you know when you're not welcome?"

"And don't you know that it's a federal crime to lie to an FBI agent?"

Faith's stomach did a little flip-flop.

"Can actually do jail time for it."

Her mouth went dry. She reached for her water but knocked it over. Ice spilled with a racket, and water dripped onto the floor.

"I've got it," Wallace said from out of nowhere and began cleaning the spill up immediately.

"Wallace, thank you," Faith said, helpless to do anything more than sit there, flustered.

"Um, you okay?" Wallace asked.

"Yes, sorry, just clumsy. Thanks for cleaning it up."

"I'll tell them to get you another drink."

"Thanks, Wallace." Faith waited for Wallace to leave and said to Mick, "Is that some sort of threat or something?"

"Actually no, because right now I'm on probation with the FBI, so I'm not even supposed to be here."

"What are you talking about?"

"Just what I said. You don't have to tell me anything. This isn't an official investigation."

Faith leaned back in her chair as Heather returned with more water and took Mick's order.

"I'll take the old-fashioned hamburger, well done. And after you grill it, I want you to put it in the microwave for one minute on high."

"Excuse me?" Heather asked.

"Sorry to be a bother, but do you think you can do that for me?"

"Um, sure. That comes with a baked potato or French fries."

"Is your sour cream kept in the refrigerator?"

"Uh . . . "

"Not just out on ice, but actually in the refrigerator?"

"I think so."

"And is it butter or margarine?"

"Margarine, I think."

"Great. Tell you what, if that sour cream is in the fridge, I'll take the baked potato. If not, then give me the fries."

Heather was trying to be polite. "Would you like a side salad?"

"No thanks."

"Faith, what about you?"

"I'll have the BLT, extra mayo. A salad, too, with ranch dressing."

"Did you know that spoiled mayonnaise can induce vomiting within fifteen minutes?" Mick asked.

Faith shook her head. "What is the matter with you? Can't you order a normal meal, or at least let me?"

"You should know that."

"No, actually, that's not something I need to know. Heather, I'll take a BLT, extra mayo, whether the mayo's been on ice, in the fridge, or baked in the oven."

Heather laughed. "Okay."

Faith turned her attention back to Mick. "Well, I don't know much about you except you're in trouble with your employer and you have strange eating habits." She sipped her water, wishing she had a more confident expression. Instead, she continued to hide behind her sunglasses. "So, you're here because I lied to you, so you say."

"Uh-huh."

"But you lied to me too," she pointed out. "You said you were with the FBI. You made it sound like an investigation."

"I did. That's why I came back. I can't expect you to be honest with me if I'm not honest with you, right?"

Suddenly Faith wished for a noisy crowd to drown out their conversation. "I don't have to tell you anything. I wish you would just leave me alone."

"But see, that's what I can't get over. Why you want me to leave you alone when I'm trying to help you."

"I can't be sure that you're trying to help me."

"Fair enough."

Heather was back. "The sour cream is in the fridge. But I forgot to ask you if you wanted cheese on your baked potato."

"Is the cheese refrigerated?"

"My goodness," Heather sighed and was gone.

"You're a pretty quirky guy," Faith mused.

"Only with anything that spoils."

Faith had to laugh a little. The whole thing was surreal. She sighed away her frustration and threw up her arms. "So you're back. Eating dinner with me."

"I'm back to tell you the truth. I'm investigating your husband's murder because I think it's linked to the murder of my brother."

Faith was reaching for her water again but stopped. "Your brother was murdered?"

"Yes. A month ago."

"How?"

"He was killed in his sleep, shot in the back of the head."

"I don't understand how this has anything to do with Paul."

"I've been investigating the murders of several law enforcement officers in the region. I'm finding some similarities among them. Your husband's is one. But unfortunately, there has not been a lot of information released on this case, so I've had to come get it on my own."

Faith listened carefully. What this man said terrified

her, but in a strange way it gave her hope. A hope she'd lost long ago. Maybe this was the break in the case that would finally solve it and set her free from this horrid prison.

"Your grandmother is quite a character."

This man was tearing at her, breaking down her walls, and it was working. He'd invaded her privacy, her routine, and her sense of obscurity. She chewed at her bottom lip to keep from crying.

"You know, Faith," Mick said matter-of-factly, "my whole impression of you changed once I met Bea."

It was one thing to mess with her. It was quite another to bring her grandmother into this. She had created a safe place for Bea, created security, and this man and his big ego had destroyed it.

"By the look on your face, I can see you're worried about what I told Bea. I told her nothing about you or what happened to Paul."

Relief flooded Faith's heart. But she could not say thank you. The irritation of being so overwhelmingly invaded still unsettled her. Faith stopped chewing her lip. "You said your impression of me changed."

"Yes, Remington Steele." He laughed. "And I can appreciate you not wanting to tell your grandmother about Paul. Or about what has happened to you. That's very unselfish, actually."

"I didn't mean why. I meant from what." Faith stopped picking at the material on her pants and folded her hands on top of the table. "What *was* your impression of me?"

"Mysterious," Mick said after some thought. "And rebellious. But now I know why."

Heather delivered their food and asked if they needed anything else. When she left, Mick said, "Shall we pray?"

"You go ahead," Faith said and began eating her salad.

"You don't thank God for your food?"

"No."

She could tell this bothered him, but he went ahead and blessed his own food and started eating as well. Faith only ate for something to do.

After a moment, Mick continued. "You don't want to know what I think?"

Faith sighed in irritation. "Agent Kline, I'm a pretty patient person, so I assumed you were going to go ahead and tell me, whether I liked it or not."

She heard him chuckle a little. "Well, you're getting to know me at least." He paused and said, "I'm a friend, Faith. You should know that too. I'm here to try to help you."

"No, you're here to try to help yourself find whoever killed your brother. I just happened to be on the path. There's a difference."

"All right," Mick said. "But in the process I could help find whoever killed your husband."

"So you could do what an entire police department couldn't. Excuse me for not holding my breath." She took another bite of her sandwich and chewed it furiously.

There was silence as Mick ate too. Then he said, "I talked to Kerri Pratt."

Faith dropped her fork, and it tumbled off the table. She instinctively reached for it, her flustered hands clutching it off the floor and bringing it back to the table.

"Kerri was a good friend of yours," Mick said.

"What business is it of yours?" Faith tried to keep her voice calm, but she knew the agitation was showing in the form of a slight quiver.

"Look, I'm just investigating here. My investigation led me to you. And to Kerri Pratt. And to Dr. Mahada."

"Who?"

"The doctor who treated you in the ER. He told me

how you were attacked. He said you were diagnosed with Purtscher retinopathy, that you—"

"It seems, Agent Kline, as if you are investigating *me*."

"Well, you are as much of a mystery as what happened that night. There are a lot of unanswered questions. I am simply trying to answer them. But strangely, I can't get a straight answer from you."

"You can find your answers elsewhere. Why do you have to drag me into this? I told you I am trying to move on with my life."

"You're not moving on with your life. You're running from your life."

"Don't you dare sit across from me and judge me," Faith said, anger scorching her words. "You have no idea what you're talking about."

"Kerri told me about the message. The one the killer left on the car window."

With one swift motion, Faith slammed down her fork, scooted her chair back, and took Sissy's harness. She clumsily maneuvered around the tables and pushed open the door of the restaurant.

Night had fallen, and the mugginess of the day had been replaced by a cool, crisp breeze. Sissy, sensing Faith's turmoil, stuck close to her. Curse words sat at the tip of Faith's tongue, but she was so angry, so frightened, not a single one, if released, would even begin to discharge any of it from her.

She had thought Dixie was going to be her biggest liability, but she was wrong.

chapter nineteen

mick let her go. He paid for their uneaten dinners, with Heather and a few others at the restaurant giving him less-than-friendly glances. Outside, he paused, letting his skin cool off a little. He kicked small pieces of gravel with his shoe, trying to understand Faith Kemper. It was almost as if she didn't want the man who killed Paul to be found. But why? He couldn't imagine that being true; there had to be another explanation.

He drove around the small town of Bakerville for thirty minutes with the windows down. It had been days since he'd let himself think about Aaron. He'd reached a point where he had to separate himself, but it was a grueling emotional feat. That drive to find Aaron's killer—and truthfully, the drive to make him pay for it—kept Mick's mind on Aaron more than it should.

The cool night breeze finally cleared his mind enough that he felt he could go back to his motel room without pacing in circles. Once inside, he checked the voice mail on his cell phone. Reggie had called. He had found nothing on Miguel Juarez. But he also said he was going to have to keep a low profile. Tom was becoming suspicious and had been acting strangely for the last couple of days.

Mick sighed and fell back onto his bed, punching the TV on with the remote. He hated motel rooms—everything about them. Their staleness did nothing more than conjure up feelings of isolation and uneasiness.

He watched ESPN for a while, then tried to find an old movie. When the images before him blurred, he realized he was more tired than he thought. In the bathroom he splashed his face with cold water, brushed his teeth half-heartedly, then went back to his bed. He laid on top of the covers, fully dressed, and grabbed his cell phone. He took a small piece of paper out of his wallet. It had Jenny's new phone number on it.

The phone rang only once before she answered. "Hello?"

"Hi, Jenny. It's Mick."

"Mick!" Relief and joy filled her voice. Mick smiled. "How's it going? Where are you?"

"A small motel in Bakerville, Texas."

"Where?"

"Exactly." Mick chuckled.

He heard her laugh, and that laugh comforted him. She was doing okay. "What have you found out?" she asked eagerly.

"I've got some good leads," he told her, deciding not to go into Faith Kemper. He couldn't think of any reason to tell a woman whose husband was just murdered that another woman whose husband was also murdered was scared out of her mind. And if the killer's threat was carried out, Jenny did not need to know that, either. Still, Mick wanted her to be cautious. "How's the apartment? Are you feeling safe?"

He knew she was smiling on the other end of the line. "Yeah, I feel safe. I keep the doors locked, the alarm on, that sort of thing. But I've been sleeping better. Started seeing a grief counselor, and that's been going okay."

"You're such a strong woman, Jenny. I've always admired that about you."

"When we are weak, He is strong, eh?"

"Yeah." Mick smiled. "Well, I just wanted to check in with you. I know it's late. I don't want to keep you up, but I will let you know if anything breaks, okay?"

"I know you will. Just be careful, all right?"

"All right. Good night."

Mick laid the phone on his chest, his eyes heavy. Soon enough he was in a blissfully deep sleep.

Mick awoke to chatter in Spanish coming from outside his room. He rose slowly and peeked out the window. The maids were outside the room next to his, laughing and carrying on as if there might not be anybody trying to get some sleep in one of these rooms. He drew the curtains closed and shuffled across the room to the sink, where he regretted the half-finished brushing job of the night before. He was more thorough this time and swished his mouth with the motel mouthwash for an extra thirty seconds. Showering quickly, he got dressed and headed downstairs for the continental breakfast, which, surprisingly, was not bad. He chose a dry bagel and a banana.

As he ate, he sifted through the files and cases, looking over the facts again, trying to find anything, any clue, that would jump out at him. He was missing something—he knew it—but he didn't know what. Whatever it was, he felt sure it would lead him to the killer.

What he had found out about Paul Kemper's murder, however, was undeniably intriguing. So was Faith. He couldn't deny that part of the intrigue came from her striking beauty. He had yet to see her eyes—he longed to see her eyes—but everything else about her was, well, nearly perfect. If he could just keep from angering her.

He finished off a cup of coffee, quickly read over the

headlines in *USA Today,* then went to his car. He started it, then sat in the motel parking lot for a long while. He laughed, realizing he had no idea where to go next.

"These mangoes, my friend, look absolutely scrumptious!" Dixie was making her way across the living room to the kitchen with an armload of groceries plus a sack of dry cleaning trailing on the floor. Dixie plopped the sacks on the counter. Faith followed her into the kitchen. "Smell this," Dixie said, holding a mango up to Faith's nose.

"Smells wonderful." Faith managed a smile. She'd been reeling since last night's horrible dinner intrusion and had gotten little sleep, but she was happy to have company.

"It's so fun to go grocery shopping for you," Dixie said, unloading everything into the refrigerator. "It gives me new ideas of things to try. Like this frozen tortellini."

Faith laughed. "Well, you can bet everything I have here is easy to fix. But I'm getting very attached to Nik's."

"It's a good restaurant. You know, if I had an excuse not to cook, like being blind, I wouldn't. I have lazy tendencies and don't push myself too much." She chuckled. "It would be fascinating to watch you cook sometime."

"Oh, it's not too interesting. I don't do too much fancy stuff."

"Well, tortellini sounds plenty fancy to me!" Dixie finished putting away the groceries and asked Faith if she would like her to mix up a big batch of lemonade.

"That would be great. Thank you." As Dixie scooped out the sugar, Faith said, "Mick Kline found me at the restaurant last night."

"You're kidding."

Faith had to get it off her chest, talk to someone about it. It seemed to be clawing at her insides like a bored cat next to a couch. And there weren't too many options of whom she could spill her guts to. What else she would confess to Dixie she did not know. She guessed it depended on what questions Dixie asked. She didn't have to wait long.

"What'd he want?"

Faith traced the grout of the kitchen tile with her finger. "Who knows. Listen, Dixie, about that church potluck . . . "

"Yes?"

Her fingers found a piece of dried-on food, and her fingernail scratched at it. "I was just thinking . . . maybe it's time I met some more people." Her heart fluttered in her chest, reminding her of how insecure she was at the thought of venturing out. But one thing she knew: she was dying a slow death here inside this house. She also knew the mind can play horrible tricks. She was not bold enough in her assessment to say that it was all in her head, but somehow, like the sun breaking through a patch of heavy thunder-clouds, logic seemed to speak to her from the far corners of her mind.

But that voice drowned easily in the screaming madness of fear.

". . . and we've got a ladies' Bible study on Friday mornings, and our services start at ten on Sundays."

Faith hadn't realized Dixie was even speaking. She dusted at what her fingernail had loosened from the counter. "One step at a time, okay?"

"I'm sorry. I get pushy. I don't mean to be. I'm just so excited. You're going to love our little church."

Faith nodded. "It'll be nice to get out of my routine a little."

"I'll come by and walk with you. It's only four blocks, the opposite direction of Nik's."

"I can find it," Faith assured her.

"Really?"

"Yeah."

"That's amazing! I mean, it is a straight shot and every-thing, but—" Dixie stopped. "Sissy, of course!"

"She's a smart dog."

"And a sweetie." Dixie said it as if she were talking to a baby. She ruffled Sissy's fur and her collar tags jingled.

"Well, don't worry about bringing anything."

"No, please, I would love to. It will give me something to do."

"Well, okay then. Is there anything else you need from me today?"

Faith rested her chin in her hand. The day was still young, and already Faith was dreading how long and drawn out it would feel in this house. "Maybe we could do some-thing together."

"Really? I'd love to! What do you want to do?"

"How about go to the park for a while? Let Sissy play. Maybe pack a couple of sandwiches or something."

Dixie wrapped a hand around Faith's shoulder. "There's hope for you yet!"

***

"Agent Mick Kline." Chief Underwood shifted in his chair but did not rise.

"Hello, Chief." Mick approached the officer's desk and held out a hand for the chief to shake.

"I figured I'd be seeing you again."

"Oh? Why's that?"

Underwood shrugged and nodded for his deputy to leave them. "You seem like a pretty persistent guy." The chief said this with little admiration for the attribute he mentioned. Mick sensed the man's plastic smile was not an indication he was happy to see him. "Well, I'm just running into some dead ends with this Kemper case. I did go and talk to Juarez. Pretty angry young man."

Underwood nodded but said nothing.

"There's something about him, though," Mick continued after Underwood remained silent. "I tend to want to believe him. I don't know . . . maybe because he *is* so angry. There's just something—something I can't quite put my finger on. Maybe it's the way he averted his eyes when I was questioning him. Kind of like you're doing now."

Chief Underwood looked up, startled by the accusation, but he quickly recovered. Mick kept his expression steady. He knew the chief was getting ready to turn the tables, and Mick wanted to knock him off balance, if even a little.

"Hmm. You think you got me figured out, do you?"

"I don't have a lot of things figured out," Mick said, careful to keep his tone mild. "For starters, I'm still not sure why Juarez was ever a suspect. I don't see a clear motive."

"There's a lot you don't know about this case, Agent Kline. And if you think you're going to get the truth out of a dumb Mexican like Juarez, you've got another thing coming."

"A dumb Mexican." The words felt heavy on Mick's tongue. "Juarez seemed like a pretty smart guy to me."

Underwood licked his lips and kept his eyes on Mick. "Is that so."

"Why don't you enlighten me about this case, then, if there's so much I don't know? Anything would help."

"I'd love to," Underwood said, standing up and moving his big frame around his desk. He crossed his arms. "But I've been doing a little checking around myself. Turns out you're a rogue."

"A rogue, huh?" Mick laughed, but perspiration threatened to break through his skin.

"Turns out, in fact, that you're not supposed to be

working at all. Not on this case. Not on any case. Bureau says you're on mandatory leave." He chuckled. "Boy, would I like to know what for."

Mick held a defiant smile. "All right. Yeah. I'm on leave. I doubt you heard *rogue*, though." At least he hoped not.

"True," Underwood confessed. "That was my word. But it's a pretty apt description, wouldn't you say? I mean, you're down here acting like you're investigating a serial murder case for the bureau, when in fact you're not even working for them right now."

"It's temporary."

"They think you need some time off or something?"

"It's none of your business."

"I see. Well, I'd have to say the same about the Kemper murder. And Juarez. That's all I need—the bureau botching a two-year investigation. We don't have Juarez yet, but we will. He makes one wrong move, and we'll have him."

"You couldn't investigate at least the possibility of another suspect?"

"You really know how to win friends and influence people, don't you? Is that what they teach over at the academy? Come stormin' in and tell everyone how to do their jobs?" The chief's voice was beginning to show anger. "You know nothing about this case, Kline. You don't know what we know and what we don't."

"Then why don't you let me take a look at the paperwork?"

The chief flashed a self-satisfied grin. "Love to, but you're on probation."

"I have a feeling you wouldn't be sharing any information with me, regardless." Mick sighed and turned to the door. "I have a personal stake in this, Chief. And if there is a serial killer out there, we have to stop him before he kills again. Whatever information you could give me might make that possible. Might help find who killed all these men."

The chief's eyes glared. "I know who killed Paul Kemper. As for your cases, you're on your own. Keep your nose in your own food bowl."

"You've been distant lately."

Carlita spoke to her husband in English anytime she really wanted his attention. She knew he had to concentrate to interpret it. He hammered at the wood without looking back at her. Four more weeks and he would have the new room built onto the back of the house. The kids would finally have their own rooms.

"Miguel." She was the only person he knew who said his name with dignity. For the rest of the world, he was merely a smudge on the bottom of their shoe.

"I've been tired."

"It's more than that." His wife came around to his side, brushing her long, black hair out of her face. "Where were you the other night? You just disappear for hours? Don't call? Don't tell me where you've been?"

"I just drove around. I don't want to worry you," he sighed, his arm hot with fatigue. He dropped his hammer and turned to her.

"Worry me about what? Our money is fine, right?"

"Yes. It's . . ." Miguel lowered his head. The words, whether English or Spanish, were hard to say. "It's Underwood."

Anger flashed through her hazel eyes. "What do you mean?"

"Another agent, from the FBI, came to talk to me about the case." Miguel slid down to a squatting position, where he fingered the dirt next to his shoe. "He said he just wanted to talk."

"What else did he say?"

"He wanted my version of the story." He looked up at Carlita's delicate face. "Don't worry. I am going to take care of this. This must stop, once and for all."

"Miguel, please, don't do anything. It will pass by."

"That's what we've said for two years now. It will pass by."

Carlita's long fingers ran through his hair. "The truth, Miguel. The truth will set us free."

Miguel's fingers scraped across the ground. In the palm of his hand, he sifted the dirt until only a pebble remained. He glared at it and wondered when someone would finally overturn the rock and find what was hiding beneath.

chapter twenty

ick stood in front of the door to his motel room, his jaw hanging open. He looked around, scanning everyone in sight. Adrenaline pumped his heart into overdrive. No one looked suspicious. Maids came in and out of rooms. Motel guests walked to and from the office, around their cars, lugging suitcases behind them. Mick tried to look carefully at each person he could see. But nothing looked out of the ordinary.

He turned back to his door and stared at the note taped to it: *LEAVE THIS TOWN*. Mick finally took his handkerchief and carefully removed the note. He unlocked his door and went inside, placing the note on the bed. He was staring at it when his cell phone rang, startling his heart to a standstill.

"Hello?"

"Mick, it's Reggie."

"Reggie," Mick breathed.

"You okay?"

"Uh, yeah. What's going on?"

"Tom knows."

"I know. The chief from Allana called him."

"Yeah. But here's what's strange. I figured Tom would be out of his mind, but he's not. He's not happy about it, and he dropped a few subtle hints that I better not be involved in any way, but then he just went back to his office, and that was the end of it. I mean, knowing Tom, I would think he'd be driving down to Houston to strangle your neck personally."

Mick sat down on the edge of the bed. "That is strange. So you don't think he's going to do anything?"

"I don't know, man. I mean, I just wanted to warn you. But it looks like you might be in the clear, at least for now. It's kind of like he had a change of heart or something."

Mick continued to stare at the note on his bed.

"So, anything new?" Reg asked.

"A lot more questions than answers right now, Reg. But I gotta keep trying."

"I know, man. Hey, by the way, Dr. Grenard came by, asked how you were doing. I told her as far as I knew you were doing fine."

"Hmm." Mick studied each word on the note. "Well, I think I just got confirmation that I'm doing something right. Listen, Reg," Mick said before Reg had a chance to ask what that meant, "I'm not going to ask you to help me anymore. I'm putting you in a precarious situation, and it's not fair."

"You know I'll go to the ends of the earth for you."

"I know that, man. That's why I can't ask you to do anything else. You and I both know there are ways around the system. But to ask you to use those would compromise your integrity, and I'm not going to do that."

He could hear Reggie sigh, whether from relief or frustration he didn't know. "Okay, brother. Thank you. But I think I'm at the end of the road anyway. From what I can tell, the information you're going to need would be coming from the bureau's Behavioral Science Unit in Virginia. They could run a lot of cross-reference information that we don't have. I wish I knew somebody there, but I don't."

Mick tore his gaze away from the note. "All right, buddy. Well, thank you. I better get going."

"Keep me updated, will you?"

"I will. Bye."

The note had been typed on a computer, in large, bold, roman type.

Bold. Now that was an understatement.

Sissy was having the time of her life fetching a Frisbee from a young teenager who had apparently lost his Frisbee partner.

"You should see Sissy!" Dixie said as they sat on a park bench eating bologna sandwiches. "She's a real good catcher!"

The dog was a free spirit indeed, and a sad reminder of who Faith used to be. Now she had to live vicariously through her dog.

"Will she come when you call her? Always?"

"Always," Faith said. "Sissy would never leave me. Even now she is aware of where I am."

"Smart dog."

"Yes."

Faith ate her sandwich in silence while Dixie rambled about the good things God was doing in her life. The indifference Faith felt toward the words *miracle* and *blessing* and *joy* that Dixie mingled into her monologue remained a grim reminder of what had been stolen from her two years before. Then again, maybe it had never been real.

Maybe God had only served Faith's purpose when good times were at hand and paradise was sure. Paradise had vanished now, along with *hope,* the word Dixie now fixated on as she told of the time she had battled a bout of depression. With perfect perkiness, Dixie concluded, "God just always seems to be there when you least expect it."

Bitterness pulled Faith's lips downward, and her nostrils

flared as she tried to restrain the vicious words that threatened to roll off her tongue. "Except in your most desperate hour, when He is nowhere to be found." She formed each word deliberately, speaking rather than spewing them. A breath of relief filled her lungs. Self-control.

But a gasp indicated Dixie didn't recognize the restraint that she had just displayed.

"My husband was murdered right in front of me. I was almost killed too." Faith swiped at her wet cheeks. "I have a right to hate God."

Dixie cried too, pulling Faith close.

Faith's throat swelled, and she couldn't speak for a moment. Her sobs left her body unashamedly. "You have no idea what it's like to live with this kind of fear and darkness."

Remarkably, the confession refreshed her. She'd figured she would tell somebody someday, and she certainly hadn't imagined it would be a woman like Dixie. Nevertheless, here she was, telling all.

Well, almost all.

"Please, Dixie, don't tell anyone. Please, I beg of you."

"My word's as good as gold. You know that, don't you?"

Faith smiled. "I do know that."

"Is that why the FBI agent was here?"

Faith nodded. "He thinks there's a connection between Paul's murder and others. A serial killer." The words came out as a whisper.

"What?" Alarm carried Dixie's voice.

"Who knows? I guess it could be. But I've told him everything I know. And he won't leave me alone."

"I can take care of that for you if you'd like."

Faith laughed. "No, that's okay." She put the uneaten half of her sandwich back in her bag. "There's one thing true about all law enforcers: If you look like you're hiding something, they'll keep after you until they find out what it is. Even if it's your age."

"Well, the guy's handsome," Dixie mused.

Faith couldn't help but crack a smile. "And annoying."

"Handsome but annoying. Well," Dixie laughed, "unfortunately you can only enjoy the annoying part."

Faith started laughing, hard, and for a moment her spirit was free to be normal. Dixie was laughing too. Soon Sissy was by their sides, wondering about the commotion.

Maybe life could be normal. Maybe there was no danger. Maybe it was all in her head. And in Mick Kline's head too.

"Paul used to love going to the park. He'd ride his bike for hours. Throw footballs with the teenagers."

"Tell me more about him," Dixie said gently.

Faith just shook her head and gathered her things. "Paul loved me. That's all I know to be true."

mick had intended to check around Bakerville that afternoon, but he decided against it. He could not be sure of who left that note. It could be that Dixie woman, but then again it could be someone else, someone with frightening intentions. He could only imagine, so he decided to go a different direction. And that direction landed him on the doorstep of Faith Kemper's home.

He knocked twice but heard nothing. He knocked again, this time identifying himself. He figured she couldn't hear his footsteps from inside the home.

"Agent Kline."

Mick whirled around and found Faith standing behind him. "I suppose I have a signature knock as well?"

"No. Dixie told me you were standing at my doorstep. We just came from the park."

"Oh. Nothing gets past you, does it?" Mick looked around for the woman who had knocked him to the ground. She was nowhere to be seen.

"What are you doing here? Again?"

"More questions."

"Gee, that's a surprise." Faith stepped next to him and unlocked her door.

"Faith, please," Mick said, touching her arm. "Please, I

just need to know some things. I'm sorry I upset you at the restaurant."

Faith adjusted her sunglasses. "You presume wrong."

"I presume what wrong?"

"I was unlocking the door to let you in. It's getting hot out here, and there's no need to discuss things on the front porch when there's a perfectly good couch to sit on inside."

"Oh. Um, thanks . . ." Mick followed her inside and shut the door.

"Lock it, please."

"Sure. Thanks for seeing me again."

"Well, Agent," she said, "I can't see you, but Dixie tells me you're good-looking, so we'll just pretend."

Mick had to laugh at that—half out of surprise, half out of sheer embarrassment. "I pay people well to say those things."

"Hmm." Faith went to the kitchen, put her things down. Her dog sniffed Mick at first, then trotted to a window and curled up to go to sleep. "I've got to start cooking a dish for a potluck tomorrow. So if you don't mind, I'll cook while we talk?"

"You can cook?"

"I can also do a song and dance, if you'd like to see that."

Mick could only smile. She was feisty, to say the least. "I'm sorry. I just didn't realize."

"Have a seat at the counter there. Would you like something to drink?"

"What do you have?"

"Diet Sprite, lemonade, water."

"Lemonade sounds good."

He watched as she opened the refrigerator door, pulled out the pitcher, opened a cabinet, and took a glass out. With little effort she poured the lemonade for him and served it as smoothly as if he were at a restaurant.

"That's amazing," Mick said.

"Dixie made it."

"No, I mean you—uh—the way you do things without seeing."

Faith shrugged as she opened the fridge and took ingredients out. "You just adapt."

"How do you cook?"

"You learn to chop slower, keep Band-Aids nearby, and organize your ingredients so you always know where everything is."

Mick watched as she broke five eggs into a bowl and beat them.

"What are you making?"

"It's a French toast casserole."

"Sounds good. You go to church?"

The whisk rounded the bowl furiously, and then it dropped on the counter. She fumbled to pick it up and put it in the sink. "Um, no. Not really. I mean, I'm just starting to think about it. Dixie's church."

"First Church of the Dixie?"

Faith cracked a smile. "Yeah. Something like that." She took six pieces of bread and put them in the bottom of a glass dish. Then she went to the cabinet and pulled out a spice. Mick could smell it as she dashed it into the egg mixture. Cinnamon. Then she put that back and took vanilla off of the shelf below the cinnamon. She continued to add ingredients while Mick watched with amazement.

"You're staring," Faith said.

Mick blinked. How did she know that? "Oh. Sorry."

She laughed. "I figured you were since you weren't speaking."

"Oh. Just watching you cook. I don't cook that well and I can see."

"Well, I'm sure you have better things to do than watch

me cook. What else do you need to know?" She kept her back to him as she prepared her dish. "It's kind of a loaded question since you seem to know everything about me anyway."

"I'm sure it feels that way," Mick said. "I'm sorry I had to dig into your life a little."

"I suppose what you're going to say is that you wouldn't have to do that if I'd tell you what you needed to know."

"True enough," Mick admitted. "But there's a lot of people telling me nothing, so you're not alone."

Faith did not say anything. She poured the egg mixture over the bread, covered it, then put the dish into the refrigerator. "It's got to chill for at least twelve hours." She put her hands on her hips and looked in Mick's direction. "Got plans today?"

"Plans? Uh, no, not really. Why?"

"I guess I don't have to tell you how to get there." A small smile formed on her lips. From the side, Mick could almost see her eyes. Her eyelashes were long and curled. He quickly put his attention back on the road.

"No, I remember."

"Good."

"How long has it been since you've seen your grandmother?"

"Since Paul died. She was at the nursing home then too. We'd moved her there a few months before. She was just starting to adjust. I didn't want to upset her, and she would've wanted to come take care of me."

"So you made up this story about going to Europe?"

Faith nodded, her head lowering as if ashamed at the thought. Mick thought it was a little admirable. From meeting Bea only once, he could tell that spunk in her eyes would not be there if she were worried about her grand-daughter.

"What are you going to tell her now when you show up? And about being blind?"

"Bea can't see too well, at least not enough to realize I'm blind. And I'll tell her I'm back from Europe, only for a couple of days. Paul's tied up on business."

"She doesn't know Paul was a cop?"

"Yes, but I told her he went into business when we left for Europe." She rolled the window down and let the wind blow through her hair. "You probably don't lie, do you, Agent Kline?"

"No, I'm a perfect saint with absolutely no stains or blemishes or warts. Except for that really big one on the end of my nose. Dixie didn't mention that?"

She smiled a little. "I did it to protect her."

"I understand that. Protect her from . . . grief?"

Faith glanced over at him, which caught him off guard. He stared at her, taking his eyes off the road to try to read what was going on. Then he heard her gasp. He looked back out the front windshield and realized he'd swerved slightly, and up ahead another car was coming. He jerked the steering wheel and pulled back to his side of the street.

"Drive much?" she asked, her hand gripping the car door.

"Sorry."

"I'm blind, but I can at least tell when you're on the correct side of the road or not."

"I barely went over the yellow line," Mick said with a scowl. He felt like he was sixteen and his mother was in the passenger's seat.

"Yes, well, getting *barely* hit head-on by another car can get you *barely* dead."

Mick glanced at her, trying to see her eyes again. But

she was facing the window. All he could see was her cheek and the back of her head.

"It was a semi."

"No, it was a—" she stopped, combing her hair through with her fingers—"a car."

"How do you know that?"

"I can hear, Agent Kline. Very well. Can't you tell the difference between the sound of a car and a semi?"

"I guess I never noticed."

"There's a lot you don't notice until you lose your sight. Then your other senses take over."

Mick listened to the wind whistling through the car for a while, trying to study Faith out of the corner of his eye. She looked like a very sad woman. And before he knew it, that very statement came out of his mouth.

She didn't reply immediately. Then she said, "I lost the love of my life. How could I not be?"

Mick realized his face was flushing. He rolled down his own window, trying to get some air.

"Are you married?" she asked him.

Mick scratched his neck, where an itch suddenly broke out. He was the one who opened the can of worms, and he figured he might just get to know this lady a little better if he obliged. "No."

"Ever been in love?"

Mick dangled his arm out the window, opening his hand to catch the wind. "Once."

"But you're not married. What happened?"

"It's complicated."

"And it's a two-hour drive to the nursing home." She leaned her head against her hand, which was propped up by her elbow against the car door.

He sighed. "I realized it too late."

"Hmm." She didn't seem to buy that answer.

"Okay, look; I just didn't know what I wanted at the time. I was immature. Thought the whole world was at my fingertips. And when I figured it out, it was too late. She was gone. She'd moved on."

"To another man?"

The words pricked his heart. "Yes."

She grimaced. "Oh. That's too bad."

Mick glanced at her. "You don't sound too sympathetic."

She was quiet for a moment. "So you're not the same man that you were then?"

Mick concentrated on the highway. "No. Not even a little."

"But she chose to stay with the other man?"

"The other man was a better fit for her." Mick tapped his fingers against the steering wheel, mentally calculating how long it would be before they arrived to see Bea. "She is one of the finest people I know."

"So you still know her?"

The hand that was grabbing at the wind curled into a fist. "I do."

"Boy, that must be tough. Losing her, but then having to see her again and again with the man you lost her to."

Mick finally looked at Faith. She knew how to hit below the belt. He swallowed away his pride and anger and put his attention back on the road. "She married who she was supposed to marry," Mick said with a purposeful definitiveness in his voice.

Faith nodded, but it was only slightly.

For years he'd told himself that, for enough years he thought he believed it. He gripped the steering wheel with both hands. He *did* believe it. Mick knew beyond a shadow of a doubt she was not to have married him.

But she had certainly set the standard, which he

believed was why so many women hadn't worked out, including his latest casualty, Gwyn.

"You're quiet," Faith finally said. He couldn't dispute that. "It's a whole other story when the tables are turned, isn't it?"

"You think I'm here about you, but I'm really here to find the truth, and for some reason my journey keeps leading me back to you."

The muscles in Faith's jaw clinched. "Maybe that's because you're not looking very hard in other places. . . ." But the way her voice trailed off, Mick knew she'd convinced neither herself nor him of that statement. She sighed away the tension in the car. "How much longer?"

Agent Kline parked the car. He got out quickly and went to the other side, opening the door for Faith. She took her white cane out first, planted it on the ground, and got out. He shut the door and said, "Would you like my arm?"

She hesitated. "Um . . . sorry, I'm not used to this. I always have Sissy with me."

"Here, please, take it," he said. "I don't mind."

"Okay. Thank you." Her fingers wrapped around his bicep, and he started forward slowly.

As they walked toward the door, Agent Kline held on to her hand with his free hand.

She was close enough to smell his cologne. Was it Aramis? "We can speed up," Faith said. "I can usually do okay walking a little faster."

"Sorry," he said sheepishly.

They finally made it to the front desk, where a receptionist said, "Hello there."

"Hi," Faith said. "I'm here to see Bea Murtaugh."

"Just sign in here."

Agent Kline said, "I'll sign it for you."

"Okay. Thanks."

The receptionist said, "I think Bea's in her room. They just finished bingo. If you hurry, you may be able to catch her before she takes her afternoon snooze."

"Thank you," Agent Kline told the receptionist. He began pulling Faith in the direction of Bea's room.

"You can wait here," Faith said.

"What?"

"I'd like to see my grandmother by myself."

He sighed a little. "Okay. Sure." He paused. "Do you need help getting to her room?"

"No. I know the way. Around the corner, second room on the right."

"That's where I found her," Agent Kline said.

Faith awkwardly maneuvered her walking cane along the linoleum. She hardly used it and really didn't know how. She reached for the wall and glided her hand along it. As soon as she rounded the corner, she covered her mouth, leaned against the wall, and let out a frightful gasp. Her breathing could hardly keep up with her pounding heart.

She pushed her windblown hair out of her eyes and tried to regain control of her nerves. She'd almost blown it.

Her palms were sweaty and she wiped them on her jeans. Removing her sunglasses, she pulled her shoulders back and walked the fifteen feet to her grandmother's room. She leaned the walking stick up against the wall outside her door and knocked.

"Grandma? It's Faith."

chapter twenty-two

mick's finger flicked his sunglasses up and down slightly as he sat in his parked car across the street from Dixie Abernathy's small apartment complex. His eyes were heavy from an exhausting night of fitful sleep. He closed them, stopped toying with his sunglasses, and tried to think.

But all he could see when he closed his eyes was Faith Kemper.

It had to have been a coincidence. "Absurd," Mick breathed. It was as if she had seen that car coming toward them on the highway. Mick picked up the coffee he'd set on the dashboard and sipped it. He was tired. Wasn't thinking clearly. But according to Tom he wasn't thinking clearly anyway. Maybe his whole theory was unsound.

But this case—Faith Kemper, Paul—everything about it, drew him. There was so much evidence, but so much he didn't know. Why wasn't Faith telling him everything? Was it fear driving her secretiveness, or was it something else?

And then there was the note taped to his motel room door, which was what brought him to see Dixie this morning. He suspected she had left it. *LEAVE THIS TOWN.* His weary eyes blinked away the image, and he finished off his coffee just in time to see the green Toyota pull into the covered parking space he'd been keeping his eye on.

Dixie emerged from the car, then went to her trunk and

grabbed three paper sacks filled with groceries. She was managing to shut the trunk with an elbow when Mick approached.

"Let me help you."

Dixie whirled around, nearly dropping everything. Mick grabbed the bottom sack from her to prevent a disaster. Dixie whipped her sunglasses to the top of her head, revealing a scowl not to be reckoned with. "Didn't you get the point the first time I knocked you to the ground?" she said.

Mick tried to smile. "I probably should mention I'm a black belt."

"In what? Annoying people?"

"I'm not sure why I aggravate you so much."

"Because I have to keep reminding myself you're the good guy." Dixie's narrow eyes blinked slowly, as if she'd had some sort of epiphany while they were standing there with the grocery sacks. "I guess I should invite you in for some coffee or something."

"You should?" Mick asked. But Dixie was already walking to her apartment, so Mick followed.

She unlocked her door. "That's what the Bible teaches," she said, opening the door wider so he could come in. "You never know when you're entertaining an angel." She gave Mick a harsh look, up and down, then said, "Though I'm doubtful you're that kind of angel."

Mick set the groceries on the kitchen counter.

Dixie said, "You'll have to excuse me while I put the perishables up. In this kind of heat, things can spoil quickly."

Mick smiled. "You won't hear any argument from me. Please go ahead."

She put away her eggs, milk, cheese, yogurt, and lettuce before finally closing the refrigerator door and giving her attention to Mick. "Can I get you something to drink?"

"No thank you."

"Okay, well, what'd you want to see me for?"

"The note."

"What note?"

"The one you left me."

"Honey, this isn't high school. I haven't passed a note in three decades."

Mick smiled a little. "So you're telling me you didn't leave me a note on my motel door?"

Dixie's face registered interest, not guilt. "What'd it say?"

"Sorry, can't tell you."

Dixie parked her back against the refrigerator door and studied Mick. "I haven't yet decided if you're here to help my friend or cause her trouble."

"Neither," Mick said. "I'm trying to solve a case."

"Where's your partner?"

"My partner?"

"Yeah. Don't you types always travel in pairs? They do in the movies, anyway."

"The movies aren't always accurate when it comes to portraying FBI agents."

"Well," she said, looking at the sunglasses in his hand, "at least you got the dark shades."

"Dixie," Mick said, "I need to know if you left that note. If you didn't, then someone else did, and I have to be certain that I can rule you out."

Dixie crossed her arms. "Is Faith in danger?"

"I can't be sure one way or the other. But the note could tell me a lot."

"I didn't leave you a note, though if I did it'd probably say something like get outta town."

Mick had to laugh. "All right. Fair enough. You're not the first person to dislike me."

"It's nothing personal," Dixie said. "But I like Faith a

whole lot, and I don't want to see her get hurt. She's a fragile woman. She's lost her faith in life, love, and God. She's like a broken reed, and it's going to take a lot of ginger nurturing to get her standing tall again."

"Has Faith ever mentioned being scared before? of someone in particular?"

Dixie's eyes darted to the floor. "I sense she's terrified, but I don't know what of. She's never mentioned anyone. She doesn't talk a lot about it. She just told me her husband was murdered. You coming around has seemed to shake her up a lot."

Mick held out his hand to Dixie, and she shook it apprehensively. Then Mick handed her a card. "My cell phone is on there. Call me if you feel there is anything else I need to know." Mick went to the door.

Dixie followed, reading the business card. "How much longer are you going to be in town?" she asked.

"Until I find out everything I need to know."

The cotton was soft between her fingers, and for a long while she played with it in her hands. She lay back in her bed and pulled the shirt to her face. The smell was faint but still there. She wondered when it would finally fade.

Old Spice.

She turned to her side and curled up with the shirt. It had been Paul's favorite golfing polo. He'd won it in a charity golf tournament. It was one of the few things she'd dared to keep. Most of the time it remained neatly folded in her sock drawer, near the back.

Tears dripped off her face and onto her arm, rolling into the fabric. "I just miss you," she whispered. "I wish I could see your face, hold you." She squeezed her eyes shut, but it would not hold in all the emotion. "I wish I could've died that day too, you know. It's cruel that you let me live."

Without consciously realizing it, Faith now spoke to God. Whether Paul or God, to her they were both in some mystical, faraway place that she could not fathom or touch. "I have nothing of him left. You wouldn't even give us a child." She sobbed, turning her face into her pillow. "At least then I would have something to live for, some reason to go on," she mumbled. "But I am a miserable, weak, beaten-down human being."

She turned over and lay on her back. "I hate living like this. I hate being afraid."

Knock-knock.

Faith gasped, lurching off her bed as Sissy barked at the door. She hurried down the stairs.

Knock. Knock. Knock.

Was the back door locked? Should she go lock it?

Knock-knock.

Sissy's barking assaulted her senses. She stood paralyzed in the middle of her living room.

"Faith? It's Mick Kline."

Mick? Oh, thank God, she breathed. She hurried to the door, unlocked it, then realized she did not have her sunglasses. She had to open the door. . . . She brushed away stray tears as she swung the door open. "Hello."

"Hi, um . . . " He seemed perplexed and hesitant. "Hi."

"Would you like to come in?"

"Sure." He moved past her. "Are you okay?"

"Yes. Why?"

"Your eyes seem a little, well, you don't have your sunglasses on, and they seem a little . . . "

"I was asleep."

"Oh. Sorry."

"That's okay. I needed to get up anyway. I have to get my casserole ready for the potluck. Please, have a seat."

"Thank you," he said.

Faith took the chair near the couch. Self-consciousness made her reach for where her glasses should have been. "So, you just can't stay away, can you?" She grinned away her reticence. She was actually getting used to having this man around, and the more he was around, the safer she felt.

"Faith, I wanted to tell you about a note."

"A note?"

"Someone left a note on my door at the motel, telling me to leave town."

"You don't know who?"

"I was hoping you might."

Faith shook her head. "I hardly know anyone in this town. Just Dixie and Sandy and a few others at the restaurant."

Mick sighed heavily. "I don't want to make a bigger deal out of this than need be, but someone wants me gone, and I have to know who and why."

Faith wanted to cry and laugh all at once. Ever since Mick came into town, things just kept getting crazier and crazier. Yet now a very big part of her did not want him to go. "So that's why you came by? To tell me about the note?"

He laughed a little. "Well, actually, to see if I could buy you dinner." He paused. "I suppose I've been a pretty big pest, and the least I could do is take you to a nice dinner."

Faith couldn't suppress another grin. "Are you asking me out, Agent Kline?"

"Um . . . well . . . "

She shook her head. "Don't answer that."

"Don't answer that?"

"I have to decline."

"Oh."

"But will *you* go to dinner with *me*?"

He cleared his throat. "You're turning my request down for dinner, but now you're asking me out for dinner?"

"Well," she said sheepishly, "it's not exactly what you think."

mick could only be thankful that the church potluck was indoors in air-conditioning, but as he stared at the long line of food, he tried to pick out the "safe" items. There were rolls. And Jell-O. And baked beans.

He watched Dixie fix a plate for Faith, who was sitting at a nearby table with Sissy. Mick moved down the line and fixed his, aware that Dixie was eyeballing his food choices. They finished at the tea table, and Dixie quipped, "Didn't your mama ever teach you about the food pyramid?"

The large helping of Jell-O wobbled on his plate as he carried it over to where Faith sat.

Dixie sat down and said, "Here you go, honey. Hope you're hungry! Got you two kinds of quiche, a ham casserole of some sort, some buttered peas, and a fruit salad."

"Thank you, Dixie."

"Now listen, I want to introduce you to people, but I don't want to overwhelm you either. So let's just eat for now, and in a little while I'll introduce you to Sara Lee, who incidentally can cook a pie like the famous one—oh, and to Barbie Mulnomy. She doesn't look anything like the other Barbie." Dixie chuckled. "And Will Russell. He's our pastor. You'll like him. Down-home kinda guy. Oh, and then there's Judith—"

"I'm already feeling overwhelmed," Faith said with a smile.

Dixie laughed. "I'm sorry. You're right. Well, we'll take it one person at a time, how's that?"

"Sounds good. This quiche is excellent."

"Thank you!" Dixie said. "It's mine." Dixie looked at Mick. "Agent Kline here isn't trying the quiche."

"You don't like quiche?" Faith asked.

"Doesn't look like it," Dixie said. "But he is fond of baked beans and Jell-O."

"Well, you do have an odd relationship with food, don't you, Agent?"

Mick tried to scoop the elusive Jell-O onto his fork. Dixie handed him a spoon with a wry smirk on her face. "Thanks," Mick said.

They all ate while Dixie chatted away about this and that. Mick found himself staring at Faith more than at Dixie, though, and tried his best to concentrate on the baked beans.

His thoughts were interrupted by a strong hand on his shoulder. Mick looked up to find a middle-aged, pleasant-looking man grinning. "Hi there, Dixie! You brought some friends!"

"Hi, Will." Dixie stood and hugged him, then pointed to Faith. "This is my friend Faith and her dog, Sissy."

"Nice to meet you," Will said. "I'm the pastor here."

"Nice to meet you too." Faith smiled gracefully. Mick's heart seemed to skip a beat every time she smiled.

Then Dixie's attention was on Mick, though her expression wasn't quite as enthusiastic. "And this is Mick."

"Hi, Mick. Glad to have you and your wife with us."

"Oh—" Mick laughed—"she's not my wife." Out of the corner of his eye, he saw Faith fidget and Dixie grimace, as if the mere suggestion was insulting.

"Sorry." The pastor smiled. "Well, when there are two nice-looking people standing together, sometimes I just assume they're *together*."

Dixie said, "Where's your wife, Pastor?"

"Over in the kitchen making some more tea and lemonade, I think."

Dixie craned her neck and said, "Faith, I really want you to meet Beverly. Would you mind walking over there with me to say hello?"

Faith nodded and found the handle on Sissy's harness. Mick watched as she took Dixie's arm and they crossed the room.

Will apparently felt bad that Mick wasn't invited, because he sat down at the table. "So how do you know Dixie?"

"I met her when she tackled me because she thought I was going to rob Faith."

Will laughed heartily. "That sounds interesting." His head cocked to one side. "So, what brings you to my church?"

"Dixie invited Faith and Faith invited me. I'm only in town for a little bit. I like Bakerville. Very warm, except Dixie, but she's growing on me."

"Dixie—she's a fire ant, isn't she? What kind of business brings you here?"

"I could tell you, but then I'd have to kill you."

By the way the pastor was smiling and frowning at the same time, Mick decided he better lay off the odd humor. "Just kidding, Pastor."

"Oh." He chuckled lightly.

"Actually, I'm taking some time off from work."

The pastor's eyes engaged Mick's in a very concerned way. "Pardon me if this is too forward, but I noticed you from across the room and you . . . well . . . you just seemed like you had a lot on your mind."

"Really?" Mick glanced up at him. "That's very perceptive of you."

"God has given me a gift of helping people and seeing when people are in need of help. Is there anything I can help you with?"

Mick was watching Faith across the room. She stood in the doorway of the church kitchen, listening to Dixie and Beverly chat. He turned his attention back to Will. "I'm having a hard time dealing with the death of my brother."

"My goodness. I am so sorry. Is this recent?"

"Yes. Just a few weeks."

"How did he die?"

"Shot in the back of the head while asleep in his own bed."

Will's eyes lit with surprise and his mouth opened a little. "Your brother was murdered?"

"Yes. And they haven't caught who did it."

The pastor was nodding, his eyes trying to show concern but still reflecting astonishment. "Oh . . . I'm sorry."

"Yeah. Me too." Mick sighed and looked at Will. "And I'm struggling with revenge. When I catch whoever did this, I'm praying I don't kill him for it. But if I do, I probably won't shoot him in the back of the head when he's asleep. He deserves to suffer."

The pastor's jaw dropped. "Uh . . . why don't we step into my office?"

━━━━━

Faith knew from experience that people often have a hard time talking to the blind, and though Beverly was very sweet, Faith sensed by the way she kept addressing Dixie that she did not know what to do with Faith. Which was fine. Faith was happier just standing nearby, quietly unnoticed, though it was hard to remain unnoticed with a dog and dark sunglasses.

Beverly's fingers touched her arm. "Faith, I am so glad you are here with us today. I do hope you'll come to our services on Sunday. Will is a fantastic preacher. He doesn't do any of that fire-and-brimstone kind of preaching, either. He likes to preach on love, and he does a lot of sermons on family and children and . . . um, and just practical things like that." Faith guessed Beverly was from somewhere east of the Mississippi by her accent.

"I'd like that," Faith said.

Then Dixie said, "Oh, it'd be perfect! You know, Faith just lives right down the—"

Faith's pressed her lips together.

Dixie caught the signal but continued on relatively smoothly. "—right down the way. Listen, before I forget, I was hoping you could give me the recipe for that chocolate cake you made for Lois's birthday."

"Oh? You liked it?"

"Very much so. I need to bake a cake tomorrow. Would you mind writing it down for me?"

"Not at all," Beverly said, and Faith was a little proud of how quickly Dixie managed to cover her blunder. They continued chatting about the cake. Faith leaned against the nearby wall and entertained herself by caressing Sissy's fur. Her fingers lazily played through the dog's hair. Her mind lazily played over the idea that there was something about Agent Mick Kline that made her want to be over by him rather than here.

"I admire your honesty," Will said as he closed the office door and offered Mick a nice leather chair next to a dark cherry drink table.

Mick realized he was still carrying his tea in the flimsy plastic cup. He set it down and eased into the chair.

The pastor moved a few things from the center of his desk and then looked at Mick. "Do you . . . um . . . plan on catching this man?"

"Yes." Mick could tell that the poor pastor had never heard this kind of confession before. Mick had never given this kind of confession either, not to a stranger. But he hadn't been able to contain his rage.

"Oh. Good." He picked at a hangnail but kept his focus on Mick. "Well . . . so . . . you said you were worried you might take revenge on whoever did this."

Mick nodded. "I've been praying about it."

The pastor's worried expression melted into relief. "You're a Christian."

"Yes."

"That's why you struggle," Will said. "Because you have the Spirit in you, telling you that revenge belongs to the Lord."

A smile crossed Mick's lips, to his surprise. He didn't feel like smiling, but just hearing that Scripture spoken aloud seemed to relieve the angst that inched itself into the part of his mind that rationalized things.

"Mick," Will said, leaning forward on his desk, "you know that you cannot kill this man if you find him. And if you think that you would do that very thing, perhaps you should stop looking for him."

The words rang in Mick's ears. "You think it is better for whoever did this not to get caught?"

The pastor nodded. "I do. If your intention is to catch him and kill him. Tell me, how do you intend to catch him, if the authorities can't?"

"With God's help," Mick said, though rather feebly. If what the pastor said was true, then maybe the Lord would not be helping him after all. Yet in his spirit there was a nagging sense that he was supposed to be in Bakerville. And the note left on his motel door was a sign that someone definitely didn't agree.

"You seem to me," Will said, "to be a man with a tremendous sense of self-control."

"Thank you." Mick wondered what it was about this pastor that made him feel vulnerable.

"Can I ask what you do for a living?"

"I'm a special agent with the FBI."

Another jaw-dropping moment for the pastor, who then shook his head and almost laughed. "I'm sorry," he apologized meekly. "I just don't hear this kind of thing every day."

Mick nodded. "It's okay. I know it seems pretty weird."

"No, not weird," the pastor assured him. "But you have to understand. I spent the entire morning counseling the women's quilting club because they got in a fight over a topstitch of some sort."

A hearty laugh escaped from Mick and he covered his mouth, waving his hand apologetically. "Sorry."

"No need to apologize." Will smiled. "But it was the longest morning of my year." He then turned serious. "I will pray for you, Mick. I can't imagine what it would be like to have a brother murdered and the murderer roaming around somewhere."

"The thing is," Mick said, "I have this theory that no one believes except me."

"What is it?"

"I think it was a serial killer."

Will's eyes went wide again, and one long, slow blink indicated this was a lot for a country pastor to process.

Mick bit his lip, wondering if he had said too much.

Before he could lament too long, Will said, "And you're in Bakerville. . . . " A hard swallow followed.

Mick held up his hands. "Pastor, don't be alarmed. I'm here talking to someone in a case related to my theory. That's all."

"Faith, Dixie's friend."

Mick sighed. "Please don't say anything."

"You have my word." Will blinked away his astonished look. "But feel free to tell me more, unless of course, then you'd have to kill me."

chapter twenty-four

it felt good to drive the long stretch of highway by himself. He didn't even turn on the stereo or the CD player. He let the wind sing to him. The sunrise, normally a distraction from all his problems, went unnoticed on this morning.

At seventy-five miles an hour at 6:30 a.m., Mick raced toward the Southwestern Canine Guide School. It was an hour's drive from Bakerville. An hour he needed to think.

At the church last night, Faith had not shown any signs of being able to see. As much as he could, he'd watched her. And there was nothing out of the ordinary. He had hoped she would invite him back to her house, but after he had walked her home, she'd cordially said good night and shut the door.

From down the street, he'd watched only a couple of lights flick on. He figured that was normal. Though a person couldn't see, perhaps they could sense light, and maybe it was a good way to let others know the house was occupied.

He replayed that scene on the way to Bea's. She'd definitely gasped. He had not imagined it. Mick blinked, the road in front of him starting to blur.

At five this morning, he'd torn off his covers, drenched in sweat, crying out his brother's name. And then he cried for Jenny.

The red numbers of the motel clock screamed at him

until finally he tore the cord out of the wall and threw the clock onto the carpet. But sleep would not be found.

He'd sat up, rested his back against the headboard, and watched two anchors on one of the morning shows discuss the latest high-profile murder case, their faces solemn, their voices straining to control their eagerness at being first to report a new fact.

At 6:00 a.m., he'd pulled the phone book from the bedside drawer and flipped it open, searching for anything nearby that would help him understand blindness more. There was nothing in Bakerville, and he wasn't having much luck in any of the nearby towns until he came across the Southwestern Canine Guide School.

At 6:15, he'd dressed and brushed his teeth. At 6:17, he realized he'd better shave. By 6:25, he was pulling through the Krispy Kreme drive-through, ordering a tall coffee.

Now the wind blew through his hair. The heat had not reached the earth yet, and the coolness of the breeze was welcome. He spent the hour-long drive recollecting his thoughts on the other cases. He'd become focused on the Kemper case, but maybe this was a dead end for him. Faith was unwilling to tell all she knew, and the clues he was getting didn't seem to be putting him closer to finding a killer.

That note, though.

Whoever wrote it had made a mistake. Mick probably would've left a day or so ago, except someone wanted just that. And he wanted to know why.

His coffee was gone just in time for him to see the large sign announcing the Southwestern Canine Guide School. In the middle of scorched land and steamy highway pavement sat a large complex. A gas station and a few scattered buildings were nearby, but the guide school was pretty much the biggest attraction.

Before 8 a.m., things were looking very quiet. Mick

parked his car near the front entrance and got out, stretching his legs and smoothing out his slacks. In the distance he
could hear the faint barking of dogs. He took off his
sunglasses so as not to appear stereotypical and found his
way into a large reception area.

No receptionist greeted him, and by the look of things—
like an empty coffee service and a television that was turned
off—school wasn't in session yet. Mick walked to a large
glass window that gave him a good view of what was out
back. A few people milled about, and he saw a dog here and
there. The lawn was immaculate, trimmed to perfection,
green as a crayon. Laid sod, he imagined. Sprinklers were
showering more sidewalk than grass, and he watched a man
step outside just in time for a misty shower.

Mick laughed a little, then heard someone clear his
throat. He turned to find a bespectacled young man holding
a stack of folders about to slide out of his grip. He smiled at
Mick and adjusted his glasses.

"May I help you?"

"I think I'm early. You're not open yet?"

"At nine."

"Oh . . . ," Mick said, glancing at his watch. "I'm way
early."

"Do you have an appointment with someone?"

"No. Actually, I'm with the FBI."

"The FBI?" The young man adjusted the folders in his
arms. "How can I help you?"

"Well, we're investigating the use of guide dogs to
smuggle narcotics across the border from Mexico." The
kid's mouth opened to say something, but no words came
out. Mick laughed. "I'm sorry. I'm joking. I have a bad
sense of humor."

The kid cracked a smile. "That's a good one. But, uh,
why are you here? We don't see the FBI out here much."

"I wonder how many people you do see. You're out in the middle of nowhere."

"Tell me about it." The young man sighed. "It takes me forty minutes to get here."

Mick held out his hand. "Special Agent Mick Kline."

"Oh, hi," the kid said, shaking his hand limply. "Roger McNickel. I work on the administrative side."

"Listen, I was wondering if there's anyone I could talk to about blindness. I just need basic information, and I found you in the phone book."

Roger shrugged. "Well, I guess you could talk to Keith."

"Keith?"

"Keith Strom. He started this school."

———

"Sandy's sick today," Wallace said. He watched Faith unwrap her silverware from the paper napkin.

"Good morning, Wallace."

"They say she has a kidney stone."

"Oh, poor girl."

"I can help out. Maybe get you coffee."

"Coffee would be great. A large. Cream and sugar."

"Cream and sugar. Large."

"Thank you."

"Cynthia will be here to serve you."

"Okay."

"They won't let me serve. Just get coffee. And wipe it up when it spills."

She smiled at him. "Thank you, Wallace."

Wallace wanted to stay at the table, but he knew sooner or later someone would shoo him away. Maybe if he acted busy, nobody would notice he was doing more than cleaning crumbs. He glanced back at Faith. She looked sad today. Tired. He glanced at the dog. *Lazy.*

"Wallace!"

Cynthia. "What?"

"What do you think you're doing? You're not supposed to serve the guests. You're a busboy. Do I need to stamp it on your forehead?"

"Sandy lets me help sometimes."

"Well, Sandy's at home, writhing in pain."

"Is she okay?"

Cynthia shook her head. "I don't know, Wallace. From what I hear, stones are painful. Never had one, never plan to. Anyway, stop harassing the customers."

"I wasn't harassing. She just needs coffee."

"Can you stop being a ghoul for once and do what you're told?"

Cynthia. Always mad.

Wallace stood nearby, watching Cynthia greet Faith.

"Hi, Faith. It's Cynthia. Sandy's sick today."

"I heard. Kidney stone. Wallace told me."

He smiled and turned his back, taking his towel and wiping eggs off table 17. *Wallace told me. Yes, Wallace told me. Don't worry. You're safe in here.*

———

Keith Strom, a tall, well-built athletic type sporting a buzz cut and a deep tan, strolled across the grass toward them, his cotton shirt flowing in the wind, casual pants to match, looking like he should be walking the beaches of Hawaii. He was holding some papers in his hand when he approached.

Roger leaned over to Mick and said, "That's him," as if introducing them had just made Roger's day.

"Hi, Roger," Keith said. "This is the FBI guy?"

Mick held out his hand. "Special Agent Mick Kline."

Keith grinned. "I guess *FBI guy* isn't the correct term, eh?"

Mick chuckled. "Well, it's okay, seeing as you're the dog dude."

Keith laughed and turned to Roger. "Will you make sure that Amy signs off on these? Sam's all ready to go except for getting Amy's signature. And we know how Mr. Turlington hates to wait."

Roger nodded and rushed off.

Keith guided Mick to a sidewalk that trailed around the entire complex. "What can I do for you?"

"I wanted some information on blindness."

"What kind of information?"

"What it's like to be blind, how someone copes. And how they use a guide dog. Things like that."

"*Dog guide* is actually the correct term. Just so you know. It's a common mistake." Keith glanced at Mick. "This in relation to a case you're working?"

Mick smiled, eyes forward. "Oh, I think I'll let your imagination take over on that one."

Keith laughed. "Come here, boy." The Labrador greeted Keith excitedly as they walked. "This is Sam. He's leaving us today to help Mr. Turlington, who became blind due to diabetes. I'm gonna miss this fellow. He's got a lot of personality. But I enjoy knowing that Sam's going to be helping a man function as normally as possible. Here comes Amy, one of our trainers."

A petite woman approached, blonde hair cut blunt, face freckled from the sun.

"Amy, this is Special Agent Mick Kline."

They shook hands, and then Keith and Amy discussed the details of Sam's final day before Amy took the dog and went to a nearby building. Keith pointed to a small garden area. "There's a bench under some shade."

They walked toward it. "So you began this school?"

"In 1984. After my wife was killed. She was a diabetic, went blind. She was hit by a car while she was crossing the street with her cane."

"I'm sorry."

"It made me determined to make sure every blind person who wants a dog guide gets one."

They sat on the bench. Mick noticed how fragrant the surrounding flowers were. *Thoughtful. Appeals to senses other than sight,* Mick thought.

"I've always heard about Seeing Eye dogs, but you said 'dog guide.' What is the difference?"

"Seeing Eye dog, dog guide, leader dog—they're just different 'brands' of dogs that help blind people. They're trained differently, but they learn the same things. The different names can be confusing."

"Interesting."

"Here at my school, I'm also very interested in teaching sighted people how to work with the blind, to help them understand how to act around a blind person and a dog guide too."

"Like what?"

"Well, for example, you should never pet a dog guide or call its name or distract it anytime it's working, which is always when the harness is on."

"Oh . . . " Mick recalled doing that several times with Sissy and noted others had too. Mick took out his notepad and pen, which did not go unnoticed by Keith, who seemed a little amused.

"And never, ever feed a dog guide while it's working, like giving it human food under the table. Since they go in so many public places, you'd hate to be there when the diarrhea hits, if you know what I mean." Mick glanced up and Keith was shaking his head, as if he'd had firsthand experience with that. "If a person is using a dog guide and you want to offer assistance, always approach on the right side, offering your left arm."

"Why is that?"

"Because a dog is almost always on the left side, unless the person has a disability, like a missing limb, that forces the dog to be on the right."

Mick jotted quickly. "The dog is never on the right?"

"Not usually."

Mick pictured Faith walking down the sidewalk, Sissy by her right side. "Okay. What else?"

Keith shrugged. "Well, blind people can do nearly everything a seeing person can do. They just go about achieving it differently. But helping a blind person is usually welcomed. For example, if you're going to tell someone what's on their plate, you would describe it using the clock method. Peas are at three o'clock. Mashed potatoes at six. That sort of thing."

Mick could not recall one time when Faith asked for that kind of help. She always just started eating.

"Once blind people learn Braille, it really opens up a whole new world for them. They can enjoy reading again, and that's a wonderful escape."

"Braille," Mick mumbled as he wrote. There were no books in Faith's house that he could see, Braille or otherwise.

While Keith continued talking about how independent blind people can be with the help of dogs, Mick suddenly found his attention on a trainer and a collie. He watched as the trainer took the dog around, instructed it, rewarded it, corrected it.

Mick leaned forward, watching intently. The dog walked on the left, just as Keith had mentioned. But it seemed different from how Sissy did it. This dog was right next to the trainer's leg, whereas Sissy seemed to always be out front a little more. Was it just a coincidence? Keith had said dogs were trained differently. Keith was explaining what breeds were common as dog guides—including German shepherds like Sissy.

Mick watched as the trainer instructed the dog where to go, and the dog obeyed. Had he just not noticed Faith doing these things? "How does a blind person learn to use the dog?"

"They go through training too. Twenty-six days. They learn the commands, learn to handle the dog. There's also love and devotion that develop."

Mick turned to Keith. "They stay here, on-site?"

"Yes. It's a very intensive, monthlong program."

"All dog guide users would have to go through this kind of training?"

"Yes. Here, or wherever they get their dog from. There are several schools around Texas. I can get you a list of those schools and their phone numbers if you want."

"That'd be great. And also a list of every student you've had in here for the past three years."

Mick's legs hurt from the drive, and he tried to stretch them as he drove the final ten miles back to Bakerville. His back muscles longed for a hot shower, and his eyelids drooped heavily, the dark and quiet highway beckoning him to sleep.

He rolled down his car window, turned up the radio, and popped his eyes open. "Ten more miles," he mumbled. "You can make it."

He'd spent the rest of the day poring over the information he had on the other murder cases. And his notes from Keith Strom. But his mind, no matter what he was concentrating on, would inadvertently drift to Faith Kemper, and he'd momentarily close his eyes and let her consume his thoughts. Then he would plant himself back into reality and into what he was supposed to be doing, which was catching a killer. And driving.

His car whizzed by a Conoco station. "Five miles," he said out loud, waking himself up as if a passenger had just started an unexpected conversation. He sat taller in his seat and stuck his hand back out the window, his fingers tingling in the wind.

It took about six minutes to finally get to the motel parking lot, where he pulled his car into one of twenty open spaces. He locked the car and stretched his hands toward the sparkling night sky. His room was up one flight of stairs, but it might as well have been ten, the way he was feeling. He trudged up the steps, holding on to the rail.

Rounding the corner, he sighed when he finally saw his room number.

"Thank the good Lord," he said, sliding his card key into the lock. He tried the door, but it was still locked. "Oh no . . . " He groaned. He put the card back into the door and waited for the green light, but nothing happened. His eyes rolled back into his head, and he wanted to scream. "I just want to go to sleep! Come on! *Come on!*" He jammed the key back and forth into the slide and was just about to kick the door in when the light suddenly turned green and the door clicked. "Thank you, thank you, thank you," he said, quickly opening the door and going in.

The frigid air greeted him like a slap in the face, and he adjusted the thermostat near the window. He closed the door behind him and was just about to switch on the light when he heard a noise.

Across the room a figure stood near the bathroom.

chapter twenty-five

mick reached for his gun, but all he caught was air. He had not taken his gun with him to the dog school. It was in one of the dresser drawers, underneath his T-shirts. Or it was . . .

He stumbled backward to the door, reaching behind him to try to open it without turning his back.

"Wait!" a male voice said. "I'm a police officer."

Mick fumbled along the wall for the switch, but then realized the only lights in the room were the lamps on either side of the bed and the one by the TV.

"Who are you?" Mick said, trying to let his eyes adjust to the dark. All he could see was a tall figure, definitely not dressed in a uniform.

"Hold on. I'll turn on a light." Suddenly the room glowed with the light from the bathroom. A tall, blond man in his early thirties stood there, face tight with apprehension.

"Who are you?"

"Greg Pratt."

"Pratt . . . ," Mick breathed.

"You talked to my wife, Kerri, at the hospital."

Mick's heart, which struggled to find a regular rhythm, now settled itself into a steady but fast beat. "Right. The nurse."

"Yes."

"What are you doing in my motel room? That's a good way to get yourself shot."

"I know," he said. "I'm sorry. It was the only way."

Mick walked forward, looking around the room, trying to decide whether or not he should get his gun. He studied the man, and from all impressions, he did look fairly harmless. In fact, he looked like this was the last thing he wanted to do.

Mick pointed to a chair near the TV stand and said, "Why don't you sit down right there and explain yourself."

"Okay," Greg said. He lowered himself into the chair carefully, but Mick did not know if it was because he was showing he wasn't going to make any sudden moves or if he was unsure of what Mick might do once he sat down. Either way, the man kept his eyes glued on Mick.

"I came to give you the case file on Paul Kemper's murder." He pointed over his shoulder to the bathroom counter.

Mick blinked, looked at the file carefully from across the room, then back at Greg. "Why?"

"Because Kerri said you had come asking questions, said you thought the murder might be connected to a serial killer. And I also know you've been to see Chief Underwood in Allana."

"You know a lot about what I've been doing. Now what I want to know is what you've been doing in my room."

"Just sitting. Though I did see the note." Greg's eyes darted to the top of the TV, where Mick had left the note this morning.

"How long have you been here?"

"Since dark." Greg's tense eyes finally lowered a little and his stiff shoulders relaxed. "Underwood is suspicious of me because I confronted him about your visit. I wanted to know what was going on. Underwood has such a ferocious ego, and I knew that whatever did happen, he wasn't going to let me know about it."

"I don't understand."

"Underwood thinks it's Miguel Juarez. Maybe it is. But I wanted to know the information you had, and he wouldn't tell me. By the way he got so defensive, I figured it was information that conflicted with his theory on Juarez."

"Something tells me you don't buy his theory either."

"I don't know what to think. There are certainly clues pointing to Juarez. But then there are clues pointing away from him too. I just want to find who killed Paul—Juarez or otherwise."

Mick walked to the counter and picked up the folder, his eyes still on Greg, who sat in the chair, both feet on the floor, his fingers fiddling with the fabric on the armrests. Hips resting against the bathroom counter, he flipped open the file, scanning the notes quickly. "How'd you get in here, anyway?"

"'Excuse me, I lost my key' works pretty well."

"Ah."

Greg smiled. "I speak fluent Spanish, so I also complimented the maid on her hair. That never hurts. I didn't want to risk being seen sitting in my car."

Mick nodded and went back to reading the file. The adrenaline surge from catching someone in his room had subsided a bit, and he felt the fatigue of the day begin to return. He walked over to the bed and sat down. "It says here Faith Kemper gave a description of the man who attacked her," Mick said suddenly.

"Yes."

Mick glanced up at Greg. "She never told me that. In fact, she said she saw nothing." Mick looked back down at the report. "Says he had dark hair and dark eyes. Juarez."

"Yeah," Greg said.

Mick rubbed his temples and scratched at his hairline. "Faith told me she didn't see him."

Greg's gaze dropped to the floor. He seemed to have nothing to say about it.

"I don't understand her," Mick continued, thumbing through more pages of the documents. "Why wouldn't she try to help me get the man who killed her husband?"

"I don't know," Greg finally said. "There's a lot about Faith we can't explain. She just disappeared on us, didn't want anything to do with us anymore." Greg's weary eyes met Mick's. "She's here, in Bakerville, isn't she?"

"Don't breathe a word to anyone, Greg. Do you hear me?"

"I wouldn't." Greg laughed a little. "I had to sneak in here, didn't I?" He shook his head. "Underwood, he's a beast sometimes. Jealous. Hates to be told he's wrong. He would probably try to have me fired if he knew I was here handing you the case file. In fact, he'd probably do more than that. I think he had me followed a couple days after Paul's murder, just to see what I was up to. That's why I had to sneak around."

Mick's eye caught something on the fifth page. "She said he was wearing a gold watch."

Greg nodded.

"Miguel Juarez was wearing a gold watch the day I visited him." Mick tapped his fingers against the paper. "A lot of people wear gold watches, though."

"True."

Mick continued reading, and something else caught his eye. The report stated that an item belonging to Miguel was found twenty feet from the Kempers. "What about this? What is it? A movie ticket stub?"

"Yes," Greg said. "Miguel verified it was his, that he and his wife had gone to see the movie that afternoon before he went to work. He said it fell out of his pocket, but he had been all over the garage that night parking cars. Which couldn't be disputed."

Mick closed the folder. "Underwood. Don't know what to do with that guy."

"He's known around these parts. Obviously we're in different jurisdictions. I'm with Houston, Underwood's with Allana. But because Paul had been a Houston officer, we tried to share information back and forth. All I have to say is be careful. He knows you're on leave from the bureau. He called your supervisor."

"I know," Mick said. "And I can't figure out why Tom hasn't called me. He's letting me do my thing. But it was a different story before I left."

Greg stood and handed Mick a card. "My home phone number is on the back. Call me if you need any more information or any help. I'll have to be discreet, but I'll do what I can to help you."

Mick handed him the folder. "This has been a great deal of help already. Now I've got to find out everything Faith saw and why she isn't telling me."

"Is she . . . um . . . is she doing okay?"

"I think so," Mick said. "She's carrying on with life, going to church, making a few friends. She's new to this town, so as far as I can tell she's fitting in pretty well."

"I can't imagine seeing Kerri murdered right in front of me. I want whoever did this caught."

"I understand," Mick said.

Greg looked at him. "I won't ask you about why you think this is a serial case. I know you probably can't give me details. But if I can do anything for you . . . "

Mick stood and took the hand Greg was offering. "Actually, you can."

"Name it."

"Distract Underwood tomorrow morning. I'm going to see Juarez."

chapter twenty-six

Something told Miguel not to get his gun when Spank, their eight-year-old pit bull, barked ferociously outside, shattering the still morning air. Miguel set down his coffee and moved the front-window curtains to the side ever so slightly and saw the FBI agent's car. Agent Kline got out of his car, eyeing Spank carefully.

"Lucky for you she's on a chain," Miguel snarled. He turned and pounded his hand against the back of the couch. A few seconds later the doorbell rang. Hesitation froze him in the middle of his living room. The doorbell rang again. Miguel finally opened the door.

"Mr. Juarez. Hello."

Miguel tightened the terry-cloth robe around his waist and narrowed his eyes at Mick. "Can't you come at a decent hour?"

"Sorry," Agent Kline said. "I wanted to catch you at home. Just a few more questions."

Miguel knew Carlita was approaching. He could smell her cherry-scented lotion.

"Miguel?"

"He's here to ask me more questions," Miguel said to her. Carlita stood by his side, slipping her arm through his. Miguel watched her study the agent.

"We have nothing to hide," she said. She looked at Miguel, then back at the agent. "My husband is innocent."

"Then let me ask you some questions to clear his name once and for all."

"Hah!" said Miguel.

But Carlita said, "Okay, come in. For just a few moments."

Miguel followed them in, watching Carlita offer him a seat at their humble breakfast table where a newspaper and two coffee cups sat. She cleared the table.

"What is your wife's name?" Agent Kline asked him as she went to the sink.

"Mrs. Juarez," Miguel grumbled.

She returned from the sink and said, "Carlita."

"Well," he said, "the pleasantries don't seem to be doing much more than annoying you, so I'll get to the point. The killer was wearing a gold watch."

Miguel glanced at Carlita, who was looking at his wrist. "I bought that for him this past Christmas," she said, forgetting her English and speaking quickly.

Miguel regarded the watch, then looked at Mick and nodded. "Yes."

The agent was about to say something when Carlita rose and went to a small shelf, from which she took a shoe box. She opened it, dug around for a moment, and then pulled out a white piece of paper. "This man always teases me for keeping all these receipts." She handed it to the agent. "There you are. A receipt for a gold watch from Sears. Bought the week before last Christmas."

Mick studied the receipt. It was genuine. He handed it back to her and smiled approvingly.

"What else do you need to know?" Miguel said, watching his wife put the receipt back.

"I'm just looking for the truth," Mick said. "That's all. And somehow it's hard to come by in this case."

Miguel stared at the white table, hardly noticing his

wife's hand on his shoulder. "The truth is something Underwood is not interested in."

"I am. Tell me what you know, Miguel, and I will find out who did this. You will be exonerated."

"Promises, promises."

"Tell him," his wife suddenly said.

Miguel glanced sideways at her with surprise. "Carlita, shush."

"No!" she said. "It has been two long years, Miguel. And I'm sick and tired of it. You have nothing to lose. Our life is already pathetic. You can hardly find work in this town. We have Underwood and his hounds breathing down our necks constantly."

His trembling hands tore through his thin black hair as he studied his wife. He could see their two children peering through the window behind her. He prayed they knew to stay outside. "I did not see who did it," he started. "But I did see the two right after they were attacked, and I heard footsteps running the other way in the parking garage. I didn't know what to do, and I was also scared for my life."

"So what did you do?"

"I hid for a moment, behind a car, watching. I decided I better get help, and so I was about to when a lady in a car that was leaving stopped and tried to help. I heard her call 911 on her cell phone."

"I read that in the file, that it was a woman who called 911. Then what?"

"Then I walked away." His wife's steady hand patted his shoulder. Miguel hoped his eyes didn't reflect his shame.

"Why?"

"You don't understand what it's like to live in Allana." The name felt heavy on his tongue. "It doesn't matter anyway. I was still targeted."

"There was a movie stub found."

"I know. I told the police everything." Miguel sighed. "We'd gone to the movies. It must've fallen out of my pocket at some point. I parked cars there all night. Who knows."

"God knows." The agent stared hard at him. "Your name, as you probably know, means 'who is like God?' God knows the truth and God knows who killed Paul Kemper."

Carlita was about to speak when Miguel held up a hand in front of her. But he kept his eyes on Agent Kline's. "Then where is His vindication? Where is His justice?"

The agent didn't blink. "It's coming."

━━━━━━━

Faith closed her eyes and smelled the candle. "This is a three-wick," the woman explained.

"I love it," Faith said. She handed it back to the woman, who handed her another one.

"Now, this is my personal favorite. Cucumber Melon."

Faith's nostrils flared. "And this one too! I'm going to have to buy the whole store!"

Dixie said, "Faith, if you're okay here for a second, I'm going to run two doors down to the post office for some stamps."

"Sure. I'll be fine," Faith said.

The saleswoman held up another candle and said, "This one is lemon."

Faith took it from her and smiled. "I really like this. Fruity but clean."

The woman was explaining that Bella's Candle Wax was started in 1984 by two sisters, Bertie and Ella, and they'd been making candles ever since. Then she excused herself to the front cash register for a moment.

Faith put the candle carefully back on the shelf and nearly jumped when she heard someone say, "Faith."

"Wallace?"

"Hi." He tried not to sway. Someone had told him once not to sway. He didn't know why he shouldn't.

"You're . . . um . . . you're in the candle shop?"

"On my way to work. Saw you come in."

Faith adjusted her sunglasses. "Oh."

"Just wanted to say hello."

"Oh. Um . . . okay. Hello."

He'd made her uneasy. He did that a lot. To all sorts of people. Emotions stirred in him, and he bit his lip, trying not to cry. Why did he make people uncomfortable? He was being friendly, just like everyone else. The more he tried to fit in, the less he did.

He knew he was going to have to leave. He didn't want to. He wanted to talk about the candles. He loved the candles too. They reminded him of the good things from long ago.

"Wallace, listen, I—"

"Have to go." His shoulder bumped into the corner of one of the shelves as he turned, and two candles came crashing down.

Faith gasped.

"I'm sorry. I'm sorry!" Wallace cried and looked at the woman behind the counter. Angry. Surprised. Irritated.

He rushed out of the store. Not even candles would bring the good memories now.

Mick drove back to Bakerville from Allana, tired of all the driving, frustrated at all the dead ends. He pulled into a gas station to fill up, wondering if he should call Jenny. He didn't have any news for her. And part of him didn't want to know if she wasn't doing well. If he couldn't help her, he didn't want to know she was hurting.

But he knew. How could she not be? His heart was still as numb as the day he found out Aaron was dead.

His fingers glided over the numbers on his cell phone, three times going through the motion of calling her but never pressing a number hard enough to activate his phone.

Then it rang in his hand, and he nearly dropped it. He didn't recognize the number. "This is Mick Kline."

"Hi, Agent Kline. This is Keith Strom."

"Keith, hello."

"Listen, no one around here or elsewhere in any of the Texas schools can find a lady named Faith Kemper in our files."

"Interesting."

"Could it be under a different name?"

"Possibly," Mick said, but under what other name he didn't know. "Keith, thank you so much for your help."

"Sure. Let me know if I can do anything else."

Mick shut off his phone and got out and pumped his gas. As soon as the pump clicked off, he dialed Faith Kemper's number. Her answering machine picked up.

"Faith, this is Mick. I need to talk to you. Meet me at Nik's for lunch at noon."

chapter twenty-seven

She was waiting for him when he arrived, which he thought was five minutes early. She sat at her usual table. He approached her quietly, to see if it would make a difference. But Sissy raised her head and grunted a greeting, so naturally Faith was made aware.

"Hello, Faith," he said, sitting down.

"Agent Kline."

"How are you doing?"

"Curious."

"I figured you would be."

"Did you find something out about the case?"

"Oh yes, indeed," Mick said.

"What?"

"Hello, you two." Mick looked up to find Sandy greeting them with a smile.

"Hi, Sandy," Faith said.

"What to drink today?"

"Water," they both said.

"Okay. Be right back."

Faith leaned forward. "Well?"

"It's not about the killer. It's about you. Every turn keeps leading back to you."

Tension pressed Faith's lips into a straight line. "You keep saying that."

"Because it's true."

Sandy returned with their water, breaking the uneasiness with order requests.

"Um . . . just a . . . just a salad . . . garden . . . ranch dressing," Faith rambled.

"A salad, too, but with vinegar and olive oil, please."

Sandy let a somewhat disapproving eyebrow arch high on her forehead before she turned and left. Mick sighed. Maybe Sandy left the note.

"Just spit it out," Faith said after Sandy was out of earshot.

"You saw his face."

The line of her lips turned downward ever so slightly. Her nostrils flared. "Who?"

"The man who killed Paul. You told me you didn't see him, but you did."

"You read the case file."

"I got my hands on a copy, yes."

An exhausted sigh heaved her chest, and she rubbed the back of her neck. "Yes, I saw him."

"Faith," Mick tried, "why didn't you tell me? Don't you trust me? Don't you see what I'm trying to do here?"

"No, Mick, I don't see what you're trying to do. You say you're trying to find who killed Paul. But all you are doing is intruding into my very private life, a life that I want to live in simplicity and solitude."

"And in fear."

Her fingers tickled at her forehead as if summoning words that wouldn't come out of her mind by themselves. Then she said, "He hit me from behind; I fell to the ground. I remember a glimpse of a gold watch. I hit my head pretty hard on the pavement. I remember seeing bright lights for a little bit. I'm not sure how long. Then I managed to roll over, onto my side, I think, and there was blood running down my forehead and into my eyes." Her voice quivered and she took a breath. "I tried to open my eyes, but there was so much blood, I wasn't sure what I was seeing. And then there was this . . . it wasn't a face . . . just eyes. And dark hair, I think. It was a figure, but I remember the eyes—they were dark. And then I guess I passed out."

Her breathing had picked up a little. Mick knew that just recounting the story was very hard for her. He wanted to reach across the table and take her hand, reassure her that she was going to be okay.

Take her hand.

He started his reach when suddenly the busboy was there with his coffeepot in hand. "More coffee." He didn't look like he was ready to serve coffee, though. His flustered demeanor put Mick on guard.

"We're not drinking coffee," Mick said.

"Faith."

Faith shook off her trauma and acknowledged him. "What, Wallace?"

"Are you okay here?"

"Of course. Why do you ask?"

"You're okay?"

"Yes, Wallace, I'm fine."

Sandy was suddenly by Wallace. "Wallace, I'm handling my tables just fine. Go get the dishes off table 12."

Mick watched as Wallace obeyed, his feet shuffling toward table 12, coffeepot held steady in his hand.

Sandy shook her head but tried to smile. "Sorry about that folks. Here are your salads." She placed them on the table.

Mick watched Sandy walk away, then go over to Wallace and gently explain something to him. Wallace looked back at their table and disappeared into the kitchen.

"What was that about?" Mick asked Faith.

"He's just sort of one of those guys, you know."

"No. What kind of guys?"

"You know, a little shy, insecure, kind of socially awkward."

"Why did he ask if you were okay?"

"He likes to watch out for me here at the restaurant. Gives him a sense of self–importance, I guess. I think he's taken a liking to me."

"Why would he think you were in trouble having lunch with me?"

Faith shrugged, piercing her salad with her fork. "I don't think he likes you. The other day he made a comment about it. I think he may have been here the day I stormed out."

Mick looked into the kitchen, but Wallace was nowhere to be seen. "Do you know him well?"

"No better than Sandy or Cynthia or some of the others here. Why?"

"Just curious," Mick said. He stared at his salad, but he'd lost his appetite.

"Mick?"

"Yeah?"

"I'm sorry I lied to you." Faith set her fork down. "I want to trust you. I want to believe you, but I don't even trust God anymore, so how can I trust anyone else? He let Paul die. He almost let me die. What is there to trust? A friend told me while I was in the hospital that all things work together for the glory of God. Well, if this is how God gets His glory, I don't want to be a part of it."

Mick pushed his salad aside. "Faith, you know there is evil in this world. And we don't understand why some things happen."

"That's supposed to make me feel better?"

"No. But deep down you have to ask yourself who you trust more—yourself or God."

"What does that mean?"

"It means that you have to probe. If you were in a dangerous situation and had to pick yourself or God to get you out of it, who would you choose?"

"That's an absurd question," Faith said. "Besides, God *didn't* get me out of a dangerous situation."

Mick sighed, trying to decide how to approach the subject from another angle, when he glanced up. The busboy was staring from a doorway. When he saw Mick look at him, he turned and disappeared.

"I want you to be careful around Wallace."

Confused by the shift in topic, Faith's eyebrows dipped below her sunglasses in a frown. "Why?"

"It's just a feeling."

"Well, Wallace had a bad feeling about you too. Whose feeling should I trust?" She took a bite of salad, as if to indicate it might take Mick a while to answer that one.

He also took a bite of salad.

Faith felt a little sorry for Mick. She knew he wanted to help. There was no doubt in her mind now. But there were things that Mick could never help her with. She didn't blame him. She blamed God.

"I guess," Mick said after a moment, "you then have to ask yourself if you are able to live with questions unanswered."

Faith wanted to retort, but she couldn't, not really. His brother had been murdered as brutally as Paul. Mick knew the feeling of being betrayed by a God he trusted to protect him. What was it about Mick Kline that he could go on when she nearly stopped living? Was she simply weak?

"Faith," Mick said gently. "I don't think less of you for your questions. For your anger."

"You don't?" Tears clustered at the corners of her eyes. His compassion was not expected.

"No." His hand wrapped around hers. "In fact, maybe you're so mad at God because you loved Him so much."

Faith covered her quivering mouth with her other hand. Tears fell quickly. "I used to."

"You still do. Anger doesn't cancel out love. It shows how much love there is. You loved God with all your heart. That's what your grandmother said."

Faith squeezed Mick's hand, her fingers trembling inside his. "I just wanted to—" Words drowned in her emotion.

"Let me take you home," Mick said, standing her up gently. As they walked out of the restaurant, Faith realized something: This time Mick Kline, not Sissy, guided her.

chapter twenty-eight

the creaking reminded her of a cradle, and the gentle rocking lulled her anxieties to a stillness she couldn't remember feeling in a long time.

Maybe it wasn't the porch swing that brought the stillness. Maybe it was Mick sitting beside her.

"Sissy is a great dog," he commented as he watched her play in the yard.

"She is my guardian angel."

Faith closed her eyes and rested, not remembering the last time she had done both. "I don't know if I would be mad at God if Paul would've died after a heart attack," Faith said. "Maybe I would. Maybe I would be asking God why He didn't protect his health."

Mick squeezed her shoulder. "I love your name."

She laughed. "My name?"

"Faith. It's a really great name."

"Guess I'm not living up to it these days," she said with a half smile.

"That's not true. Our faith is so often tested. Some people's more than others. There were those who were martyred for their beliefs. And there were those who God allowed to live out their days in perfect peace. The mystery isn't why God allowed men to be martyred. The mystery is why only some."

Faith's eyes felt heavy, but for the first time it wasn't with grief or fatigue. It was almost . . . peace?

"At least you don't sound like a chicken when you say your name."

"Excuse me?" Faith laughed.

"Well, my name—you know, Mick Kline—if you say it slowly and pronounce all the vowels and consonants, you sound like a chicken clucking."

"Huh-uh . . . "

"Sure. Try it."

"Mick. Kline." She laughed. "It's true!"

He made chicken noises that made her laugh even more. She held her stomach and laughed so hard that Sissy came over to investigate, rubbing her nose against Faith's arm.

"It's okay, girl," Faith said between breaths. "It's the chicken over here you should be worried about."

Faith could hear Paul's laughter mingle with hers, but she didn't want to cry. She wanted to laugh more, and so she did.

━━━━━━━━

They'd spent the better part of the afternoon rocking in the porch swing, letting Sissy explore the outdoors, and sipping lemonade.

It was therapy, more than he could've ever received from Dr. Grenard or another counselor or anyone else. Faith talked about Paul; he talked about Aaron. He realized that one reason it looked as if he was dealing with Aaron's death better than she was dealing with Paul's was because he was kept busy trying to do something about it. He was hunting a killer. She was hiding from one, or at least the thought of one.

They kicked their feet back and forth on the swing like little children, their arms brushing every now and then, pretending not to notice. Mick loved her voice. It was a little deep but soft. He could tell she had once been a self-assured woman. Her slender neck held a perfectly proportioned head with long, blonde, shiny, flowing hair, fine and wispy like a baby's.

Faith was telling the story of how she and Paul met, and Mick listened intently. Then something caught his eye in the wooded area behind her house, and he heard a noise. And as he focused into the shade beyond the first few trees, he saw darkness. Then the darkness moved, and in a second's time a figure whisked through the brush, disappearing into the foliage.

"Stay here."

"Mick? What is it?"

The walls of his chest barely held his pounding heart, yet his mind urged him on. He didn't have his gun, but he could maybe get a glimpse of who or what it was. His gut, though—his gut told him to stay put. He stood on the edge of the porch.

Faith did not need to be disturbed now. For the first time since he'd met her, she was relaxed. Laughing.

But who was in the woods? A neighbor, maybe? A kid playing?

He turned to reassure Faith that it was nothing, but she wasn't looking at him. Her attention was directed at the woods. Had she heard it too?

She turned to him, but now her demeanor was different. That guard she seemed to always have up, that stiffness that settled on her shoulders like dampness from a rain, was back. Her lips were pursed. The wall had returned.

Mick glanced down at Sissy, who lay lazily asleep on the porch. If only Sissy had been romping around on the grass.

"It's getting late," Faith said suddenly, standing and reaching for Sissy, who came immediately. "I better go inside."

Mick stood too. He watched her make her way to the back door. She smiled at him briefly, said good-bye, then went inside, pulling the curtains and shades.

Mick sighed, running his hands through his hair, studying the woods for any further movement. There was nothing but the soft rustling of leaves in the wind.

And the feeling that he was being watched, this time from inside the house.

━━━━━━━

Mick drove the few blocks back to Nik's and parked by the curb. He entered, scanning the restaurant for Wallace. It was the early evening crowd, mostly elderly. A few waitresses milled about, but he could not find Wallace. Or Sandy.

Then the kitchen doors swung open, and Sandy made her way out with her purse, obviously ready to leave. She spotted Mick from across the room and rolled her eyes as he approached her.

"What do you want?"

"Where is Wallace?"

An eyebrow cocked with surprise. "Wallace Bledsoe?"

"Is he here?"

"Why?"

"Is he *here?*" Mick tried his best to seem urgent but not panicked.

Sandy folded her arms together. "Ever since you got to this town, all you've been doing is asking a lot of questions and upsetting my customers."

Mick looked around her, trying to spot Wallace. He didn't have time for this.

Then Sandy said, "He's here. He works until seven." She glared at Mick before walking out.

Mick stood there, trying to spot the busboy, but he was nowhere to be seen. He wondered if Sandy would lie for him.

He was about to leave, convinced Wallace wasn't there, when the busboy appeared from the kitchen. Mick moved slightly, out of his direct line of sight, watching him for a moment. He seemed a little zombielike, going through the motions, though what busboy wouldn't?

A tap on Mick's shoulder caused him to whirl around.

"Sorry," said a bright-eyed woman with a small smile and a name tag that read *Cynthia*. "I heard you asking about Wallace." She glanced in the busboy's direction, disdain melting her smile away. "He's a weirdo, I'll tell ya that."

"What makes him weird?"

"He doesn't look me in the eye when I talk to him. I think he's mentally . . . you know—" she twirled her finger around the side of her head—"a little slow."

"Why do you think that?"

"He just answers questions weird or sometimes doesn't answer at all." She shrugged. "I mostly just avoid him. Sandy's nice to him, but Sandy's nice to everyone. Except you, I guess."

"Has he ever threatened you or anything like that?"

"Oh, no. He's just strange. But he keeps to himself. I figure he's like a Trekkie or something, you know? Probably has five computers at home and can hack into the Treasury Department."

Wallace had disappeared into the kitchen, never noticing Mick.

"All right. Well, thanks for the information."

"Sure," she said.

Mick started to walk out, but then she added, "Wallace has been here all night."

"Yes, Sandy told me," Mick said. "Thanks."

"But he did have a break about twenty minutes ago."

Mick pinched the bridge of his nose, his eyes straining to focus on the road. It was only a three-minute drive to his motel, but his thoughts caused time to expand exponentially.

Wallace was strange—there was no doubt of that. But he couldn't quite make the leap to the conclusion that he was dangerous. Yet, there was something about him that wasn't right. . . .

Mick's fingers slid down his face and pulled at the skin on his right cheek, then tapped his jaw lightly for a bit of invigoration.

He made himself entertain the idea that perhaps his perception was jaded, and maybe he wasn't able to look at this case with objective eyes. He wanted to find a killer, and anybody and everybody could fit the profile, including a simple busboy. Mick's desire for vengeance was controlling him. His mind, his rationale, perhaps they were being directed by something that was growing increasingly out of control.

Was he out of control?

Not yet.

Could he be, if he found the killer?

He sat in his car in front of the motel, engine turned off, and wondered. He dare not pray. He wasn't sure if he wanted God's answer. Instead, he let his mind play out the possibilities, work through the scenarios, and try to find even a small answer in all of this.

But his mind would not cooperate. It leapt from one murder case to the next, not wanting to concentrate, like a child in a room full of too many toys.

He finally let his mind go where it wanted, and it took him to Faith Kemper. What it told him was that he needed to find out, beyond a shadow of a doubt, whether or not this woman could see. How he was going to do that was another story. He needed to know how to protect her, and her ability to see or not was vital.

Mick's back muscles ached suddenly, so he finally got out of his car, ready to crash on his bed. He climbed the stairs wearily, deciding whether or not to change into his T-shirt and shorts. By the time he reached the top of the stairs, he thought he'd probably just go straight to bed and, if he were lucky, take off his shoes and socks before his head hit the pillow.

One of the lights over the balcony was out, creating a dark spot right in front of his door. He got out his key card before he got there so he wouldn't have to fumble for it in the darkness.

When he got to his door, there was another note. He ripped it from the door and turned toward the next room's light.

GO AWAY OR YOU WILL BE SORRY.

After unlocking the door, he went inside, throwing all his clothes into his duffel bag. He went to the bathroom and scooped everything into the bag with one swift swipe.

He opened the door and stopped. The letter dangled from his thumb and forefinger, rattling in the night breeze. If he left, he would be doing exactly what the killer wanted.

He hurried down the stairs to the front office, where a college-age boy greeted him with a practiced smile. "Hi there. What can I—"

"I need to check out. Now." Mick slid his key and credit card across the counter.

"Uh . . . yes, sir." The boy clicked away at the computer and soon had a piece of paper for Mick to sign.

"Hope your stay was—"

"You might want to get the light fixed on the north side

of the building near my room. It can compromise safety when you have a lot of lights out."

"Sure. Okay. I'll call maintenance right now. Have a nice—"

Mick didn't hear the rest of it. He was already outside, halfway to his car.

He wasn't leaving town, but nobody needed to know that.

———

"The fair?"

"Of course!" Dixie exclaimed, guiding Faith with skill.

"You're bringing me to the county fair," Faith said, shaking her head in disbelief.

Dixie laughed. "Hey, anyone can enjoy the tilt-a-whirl. I have my eyes squeezed shut the whole time I ride it anyway." She pulled Faith along. "And the smells. Oh, the food can't be beat. Indian tacos. Corn dogs. Cotton candy. Fried candy bars."

"Fried candy bars?" Faith tried to keep her cane moving in front of her as best she could.

"Oh yeah. They take a Snickers bar and deep-fry it. Honey, it'll almost kill ya with one bite."

"Sounds like it."

Faith kept moving alongside Dixie, trying to be appreciative of Dixie's enthusiasm for taking over her mundane life. But the idea of being at a county fair did not seem like the way she wanted to start gaining her life back. A roar of screams and the giggles of overly excited children swirled around her.

"You're not actually expecting me to ride on the tilt-a-whirl, are you, Dixie?"

"You don't have to see to scream like a crazy woman."

Faith screamed, then gasped for air. "Dixie!"

Dixie clung to her hand and laughed hysterically as the tilt-a-whirl flung their backs against the metal. Faith couldn't even scream. She swallowed air but managed somehow to laugh and tell Dixie she was going to kill her as soon as they got off.

In a few minutes, the ride slowed to a stop.

Dixie was hollering a laugh as she helped Faith out of the car. "Oh me, oh my!" Dixie said as they stepped back into the crowds of the fair. "That was something else! What next? They've got that one ride where it drops like you're free-falling and puts your stomach up in your throat."

"Hmm," Faith said, patting Dixie's arm. "How does the Ferris wheel sound?"

"Boring, but I guess I've tortured you enough already."

Faith smiled and took Dixie's arm. They walked through the busyness, Dixie stopping here and there to check something out. She bought herself a pickle; Faith declined. As Dixie munched on her pickle and Faith walked beside her, they discussed normal, everyday things. Dixie talked about her plan to start selling Pampered Chef, and Faith told her of her dreams of someday going to Paris. Dixie shared more about her husband and her two grown daughters, who lived in Kansas and Arkansas. Faith talked about her own parents, how they'd died only a year apart, six months after she and Paul had married.

Tonight it seemed like Faith had a normal life. Going to the fair. Talking with a friend. Eating good-tasting food that one should really never eat.

Paul had never taken her to a fair. He always said weird people hung out at fairs, and he could never relax because he was always looking people in the eye, trying to decipher their intentions. That was a cop for you.

They rode the Ferris wheel twice. Faith loved the way the wind at the top was warm and soft, almost enveloping her like a mother's arms. She'd patted Dixie on the knee and said, "Thank you." No further explanation was needed. Dixie knew the many things she meant.

They sat on an empty bench and listened to a local jazz band play. They were pretty good, and Dixie said she'd like to find out more about them, see where else they'd be playing throughout the year.

As the band wound down, Faith said, "Funnel cake."

"Funnel cake?" Dixie laughed.

Faith laughed too. "I think the last time I had a funnel cake was when I was nine years old."

"Well," said Dixie, "by all means, let's go get you a funnel cake! Now, you gotta get it the right way: smothered in whipped cream and strawberries."

"Really? I just remember it having powdered sugar on top."

"Honey, that powdered sugar version is for people who hate excitement in their lives. And you've ridden the Scream Machine tonight, so I suggest you go over the top and get the whipped cream."

Dixie was right. The funnel cake topped with whipped cream and strawberries was out of this world. And they'd even dared each other to try a fried candy bar. Neither wanted a whole one so they ended up splitting it.

"My stomach is going to hate you tomorrow," Faith said, jabbing Dixie in the ribs as she finished licking the candy bar off her fingers.

"Hey, listen, I did your stomach a favor by going on the Scream Machine first!"

"Amen, sister," Faith said. "What'd you think of the fried candy bar?"

"Hmm. I'll have to let you know tomorrow when I'm sure it's made its way out of my stomach." Dixie took Faith's plate to throw away in a nearby trash can. Then she said, "Hey, why don't we play one of those games?"

"Games?"

"You know, where you throw the thing on the lily pad or try to shoot the arrow through the tire."

"Dixie . . . " Faith pointed to her sunglasses.

"I know! But what a hoot it would be if you did it! I bet they'd give you double prizes!"

Faith laughed but shook her head. "I better be getting home. I can't imagine what Sissy's doing right now. She's not used to me being away from her."

"Sissy's fine," Dixie said.

"I know. But I'm a little tired." Faith hugged Dixie. "I haven't had this much fun in a long time."

"I think it's my job to bring some fun into your life." Dixie stood, helping Faith to her feet. "Listen, we got an auction next week at the church to benefit the missions trip. You'd love that."

They walked toward the front gate. "You're bound and determined to get me to go to church, aren't you?"

"You betcha," Dixie said. "You betcha."

The county fair was twenty-five minutes from Bakerville, and by the time they arrived back home, it was nearly ten in the evening. Faith was tired. She was not used to this much excitement. Even her feet and back ached, but she didn't mind.

"Don't forget your frog!" Dixie said as she pulled the car to the curb outside Faith's house. Dixie had bought her a souvenir and a pie from the baking-contest table. She plopped the frog gently on top of the pie. "You want help getting to the door?"

"No, I'll be okay. Thank you."

"Are you sure? I don't mind."

"I'll be okay. You parked right in front of the walkway to the door. Right?"

"Yes."

"Good. Then I'll be fine." Faith got out of the car, holding her pie and her frog carefully, and then waved at Dixie with the fingers around her cane. She made her way up the sidewalk and to her front door, where she inserted her key until the dead bolt clicked. She turned one more time to wave at Dixie to let her know she was okay.

Dixie drove off and Faith went inside, closing the door behind her and locking it.

"Sissy? Sissy?" Faith found the switch on the wall and turned on the light in the living room.

Then screamed.

chapter twenty-nine

mick sat on Faith's couch, staring at her, as startled as she was. Faith's back was against the door, her chest heaving up and down, her breathing more like gulping. She still clutched the frog. The pie lay splattered on the entryway tiles.

Mick slowly stood from the couch. He took a deep breath to try to calm his own nerves. "Hi, Faith."

"What are you doing here?" she said harshly.

"Protecting you."

"Protecting me?"

"Take off your sunglasses."

Faith didn't move. For a moment Mick thought she might actually turn and run out the door.

But then she said, "Where's Sissy?"

"In the garage. Take off your sunglasses. Now."

She bit hard into her bottom lip. Her long fingers moved slowly to her sunglasses, her index finger tracing the corner of the left side. After a few moments, she slowly removed them and for the first time looked Mick in the eye. Her iridescent blue eyes, almost aqua, filled with tears.

Mick looked away. He wanted to scream at her. He wanted to hold her. She was sobbing now and moved from the door across the room to the kitchen. She kept her back turned to him, which was fine with Mick.

Sissy whined and scratched at the door to the garage.

"When you're ready to tell me the truth, I'm ready to listen." Mick went to the front door, quietly went out, and walked to his car, parked three houses down on the opposite side of the street.

He drove around Bakerville for a while, stopped at a convenience store for a cup of coffee and a package of powdered donuts. An hour passed, and the fatigue of the entire day was now about to do him in.

He found a quiet wooded area off the highway, a farmer's field where nobody would notice him in the middle of the night. Parking the car on the side of the road, he locked his doors, pulled out his gun from his duffel bag, and reclined his seat a little.

There, in the distance . . .

Breathtaking.

The air had been thick, heavy, almost angry, nearly all day. He'd noticed the early afternoon appearance of altocumulus clouds, a sure indication that thunderstorms would follow.

Now they were approaching, still at a distance, humming instead of roaring. Mick rolled down his window, the unmistakable aroma of rain beckoning his eyes closed and his other senses to come alive. He rested a bit, only listening. But soon enough a grand display of power and light that could make a human's knees weak would dance on the horizon.

Heat lightning, the kind one can only observe at ten miles or more away from the storm, made the tops of the towers of clouds glow and fade in complete silence. Very soon though, the thunder would be heard as the storm neared, and then it would be sheet lightning. If Mick got lucky tonight and the storm was traveling due south, forked lightning would climb down the wind and the rain, and the thunder would shake him to his core.

He smiled.

He'd loved lightning his whole life. A few weeks before Aaron's death, he'd gotten on a kick researching high-altitude lightning, such as red sprites, blue jets, and green elves, three mysterious types of lightning that shoot up from the cloud rather than down. They had been only recently discovered.

Mick settled himself into the seat of his car, his fingers entwined around his coffee. This was going to be the ulti-mate lullaby, and he knew he would eventually drift into a sleep that would last until morning.

"Ah!" Mick awoke to the sound of someone trying to open his car door. He grabbed for his gun, dropping it twice before getting a grip on it. He sat up straight, his elbow knocking over last night's coffee, spilling some of it in the cup holder.

Then he saw it. A bird. On the hood of his car, batting one of its wings against the wet glass. He slid back into his seat, throwing his gun down and swallowing back the anxiety. He rubbed his eyes and checked his car clock. It was six-fifteen. The storm had passed. Mick started the car to get the air going. His skin was clammy and moist from the humidity of the night. Rumbling in his stomach prompted him to reach for a stale donut and pop it in his mouth.

Cold coffee was another story. He drove back to the same convenience store and bought a small coffee and a bottle of water. On his way to Nik's, he finished off the rest of the donuts. Reminded him a little of college. Then he parked his car a block away, where he had a full view of the restaurant.

His fingers tapped against the steering wheel as he tried

to decide whether or not to confront Wallace. Confronting him would let Wallace know he was being watched.

But it could also trigger him to do something irrational if he was dangerous or demented. Mick wished he knew more about profiling. What was the best way to approach? Would it turn violent? Mick could only guess.

He played through the different scenarios of how he might confront Wallace if he chose to do so. Should he do it in the restaurant or elsewhere? Should he follow Wallace home, watch him awhile, see what his routine was?

Urgency pumped through his heart, but he didn't know why. Was it because he thought Faith was in danger?

Faith.

He'd thought little of her last night, fatigue winning the battle for clarity of mind. He didn't want to think of her. He wasn't sure he wanted answers to his many questions, either. If someone could fake blindness, they were capable of other things. Like leaving notes.

Mick stared at the parking lot, waiting for any sign of Wallace. He let the corridors of his mind open wider to the possibility of Wallace being connected to these cases. He'd considered it before, but not seriously.

Wallace was obviously disturbed by Mick's involvement with Faith. Still, it was hard for him to connect what few dots he had and tie Wallace in to his investigation. It was just too much of a stretch.

Furthermore, if Faith could see, wouldn't she recognize Wallace's face? She had seen the killer's face, she said. She'd described him as dark eyed and dark haired. Wallace's eyes were brown, but his hair was blond. Light blond. Possibly dyed. But surely Faith would recognize his eyes.

Or would she? Two years later? Maybe her mind had blocked out some things.

Indecision on whether or not to confront Wallace now

came out in the form of a Broadway-worthy foot tapping, quickly and precisely against the floor mat.

He could see the side door from where he sat. Where was Wallace? It was nearly seven. Surely the busboy arrived when the restaurant opened.

Mick got out of his car, unable to pace, unable to stand still. The indecision about whether to stay here or check on Faith knotted the muscles in the back of his neck. His mind whispered the song he'd heard in the woods.

Mick stared at the restaurant's front doors, then decided without further hesitation to go in and check. As he shut the car door, he heard a noise behind him and turned.

It was Wallace.

A prickling sensation climbed over Mick's skin, but Mick remained calm. He wasn't often caught off guard, but he knew his reaction more than his words was important now.

Wallace was sitting on a bicycle, staring at Mick in the most uncanny way. His head was tilted, his eyes a little glassy.

Mick didn't move.

"Agent Kline." Wallace spoke softly, blinking away the window Mick wanted so desperately to peer into.

"Wallace."

Wallace regarded Mick's car, then looked toward the restaurant, amusement ever so slightly sliding over his features. "She doesn't come for breakfast before eight. It's usually between eight and nine. You'll see her coming. She walks down that sidewalk with her dog. Never before eight."

Mick was about to tell Wallace it wasn't Faith he was spying on, but he shut his mouth. Something . . . someone . . . was telling him not to say a word.

The sun glinted off Wallace's wristwatch. Mick

glanced at it. Gold. Though it looked too petite to be a man's. Mick also knew what was on his own wrist . . . a gold watch.

Wallace rang the bell on his bike and peddled across the street to the restaurant. He parked next to the wall and chained it to a pipe coming out from the building. He glanced back once at Mick before vanishing into the restaurant.

Mick realized he had been holding his breath. He leaned against his car to try to regain his composure and figure out what to do. "You creepy little twit," Mick nearly spat, but he didn't. He couldn't say for sure what Wallace was.

His cell phone rang. Sighing, he opened the car door to answer it. "Yeah?"

"Mick?"

"Yes."

"It's Abigail Grenard. I need to meet with you."

Mick almost laughed. "Excuse me?"

"Please. Today if possible."

Mick paced next to his car. "Today is going to be difficult. I'm nowhere near Dallas."

"That's okay. I'll come to you."

Mick frowned. Her voice was tense with urgency. "What's this about? Did Tom sic you on me?"

"No."

"Tom has you up to something."

"Mick, you are just going to have to trust me. Tom doesn't know I'm calling you. Nobody knows I'm calling you. But I need to see you, and I'm willing to come wherever you are."

Mick laughed a little. "On-the-road therapy."

"This isn't about you. Are you going to meet me or not?"

Mick stared across the street at the restaurant, wondering if Wallace was peeking out the window at him. All he could see was his distant reflection, warped in the shiny glass. Did Wallace lurk invisibly behind his own image, watching? Curiosity about Wallace kept his eyes glued to the reflective windows. Curiosity about why Abigail Grenard was calling him kept him from hanging up the phone.

"Mick," she said, "you can trust me."

Mick had Abigail meet him fifty miles north at a diner that he'd stopped at on his way to Bakerville. He didn't want her to know what town he'd been in. He was still hesitant to trust her, but curiosity kept him speeding toward the little town that was home to Eddie's Eating Stop, a step above Allana's sub shop.

He was at the diner a little after ten, wondering how long it would take Abigail to get there. She had a much longer drive. But she also had a much faster car. He'd noticed she drove a Jaguar with a license plate that read MINDOC, which he thought was a little crass.

Eddie's was emptying of the early morning crowd. A sign instructed him to seat himself, so he found a booth near the window and waited for Abigail and a waitress. When the waitress finally came to his table, he ordered coffee, black, and said he was waiting for a friend.

Three cups of coffee later, he saw Abigail pull up in her silver Jag. She was out of place at this kind of joint, that fact punctuated by the gawks from several rig drivers as she stepped out of her car, sporting a dark purple suit, high heels, and the same perfect French twist. Inside, she pulled her sunglasses up as she spotted Mick.

"Hi. Thanks for meeting me." She slid her hand over the vinyl seat, swiping stray crumbs to the floor.

"Well, it takes a lot to steal a man from his monthlong vacation at the beach."

She cocked an eyebrow and grinned. "Uh-huh. What's good here?"

"No idea. I usually just eat toast for breakfast."

"Oh? Why's that?"

"Well, nearly everything on the breakfast menu can poison you with bacteria if it's not cooked right. Except maybe the oatmeal. But I hate oatmeal."

She glanced up from her menu, her eyebrows forming a worried arch. "Sounds like a phobia to me."

"Oh, yes. You can definitely call it that."

She smiled and went back to reading the menu. "Well, for $250 an hour I can fix that for you."

"No thanks. I'll just eat toast."

"Don't tell me you wash your hands incessantly."

"Only on the third and fifth Tuesday of every month, unless it's a full moon, and then I soak them in water and vinegar."

Abigail closed her menu and shook her head playfully. "You are something else."

He shrugged. "Just gotta be me."

The waitress approached, and Abigail ordered a vegetable omelette with a large orange juice. Mick ordered four pieces of toast, no butter. After they handed their menus back to the waitress, Abigail leaned forward and said, "You're probably curious."

"Skeptical," Mick said. "I have a feeling you're up to something regarding Tom."

"I'll admit I have talked to Tom about you recently. Tom knows you're not using your time off to relax and settle down. Some chief of police in Allana called to let him know you were pursuing your investigation."

"I bet the top of his head started smoking."

"Oh, it wasn't quite that bad. Tom trusts you, Mick. You should know that."

Mick laughed. "Really? Didn't quite get that feeling when he sent me packing."

"You're being overly dramatic. He told you to take some time off."

"*Ordered* me to take some time off."

"Because he knew you wouldn't do it yourself. Which," she said, a smug smile on her face, "he was right about."

Mick sipped his coffee. "So why didn't Tom send agents after me?"

"I told him not to."

"Really . . . " Mick set his coffee down. "And why would Tom listen to you on that?"

"Because I told Tom that I thought there may be some validity to your theory on these cases."

Mick's eyes narrowed. Was he hearing her right?

She pulled out a folder from her briefcase. "I've been studying these."

"You've been studying the cases that I . . . ?"

She nodded. "When you were in my office, I ended up taking a few more notes than you probably expected." She shrugged. "I jotted down some of what you said about your theory."

Mick could not hold in his surprise. His mouth hung open and he blinked several times, trying to decide if he was still asleep in his car on some vacant dirt road. "Abigail, why in the world would Tom listen to you about my theory?"

She slid the folder over to him, folded her hands together gently, and said, "I've been with the FBI a little longer than you might be aware of."

"You haven't always been a shrink?"

"Psychologist. And yes, I have. I hold a doctorate in

counseling psychology and human development from Sam Houston University."

"Okay . . . "

"After college I went to work for the bureau at the Behavioral Science Unit at Quantico."

"The BSU? Are you trying to tell me that you're familiar with serial killers?"

"I'm an expert."

chapter thirty

faith's heart continued to beat in her chest like the bass drum in a marching band—heavy, constant, pounding. It had not stopped beating that way since she had found Mick Kline in her house the night before.

Growling out her thoughts incoherently, Faith paced the floor, suspecting she sounded like a lunatic. It didn't matter anymore. He'd exposed her secret. He'd made her vulnerable. Knocked down a wall in her room of safety.

Now all she could do was crouch in the corner shadows, hoping not to be seen. But the light had exposed her. And would expose her again.

She sat down and pounded her fist into the armrest of the couch, screaming out Mick's name, rage blowing from her soul like the winds of a hurricane. Tears fell uncontrollably. She wanted to pull all the hair from her head, to redirect the pain that stabbed her heart. Another scream, guttural, like a savage beast crying out, filled the room. She fell to her knees, then collapsed on the ground. She rolled to her back, staring up at the ceiling's white stucco patterns.

Sissy sat in a corner huddled against herself, her eyes worried. Faith could do nothing to comfort her companion. Her fingers clawed at the floor, the repetitive sound almost soothing. Almost.

"I should leave," she whispered. "I could leave." She could be gone tomorrow, but would he find her? Would he come after her? She blinked. Who was she talking about? Mick? Or . . . the killer? Mick could never understand this. He would judge her. He already had judged her.

Faith sat up, resting her forehead on her bent knees, clasping her hands around the back of her neck. The floor beneath her blurred more and more with each thought of what she'd done and of how she'd been exposed.

For two long years she'd been a fugitive from a normal life, running, looking over her shoulder when no one was watching, staring into space when someone did watch her. Hiding behind dark glasses. Never returning smiles offered. How often she had just wanted to smile at people.

The pathetic thing she called her life. Empty without Paul. Dangerous without boundaries. And a lie. Her eyes squeezed shut, her hands covered her ears. But she could not stop the word from murmuring its ridicule. *Lie.*

With her long fingers she rubbed either side of the bridge of her nose as if that might stop the tears from flowing, but it did not. She picked herself up off the floor. It was a task. Knees wobbling from fatigue, she walked to the hall closet and pulled out a box. Inside, near the top, was a picture frame. She picked it up delicately and turned it over.

It was her favorite picture of Paul, standing on the beaches of Lake Michigan, his sandy blond hair swept to the side by the wind. That mischievous, ornery grin on his face, the one that made him look boyish and charming, gleamed in the sun. His blue eyes, always sparkling with life and love, were hidden by his favorite dark sunglasses, just like the kind they wore in *Top Gun*. He loved that movie.

If it had been winter, he would've been wearing his favorite bomber jacket too.

Knock-knock.

Faith threw the picture back into the box, shoving it into the closet with a push so fierce it rammed against the back wall with a thud. She slammed the closet door shut.

Knock-knock.

Rushing into the living room, she scanned every shelf and table for her sunglasses. She couldn't find them. Her eyes were sore and bloodshot.

Sissy barked softly as she was trained to do. Faith spun around, her eyes darting from one place to another. She'd been so distraught last night. She'd taken them off when she came in and saw Mick, and then Mick . . .

Where did they go?

She couldn't even remember most of last night. Crying and rage. That is what she remembered. Fury. Scorn. Hate—

Knock. "Faith? It's Dixie. Are you all right?"

"Dixie," Faith breathed. She would not go away and would begin to worry if Faith did not go to the door.

Faith's hands tapped her cheeks; they were still sticky with tears. Her jaws ached from the way her teeth were clenched together.

"Faith?"

She could go to the door . . . tell Dixie the truth . . . look her in the eyes.

Faith reached for the doorknob. It nearly turned itself in the palm of her hand. *Look at her.* "Hi, Dixie."

"Hi there! I was starting to worry something was wrong."

Faith blinked lazily and smiled, staring to the left of Dixie's face, aware of her surroundings but seeing nothing in particular. She made the images her eyes wanted to focus on blur, and she reminded herself to see with her ears.

"Everything's fine," Faith said. "I've misplaced my sunglasses. Maybe you can help me find them."

"I joined the Behavioral Science Unit about eight years after they formed the National Center for the Analysis of Violent Crime. In 1986, NCAVC was split. There was the Behavioral Science Instruction and Research side, and the Behavioral Science Investigative Support side. The BSIS administers profiling, consultation, and the Violent Criminal Apprehension Programs. I worked alongside some of the most well-known profilers in the bureau."

"What made you leave?"

Abigail shrugged, poking the omelette with the prongs of her fork. "It gets to you after a while. Some can take it. Some can't. I'm not ashamed to say that I couldn't."

"I'm sorry."

"Don't be sorry," she said, looking up at him. "I'm not. I did a lot of good work for the bureau when I was there."

"And now you counsel agents. Odd." Mick smiled.

"Yeah, I know. But that's what I had my degree in. Counseling. I never thought I'd use it to profile serial killers. When I decided my time at the BSU was up, I knew I hadn't lost my love for the bureau. I couldn't think of a better way of using my knowledge than helping agents." She paused to take a bite. "And I was influential in convincing the bureau they needed in-house psychologists. It's been an uphill battle, but we're getting there."

Mick had already finished three out of his four pieces of toast. "What an experience that must've been. The BSU, I mean."

She laughed. "Oh, the stories I could tell. Mostly about my mentor, Special Agent Ressler."

Mick smiled. "No kidding. Robert Ressler. He certainly has a reputation."

"I adore him," Abigail said. "I think he's the best in the

business. I learned so much from him." She pushed her half-eaten omelette aside and said, "But enough about me. I'm here because of you."

"You said on the phone this wasn't about me."

"Well, not in a profiling, psychoanalysis sort of way."

Mick grinned. "I can only imagine the profiling you've been doing on me."

She leaned back in the booth, her face growing serious. "I couldn't get our conversation out of my mind. You have this passion about you. I know it stems from your drive to find Aaron's killer. But there was something more. So I started doing my own research."

"And?" Mick asked. Eagerness pushed away other distractions.

Abigail slid the folder across the table to him. "And I think you may be onto something. I can't say definitively. But there's something worthy of concern, let's just say that."

Mick opened the folder and sifted through all the notes and pieces of paper. She had gathered information on each of the cases, writing notes and highlighting specific points of interest. He scanned each page but couldn't see where she was going. Her notes seemed to be jumbled thoughts.

"How about giving me a road map?" he finally said. "I'm an accountant, remember?"

"First of all, I tried to zero in on the MO, then isolate a signature. I couldn't quite get all these to fit. You're right in that the victims were all law enforcement, but the MOs cannot be definitively connected because there seems to be too little information about the killers. But it could also be that if we are talking about one killer here, his MO is that he is never seen by the victim and vanishes without a trace. Maybe he watches them for weeks, knows their schedule, knows where they'll be and when. In all the cases you cited, this is a possibility."

Mick nodded. He wished he could speed up her Texas drawl. "Yes, I can see that. Especially with Aaron."

"But no signature," Abigail said apprehensively. "And that's where we have a problem."

"I don't understand."

"In a serial homicide of this magnitude, we're going to be seeing some kind of signature." She paused. "Okay, let me explain it this way. A man robs a bank, and while doing so, he instructs all the tellers to undress. He leaves with a bag full of cash. Another bank robber does the same thing— instructs the tellers to undress. But before leaving, he takes all the men, stuffs wads of money in their mouths, and gags them. What's the difference?"

Abigail answered her own question. "The first robber's MO is making the tellers remove their clothes, because that allows for more getaway time. The tellers will get dressed before they call the police. The second bank robber goes beyond robbing the bank. His signature demonstrates a psychological need."

"Stuffing money in the mouths of the men."

"An MO can develop as a killer gets more experience and more confidence. But it is the signature that most often links serial homicides. In these cases, we have all the victims in law enforcement. It's not the victim's physical appearance that is important, especially if the crime is motivated by anger, which these must be in some form, as they are not sexual in nature. And it is also rare to have male victims. Normally it is women or children."

"Okay, so what does all this tell you?"

"Well, number one, we know that most often the killer will attack a victim out of rage or anger and express those through his rituals, i.e., his signature aspect, and not by certain characteristic or traits. So that is why there is hesitation on my part to link these by the fact that these men were law enforcers."

"So in terms of profiling this killer, you're looking at the signature, not the MO."

"Right. And in these cases, the signature is nearly nonexistent. The victims weren't even killed in the same way or with the same kind of weapon. What links them is the way they seem to have been killed by a phantom. Either that *is* the signature, and we have to work on an MO, or these are all random cases of violence, presently unsolved."

Mick leaned back in his chair, sighing. "What does your gut tell you?"

She grinned. "Thank you for that compliment."

"That's a compliment?"

"Well, for a while psychologists and cops weren't even on the same planet when it came to these things. Now we work together, but few consider this real 'cop' work." She laughed. "But going by your gut instinct, as you like to say, now that's the real deal."

Mick laughed. "Okay, well, play the cop."

She turned serious again. "Well, I have to be honest. I have looked these cases up and down, side to side, and I can't link them. There may be a missing link, I don't know. VICAP has not picked up on it, if so." She glanced sheepishly at him. "I had some of my old contacts take a look, see what they could find. Five of these cases are or have been entered into the VICAP system, but as of yet there hasn't been any sort of link. Even with the ones that have arrests. I don't think that's any surprise to you. If you'd had more, Tom may not have been so hard on you."

"True."

"But one case in particular grabbed my attention, and working backward from this case, I may be able to expand the killer's profile a bit, and that may lead to the missing link. This case has me truly engaged."

"Which case is that?"

"The Kemper case."

chapter thirty-one

there were days that Dixie's company was a delight, like fresh mint in iced tea. But there were other days when the fatigue of keeping up the facade made a conversation with her suffocating.

Thankfully, Dixie had found Faith's sunglasses under the coffee table. It had been a terrible strain to control her eyes in a way that made her look like she wasn't seeing anything with them. Her sunglasses allowed Faith to relax a little, to see but keep it hidden. And to tolerate the walls that closed in around her.

Faith realized Dixie had stopped talking. "Faith? Are you okay? You seem distant."

The smile reserved for placation swept her lips into a soft, barely curved line. "Tired. Didn't sleep too well last night."

"I'm sorry. Bad dreams?"

"No. Just didn't sleep well."

"Will asked about you this morning."

"Who?"

"Our pastor."

"Oh." Will. The evening of the church potluck, she'd watched him from across the room as he spoke with Mick before they walked down the hall together and out of sight. He seemed to be a man with a big heart.

"I spoke with him this morning about the children's

choir, and he wanted to know how you were and if you were thinking of coming back to the church." Dixie was busy arranging some flowers she'd brought in a vase. They were bright and cheery, but she had picked them for their strong scent, which could be smelled all the way across the kitchen.

Faith's mind drifted. The heat of the season made her drowsy. She sensed the stress of her life pulling her mind in different and exhausting directions. "Those flowers are beautiful. I love red," Faith said.

Dixie spun around. "What did you say?"

"The red ones, they're beautiful. And the yellow ones, too."

"You can *see* these flowers?"

"You should wear blue more often, by the way. It really goes well with your complexion."

The vase dropped, shattering onto the kitchen floor, water splashing up and tickling Faith's face. She tried to smile at Dixie, whose skin had been drained of all color and whose wide eyes registered both astonishment and fear. "I've been meaning to tell you that I can see."

"You want something to drink?"

"What?" Faith blinked away the scene in her mind, her head foggy with the effort to try to find reality. She could only imagine what would happen if she told Dixie in that way.

"You want a cola or something?" Dixie asked. She'd finished arranging the flowers, and they sat on top of the kitchen counter boasting their beauty.

"Sure," Faith said. But a drink could not relieve her scorched conscience. How could she ever tell Dixie? It was a betrayal to lie to her like this, but it was even more of a betrayal to tell her that she'd seen all this time. The things people did when they thought no one was looking. The stories she could tell.

And this, Faith reminded herself, was why she limited her contact with people and never formed relationships. She knew if she did, guilt would come knocking. And it had now arrived at her door, pounding out its request for her attention, her heart tapping heavily inside her chest.

"What in the world?" Dixie said, her eyes focusing toward the back door.

Faith's neck muscles ached, resisting the urge to turn her head to see what Dixie was looking at. "What is it?"

"Stay here," Dixie instructed, walking past her briskly. Faith carefully turned herself around on the barstool on which she was sitting.

Dixie was at the back door, looking out.

"Dixie? What's the matter?" Faith demanded.

"I thought I saw . . . " Her voice trailed off. She was scanning the backyard.

"Dixie?"

"It's nothing," Dixie said finally, turning and coming back to the counter. "I just thought I saw someone."

"In the backyard?"

"It was probably nothing."

"What did you see?"

"Oh, you know . . . . I glanced up and thought I saw someone walking around the corner of the house. It was just a blur, though. I mean, it was probably just my imagination."

Faith glanced sideways. Carefully. Sissy sat next to the dining-room table, close enough for Faith to feel secure.

"Maybe it was the meter guy," Dixie said.

"He comes on Mondays."

"Oh. Well, who knows. I can go outside and look around if you want."

"No. That's okay. I'm sure it was nothing. Maybe a kid taking a shortcut or something."

"Yeah, a kid," Dixie said with a half laugh. "Here's your cola."

"Thanks." Faith welcomed the sting of the carbonation down her throat. "Dixie?"

"Yes?"

"I probably haven't told you this, but thank you."

"Thank you?"

"Yeah. For being my friend. I don't deserve a friend like you."

Dixie propped her elbows on the breakfast counter across from Faith. "What in the world would make you say something like that?"

"I just wanted you to know that."

"Faith, I'm honored to be your friend. I enjoy your company." Dixie snickered. "You're the only person I can feel comfortable being around without my makeup on!" She had a good laugh over that one.

Faith, on the other hand, could only manage a meek smile.

The waitress had cleared the dishes, and now the tabletop was white with papers spread over it.

"Is the Kemper case in the VICAP computer?"

"Yes." Abigail was looking over some of her notes. "Now, it could just as easily be someone who was out to get Paul Kemper as it could have been a serial killer. But it was certainly violent, and there doesn't seem to be a motive. If we're looking at serial, whoever did this could be classified as disorganized."

"Disorganized? What does that mean?"

"In 1978 a grant was given for the first research-oriented study on serial killers. Thirty-six of them were interviewed, and one of the most important findings of the research was the distinction between killers who are organized and disorganized. An organized killer will clean up the scene, make himself an alibi, hide the body. He is usually intelligent, educated, drives a nice car, has a stable job, may even have a family and normal relationships. A disorganized killer is subintelligent, socially inferior, works in low-paying jobs, moves around a lot. Maybe a drifter."

Mick looked at the crime-scene pictures from Paul's case. "Disorganized."

"Yes. Kills out of rage. He even had a chance of being caught, right in the middle of a parking garage. The killing was swift, you see? Angry."

"Paul and Aaron were both killed from behind, never having a chance to see who attacked them. Is this important?"

"Possibly. But Aaron's murder looks more planned. Paul's seems unplanned. Did he plan on the victim's wife being there? And it is also unclear if he intended to kill her. She was brutally attacked, yet the killer left the message, indicating he thought she would live."

"You know about the message?"

Abigail paused. "Like I said, I've got contacts."

"So what kind of person am I looking for here?"

"There is a high probability that the killer is shy, quiet, nice. Probably not married, inadequate with interpersonal relationships. He has a poor self-image. A lot of anger. Maybe poor hygiene. He is probably Caucasian. Between the ages of seventeen and twenty-five. He tends to attack from behind and can be confused and distressed during the killing. He is spontaneous, impulsive. And usually low in the birth order."

Mick smiled. "Wow."

"One of the first things you learn doing this stuff. I know it like the back of my hand."

Leaning back, Mick looked over some more of Abigail's notes, but inside he was deciding whether or not to tell her that he was on the Kemper case. He also wondered if he should tell her of his increasing suspicions about Wallace.

"You okay?" she asked.

Mick glanced up, then grabbed for his coffee. "Yeah. Just a lot to process, you know?"

"I know." She smiled. "When I was working at the BSU, I had to learn to become emotionally uninvolved or I'd go crazy. I had to look at the facts and keep them facts. But it takes a lot of training to rattle off the profile of a serial killer without feeling something. And I always did feel something, which is why I'm working elsewhere now."

Mick nodded, trying to seem engaged while also processing his thoughts on Wallace. Half of him thought he was being paranoid about the man. The other half of him thought Wallace was more than just "different." And he fit the profile Abigail had just described.

"On the Kemper case," Abigail said, "one thing that is striking is the note the killer left. That seems to be more of an organized trait. It indicates he was thinking about the future, making sure to cover his tracks by warning her. Written with her own tube of lipstick. He could have been caught, yet he took the time to threaten her. And then he wiped the lipstick tube clean."

Mick closed his eyes, trying to think. *Faith can see,* he reminded himself. *And if she can see, that means she can see Wallace. And she does not recognize Wallace as the killer.* The thoughts paraded through his mind one by one. Then came thoughts of Miguel Juarez. A family man. A hard worker.

"Tell me more about the organized traits."

"Um, relationships appear normal. He has a skilled occupation, though his work history may be uneven. Has an average to above-average IQ but tends to work below his capabilities. Tends to be a manipulator, wants to get even, punish and shock society. Tends to be average to above average in appearance, height, and weight." Abigail thought for a second. "His crime is carefully planned to avoid detection. His mood is controlled during the crime—there is a sense of order. That is why there is often a lack of evidence at the scene. An organized offender will most likely follow the coverage of his crime in the news media, visit the crime scene on the anniversaries of the killings, and may even inject himself into the investigation."

Mick looked up from his thoughts. "Inject himself into the investigation? Really?"

"Sure. Sometimes by following the police. Sometimes by being a witness. Those are the killers we can appropriately call *maniacal.*"

Did Miguel Juarez fit this description? A family man. Works odd jobs but seems intelligent. Mick clasped his hands over his head, trying to think.

"Mick," Abigail said, "we have a missing link, and I want to be honest about that. But if I had to choose out of these cases, the Kemper case, the Lubbock one, and the other Houston one seem to be the most connected. However, I cannot find a signature that links these cases, unless that signature is the fact that they are all law enforcement, which is highly unlikely, for the reasons I stated earlier."

"But what about these guys who kill prostitutes?"

"Well, then you're talking about sexual homicide, and that's another ball game. It's even highly unlikely that a male would be killing all male victims."

Mick lowered his head, processing his scattered thoughts.

"But," Abigail said, causing Mick to look up, "it was also highly unlikely that the D.C. sniper would turn out to be two black males, one a juvenile." She smiled a little. "That case threw the whole profiling community for a loop. They were sure it was a white male, seventeen to twenty-five, blue collar, working alone, ex-military. When they found those two guys, a whole bunch of profilers were scratching their heads and going back to their profiling manuals."

Mick blew out a sigh. "So, what do we do?"

She leaned forward. "Tell me what you are doing now. I know you're not sitting on a beach reading Oprah's next pick. Have you made any progress tracking Aaron's killer?"

Mick stared through her, seeing the consequences of telling her what he knew if she wasn't trustworthy. He shifted his gaze to her eyes. They were kind, compassionate, and well trained to look that way. He blinked and looked away.

"Mick, you can trust me. What do you know?"

"How do I know for sure I can trust you?"

"You don't." She smiled. "That's why it's called trust. Trust is earned. And I'm here, aren't I? Telling you what I know."

"Fair enough," Mick said. "Do you know anything about Aaron's case? anything at all?"

"It's still in the headlines. There've been some leaks, but nothing substantial. I'm not privy to the information anyway."

"I know. I was just hoping."

"They would call if they knew."

"I don't know about that. I think they want me as far away from the investigation as they can get me."

Abigail's slow blink indicated she didn't agree. "Mick, they're just trying to solve the case."

"Yeah." Mick rubbed away the fatigue from his eyes and looked around for the waitress, hoping to get a fresh cup of coffee. They'd been at Eddie's for two hours.

"So . . . are you going to spill the beans as to what you've been up to?"

He clicked his tongue on the roof of his mouth as he watched an eyebrow rise on Abigail's forehead. She grinned. "You *have* been investigating!"

"Of course I have. Do you think I'd really be taking it easy?"

"No, I never thought that. I knew when I first met you that you were a man of character *and* passion. A fine mix of strong qualities."

"Does Tom know you're here?"

"No. But he does know my theories as I have discussed them with you." She paused, as if waiting for Mick to ask another question. When he didn't, she said, "Aren't you going to ask me if I'm going back to Tom with the information I learn from you?"

Mick shook his head. "No. I guess I'm just going to have to trust you."

"Okay."

He allowed a few moments of silence to give his conscience one final chance to back out. Then he said, "I am working on the Kemper case."

Her eyebrows shot high up on her forehead. "No kidding."

"It was the first case I started working. I felt it had the most clues, the best chance of leading me to Aaron's killer."

"So what have you found?"

"A lot more questions than answers. But . . . "

"But what?"

"Well, I have interviewed Miguel Juarez."

Abigail looked at her notes. "Juarez. A suspect, but never arrested."

"Yes. His story doesn't completely add up, but there's

something about him . . . I can't put my finger on it. He's
not been completely truthful. I don't know. He claims he's
being framed by a racist chief of police."

"Of Allana. Underwood, right?"

"Yeah. I found Faith Kemper. She's a scared woman,
I can tell you that. She is taking that threat seriously."

"I can only imagine," Abigail said, compassion replac-
ing the intrigue in her eyes. "Well, has she been helpful?"

"Yes and no. Like I said, she's scared."

"So have you found anything that would link any of
these cases together?"

Mick shook his head. "But . . . "

"But what?"

He could not hide his hesitation, but he also knew it
might be enlightening to talk it over with Abigail.

"There's this man. He works as a busboy at a restaurant
Faith frequents. He fits your disorganized profile. Socially
incompetent. Low intelligence."

"Why has he caught your attention?"

"He seems bothered by the fact that I'm helping Faith.
Doesn't like me being around her. Even caught me off
guard while I was waiting for him, came from behind on a
bicycle."

Abigail had pulled out a notepad and was writing. She
glanced up when Mick stopped. "And? What else?"

"One waitress thinks nothing of him. Another thinks
he's a weirdo, as she put it."

"What about Faith?"

"She thinks he's just a lonely fellow."

"And you think differently."

Mick nodded, his eyes going to the crime-scene photos
of Faith's case on the table. He stared at the picture of the
writing left on the car window. "I've received two threatening messages on my motel door."

Abigail's pen clattered to the table. "What?"

"Telling me to leave town or else."

Abigail stared at the ceiling in shock. Then she looked at Mick eagerly. "This is nothing to take lightly."

"I know. But I wasn't sure who it was from. I can't be sure it's the busboy. It could just as easily be Miguel Juarez. Or Underwood. Or someone else entirely."

Abigail chewed a finger as she thought. "The case file says Faith described her attacker with dark hair, dark eyes. That fits Juarez?"

"Yes. Wallace has dark eyes but blond hair. Could be dyed, though."

"And Faith is blind, so she can't see him to recognize him."

Mick's heart whispered a warning not to reveal the truth about Faith's sight. He opened his mouth to speak but nothing came out. Abigail didn't notice. She was busy sifting through notes while mumbling her thoughts, " . . . and she can hear, but maybe the attacker didn't speak."

"Would a killer follow one of his victims?"

Abigail stopped to think out her answer. "I don't know. He could've attacked all those other men, but there was never a woman involved. Maybe he hadn't counted on her being there. It's hard to say." She finally focused on Mick. "It's a higher probability that this busboy is just a weird dude."

Mick nodded. "Okay."

"There was this case in the midnineties. Killer gets caught after murdering nearly a dozen women in the Carolinas. When they finally catch him, the profilers realize he does not fit neatly into the organized or disorganized categories. He was organized in that he left little evidence. Yet he would take items from the crime scene, go home, put them in the oven to destroy them, and then forget to turn the oven on. We never got a clear statement about a motive."

"Okay?"

"What I'm trying to say is that profiling is an art, not a science. A cop's best weapon is still his gut instinct. Would a killer follow a surviving victim? Probably not. But who would have suspected that two black men were gunning down people from the back of a car in the middle of Washington, D.C.?"

Mick nodded.

"I'll run some background on him, see what I can come up with," Abigail said.

"Really?"

"Yeah. It may take me a few days. I'm going to have to . . . well . . . get creative, let's just say."

Mick laughed. "Okay." He bit his lip and regarded Abigail before saying, "I don't know what I'm going to do if it's Wallace. If I've looked the man who killed my brother in the eyes . . . "

"You'll do the right thing," Abigail said quickly. But the swallow that followed her statement belied the confidence in her eyes.

They both looked away.

chapter thirty-two

h i, Faith. I just . . . um . . . just wanted to know if . . . you needed your house number painted on the curbside? I do that for people."

Faith stood in the doorway of her home, sunglasses on, startled to see Wallace on her steps.

He fidgeted with his hair, then the bottom of his T-shirt, shuffling his feet like an eight-year-old boy. "I don't charge much," he added when Faith didn't respond. "And I'm quick."

"Wallace, how did you know where I live?" Sissy poked her head out the door, and Faith grabbed her collar.

He scratched at his face, gazing at the grass. "I'm sorry. I . . . uh . . . I saw you one day, on my bicycle . . . one day. You know, I was going to the diner. And, I'm sorry . . . I just saw you."

"No, Wallace, it's okay. I just wasn't expecting anyone." Faith paused. "Um, were you just in my backyard by chance?"

Wallace looked startled. "No."

Behind her, Dixie approached. "Faith? Oh . . . you're from the diner."

Wallace regarded Dixie, his manner suddenly less enthusiastic.

Faith said, "This is Wallace. He just wanted to know if I needed numbers painted on the curbside."

"It makes it easier for 911 to find you." He said it like he was reading from a script.

"I thought he might be the person you saw in the backyard," Faith said.

Dixie stepped to Faith's side. "I'm the landlord, and I'm sorry, but we won't be needing that service."

Wallace's fidgeting stopped. He turned and went to his bike.

Faith called out to him, "See you at Nik's."

"Kind of weird, eh?" Dixie said once they were back inside.

"Yeah, he is a little weird. I feel sorry for people like that. They're lonely. Not very good socially." Faith couldn't shake a nagging feeling, though, that told her Wallace's visit was about more than painting numbers on the curbside.

Dixie was gathering her things. "You okay? Need anything?"

"I'm fine," she said, tangling her fingers into Sissy's fur. "But thanks for the flowers. They're beautiful."

"Beautiful?" Dixie laughed.

Faith pinned a smile on her face. "Yeah. Beautiful."

"I guess anything that smells as good as these have to be beautiful, right?"

Faith nodded. She knew she was losing focus. She'd made a slip. That wasn't like her. But she'd made a slip with Mick, too, when she'd reacted to the oncoming car. And that had cost her dearly.

"Well, honey, I'll check in with you tomorrow, see how you're doing. And think about coming with me to church, will ya? I promise you won't regret it. You'll love our choir. Some of the best voices in the Southwest. And there's always free coffee and donuts and—"

"I'll think about it."

270

"I'm being pushy, aren't I? My husband always said I was pushy. I'm sorry. I just know you'll love our church, once you get to know the people, and everyone is so kind and considerate and caring, and I think—"

"Dixie . . . "

"There I go again! It's like a disease!" She laughed and shook her head as she made her way to the door. "Well, I'm out of your hair."

"Dixie, thank you. I'm glad you stopped by."

"Me too. See you tomorrow."

The door closed softly, and Faith waited until she heard Dixie's car back out of the driveway before going to the front door and locking the dead bolt. Then she went to the sliding-glass door and put the safety bar in place.

Sissy indicated she wanted to go for a walk, but Faith wasn't up for it. She threw her glasses on the dining-room table and fell back onto the couch. She would have to start looking for a new place to live. She thought of Florida. She'd always liked Florida. Or maybe Washington State. She heard it was pretty up there. And there were plenty of isolated towns.

But first things first. In the kitchen she pulled out a drawer and found Mick Kline's business card. She grabbed her phone and dialed the cell-phone number.

"Mick Kline."

She could tell by the windy sound in the background he was in his car. "It's Faith."

There was silence. She guessed she could've predicted this.

"I was wondering . . . I just wanted to . . . I was wondering if you would meet me somewhere, allow me to explain . . . um, explain some things."

"Sure."

"Thank you," she breathed.

"Where do you want to meet?"

Faith smiled. Somewhere wonderful.

Mick's leg ached from the long drive. He was now fighting through Houston traffic on his way to the beaches of Galveston Bay.

He looked at the directions he'd jotted down. I-45 south out of Houston, then exit on NASA Road 1, east. Turn left on Todville Road. Follow the bay until you reach the El Jardin subdivision. Turn right on El Jardin.

Mick followed the directions precisely until El Jardin dead-ended at a park next to the bay. He slowed his car and looked for a good parking spot. It was three o'clock in the afternoon.

He walked slowly through the park, the wind coming off Galveston Bay messing his hair like a playful hand. He propped his sunglasses on top of his head and looked around. Windsurfers and sailboats were taking advantage of the choppy water and decent-sized waves. The edge of the park stood slightly above the bay, and from there it was easy to watch the young men in their wet suits tackle the water with their boards.

"Hi, Mick."

Mick turned. Faith stood behind him, smiling a greeting, her dark sunglasses reflecting the rays of a hot spring sun.

"This is quite a place," Mick said, turning back to his view of the bay.

Faith stepped to his side and looked too. Mick was just about to make more small talk when Faith took off her sunglasses. At first she didn't look at him. She simply let her gaze wash over the beautiful crashing waters on the shore.

But Mick wasn't watching the waters. He was watching Faith. It was as if he were looking at a totally different woman. Her eyes engaged things before her, moved with objects, blinked emotion. Before, he had always watched her mouth. Her eyes had seemed dead. Now they were alive.

And looking at him.

He held back a gasp. It was the oddest thing to stare into her soul. Yet the windows were open, beckoning him to look. So he did. He took a long, hard look.

And she let him. Then she turned away. "Come, sit with me over here."

He followed her to a wooden park bench. The wind had the coolness of the water in it, the perfect complement to the muggy heat that was so typical of southern Texas.

"Thanks for meeting me here," she said.

Mick nodded. He still felt awkward looking her in the eyes. They were dazzling, almost iridescent, alive with sensation. She was one of the most striking women he'd ever seen. He stared at her a moment longer than he should have, then focused his attention on the water. "Why here?"

"Paul and I used to come here. It was a special place for us. He proposed to me over there, on that beach." She pointed north. "He loved to windsurf. I tried it a few times, was never very good at it." She smiled at a private thought. "The most gorgeous sunrises you have ever seen are right here over the bay." She glanced at him and said, "I just didn't want to leave things . . . I didn't want you thinking I'm a terrible person."

Mick turned to her. "I would never think that."

"But I need you to understand. I don't know why, really. But it means something for you to understand me." She swept the hair out of her face, holding it back with one hand. She looked at him. "You probably don't know what it feels like to be weak."

Mick chuckled. "Yeah. Big bad Mick." He shook his head. "I'm an accountant."

"Excuse me?"

"People have the perception that FBI agents are just a bunch of meatheads toting guns. But the bureau recruits a lot of accountants and lawyers. How's that for being big and bad?"

Faith laughed heartily. "You're pulling my leg!"

"I'm not."

"You're an *accountant?*"

Mick shrugged. "Yeah. Although I do have other interests. I also coached football for a while. That was my real dream. To be a football coach."

Her forehead crinkled skeptically. "An accountant/football coach? who is now an FBI agent?" She laughed again. "That's a little hard to believe."

"And in my free time I'm a storm chaser."

"Seriously?" Faith laughed again.

"Yeah . . . " Mick gazed at the ocean. "Once you see a tornado, it's something you'll never forget. It's so ferocious and enormous, but at the same time almost elegant. To me, it's one of the greatest phenomena this earth has to offer."

"I've only seen pictures, thankfully. Not too many people want to see a tornado up close," Faith said.

"I was in Oklahoma City on May 3, 1999. I was actually at the field office going over some cases with agents there. They came in and warned us a storm was coming and everyone needed to go home. Of course I didn't go to my hotel. I went chasing the thing."

"That was one of the worst tornadoes in history, wasn't it?"

"Yes. It stayed on the ground for hours, sometimes over

a mile wide, which was how big it was when it hit a suburb of Oklahoma City. Some estimate the winds topped 318 miles an hour. It wiped out entire neighborhoods." He shrugged. "I have some really great pictures. *Newsweek* magazine used one of them."

"Really? Wow. Sounds dangerous."

"The more we know about things in life, the less scary they are. It is the unknown that scares us the most. We still don't completely know how a tornado works, and maybe that's what makes them so terrifying."

"That, and they can blow away an entire city."

Mick laughed. "Yeah, that too."

"So how did you get into the FBI?"

Mick grinned. "Well, that's a really long story. Maybe I'll tell you another time."

"I'd certainly love to hear why anyone in the FBI would want the extra danger of chasing tornadoes. I don't suppose you want to tell me what your weird eating habits are about?"

"That's an even longer story, but let's just say that food poisoning reminds me of the most desperate hour in my whole life." He touched her hand. "But I think it's time you tell me your story."

She leaned back on the bench, crossing her legs and folding her arms loosely on her lap. "I couldn't always see," she began. "I was blind for two months after the attack, and the doctors told me that I would probably never regain my sight. The police told me about the message left on the car window: If I ever saw his face again, I would die."

The pain in her voice was hard to ignore.

"Then one day I saw a little light. And then a little more. And so on, for three weeks, until one day I could see everything. And that frightened me more than being blind. Because I feared . . . " Her nostrils flared, and escaping emotion made her bottom lip quiver.

"That you might see him again."

She nodded. "And I felt like he was going to come after me. And so I moved away, and I stayed blind."

"That must've been so hard—to trick everyone."

"There was no one to trick. I stayed to myself mostly, except for Sissy, and tried to settle in, feel secure. But I never could feel secure. When I moved to Bakerville, I had the same intentions." She laughed a little. "I thought I had a pretty good thing going. And then I met Dixie. Never met a stranger she didn't like, you know."

Mick laughed. "Except me, but I'll forgive her for that."

Faith grinned, her eyes smiling too. "Anyway, Dixie became my friend, and I guess I didn't realize how lonely I really was. But I latched on to her, and then I started going to Nik's, and that became a nice routine. I don't know, maybe it got out of hand. I wasn't trying to deceive people. But I was just trying to . . . " Her words were lost in the wind.

"Protect yourself?"

She nodded. "From a ghost, or the idea of a ghost. I don't know."

"Faith, no one can blame you for being scared. What happened to you was traumatic."

"I just wish I could've been stronger. I know Paul would've wanted me to be stronger."

"Paul would want you to be happy."

Her lips puckered with acknowledgment, and she stared at her hands. "Yeah. He'd hate to see me living like this, living in the shadows, hiding behind the darkness." She looked at the sunglasses in her hand. "I lived behind these sunglasses, pretending not to see, but seeing everything. If I had to take them off, I tried to fade out everything in my sight. I would see with my ears, I guess you could say, which I did when I really was blind. It is amazing how your other senses take over. I still use those senses a lot more than I ever did."

Those misty blue eyes held both sadness and joy. "And maybe I stayed this way because missing a normal, easy life helped me not miss Paul so much. But I do miss him. So much." Her eyes followed the coast up north to the spot she'd pointed to earlier. "You miss your brother too."

"Yes. Very much. But maybe I'm doing what you're doing. Maybe I'm hunting the killer so I don't have to spend my time thinking about how much I miss him."

Faith briefly nodded. "How do you do what you do? Face evil every day?"

"Well, it's not quite like *Silence of the Lambs* every day, you know. Most days I spend behind a desk, poring over paperwork. It's a real busy day if I have to go out with my partner, Reggie, and interview a witness."

"But you see a lot of bad things."

"I guess," Mick said. "But you know what really bothers me? When someone is unkind to an old person. Or I see a mother screaming demeaning things to a child. Or I watch people at Wal-Mart put food back on the shelf because they don't have enough money or food stamps to buy what they need. The stuff some FBI agents see every day—murder, theft, I guess I expect. But I can't fathom why any normal person would yell at an old person for driving slow."

Faith scratched her forehead. "You're a terrific guy, Mick. I can't imagine why you haven't found the right person yet."

The sounds of dancing water and wind interrupted the conversation for a while, then quieted down for them to continue.

Faith said, "How long are you going to be staying in Bakerville?"

"Until I find who I'm looking for."

"Do you know anything?"

Mick stood, needing to walk a little, stretch his legs. He stepped a few paces closer to the water. Mick had to decide whether to tell Faith about the second note left at his motel and his suspicions about Wallace. Wallace . . . or Miguel? His mind teetered like a seesaw.

Faith was behind him. "You do know something!"

Mick turned to her. "I don't know enough to say for certain. I'm making some headway, I think."

"Tell me." Her eyes shined with urgency.

"I'm not sure I should."

"Mick . . . " She stepped closer to him. "I deserve to know. Do you know who attacked me?"

"No, I don't know that. Not yet."

"Then *what?*"

Mick shoved his hands into the pockets of his pants. His fingers twiddled nervously against the fabric. "I've interviewed Miguel Juarez. More than once."

Her partially opened mouth and a soft gasp indicated to Mick that he didn't need to explain to Faith who this was. "And?"

"Hard to say. I'm getting mixed signals from him. He's not telling me everything he knows."

Faith wrapped her arms around herself, letting the wind from the water blow her hair back out of her face. She stared forward, her face resolute. "They never could arrest him."

"They didn't have enough evidence."

She shook her head, then looked at him. "What else?"

Hesitation caused him to fumble for his words a moment. Then he said, "There have been two notes."

"What are you talking about? Another note threatening you?"

"Yes. You could definitely say that."

Fear seized her features, and she turned away. Mick put his hands on her shoulders.

"What does this mean?" she asked quietly, settling under his touch. "The first note, I thought it was maybe a joke . . . or just . . . It doesn't mean anything by itself. Bakerville is a small town. Small towns don't like federal agents snooping around."

"You think it's more, though."

"I have to be cautious and assume that, yes."

Beneath his hands she was trembling. He hated to see this fear consume her. If he told her about Wallace, it might overwhelm her.

"What else?" She turned around and stared at him hard.

"Faith, don't let this get to you, okay?"

She nodded, but he knew that was a hard thing to ask. "Anything else?"

"Just take the precautions you know to take. Keep your doors locked. Don't answer the door to strangers. Things like that."

"Okay."

His hands still held her shoulders. "You've got my cell-phone number. If you need me, I'll be there in an instant. I'm getting close, Faith. I can feel it. I just need a little more time, a little more information. We're going to find who killed Aaron and Paul."

She pulled him close and buried her head into his shoulder, sobbing softly. He didn't know what else to do but hold her, so he did.

Finally looking at him, Faith wiped at her tear-streaked cheeks. "It would seem like a miracle if it did happen."

Mick smiled. "God knows who did this. He's in control."

She smiled a little. "I believe you're in control, and you have faith in God, so that's enough for me right now."

"Okay." He released her from his embrace.

She stepped back, trying to recover her emotions. She turned for a moment, wiping her eyes. "What are you going to do if you find this person?"

Mick wanted to say he'd call the police, call for backup, contact the bureau, arrest him on the spot, and wait for help to arrive. But he didn't know if he would do any of those things. "Don't worry about me, okay?"

She looked at him one long moment, then glanced down at her watch. She looked back at the road, where a taxi was waiting. "Right on time." She smiled. "I have to get back."

"I could drive you home."

"That's okay. I need some time. . . . "

Mick nodded. "I understand."

"Okay." Her hand touched his arm, then slid down to his fingers. She squeezed his hand, then turned to walk to the waiting cab.

"Wait, Faith," he called after her, and she turned. "When I see you again . . . will you *see* me?"

Her dark sunglasses masked her eyes. A faint smile indicated only sadness. "You won't see me again. I'm leaving Bakerville. But wherever I go, I will be able to see again. I'm tired of hiding."

He watched her walk, graceful with the wind behind her, her summer dress blowing to her side. The wind lifted her shimmering hair, carrying it for a few seconds with great tenderness.

She got into the cab and looked at him from the car window. Just the idea that she could look at him palpitated his heart. He gave a short wave before turning back to the bay.

Mick sat down on the lush grass of the park, a few yards from the water's edge, and watched the waves crash and soar. He'd forgotten this sound. It had been years since he had been to the ocean. The thunder of the waves soothed his soul somehow, reminding him there was someone greater than himself commanding the galaxy.

Mick only knew time had passed by the way the sun had now edged closer to the horizon behind him. Its warmth against his back was a simple pleasure. In the time he had been sitting, his mind had been far from idle, and he knew he had to call Reggie. He looked at his watch. Hopefully Reg would be home. He dialed the number from his cell phone, thankfully getting a good connection.

"Hello?"

"Reg, it's Mick."

"Mick! Brother! It's good to hear your voice! Where are you, man?"

A grin crossed his face. "Where else? On the beach."

Mick stretched his body across the grass, his arms acting as a pillow for his head, his feet crossed at the ankles. The night air was chilly, but he'd brought a jacket, which provided enough warmth to allow him to stargaze.

And pray.

He hadn't prayed in a while. Not really prayed . . . the kind of prayer that's uttered from the soul, not the mouth. He never even opened his mouth. Instead, he stared at the stars, imagined God looking down and listening.

Tears fell on either side of his face, running down into his ears, as he allowed himself to think of Aaron. It was too painful to do much. But what he saw in Faith, a desecrated life, he didn't want to happen to him. And he knew it could. There were always ways to deaden the pain. But he knew God did not want that. Somehow inside himself he found the courage to face it. He didn't feel the pain any less, but he now shared it. And there was something comforting about not being alone and knowing that in God's design for human destiny there would be pain, loss, suffering, but also redemption and peace.

Mick cupped his hands over his mouth and blew warm breath into them. He sat up, his head heavy with the deep burden of emotion. He could feel a headache coming on. A couple walking the beach, hand in hand, regarded him momentarily before embracing and continuing on their way.

Loneliness crept into his thoughts, and he turned it away. He zipped up his jacket, rose to his feet, and walked toward his car. Right before he got in, his cell phone rang, loud and clear in the stillness of the night. He quickly answered it, hoping it was Abigail with some new information. "This is Mick."

"This is Miguel Juarez."

chapter thirty-three

m iguel, what can I do for you?"
"I have more information for you,"
Miguel said. His words warbled quietly
through his thick Spanish accent.

"I'm listening."

A pause. "I wasn't completely truthful with you before.
I was afraid. My wife, she told me I should tell you everything."

"Your wife is a smart woman."

"She has a sense when it comes to people. She sensed
you would be true to your word. Chief Underwood, he has
come sniffing around again, causing trouble. He is going to
try to get me, Agent Kline. You understand now that you've
reopened the game."

"Tell me what you know."

"I don't know if this is going to help you catch whoever
did this to these people, but I will tell you anyway. I lied
when I told you I did not approach them. I did approach
them."

"Go on."

"I guess I stumbled upon them right after they were
attacked. The lady, she was moaning and crying. I knew she
was alive. I ran over to them, just by instinct, I guess. I
looked up. I saw someone, just a shadow, running away. I
rolled the lady over. There was blood all over her face. It

scared me. I ran. Then I hid behind a car, not knowing what to do. I thought I was going to be next. Then I saw the lady, the one who called the police. And so I knew that help was coming. That's all I did." His words were strained and softened. "I should've done more. I don't know. I just got scared. Maybe if I had not been such a coward, things would've turned out differently. I don't know."

Mick sighed, shaking his head as he listened to Miguel. "All right. This is good to know. You did the right thing by calling me."

"I don't know, but all I do know is that if you don't find who did this, it will be put on me. I know it will."

"I'll be in touch, Miguel." Mick turned off his phone and stared into the night sky. He didn't know how useful this information would turn out to be, but one thought ricocheted around the corridors of his mind in the form of Abigail's voice: *"He may insert himself into the investigation."*

***

Faith's stomach rumbled with hunger. Nik's had quieted after the evening rush, and she was nearly alone in the restaurant except for a teenage couple sharing a sundae and two older gentlemen discussing a fishing trip.

Sandy, who'd switched shifts with Cynthia, brought her an iced tea. "You waiting for Dixie?"

"Yes. She should be here any minute," Faith replied.

Sandy smiled and said, "Okay, I'll check back."

Faith was going to miss this place. She'd only been in Bakerville for a short period, but she felt a warmth here. Nik's had become like a friend. Sandy *had* become a friend without knowing it. Faith's definition of *friend* had changed in the last two years.

She sipped her tea, and her mind drifted to a different time . . . a different friend. She missed Kerri Pratt and knew

Kerri didn't understand why Faith had seemed to be carried off by the wind. Maybe she would call Kerri from her new town, wherever that would be. Faith had spent some time looking at a map. She had considered leaving Texas altogether. She loved the state, was born here, and had the twang to prove it. But maybe it was time to go.

Deep in thought, Faith did not notice Dixie approaching until she spoke. "Hi there, friend."

"Dixie." Faith smiled. "Thanks for meeting me."

"Hey, I'm always up for good food and good fellowship!"

Sandy came to take their orders, and Faith decided on the country fried steak, loaded mashed potatoes, and corn on the cob.

"Whew! What are we celebrating here?" Dixie said.

Faith laughed. "Just hungry. Haven't eaten much all day."

"All right, well, I'll take the same. Extra artery clogger, please."

"What?" Sandy looked perplexed.

"Interpret that as more gravy, but if you feel like you might want to interpret that as more butter on the potatoes, feel free to do that too."

"Gotcha." Sandy giggled.

"How's your day been?" Faith asked.

Without hesitation, Dixie jumped at the opportunity to exercise her fondness for language, and Faith relaxed into her chair, enjoying the opportunity to rest and listen. She noticed Wallace out of the corner of her eye, busy cleaning up a mess under a table where children had sat. He glanced at her once, staring awkwardly as he normally did, but then he went about his business.

" . . . and then the pastor asked me! Can you imagine? ME! To sing the solos. I mean, I can sing and everything, but not as well as Belinda Waterbee, who almost always gets the solo. But she's been a little prideful I think lately, and maybe God is just showing her she needs to be not so prideful. Anyway, I'm singing this song that has quite a bit of range. . . . "

Faith nodded, catching every fifth word between thoughts of how she was going to tell her she was leaving. It would crush Dixie, and Faith knew it was going to do a number on her too. She had to start over . . . again . . . but this time things would be different. This time she wouldn't run; she would live. Face the fears. Face the anguish. Face the grief.

Sandy had served the meals, and Dixie was on to a new topic—the weather and how it affected her hair. Faith nibbled on her corn while Dixie explained the different stages her hair goes through during humidity. She found it fascinating that somehow Dixie could carry the conversation at a meal and somehow still eat without being impolite. It was quite a talent.

By the end of the hair explanation, Faith was getting full, so she set her fork down and drank some tea.

Dixie was finishing off her potatoes. "You know," she said, after five seconds of silence passed, "I'm glad we're friends."

Faith nodded. "Me too, Dixie. We always will be."

"Yeah. I think God had something to do with bringing us together."

"Well, whatever the reason, I'm glad to know you." Faith folded her napkin and pinched at the edges underneath the table, little shreds falling to the floor. "Dixie, I wanted to talk to you. That's why I had you meet me here. There's something I've got to tell you."

"Well, my goodness, go right ahead. I'm sorry, listen to me babbling on like I'm the only one with something important to say. My husband, he always said I could talk to a stump, not that you're a stump, but you get the idea. I sometimes have a hard time keeping my mouth shut. Sorry. Go ahead. You were saying?"

Faith smiled. Yes, she was going to miss Dixie. "Dixie, I'm going to have to leave."

"Leave?"

"Yes. I know I signed a six-month lease to rent your house, and I would be more than happy to pay that out to you, plus you can keep the deposit—"

"Forget that," Dixie said with a wave of her hand. "Why are you leaving? You just got here, honey. I mean, what, just a few weeks? Why are you leaving? Is it me?"

"No, no! Dixie, no. Not at all."

"Then why?"

"It's complicated. I can't really explain it. But I have to go."

"Honey, you're running from something, but whatever it is, it seems to be following you no matter where you go. Maybe you should stop running and turn around to fight the beast."

Faith sighed. "I know it seems that way, but the truth is, this time is going to be different."

"What can you do elsewhere that you can't do here?"

"I don't expect you to understand. I know this is hurtful. We've become friends, and I cherish that friendship, Dixie. I really do. We'll always be friends."

Dixie hung her head, shaking it. "I guess I can't stop you."

Faith's throat ached with compassion for her friend. "Dixie—" she tried not to let her voice quiver—"I wish I could tell you why I'm leaving. But I can't. Just trust me. It's the best thing."

Dixie, for once, didn't seem to have anything to say.

She pushed her fork around in the mashed potatoes that remained on her plate.

"Dixie? Are you okay? Are you mad? You're, um, quiet."

Dixie scooped up the last of her potatoes and shoved them in her mouth. "I was just thinking, I know a guy out west of town who sells moving boxes really cheap!"

Faith smiled as Dixie went on to explain how he was actually a distant third cousin.

Mick finished off a well-done burger, French fries, and a Coke at a small sports bar. Five TVs lined the smoky room, all with the NCAA men's basketball tournament on. When Aaron died, so had Mick's desire to watch the tourney. It was something they had done together since they were young. Mick couldn't bear the thought of watching it alone.

Like Faith, he needed normalcy to return, and this was a first step. In the background on the TV, the crowds roared as the game began. Mick sipped his Coke and looked over the list he'd been working on. He'd made two columns. At the top of one column was Miguel Juarez's name. At the top of the other was Wallace Bledsoe's name. Miguel Juarez would be classified as organized, Wallace Bledsoe as unorganized. He listed their traits, then at the bottom drew a diagram relating how each trait might be significant in the deaths Mick felt were linked, circling the three Abigail had mentioned.

He still had not come up with the missing link. Nor a conclusion as to who might be responsible for Paul Kemper's death. Where *was* the link? What was he missing here? He had to believe God had sent him down this trail for a reason, but now what? It seemed he had hit a dead end.

"More to drink, hon?" The gruff, wiry-haired waitress stood above him with a pitcher in her hand.

"No, thanks."

"A little old for homework, aren't we?" She glanced down at his steno pad. "Let me know if you need anything else."

Mick dropped his pen to the table and stared up at the TV nearest him. The game had begun, so he watched it lifelessly, but he watched it nevertheless. The bar crowd cheered at each basket. Mick probably looked awkward just sipping his Coke, but he couldn't care less about the game. Too much plagued his mind.

Especially that missing link.

He paid for his dinner and left. He drove straight to Wallace Bledsoe's apartment. He parked his car on the side of the street, turning the ignition off. Even the quiet rumble of his engine seemed loud against the night's stillness.

He watched the window four stories up, three from the right. He knew it belonged to Wallace. He'd looked up his address a few days ago but had only permitted himself to drive by long enough to confirm which apartment was his.

Tonight he couldn't stop himself from returning. He rolled down his car window and waited. A white, sheer curtain hung in front of the window, but it did little for privacy. The building was old and run down. Mick thought it even looked like it tilted a little bit.

There. A dark shadow moved across the window. Then again, back the other direction. Mick's chest constricted. Wallace crossed in front of the window several more times. Then nothing. The window glowed a warm light but nothing more.

Mick grabbed the handle to his car door. It clicked, releasing, but Mick didn't open it. Not yet. He reached for his holster and took out his 10mm Smith & Wesson semiautomatic. He looked it over, felt its body and all the crevices and curves. He knew he should leave it in the glove box, but no decent cop would ever leave his pistol behind. That's how he justified it as he got out of his car and put his gun back into its holster. He walked across the street and toward the front door, which was locked. A key or pushing the call button was the only way in.

Mick studied the door for a long moment while standing in the shadows of a large elm. During the day, he could probably talk his way in if a resident came to the door, but this late at night, the chance was small. There probably was a fire exit in the back. He might be able to pick the lock, but an alarm could sound, though in a building this run-down, he doubted the alarm was even working.

His thoughts were interrupted by the sound of tires on the pavement. Mick slipped behind the tree he was standing by and noticed a car turning into the small parking lot on the west side of the apartment building.

The old Cadillac stopped, its lights dimming and then turning off. A woman got out. Mick's hopes sank. A woman would not be easy to approach, especially at night, even for a clean-cut-looking man. Mick rubbed his stubble. This was going to be next to impossible.

But not totally impossible.

He watched her gather her things from her car, including a book bag and two grocery sacks. He could approach her, credentials out, ask her if he could speak with her about one of her neighbors, maybe offer to help her carry her groceries.

This wasn't going to work. He'd scare the daylights out of her just by approaching. And the chances of her inviting him up were slim. He hoped a woman wouldn't be so naive! Plus, Wallace might hear the conversation.

He watched the woman approach the front door, fum-

bling with her keys. Mick swallowed. She wasn't paying
attention. He could make a dash for the wall, wait until he
heard her unlock the door. Maybe it had a slow hinge on it.
If he timed it right, he could wait for her to enter, go
around, and grab it before it locked again, and hope she was
too distracted to notice.

Mick's fingers twitched with indecision.

She'd found the right key. She was trying to put it in the
keyhole.

Now, he screamed to himself.

He dashed quickly, quietly, to the front of the building,
turning so his back was against the wall. Breathing shal-
lowly, he waited. He could hear her keys clanging, frustrated grunts with every attempt to get the key in the hole.

"Come on . . . ," the lady said. "Yes! Got it!"

Mick moved a little toward the door, waiting to hear a
click. Mostly all he could hear was the rattling of grocery
sacks.

Come on . . .

Mick heard the squeaking door open and the woman
make her way inside. With all the racket the sacks were
making, there would be a good chance she wouldn't pay
attention to whether the door latched behind her. He
dashed around the corner and caught the door, praying she
wouldn't turn around. She didn't. She shuffled upstairs and
out of sight.

Mick stood there, holding the door, wondering if this
was the right thing to do. He knew that lying underneath
his nervousness was a solid layer of anger.

Would he be able to talk to Wallace? Would Wallace
talk to him?

Mick's fingers glided over the gun's metal.

Suddenly he stepped back out into the night air, allow-
ing the door to close. He moved along the wall of the build-

ing and was now right under Wallace's window. He looked up, the window's glowing light streaming into the darkness.

The shrill ringing of his cell phone raised the hair on his neck, and he fumbled in his pants pocket while moving against the wall and around the opposite corner. He couldn't get to it while moving. Again, it rang. A few yards away a grouping of trees stood shadowed in the night.

Mick ran for them. He entered the small wooded area on the third ring of his phone, looking back to see if anyone had decided to go investigate. There was only silence.

He had one more ring to answer it before his voice mail did. He retrieved the phone, barely able to breathe. "Mick Kline."

"It's Reggie."

"Reg . . . " Mick was still catching one anxious breath after another. "Reg." Mick stared at the building, a few yards away. He couldn't see Wallace's room, but there didn't seem to be any activity.

"You okay, man? What's wrong?"

"I'm fine. I was just . . . running. What's up?"

"Brother, are you sitting down?"

"No, I'm standing . . . uh, outside."

"I've got news for you. You better sit down."

"What is it?"

"It's about Aaron's case."

"What about it?"

"They've made an arrest."

chapter thirty-four

mick slumped against a tree, trying to decide if he'd heard Reggie right and if his heart was going to slow down so he could speak.

"Mick? You there?"

"What do you mean they made an arrest?"

"Just tonight. I called you as soon as I got word. Tom called me. Brady called him—"

Mick groaned, clawing at his forehead with his thumb and index finger, kicking his toe against the bark of the tree. "Reg, this can't be."

"Why? What's wrong? I thought you'd be happy."

"I just can't . . . I just can't believe it." A surprising rush of emotions made Mick pause.

"Um . . . anyway, his name is Bart Jackson."

"Bart Jackson."

"Yeah, man. Aaron wrote him a ticket about ten days before he was killed."

Mick had squeezed his eyes shut, trying to hold back looming tears. His eyes popped open and he said, "Are you trying to tell me the man shot Aaron because Aaron wrote him a ticket?"

"It's a sick world."

Mick circled the tree he'd been leaning on. "Well, are they sure they have the right man?"

"It was easy to overlook him the first time. He didn't

give Aaron any problem other than a couple of comments as Aaron was writing the ticket. But later he started telling friends how he wasn't speeding, and this cop just pulled him over because he was in a fancy car."

"This has to be a mistake," Mick said.

"There's no mistake," Reggie replied. "Mick, the guy confessed."

"He confessed?"

"Yeah. A couple of days ago they got an anonymous tip about Jackson. I guess he'd slipped and said something one night at a bar. When the police went to question him, he broke down and confessed to the whole thing."

Mick covered his mouth. His stomach felt queasy. At least he was outside.

"Mick?"

"Sorry . . . this is just a lot to take."

"I know, man. Tom thought it best I call you. He knew this might shake you up a little."

"Jackson just walked into Aaron's house and shot him."

"Got in through the back door that was open. He watched Jenny leave, then went and did it. He keeps saying how insane he was. He was going through a divorce or something. Doesn't matter. Anyway, they got him."

Mick's shaking fingers ripped through his hair. He could hardly talk. "Okay. I better go."

"You coming back soon?"

"Yeah. Sure. Soon."

"Okay."

"Reg?"

"Yeah?"

"Does Jenny know?"

"Brady called her about twenty minutes ago."

"All right."

"Man, you okay?"

"I'm okay. I'll see you soon, Reg."

Mick dropped his phone back into his pants pocket. He looked around, shaking his head. Here he was, in the middle of a small forest. Maybe it had been like this all along. He couldn't see the forest for the trees.

How could he have missed something like this? How could he have been so off? Back at his car, he got in quietly, started it, and drove slowly through the residential area.

It was 11:18 p.m. But he had to go see her.

The house was dark. Before, thinking Faith was blind, a dark house wouldn't mean anything. But now he knew she was asleep.

Hesitation mingled with the other emotions he was experiencing. He needed to be with her. So he parked his car in the driveway and went to the front door. He rang the doorbell, but only silence answered.

Then soft, controlled barking. Sissy.

"Faith, it's me," Mick called out. "I'm sorry it's so late."

Sissy was at the door now, barking and whining. Light flickered through a window upstairs, and then downstairs.

"Faith? It's Mick."

A couple of clicks indicated she was unlocking the door. When she opened it, she stood in her nightgown, hair a little tangled. Her gaze swept the front yard. "You're alone?"

"Yes. I need to talk to you. I'm sorry it's late." His voice quivered. He felt like he was going to break down.

Those dazzling eyes that had been hidden for so long now glowed with concern. "Come in."

She offered him a seat on the couch. Mick noticed boxes were out and about, half filled. Life was getting ready to move on for Faith. When Mick looked at her, she glanced away, shrugging and sitting across from him.

"What's wrong?" she asked him.

Mick lowered his head between his hands. "It's just so unbelievable."

"What?"

"They arrested Aaron's killer tonight."

Faith's hand covered her mouth. The only sound in the room was Sissy's whimpering inquiries, her nose against Faith's hip.

"They just called me."

Astonishment glowed from her eyes. "You said Aaron's killer."

Mick nodded, his throat so tight he could hardly speak. "I'm sorry."

"They're not connected?"

Mick shrugged. "He was this guy—this stupid guy—who shot Aaron because he wrote him a traffic ticket."

Faith rose, going to the kitchen, busying herself with a glass of water. But then she stopped, and Mick heard her crying.

He went to her. "Faith," he said, turning her to him. "I'm sorry."

She shook her head, wiping at her tears. "Don't be sorry. This is a good night for you."

"I don't know," Mick said. "I don't know what I'm feeling. I'm numb." He took his thumb and caught a stray tear dripping from her cheek. "Are you okay?"

She nodded and walked to the freezer. Ice clanked against the sides of her glass. "I'm sorry," she said. "I'm being selfish. I don't know why I'm so upset."

"Because," Mick said, "there was hope of finding who killed Paul. I made that hope alive in you."

Faith turned to him, setting her glass down. "I just can't

believe all this was . . . I can't believe your coming here was an accident. Ever since you arrived, I've felt so much safer. And I felt like there was a chance. . . . "

"I know." He drew her near and hugged her tightly. She embraced him eagerly. When she released him, she went to the couch and collapsed onto it.

Mick joined her in the living room. An exhausted laugh left his lips. Faith looked at him. "God did know what He was doing," he said.

"What do you mean?" she asked.

"I mean, the whole time I was here, all I could think about was what I was going to do to the guy who killed my brother, once I found him. God got me out of the way."

Faith's expression turned solemn. "Yes, God does seem to know what He is doing with you. For me, it's a different story." A disgruntled sigh left her lips. "You want some coffee or something?"

"No. I'm okay." Mick stood. "I should probably let you get some sleep."

Faith nodded. Her demeanor had turned cold. "Well, thanks for coming to tell me."

"I'm sorry if this has upset you. It has upset me too."

She silently stared at the carpet.

Mick didn't know what else to do. Sensing she wanted to be alone, he went to the door. "Faith," he said, before leaving, "God is as much in control of your life as He is of mine."

"Have a good life, Mick Kline. I hope you catch a storm someday."

mick did not have the energy to drive home, so he checked himself in to a motel forty-five minutes outside Bakerville. He didn't unpack his bag. Instead, he threw it against the wall and fell into bed.

His mind went to Jenny, and he wondered how she was doing. What she was doing. He hoped she was coping. He knew the news would rattle her too. How could a man shoot another man over a traffic ticket?

In a faraway place in his mind, he thanked God for His intervention. God knew Mick Kline well, and He knew wherever Aaron's killer was, Mick should be as far away as possible. But had God sent him on a wild-goose chase for nothing? Was Mick in Bakerville for no good reason except to bring false hope to a hurting woman?

Mick knew God's purposes stretched far beyond what his eye could see.

Thoughts of Faith, Juarez, Wallace, God, Bakerville, and Bart Jackson swirled inside his head, a vortex of emotions drawing him inward. Now he would have to face his grief head-on. There was nothing to chase. No one to save. Just an empty plain before him, to be filled with a life void of Aaron.

"Maid service!"

Mick sat up, squinting his eyes. The light filtering through the window blinded him.

"Maid service!"

"Hold on!" Mick fell off the bed, picked himself up, and stumbled to the door. He opened it, and a petite woman stood there with a stack of towels.

"You should put your sign out if you don't want to be disturbed," she instructed, then pushed her cart to the next room.

Mick stood in his doorway, blinking away the bright sunshine. It was ten after nine. Inside, he dragged himself to the bathroom, where he splashed his face with cold water and ran his toothbrush over his teeth.

Downstairs he found the continental breakfast. He poured himself a cup of coffee and took a seat at one of the empty tables. An abandoned morning newspaper lay nearby, and he stood and grabbed it. Sitting back down, he saw his brother's picture next to the headline "Traffic ticket caused man to kill."

He threw the paper to the floor. When in history had a traffic ticket ever caused anyone to kill?

Mick watched a few vacationing families mill about the hotel lobby, eager to start their day. There wasn't an ounce of eagerness in him. All he knew was that in three days, it would be time to get back to work. He'd return home today. Maybe go see Jenny.

"Hi, Faith," Sandy said. "Hold on. I have to clean your table."

Behind the safety of her sunglasses, Faith studied Sandy. She was a cute woman, probably in her late thirties but still youthful. Bright. She wondered what Sandy's aspirations were. Some people like the comfort of staying in their small towns forever. Their aspirations are simply to enjoy family and friends, not fame and wealth and prestige.

She watched Sandy wipe the table carefully, methodically. What would Faith's new life hold? She would see. Interact with people. She regretted lying to everyone here and not being able to tell them the truth. But in the end, she thought it best.

Still, she mourned the fact that there was no one she could share her triumph with. Nobody would know what an amazing thing it was going to be to take off her sunglasses, start a new life, decide not to fear the unknown but to embrace it. And most of all, she would know that she was in control of her life, not some sick lunatic she imagined stalking her day and night. This was a milestone, but it would be celebrated alone.

"Okay, your table is ready," Sandy said.

"Thank you," Faith said, sitting down. "Where's Wallace today?"

A disgruntled sigh turned Sandy's charming smile south. "He quit. Just up and quit. No warning. Said he's moving. Family problems. I don't know. You know Wallace. Kind of an odd guy. Hard to read. Anyway, now we're all having to take up the slack until Danny can find someone. What to drink today?"

"Coffee."

Sandy nodded and was about to turn when Faith said, "Sandy?"

"Yes?"

"I just wanted you to know . . . just that . . . thank you for your friendship."

Sandy patted her shoulder. "You're welcome, Faith. You're an easy person to be friends with. I always look forward to your coming in to eat."

Faith swallowed. "It's just that I'm moving soon."

"Oh, no. Really?"

"Yeah. I wanted you to know. I also wanted to thank you for taking good care of me. You're a really kind person."

"Why are you leaving?"

"Various reasons, but all of them good."

"Okay," Sandy said. "I guess I'll have to trust you." Faith smiled warmly, and Sandy squeezed her hand. "Well, until then you're going to have to eat. What's it going to be this morning?"

"French toast. Blueberry topping."

"Great choice! I'll be back with your coffee."

Faith settled into her chair. Leaving this small town was going to be harder than she thought. There were people here she was never going to forget.

And then there was Mick Kline. Contradicting emotions wove themselves together in her heart. Part of her wanted to be bitter. He'd found out who killed his brother. Now he was leaving. But another part of her knew bitterness would not bring about anything good, and she knew Mick Kline was a man of deep character. God had rewarded him by exposing the beast who took his brother from him. How could she be mad about that?

She sighed and sipped the coffee Sandy had returned with. Closing her eyes, she imagined herself riding the bus out of town, finally taking off the sunglasses, staring out the window, and smiling at anyone who smiled back.

She'd decided to find a place near her grandmother. She missed seeing her, knew she didn't have too much time left. How she would explain what happened to Paul, she didn't know. But that was something she could work out later. Maybe she would tell her the truth.

If Mick had done anything for her, it was to teach her that living in fear was going to rot her like an apple on a hot sidewalk in July. First you shrivel. Then you mold. Then you're worm food.

She regretted the fact that she'd torn up Mick's business card and thrown it in the trash. She'd done it angrily. She wasn't angry anymore. But she also knew there were certain people in this life who are meant to come and go, and you have to be brave enough to say good-bye. She just wished she'd been a little nicer about it.

"Here's your French toast, blueberry topping," Sandy said. "Let me know when you have your last meal here. Danny said it's on us, for being such a good customer."

"That's so kind," Faith said. "I won't be leaving for a few more days."

"Good. I'll check back with you in a little bit. Gotta go clean up another table."

Mick threw his bag into the trunk of his car, then stopped at the nearest convenience store for more coffee. But what he was really doing was stalling. Indecision pulled at him like a nagging child. Should he go see Faith one last time?

In a rare moment of complete honesty, Mick knew he'd begun to have feelings for this woman. He'd blocked the idea from his mind. His track record with women wasn't exactly worth bragging about. Plus, this was a woman whose husband had been brutally murdered. He doubted she had love on her mind.

Still, they had a connection, the kind that couldn't be ignored. Mick mindlessly stuck his cup underneath the machine that makes fake cappuccinos. When it was filled, he realized he'd picked Vanilla Nut rather than Irish Creme. Oh, well. Nut it was.

He paid for the drink and stepped outside. The day was warming up, and he let the sun's rays soak into his skin as he leaned against his car and sipped his coffee.

His cell phone rang.

"Mick? It's Jenny." Her voice was strained with emotion.

"Hey. I'm headed home. I was going to call you as soon as I arrived."

"I can't believe it," she said, and her words turned into sobs. "It's just so unbelievable that someone would do this over a fifty-dollar traffic ticket."

"I know," Mick said. He stepped inside his car and started it, rolling up the windows and turning on the air. "Are you okay?"

"I don't know," she cried. "I'm just so stunned. I had to call and tell your parents, you know, and they were very upset. Your mother, especially, doesn't need this kind of stress."

"Yeah . . . ," Mick sighed. "Well, at least they got him. He's not going to get away with murder."

"I know. That's the good thing. There's justice."

"Yeah, not everybody gets justice."

"So you're coming home soon?"

"Right now. I'll come by this evening, okay?"

"That sounds good," Jenny said, her voice easing up a bit. "I need to be with someone who understands this."

"Okay. I'll talk to you soon, okay? Call me if you need anything."

"I will. Thanks, Mick."

Mick sat in his car, the steam from his coffee making his face perspire. He stared forward, Faith's beautiful face still lingering in his mind. The last time they had talked, she had been angry. He didn't want to upset her again. And seeing him now might do just that.

He put his car into drive. She had his number. If she wanted to talk, she could call. And with that final thought, the nagging child of indecision went to her room, and Mick headed toward the highway.

chapter thirty-six

h ey there," Jenny said. She smiled as she opened
her apartment door farther. Her eyes were puffy
and red. She looked completely exhausted.

"Hi," Mick said. "Something smells good."

"You're just in time for Chinese. I ordered enough for
two. I was hoping you'd make it for dinner."

"Great. I'm starving. The drive seemed to last forever."

Mick headed for the table, hoping to find lo mein.
There it was. Along with a big carton of fried rice. She
knew that was safe enough for him. He smiled.

"Here's a plate," she said, handing it to him. "Feel like
watching a movie or something? I can't stand to have the
TV on. They're covering the arrest pretty big."

"I saw it in the newspaper this morning."

Jenny shook her head, grabbing an egg roll. "The guy
looks so normal, Mick. I mean, like a neighbor. A cousin. A
church deacon. You'd never guess he could kill someone."

"Anger got the best of him, I guess." Mick sighed. The
reminder that he had been just as close to having anger get
the best of him tickled his backbone. Flashing before him
was Wallace's apartment building, Mick standing below his
window. He shut his eyes tightly.

"Mick? You okay?"

"Yeah. Just a headache."

Jenny scooped rice onto her plate and dashed soy sauce

across it. "You look like you've been holed up in the wilderness somewhere. Without a razor."

Mick laughed. "Look pretty bad, huh?"

"Just a little rugged." She made her way over to the couch, sat down, and put her plate on the coffee table.

Mick heard a loud sigh escape from her as he joined her. "This will bring some closure, you know," Mick said. It's shocking right now, but at least you know the man responsible for killing your husband is behind bars."

She stared at her plate. "My appetite comes and goes. Sometimes I'm really hungry, then by the time I get the food on my plate, the last thing I want to do is eat."

"You've lost weight, Jen. Eat it anyway."

Mick's cell phone rang from where he had set it on the entryway table. Jenny raised an eyebrow at him and Mick tried to decide whether or not to get it. On its third ring, he moved swiftly, hoping it was Faith. "This is Mick."

"Mick, it's Abigail."

Mick glanced at Jenny, who was busy twirling lo mein around her fork. "Um, hi."

"You okay? You sound—"

"No, I'm fine. What's up?"

"Where are you?"

"In town."

A brief pause was followed by, "Meet me at the office in ten minutes." The phone then went silent.

———

A few agents were working, but for the most part, at eight o'clock at night, the office was empty. It felt good, familiar, to be walking across the floor, passing by his desk, hearing the faithful sounds of the ever working machines. The fluorescent light that hummed a constant buzz had still not given up the ghost.

Mick took the stairs to Abigail's office. Her light was on. "It's Mick," he called.

"In here," she called back.

Mick approached and entered her office. "Hi."

She looked up at him and smiled, but the tension in her face caused the smile to be less affectionate and more courteous. "Thanks for meeting me," she said, shuffling papers back and forth across her desk. "I'm glad you're back in town. I heard about the arrest. I don't know what to say." Her eyes finally focused on him.

Mick nodded but said nothing. Abigail's behavior was making him nervous. "So, what's this about?"

Abigail leaned back in her chair, clasping her arms behind her neck in a poor attempt to look casual. "I'm just going to shoot straight with you. I've got some info on Bledsoe."

"And?"

"And we may have something." Abigail held up a hand as Mick was about to speak. "Now, Mick, I want you to listen to me very carefully. You have got to get yourself together here. I don't want you jumping to any conclusions. Okay?"

"Tell me what you know."

A terse sigh indicated she was not happy that he didn't acknowledge her request. "Looks like Wallace Bledsoe may have some mental issues. He was in a psychiatric ward."

"For what?"

"It's hard to say."

"Why?"

"Well, he was being evaluated when he escaped. No one could locate him."

Mick leaned forward. "Being evaluated for what?"

Abigail pressed her lips together. "Schizophrenia. Possibly paranoid delusions."

Mick closed his eyes and dropped his head. "You have got to be kidding me."

"Now listen. There are a lot of pieces of the puzzle missing. But I have some more information to share with you. I just need to make sure you understand this is just information. It doesn't necessarily mean—"

"What is it, Abigail?" His face flushed with frustration.

"All right. There is some evidence that Wallace was in the area of Lubbock when the sheriff's deputy was killed. And then in Houston when that DEA agent was found dead in his backyard."

Mick's heart seemed to squeeze itself into a tight ball. "And what about in Houston, when Paul Kemper was killed?"

Abigail nodded. "There is a possibility."

Mick stood up. "I knew it!"

Abigail's face was wide with surprise. "Mick, you've got to calm down. Just sit down. There's more to this than meets the eye."

Mick looked at her. "Like what?"

"I'm just saying, you can't draw conclusions here. You know that. You've got to have evidence."

Mick rubbed his eyes and paced in circles, listening to Abigail.

"He was in the *area*. But that doesn't mean anything, okay? We need more evidence. We're working on getting that right now."

"Abigail, if this is true, he's stalking Faith Kemper. Don't you understand that?"

"Yes, I understand it, Mick. I understand it." Her voice softened.

"Well, what are we dealing with then? Organized or unorganized?"

"It's hard to say. It depends on what kind of mental situation we're dealing with. Wallace wasn't at the hospital long enough for them to do a thorough evaluation of him. Even though they suspected schizophrenia, they didn't get enough tests run. Schizophrenia can be very hard to diagnose. It could be that he's just one messed-up guy."

"What's his background?"

Abigail paused and looked away.

"Abigail?"

Her eyes darted up to his. "His father killed his mother right in front of him when Wallace was twelve. Had abused her for years before that."

Mick shook his head, hardly believing what he was hearing.

"His father was a Seattle homicide detective."

Mick wanted to kick something. "I had him! Right there! I knew it! I knew there was something off about this guy!" He rubbed his neck furiously, clenching his teeth. "So why Faith?" He paced the floor, trying to grasp at anything that made sense. "The other two victims weren't married, were they?"

"No."

"Paul had a wife. . . . " It was beginning to make sense. "And Wallace felt like he needed to take care of this woman, watch out for her, because she was married to a law enforcer, and they are all evil. . . . "

"Mick, you're jumping to a lot of conclusions here."

Mick turned a fierce stare in her direction. "I can't figure out why you are acting more like a spin doctor here."

Abigail rose and went to the front of her desk. "Mick, it's more complicated than just going and getting this guy. I mean, I had to do a little finagling to get this information, all right? And we can't just storm the town and take this guy down without making sure we've got everything right. I don't think I have to remind you that you're not actually working a case here. You're supposed to be on a beach."

Mick calmed himself. He wasn't going to get the information he wanted by putting Abigail on edge. Sitting, he folded his hands in his lap. Abigail indicated she'd relaxed by returning to her chair behind her desk.

"What about the other cases?"

Abigail shook her head. "I cannot find a link with those. Just these three. And of course your brother's case was eliminated yesterday."

"So what do you think? I want your opinion."

Abigail sighed, as if dreading that very question. She tapped the pencil she was holding against the wood of her desk, scratching her hairline with the other hand. "It could be coincidence, but it could be the real thing. We just need a little bit more. If we're going to do this, we're going to do it right."

"What about Wallace? What are your gut instincts about him?"

"He's all over the board, Mick. I mean, the Kemper crime was organized/unorganized. The other two crimes showed signs of both as well. Wallace's charts indicate borderline schizophrenia. That may be why we're not getting a clear reading. The guy has had problems ever since he was a teen. Nothing with the law, but poor grades in school, few friends. We talked to one guy in his hometown who knew him."

"A friend?"

"No. He owned a comic-book store Wallace frequented."

"What'd he say?"

"Not much. Just that Wallace was odd but a good customer. Thought he wasn't always in tune with reality, though."

"So you're convinced he's schizophrenic?"

"No."

"No?"

She looked at him, then shook her head. "Mick, I am telling you this because I think I can trust you with this information."

"What?"

"There is just as good a chance that Wallace Bledsoe is a man who is intelligent enough to make his crime seem one way and then act another way. Do you understand?"

"Not really."

"What I'm saying is that his father was a detective. Wallace Bledsoe has above-average intelligence, according to his records. He might know to kill organized but act unorganized. He might know they're looking for a certain personality type, so he becomes another personality type."

"A sociopath?"

"There's a fifty-fifty chance. I can't say either way. He could very well be a schizophrenic. There is Wallace the mild-mannered, socially inept busboy, and then there's someone else, the little boy enraged by his mother's death."

"So we have no idea what kind of beast we're hunting."

"That's what I'm working on."

"And in the meantime, he's following Faith Kemper around."

"Don't get ahead of yourself, Mick. If you make a move, it may make it worse." Abigail's eyes dimmed in serious thought before she said, "If we are talking about someone suffering from schizophrenia, then the most likely scenario is that he's one part mild-mannered, socially inept guy and one part killer. You should know, schizophrenia doesn't make a person violent. And violence doesn't cause schizophrenia. There are a lot of misconceptions about the disorder. However, someone suffering from paranoid delusions and a host of other mental and emotional disorders, which appears to be the case with Wallace, could turn to violence."

Mick swallowed the sour bile back down. "How do we know when he will turn violent?"

"You have to know the triggers. And we don't know those yet."

Mick stood and headed for the door.

"Where are you going?"

"Back to Bakerville. I can't leave Faith there, knowing what I know."

"Mick, please, give me five more hours. I need more to get the police on this. Just a little more time."

"It takes two hours to get there."

"Mick!"

But Mick was already making his way down the stair-well.

chapter thirty-seven

the guilt Faith was feeling by not packing her things herself was superseded by the company she was enjoying. Dixie hummed happily as she organized box after box, careful to receive instructions from Faith about where she wanted what.

She was telling Faith about a couple of prospective renters she had in mind. One was a little old lady at her church whose husband died and left her with a four-thousand-square-foot home. The other was a college boy, but as Dixie put it, "very responsible, not the partying type." Faith had to laugh. Was there any such thing as a responsible college boy?

They'd been working for nearly four hours and had taken a break only to order pizza. While Dixie had her back turned, Faith glanced up at the microwave clock in the kitchen.

"Dixie, it's getting late. Why don't you go home and get some rest. You've been working so hard."

Dixie shook her head. "You amaze me how you can keep track of time internally! I'm always losing track of time. Oh!" Dixie glanced up at the clock. "It *is* getting late. I better get home in time to see the news. I hate missing the news."

"I know," Faith said, smiling. "And I know how you don't go to bed past eleven."

"Well, I'll be over here bright and early in the morning!" She looked around the room. "I've got everything pushed to the side so you won't trip over anything." Dixie gave her a big hug, then patted Sissy as she walked to the door. "I can't believe you're leaving. I'm going to miss you so much!"

"Me too," Faith said, making her way closer to the door. "We'll keep in touch by phone, okay?"

"Okay."

"I'll make us a fresh pot of coffee in the morning."

"Sounds good."

"Dixie?"

"Yes?"

"Can you do me a favor and close the curtains?"

"Sure I can!" Dixie quickly closed the curtains on the two windows in the living room. "Get a good night's rest."

"Good night."

Dixie closed the door behind her, and Faith grinned. What a delight that Dixie was! Faith took off her sunglasses and stretched her aching neck.

Sissy was pawing at the back door, a little more eager than usual to go out for her final bathroom break. Faith had forgotten to let her out sooner. Faith opened the door for her. "Take your time, girl. I'm gonna be up for a while." Faith knew Sissy liked to explore in the cool air.

Sissy happily bounded onto the porch and into the darkness. Closing the door, Faith sighed, looking at all the packing that needed to be done yet. Fatigue was setting in, and all she really wanted to do was sit on the couch and soak her feet.

A stray piece of packing paper caught her eye by the front door, and she decided she could at least manage to go and throw that away. She was about to pick it up when she heard someone on the other side of the door. She smiled;

Dixie almost always forgot something. She swung open the door, saying, "You silly—"

Wallace stood there, his eyes bright with surprise. Faith recovered quickly, making her eyes stay completely steady in front of her. Pulsating blood swelled her veins.

"It's me. Wallace."

"Wallace." It was barely a whisper. She'd almost blown it, almost blown her cover. Her wilting lungs were reminding her of it.

"Are—are you okay?" he asked.

"Sorry. I was just expecting someone else."

"Dixie?"

Faith regained control of her shaking limbs. "What can I do for you? It's kind of late to be coming by."

"From town to town."

"Excuse me?"

"It's just that you keep moving."

The tendons in Mick's leg and foot ached at the restraint of having to go the speed limit. But it wasn't going to do him any good to try to save a couple of minutes only to lose fifteen by being pulled over for speeding. The muscles in his left hand cramped from holding the steering wheel too tightly, so he switched to his right hand and popped the knuckles of his fingers with his thumb.

The forty-five minutes he'd been on the road seemed an eternity. He glanced at the clock every two minutes. But his mind continued to chew over one detail like a dog would chew a rawhide bone. If Wallace was the one who had attacked Paul and Faith, why didn't Faith recognize him? She saw his face every day, heard his voice. Had she blocked it all out?

Mick rolled down the car window, and the fresh air

brought a sobering realization: God had not sent him to Bakerville to find Aaron's killer but to save Faith.

Save Faith.

He upped his speed to ten miles over the limit.

The incompetency! How could he not have seen it? Such denial! The anger that smoldered inside cooled ever so slowly, starting with a frightening chill at the top of his head.

Suddenly he understood why Faith did not recognize Wallace Bledsoe. She never saw Wallace. Mick's conversation with Miguel flashed through his mind. She had seen Miguel Juarez bending down to try to help.

Mick's car roared over the pavement at ninety miles an hour.

"I have a gun. Get in the house."

Faith could not see a gun. But she also couldn't look down. Besides, tears had fogged her vision several seconds before. "Wallace . . . please . . . " Faith's knees were shaking so badly she could hardly move.

"Let's go in the house, Faith." Wallace's tone was gentle and eerie—quiet. Controlled.

Faith stepped backward. She stumbled a little, out of nervousness.

Wallace's eyes lit up.

A black, shiny object in his left hand caught her attention. She still couldn't tell if it was a gun.

"Over on the couch."

Faith turned, stretched out her hands, walking slowly, then sat on the couch. The tears that dripped down her face begged to be wiped. She let them be, afraid to even let her chest rise with a single breath.

Wallace paced in front of her, rubbing his head like he

was battling a migraine. He never looked at her as he spoke. "You shouldn't be afraid of me. You should be afraid of them. They're the wicked ones. Wicked. Wicked."

Faith heard Sissy at the back door, whimpering, wondering why she wasn't coming to let her in. Wallace heard it too. He looked up, then did not regard it.

"Don't hurt me," Faith cried.

"I'm not going to hurt you." Wallace's speech was as stilted as it had always been. His dark eyes melted with a strange compassion. "Don't you understand that I have been helping you all this time? Trying to protect you."

"Please let me go."

"No, no, I can't do that." Nervousness quavered his voice. "No. You're not safe without me. You betrayed me."

"Betrayed you?"

"With that FBI agent. I thought you were going to trust him. But he left, luckily for you. But you cannot be alone anymore. You are too dangerous. To yourself. You trust all the wrong people."

"Why are you doing this?" Faith could not hold the sobs in. Fear stung her lungs as she gasped for breath.

"I need you to be quiet now."

"Please, don't do—"

"Quiet. They are watching. Always watching."

Mick passed a car on the left. He needn't look down at the speedometer. The pitch and volume of wind flowing through his car told him how fast he was going. His cell phone rang.

"It's Abigail. Mick, I've got some more information."

"What?"

"We found out what got Wallace committed in the first place. A police officer had pulled him over for making an illegal lane change. Wallace protested; the officer gave him a ticket anyway. Things got heated. He got thrown in jail for assaulting the officer. At his court hearing, he was babbling incoherently. His court-appointed attorney told the judge he thought Wallace needed a mental evaluation."

"That's when he got put in the hospital."

"Here's the kicker. That officer was killed."

"By Wallace?"

"No. He was killed in an unrelated traffic accident while on vacation. But anyway, in court the prosecutor mentioned that the officer was deceased."

"What are you saying here?"

"I'm not sure." Abigail sighed. "But sometimes people with paranoid delusions can draw the wrong conclusions from incidents like that. Wallace may have seen that as a sign that God killed the evil man. Two months after he escaped from the hospital, the man in Lubbock was killed."

"All right," Mick breathed.

"I am working as fast as I can. We're trying to get a warrant for Wallace's apartment. They're trying to find the judge right now. Just don't do anything crazy. They're contacting the local police. Things are coming together. But it's got to be done a certain way."

"Call me if anything else develops."

Mick hung up and glanced at his clock. Another eighteen minutes and he would be there.

chapter thirty-eight

i knew that about you. That you were too trusting. You don't know. You don't know how they can be. Dangerous." Wallace turned to Faith, his shoulders slumped, one hand in his pocket, like a little boy on his first day of school. A boy who knew hatred. His eyes told stories his tongue could not.

Faith continued to sit on the couch. Her whole body trembled uncontrollably. She steadied her eyes in a place where she could see what was going on. "Wallace, what are you doing?"

"I'm protecting you. I've protected you once. And I'm protecting you again." His matter-of-fact tone crawled over her sensibilities like a thousand spiders.

Heavy tears followed the ones that had streamed just moments before. "You killed Paul?" she whispered.

Wallace twitched, his eyes blinking in an odd way.

Fear ripped through her heart. Then rage shredded what was left. She could not control herself. "You killed Paul!"

He stuttered. "No. No. He is bad. He is the bad one."

"You killed my husband!" She screamed like a wild animal caught in a trap on a cold winter night.

"I-I-I protected you. And I'm protecting you again."

"You sick and pathetic worm! You maggot!"

Wallace's face, wrecked with indecision and confusion, flushed. "You sit down!"

She gasped, almost forgetting not to look at him. *She was sitting down.*

"You sit! Now! Sit down!"

Her fingers clutched the fabric of the couch.

"I told you to sit down." His calmness chilled her to the core. His gun shook in a trembling and uneasy hand. It pointed at her slightly.

Faith gritted her teeth. "I want to hear you say it. Say that you killed him. Do you hear me? *Say it!*"

Wallace's eyes bulged. "You do what I say! I'm the one. I'm the one!"

"Say it!"

Now the pistol glinted in the lights of the room as it rose and pointed directly at her. She didn't care. In fact, she oddly welcomed the thought of dying at this moment. Her spirit had little more fight left. She made herself look at the gun, stare it down. Paul never saw what killed him. She would.

Wallace did not seem to notice.

Her eyes roamed upward, slowly, to Paul's killer. Emotions seemed to be the only thing holding her upright, and they fluctuated as she stole subtle glances at Wallace. There he was, a madman holding a gun. But in his eyes she could see a little boy. Fragile. Weak. Scared. He swayed slightly, just as an insecure child would. His free hand tugged at the wisps of hair over his ears. But he was not all little boy. There was something else in there. A ravaging beast, caged but wild.

Faith stood up.

His eyes looked at her, but they were vacant now, lost somewhere inside himself.

"Say you killed him."

His expression contorted, registering that he'd returned from wherever he had just been. "I am going to have to do something."

Fury squashed Faith's fear. She flung her arms up. "Do what? Kill me? Then kill me! You already killed me two years ago when you took Paul from me!"

The gun pointed toward her head.

Her tongue stuck to the roof of her mouth. She didn't have enough moisture to spit. Her heart felt too heavy to beat. Was she ready to die? Like this?

"I'm your friend," Wallace bumbled. "Your friend. You don't know. I've been watching, watching you, protecting you."

That realization almost made Faith faint. She'd been watched for two years. Stalked. Her eyes closed and opened slowly, that single thought weighing her shoulders down like a bag of bricks.

"You are not my friend. And whether or not you kill me does not matter to me. If you kill me, I will be with the one I love."

Then the hair-pulling stopped. The unsteady, bashful eyes she'd seen just moments before vanished. In its place a dark, hungry, vengeful stare stabbed through her.

She was preparing to die. And as she stood there waiting for the sound of the gun, her mind vacillated between saving her own life and one other thing: Making sure Wallace knew she could see him. If she was going to die, she wanted to see her killer's face.

Mick's car tore around the corner that led him off the highway and onto the street that would take him into Bakerville. Five minutes.

He hit callback on his cell phone. It rang only once.

"Abigail, I need to know something. I need you to think something through. He killed the other two men first—"

"Allegedly, Mick."

"Abigail, please, just listen to me. The other two, then Paul. But Paul had his wife with him."

"All right."

"Do you think Wallace Bledsoe has been following Faith around ever since he killed Paul?"

Silence indicated Abigail was giving it careful thought. "Yes."

"So why now, at Bakerville, does he become more bold? insert himself into her life? What's the difference?"

"It's hard to say, Mick. If I had to guess, I would say it was coincidence."

"Coincidence?"

"I think Wallace came to Bakerville, following her, and took the job as a busboy. By coincidence, Faith started eating there. It probably took a certain amount of boldness for him to start talking to her. But that's what concerns me. That he has formed a relationship with her, at least in his mind."

"Okay . . . ," Mick sighed.

"Are you in Bakerville?"

"I'm about to drive into the city limits."

"Mick, listen to me. Do not go over to Wallace's apartment. Do you hear me? You could jeopardize everything."

He was approaching the street to Wallace's apartment. If he went straight, he'd be at Faith's in three minutes. A few days ago, he would've taken the road to Wallace's. But something had happened to his own need for justice. It had vanished when he realized God's amazing power of control.

"I'm going to Faith's house."

A relieved sigh. "Good. That's very good. Tell her whatever you want, but stay there. I think we're about thirty minutes away from getting that warrant."

"Okay."

Mick hung up and obeyed the warning that the speed limit was getting ready to dramatically reduce. In every

small Texas town he'd been to, there were speed traps.
Thirty miles an hour. Mick felt he could run faster.

What would he say to Faith once he got there? How
would he explain to her that Wallace the busboy had killed
her husband? It was going to devastate her, not to mention
freak her out of her everlasting mind.

Mick let his speed creep up to thirty-four miles an hour.
Thirty seconds later heard the siren.

Mick bit his tongue. He knew it would delay him even
longer if he tried to explain where he was going and why.
To simply nod and smile and say thank you, which was
always a stupid thing to say to a cop writing you a ticket,
would get him there sooner.

The cop was on a motorcycle, a young guy with a
skinny mustache and a thin frame. Luckily he didn't have
an attitude, and he seemed almost apologetic for writing a
ticket for only four miles an hour over the speed limit.

Within seven minutes, Mick was back on his way—
thirty miles an hour.

Mick pulled his car up to the curb in front of Faith's house.
The lights were on. That was a good sign. He had not
wanted to wake her up.

He turned off the ignition and gathered his thoughts
and apprehensions into a ball of courage. Telling her was
not going to be easy. Seeing her again wasn't going to be
easy. They had not parted on good terms. And he knew she
resented him some too.

Mick secured his gun at his waist and locked his car.
For a moment he watched for any kind of movement in the
house, but the curtains were drawn.

"Okay, just do it," he mumbled as he walked up the
sidewalk. Nervousness palpitated in his heart, but it was not

the only thing pumping his blood. The way she had looked at him with those beautiful blue eyes . . .

At the front door, he chewed at his lip. Maybe he should wait until morning. She was probably getting ready to go to bed. Fingering the whiskers on his cheek, he shook his head.

Kline, for crying out loud, make a decision! Just knock on her door!

Forgive me, God, Faith prayed while staring at the carpet, pretending she could not see the man waving the gun in front of her. *Forgive me for everything.*

An absolute calm washed over her, an unexplainable peace crashing into her soul like a wave. The trembling stopped. The grief she had not allowed herself to feel when she had denounced God did not bring tears. She felt relief. The honesty of acknowledging her God again tore open her soul, leaving a gaping hole. And God eagerly filled every square inch of it.

Flickering through her mind was the strange thought that she did not have to understand everything, that she did not need answers to the hundreds of questions that had eaten away at her will to live. Suddenly she had an answer to questions not yet asked. She had security to dwell in the chasm of the unknown.

Somehow through the chaos of revisiting Paul's death, Mick Kline had shown her how to trust again. And now she realized that she trusted in the eternity that God had promised her . . . the eternity her beloved Paul now enjoyed.

With one last ounce of courage and strength, not realizing she had either one, Faith Kemper raised her gaze to meet her husband's killer's eyes. She would stare into them until she was gone.

But Wallace was not looking at her. He was turned toward the door, where someone was knocking.

"Faith?" Mick knocked again. "It's me, Mick."

He waited, but there was no reply. "Faith, please, open the door. I know you're upset. But I need to talk to you. It's important."

Mick listened carefully, but there was only silence. He raked his fingers through his hair and turned to look out into the darkness. Was she ignoring him? Was she already asleep? in the bathroom?

He knocked once more. "Faith?"

Scratching his head, he dragged his tired body back to his car and got in, reclining into a relaxed position. He looked back one more time at the door to see if it would open, but it stood quiet and still. Pressing his lips together in frustration, he debated about what to do next.

He dug into his pocket for his keys. Then he glanced across the street—and saw something that stopped his heart.

A bicycle. Parked under a tree.

Mick stumbled out of his car. He scrambled to the front door, his feet unstable beneath him. Then he paused, trying to decide what to do next. He'd already knocked, called out his name. They'd been alerted to the fact that he was out here.

He didn't have time to think out a plan. Mick raced around the back of the house, opening the gate. Sissy greeted him with a wagging tail and perked ears.

"Calm down, girl," Mick said, scooting against the side of the house. He rounded the corner, hoping for a break between the back curtains. But they were drawn together tightly.

"Mick!" The startling cry nearly buckled Mick's knees. "Mick! Mick!" Sissy raced onto the front porch.

"Dear God . . . ," Mick breathed. He turned to run to the other side of the house, where he could kick in the front door.

A blow to the forehead, right between his eyes, knocked him to the ground. A faint ringing in his ears and bright spots of light in his vision told him he was about to lose consciousness. The only sensation he could feel was dirt scraping against his back as he was being dragged.

Excruciating pain splintered through Mick's head as he tried to open his eyes. He could hear voices, but they were indiscernible. He forced one eye open, and the room spun. His stomach lurched with nausea.

" . . . evil is his way. All their ways. They are not who they seem to be. . . . "

The voice echoed in the chambers of his thoughts, making no sense to him, garbled as if spoken underwater.

" . . . they all must die . . . must be . . . exposed . . . "

Mick squeezed his eyes shut, trying to block out the pain that dominated all his senses. If he could just open one eye, figure out where he was. One thing he knew immediately—he could not move his legs or arms. His neck was strained and weak, falling forward at any attempt he made to raise it and look around.

He slipped into a drowsy slumber again, for how long he didn't know. But when he regained consciousness, the slicing pain in his head was down to a distinct throb. The heaviness in his eyelids had lightened. As one eye peeked open, soft light filled his vision, and he could make out a few things around him. First he saw his knees, then his feet. The carpet. He was sitting in a chair.

Something tickled his forearm. He stretched his fingers to explore it. Rope? No. A leather strap. What kind of leather strap? His hands were tied behind his back around the back of the chair.

He kept his neck bent, trying not to show that he was awake. His vision was still blurry, but he cast his gaze to the side and realized he was at the edge of the living room. Then he saw Faith. She was sitting in a chair in the kitchen near the breakfast table. Mick tried to see if she was tied up, but her image split in two, his mind swirled, and he had to close his eyes again.

" . . . please don't hurt him. . . . "

That was Faith's voice, strained and timid. Mick opened his eyes again, trying to look at her. She was too far away to notice he had his eyes open.

" . . . you don't know what he is!"

Mick's mind yanked him awake. The second voice was male. Mick saw a figure pass by him. Dark clothing. But the image swirled, blurred, and then the light faded. *Stay awake*. But the darkness fell again.

chapter thirty-nine

i t was hard to describe. He had tried. But when he did try, there was always that look from the doctors. The eyes narrowed. Then the head would tilt. They wore white, as if they were pure somehow. He hated white. Always probing with instruments. Asking questions. Saying they were there to help.

But if he had to describe it, he would say that his thoughts would pass him by, floating through his mind. He could see them but not touch them. And they got mixed up and out of order. Perhaps he could catch one, but then it would be the wrong one. His mind was like a busy highway with the heavy traffic of words and feelings and ideas that came and went without any order.

It was not always so.

There were times that the road was clear and the vehicles moved to and fro in an organized fashion. They were all red. Or all trucks. Or all going the same way. But then, for no reason he could determine, a pile-up. Confusion. Distortion.

Now, though—now he could reason. He knew things were right in the world. He could rest in that fact.

Things had been unsettled. For a while. The cars, they would speed up, go the wrong direction, turn where they weren't supposed to. He'd managed, though. Until . . .

No, don't think about it. It is under control now.

But . . .

No, do not look. Evil is behind you. Lurking. Ready to prey on you. And her.

He studied her. So sad. So lonely. He'd tried to comfort her, but she had yelled at him. She didn't understand. He had to make her understand how much danger was around her. She didn't understand.

"Can you get the can of green beans from the pantry, honey?"

"Yes, Mama."

No to the voices. No no no. Go away. Calm. Flowing all one way.

"Thank you, honey."

"You're welcome."

"What are you talking about?"

He opened his eyes. Had his eyes been closed? She was there, in front of him, still crying. He remembered . . . yes, his mama . . . she cried a lot too. Just like hers. Big blue tears. Baby blue eyes.

"I'm helping you. You see that? You see him? Trying to hurt you?" Wallace spoke to her softly.

"Wallace!" The monster was awake.

He turned. He'd spoken too loudly. No matter. It would be silenced soon. Then she would stop crying. He hated to see his mama cry.

"Wallace!"

He didn't want to turn around. He knew that the traffic would run faster. Harder. The wrong way. But he had to look at it, show it that it had been defeated. So he turned.

"Wallace, what are you doing?"

The monster spoke to him, as if they were equals, as if it weren't a monster but a man. That's how they said it would be. He would come in the form of a mere man. The voices spoke to him. Sometimes they shouted. He didn't like when they shouted. But other times they instructed him. And see where it had gotten him? In a place of control. Complete control. Where Mama would be safe.

But Mama was angry. He looked back at her. Those blue eyes, they weren't kind, like he knew them to be. They were angry. And scared. Didn't she see the monster tied up? how he had defeated the monster?

"Wallace, listen to me. Listen. You need to let her go. Let her walk out of this house."

"Don't . . . you . . . speak." But that is not what concerned Wallace. "And don't look at her."

Oh, the control! Look! How his eyes obeyed, returning to him!

"What are you doing, Wallace? Why are you in Faith's house?"

"The sword will kill you!" The monster, Wallace observed, spoke in riddles. But the monster and the maiden both understood the sword. Yes, the sword—that would make the monster bow. Wallace gasped. The monster had looked at his mama again. He marched over to it.

There. Silenced. Wallace turned from the monster, his fist tightened, trying to relieve his aching knuckles. Pain surged through his arm.

"I know your father killed your mother, Wallace."

Wallace turned quickly. The words! The words! They betrayed the monster! The highway, it was filled with chaos. The traffic, a collection of streaming pandemonium. No, no, slow down! "Slow down! Stop! Turn around! No, don't go there!" Wallace held his hands up, trying to get all the thoughts to go the right way, but they were not obeying. No, please. "Please!"

He gasped. There, the monster was looking at her! He looked at his mama, and she was talking! Saying something to the monster. Wallace screamed. When would his mama understand she didn't have to be under the monster's control? But there she was again, speaking to it as if she were its slave. Doing what it said.

"Get me my eggs!"

There. A napkin on the table. He swiped it. Good. Soft cloth. It would be comfortable. His mama trembled. But there was no time for comfort now. He would have to teach her a lesson, that she could never, ever speak to the monster.

For the monster told lies.

"I shouldn've hit ya. If you would've just brought me the eggs."

"No, Roy, I should've brought them to you. It's okay."

She would always say it was okay. Why had she said it was okay? The monster bruised her body and broke her bones. He crushed her as if she were merely one of his beloved beer cans.

She would make the excuses, invite the monster to the throne of power. "I shouldn't have done this, I shouldn't have that."

"You shouldn't have done what, Wallace?"

Wallace laughed. The monster would not be in power long. He tied the knot softly around her face. She struggled. Helplessly. And for a moment, he felt that power the monster must have felt. Her head whipped from side to side, but it was in vain. His hand rested gently on her shoulder. He was not a monster. Just the guardian.

There. Now she would no longer be able to speak to the monster. The soft white napkin hid her gentle lips. Tears poured from her eyes, and for a moment Wallace thought twice about restricting her speech. Yet it was for her own protection. She could never protect herself.

Now. What to do with the monster.

"Wallace, what are you doing?" the monster hissed. Wallace knew the fire just beneath the surface of its eyes, waiting to rage, waiting to consume.

Many years ago it had looked at him in nearly the same way. But then he was small. A boy. Never had he imagined that his life would be spent slaying the monster. But it had. And it would continue. He had been chosen for a great purpose.

Back then, the monster hardly saw him as a threat. Barely noticed him. What a mistake. What a grand mistake.

The monster's eyes roamed to his mama, and Wallace knew that he had taken a significant amount of power from it. She could no longer speak to it and that, he knew, was the beginning of its demise.

Wallace studied the new form the monster had taken. Many he had seen. All dangerous. He had defeated the monster many times, yet never could he kill it completely. The monster always came back.

And so Wallace continued to draw his sword.

"Mama, it's okay," he said without glancing over his shoulder at her. "Don't cry. It's going to be okay." But the crying continued. Wallace tried not to let it distract him. Soon she would be safe.

It was something about the eyes. Severe. Harsh. Determined.

"Don't look at her!"

Obedience. Again. He liked that.

The voices came. They clearly pointed to the white napkin left on the table. The monster was saying something to him, but the voices wanted his full attention. They had not steered him wrong before.

He took the white napkin off the table. The monster did

not deserve the comfort of its softness, but it was the only choice he had. It would be the last comfort the monster would ever know. Soon it would be destroyed, once and for all. The voices would show him how.

He did not use the gentleness as he had with his mama. He tied the knot, pulling the napkin tight around its head. For a moment, he thought he heard the voices instruct him to let it drop around the monster's throat. How easily he could cut its life off.

He heard no further instruction, so he continued the task at hand. He knew he'd driven fear into the monster's heart. Whatever fire had been kindling behind those eyes now smoldered to darkness.

Perhaps that was the key. The eyes.

chapter forty

Sweat collected in the hollow of Mick's neck. Dampness was on every inch of his skin and stuck his shirt to his back, his hair to his forehead. The napkin that blinded him was secure, tight across his eyes, though soft. He gasped for breath, as if his mouth were bound as well.

Jesus . . .

He uttered a cry for help. The shadow of death crept into the darkness before him. Did Wallace intend to kill him? or worse, kill Faith? He wanted to cry and scream all at once. Everything was out of control. He didn't know what was happening.

Listen.

Mick swallowed. *Listen. Listen.* For a moment, all he could hear was his own blood pulsing through his body, ringing in his ears. The horrible sight of it spilling onto the floor filled his mind's eye.

Listen.

He deliberately slowed his breathing. It was a small first step in gaining some sort of control. After what seemed like an eternity, his heart only raced like he'd run a long sprint. In a matter of seconds, it fell into a fast but tolerable rhythm.

Faith cried. He could hear it. Soft, like a scared little girl. Mick clenched his teeth together.

"I never forget how a person's footsteps sound," Faith's

335

gentle voice whispered to his soul. Mick sat up straight, listening intently. He could hear Wallace. He dragged both his feet across the floor in a very identifiable pattern. He was near Faith, causing Mick's muscles to seize in panic.

He knew Faith could not say anything. Her mouth was bound. *Listen,* he commanded himself. *Be still. Silent.*

He heard Wallace mumbling, and at first it sounded like the rambling gibberish of a madman. But Mick could do nothing else so he focused on every word.

"Mama, don't be scared."

Mama?

"I've just had to do this because you are powerless against the monster. You always want to cave in to the monster's insistence. You must not. It left you dead once."

Mick started to speak, but then held his tongue against the roof of his mouth. He closed his lips. Any sudden move, he realized, could be the wrong one. If he was going to do something, he would have only one chance to do it. What he could do, he didn't know yet.

Wallace continued to converse with Faith, or maybe with himself. Mick knew he was over on Faith's side of the room.

Though Mick couldn't see a thing, he still squeezed his eyes shut, trying to block out what his common sense was telling him: to sit quietly and analyze the situation with sound seemed absurd. But his choices were limited.

Sissy scratched at the back door. He hadn't heard her before, but he knew she must have been doing that the whole time. She must wonder why Faith had not let her back in.

A clock ticked from somewhere nearby. Not the wall, though. The floor. From a box. Yes, she'd packed it.

Wallace was still talking to his "mother." The way his

voice resonated with gentleness and compassion gave Mick a little comfort that nothing violent was going to take place immediately. At least not to Faith.

He listened but could hear nothing else. Smell. Yes, he could use his other senses. He tried to focus on scent. There. A floral scent. Probably a candle from one of the nearby boxes. What else?

Faith. He could smell her perfume. Just barely. It was mixed with something else, but he didn't know what. And there was a more pungent smell slicing through the others. Wallace. Sweat. Body odor. It came and went, and Mick guessed that was due to how Wallace was moving in relation to the air vents.

He waited, trying to identify more scents, but he could not. There was touch, but his hands were still tied behind the chair. His fingers moved along what he had identified earlier as leather. What could Wallace have used to tie him up? Something Wallace had brought with him? Or something Faith had in the house? He knew there was a collection of moving boxes around the room.

His fingers ran up and down the loose piece of leather that dangled against his forearm. He noticed suddenly that his arms were tied in an odd way, not the way you would tie someone if you had rope. The leather laid smoothly against his entire left forearm but not his right. Then there was this odd piece dangling down. He tried to maneuver his wrists to feel up his arm, but could only reach about halfway. On his right arm, the leather seemed to be bunched against his wrist, and there was something hard against the inside of his arm, metal maybe.

Suddenly his ears tuned back in to Wallace, whose voice seemed clearer and more distinct now. Mick listened to the way his footsteps brushed against the floor and carpet, and he knew Wallace was coming closer.

" . . . the sword is what you fear. The sword will be your demise. And I have listened to the voices, and they have told me how to rid the earth of you for eternity."

Mick forced himself to stay calm. At least if death was near, he wouldn't be able to see it coming.

Suddenly his neck screamed with pain, and his cheek burned from skin slapping skin. Wallace stood over him, battering him with the rage that had brought him to this point. Mick slowly sat back up, but he was again struck with a forceful blow, this time causing bits of white light to soar through his mind and blood to trickle into his mouth.

"Wallace . . . ," Mick managed weakly, "I did not do anything to your mother. I will not do anything to Faith. Your mind is playing tricks on you." Mick couldn't think of anything else to say, and the compartments of his brain seemed in a crooked mess of pain. Could he somehow get Wallace to snap out of the idea that he was protecting his mother?

"I trust them, not you," Wallace said, "and they tell me that you are the one that must die."

Mick had never paid much attention to the difference between his soul and his body. To him they coexisted. But at this moment he realized how very separate they were, how one might go on and the other might stay, and it would be Wallace Bledsoe who would determine that moment.

Unless God intervened. Mick's soul, the part the Spirit had comforted in the last few days, had mourned deeper than the flesh knew how, groaned a plea to the heavens that could not be interpreted by words.

In the most helpless state he'd ever known, Mick felt a strange peace that empowered him to raise his head one more time.

Wallace stared at the monster. He had full control of it. He smiled, even laughed, at how large he'd built it up to be. Now to see it panting, trembling like a scared pup . . . it perplexed and exhilarated him in a most uncanny way.

He left it alone momentarily. There was no reason to end its suffering quickly. His mother's suffering had lasted a lifetime—almost a lifetime.

"Now, Mama, I'm going to untie you. I don't want you to run. I don't want you going anywhere. The monster, he is close. He is so close." Wallace took the gun off the table. It made him feel secure to know he could pull it out any second, even though the voices had told him that this weapon was not the way to eternal extinction. He pulled at the knot of the napkin around her wrists until it fell to the floor. Mama's fingers wiggled a little, stretching themselves out of what was sure to be an uncomfortable position.

For a moment he entertained the thought of untying the napkin around her mouth, but then he thought differently. Mama was notorious for her loyalties to the monster, of being weak and vulnerable in a way that always put her in danger. That mouth of hers was always so submissive.

So he left it on.

Wallace knew he was going to have to take care of the monster, but he didn't want his mama in the room when he did it. Even though she couldn't see, she would hear, and it was going to be nothing a sweet mama needed to hear.

He tried to decide what to do with her while he did the deed. Maybe she could stand out on the back porch. But what was to say she wouldn't try to run? Mama was different these days, and he couldn't predict what she would do.

He looked at her and realized she was trying to tell him

339

something. Her words were muffled, but she was gesturing with her body. Toward the back door. Wallace turned.

He could hear the dog. Sissy. Yes. She needed Sissy. Wallace knew he couldn't be her guide forever.

"Your dog. Of course." Wallace patted his mama on the shoulder. "We won't forget her, I promise."

But his mama's eyes seemed full of worry, and his heart melted at that sight. He hated his mama to worry. He smiled, then laughed. "Mama, don't worry. I won't forget Sissy."

Mama's eyes filled with tears, though, so Wallace sighed and decided if she was going to be that upset about it, he might as well go ahead and get the dog for her. He went to the door and let the dog in. Sissy was normally a happy dog, but the way she hung her head and lowered her ears now, Wallace knew Sissy was not happy about being outdoors for so long. But Sissy was just a dog. Who cared?

Wallace walked over to the coatrack where a leash hung. He took it off and hooked it onto Sissy's collar. Then he handed the leash to his mama. "There you go," he said. "Now will you stop worrying so much?" He glanced at her, then studied the monster on the other side of the room. "You always worried about the wrong things, you know. Whether the meat was done right. The clothes perfectly ironed. The sheets clean. And what you should've been worrying about—"

Wallace froze. Outside, he heard . . . no . . . his heart sunk at the same time adrenaline rushed through his body. A car pulling to a stop in front of the house. And then another. The time was now. He had to move—and move fast.

And he also knew he had a choice to make: Save his mama or kill the monster. There was not time for both.

The voices screamed instruction inside his head, but when they got upset, he couldn't understand a single one of them. The thoughts he needed to make a decision sped through his mind in a hundred different directions.

He grabbed his mama's arm. She gasped and cried, but he didn't have time to be gentle.

In the midst of the shrieking inside his head, he knew there were orders to kill the monster. He could hear them faintly, like someone hollering beneath the wind. And though he didn't want to listen, he knew he must, because he knew they were giving him instruction on how to wipe the beast from existence. Permanently. They had been preparing him for it, whispering pieces of the plan here and there for months now. His body trembled.

The plan was complete. They were calling him to be a martyr. It would be over quickly, they assured him. Kill the beast, then kill himself. The voices would be silenced, the war would end, and the monster would be gone forever, never to hurt another human being.

Wallace glanced at his mama, quivering in his grip. How could he leave her? How could he let her go in this dark world? She knew nothing of survival, nothing of evil. She only knew how to be a servant to whoever called her to it.

Outside, a car door shut. He struggled to catch his breath. Save his mama or kill the monster. How could he make the choice? The voices urged him in one direction. His heart urged him the other way. He looked toward the back door. He could take her out there, through the gate that went into the trees, and vanish.

Or kill the monster. Kill the monster. Kill the monster. Squeezing his eyes shut, Wallace determined his way.

Mick heard one car door shut. Then he heard Wallace, Faith, and Sissy moving. He controlled himself with everything in him. *Listen.*

341

He could tell by their footsteps that Wallace was guiding Faith, rather hastily, toward the back door. But he also could hear Sissy's nails tapping against the wooden floor that led to the back door. By the gentle jingle of her collar, Mick knew Sissy was staying obediently beside Faith. He heard Wallace slide the glass door open, all the while assuring Faith this was what was best, but they needed to hurry. Mick had to assume Wallace had the gun with him.

Tuning his ears to the noises outside, Mick heard another car door shut. The authorities had arrived. But by the time they knocked, then knocked again, knocked a third time, and then huddled to try to decide if they should go check around back, Wallace and Faith would be to the trees and into the darkness. What his intentions were then was anybody's guess.

Mick's mind raced through possibilities, all of which became instant impossibilities with a second's more reflection. He knew by the way Wallace's voice wasn't reverberating off the walls inside that they were now out on the back porch.

Maybe Sissy would bark, make some noise. But the dog was obedient, well trained. How confused the dog must be at this moment, though. Then a single thought shot into Mick's conscience like a bullet, shocking his heart to a stop. Sissy. Faith had called her a guardian angel.

"A dog guide is off the clock without its harness." Mick's fingers clinched the leather strap. Guide dog. He knew there was something off about Sissy . . . the way she walked more in front than guiding beside . . .

She didn't have her harness on . . . it was used to tie Mick up. . . .

Blazing through Mick's mind were thoughts and images that seemed to be sorting themselves out, arranging letters into a single word. Then one word presented itself in his mind.

"Sissy!" he called. He heard Faith's surprised gasp and Sissy's collar ringing, indicating she'd turned her head.

Mick yelled, "Attack!"

it seemed to happen instantaneously. She heard Mick yell, and a split second later her hand stung from the rope burn left on her palm when Sissy jumped up with a horrific and frightening growl, clobbering Wallace to the ground. She knocked Faith over too. Faith scrambled out of the way, watching her dog chew at the man without mercy.

Faith wanted to scream, but she couldn't. Her mouth was still bound. Yet there was screaming. It took her several seconds to realize it was Wallace. Blood spilled onto the cement porch as Sissy's jaw snapped around Wallace's arm and tore at it as if it were weightless.

Faith looked away, then back at her dog. She knew Sissy had been trained as an attack dog. It was why she'd gotten her. But to see her like this was like watching a completely different dog.

Then Wallace locked eyes with her. Faith scrambled backward, as if his eyes could harm her. She glanced to his left, and there, several feet away, was the gun. He couldn't reach it. She looked back at him, and those terrifying eyes begged for mercy.

Faith knew the command to make Sissy retreat. But this was the man who had killed her husband. This was the man who probably would have killed her. Didn't he deserve to die slowly in the jaws of an unrelenting, vicious dog?

Then Wallace whispered, "Please . . . please . . . Mama . . ."

The man was insane. She knew it. Maybe this would put him out of his misery. The low, guttural growl of Sissy's savageness filled the silent night air. But the eyes Faith stared into were not those of a killer. They were of a meek and mild busboy who had the social skills of a gnat. Blood trickled out of the corner of Wallace's gaping mouth, his eyes wide and pleading.

Faith turned her head again. No! She would not call Sissy off! But at the same moment her mind issued that thought with finality, her heart succumbed to the deepest part of her humanity, the part where God dwelled. There a compassion that could not exist by human effort rose up and reigned in every maddening emotion, every ounce of grief, and every thought of hate until she found herself clawing at the back of her head, trying to untie the knot. Her hands shook horribly, and the knot was tied so tightly. She stared with horror at Wallace's body, now a mangled mess of blood and flesh. He was fighting less, his strength draining by the second.

At last a thumbnail loosened the knot behind her head, and within a matter of seconds, she'd freed the knot enough to pull the napkin away from her mouth. It dropped around her neck. She opened her mouth to shout the command. But what filled the air was not her voice.

It was a gunshot.

Then the night was silent, until all she could hear were her own screams. Next to Wallace's limp body was Sissy. She heard her dog whimper; then Sissy laid her head down, unconscious.

Two men worked feverishly behind Mick, trying to get his hands loose from the harness that bound him.

"Hurry!" Mick yelled.

All he could hear was Faith screaming, which in one sense comforted him because he knew she was still alive. He craned his neck, trying to see what was going on outside. There were police officers darting here and there.

The front door of the house was still open from where the police officers had kicked it in, and as Mick glanced to it, Abigail rushed in, eyes roaming the room until she spotted him.

"Are you okay?" she asked, running to him and falling to her knees at his side.

"What's going on out there?" Mick asked. "Is Faith okay?" But Abigail didn't have a chance to answer. The officers loosened his hands and Mick leapt up, knocking the chair over as he ran outside, where he saw Wallace on the ground, surrounded by EMTs. A couple yards away Faith was crumpled against the side of the house, shivering and crying uncontrollably. A female police officer was kneeling beside her.

"Faith!" Mick called as he rushed to her side.

Faith's hands clung to his shirt as she buried her face into his shoulder. Mick made her look at him. "Are you all right?"

She nodded, still crying. She glanced over toward where Wallace was lying. "I can't believe it. . . . "

He embraced her. "Don't think about it. Everything's okay."

"They shot Sissy," Faith cried. "They shot her."

Mick looked around. He couldn't see the dog. There were three people standing around her. Mick stroked

Faith's hair, watching her wet eyes glimmer in the moon-
light.

"How did you know?" she asked.

"Know what?"

"About Sissy? How did you know she was an attack
dog?"

"I'm not sure. Without being able to see, I guess my
mind went into overdrive. I knew Wallace had tied me with
her harness, and I remembered a guy told me guide dogs
are off the clock whenever they don't have a harness on. It
just came together at the right time, I guess." Mick pulled
her hair away from her face. "God saved us tonight, Faith."

Faith nodded, more tears spilling from her eyes. Just
then a man approached them and looked at Faith. "What's
your dog's name, ma'am?"

"Sissy," Faith whispered.

The man smiled. "She's going to be fine. We just got
her with a tranquilizer gun."

Faith's eyes widened with surprise. "She's not dead?"

"Nope. Just gonna be asleep for a while, that's all."

Mick looked at the huddle of EMTs. "What about
Wallace?"

The officer glanced over his shoulder. "Too early to say.
They're working on him. But both of you need to get to the
hospital to get checked over."

"I'm fine," Faith said. She looked at Mick. "You don't
look so good, though."

"I'd feel better if you both went," the officer insisted,
helping Faith to her feet. "You can ride together with Officer Sherman if you'd like." He gestured toward the female
officer standing a few feet away.

Mick took Faith's hand. "Come on. Let's get out of
here."

"What about Sissy?" Faith asked the officer.

He grinned. "Well, I'll stay with her until she wakes up. Go take care of yourself, ya hear?"

Mick led Faith around the corner of the house as they followed Officer Sherman. As they walked across the front lawn, Abigail approached them. She looked at Mick. "Are you all right?"

"I'm fine. Abigail, this is Faith Kemper. Faith, Dr. Abigail Grenard. She figured out that Wallace was the one we were looking for."

Abigail shook her head. "Notoriously humble, this man. Mick, we should've done more sooner. I'm sorry."

"Don't be sorry. It turned out okay. Thanks for believing me."

"Tom and Reggie are on their way. I'll send them to the hospital." Abigail stepped aside and patted Mick on the shoulder as he walked past.

Mick helped Faith into the back of the police cruiser. A small crowd of neighbors had gathered, but a police line kept them back.

"You look like you've been hit by a truck," Faith said with a small smile. "Sissy is a retired K-9 dog I adopted. She's so well trained that she wouldn't have attacked Wallace until I gave her the command. But she knew. I saw it in her eyes. She knew I was in trouble."

Mick squeezed her hand. Too many emotions were crawling up his throat for him to say anything. For the first time in his life, the wailing of sirens brought him comfort. He listened quietly as he held Faith's hand in his. The noise faded as they drove out of the neighborhood and toward the hospital.

chapter forty-two

mick opened the front door of the house for Faith, noticing that some of the officers must've fixed the doorframe they'd busted the night before. The glory of morning seemed to have wiped the slate clean. Sissy excitedly greeted Faith at the door.

"Hey, girl!" Faith squatted and let the dog lick her face. She hugged her neck and scratched her ears. "Good girl! Good girl!"

"She looks good," Mick said as they watched Sissy bound across the living room.

"Officer Johnson said she might not eat too well today, but tomorrow she'll be back to normal." He watched Faith walk to the back porch and stare at the empty cement. "I guess they washed it off with a hose. It's like nothing happened here. Look, even the chairs are put back into place."

"They did all the crime-scene investigation last night."

She turned to him. "You look terrible!"

Mick rubbed the cuts and bruises along his face. "Yeah. I finally got a glimpse of myself in the mirror. Did you get any sleep?"

"A little. You?"

"Maybe a couple of hours. Reggie's going to drive me back home today."

Faith glanced away, her face solemnly responding to his words. She turned and straightened a pillow on the couch. "Did you hear anything about Wallace?"

"He was in surgery last night for a few hours. But he's going to make it."

Faith nodded, then looked around the house. "I'm going to stay here. In Bakerville."

Mick grinned. "Really?"

"Yeah. I feel more at home here than anywhere. I don't know why. Maybe I'm tired of running. Dixie's a great person, a great friend. And I like her pastor. And that church. I think this is a good place to start the first day of the rest of my life." Faith fell onto the couch and stared at the ceiling. "Dixie called me at the hospital. I told her not to come and that I'd call her when I got home." She glanced at Mick, who sat down in the chair next to the couch. "I've got to tell her."

"Tell her?"

"I'm not blind." Faith hid her eyes with her hands and growled out a sigh. "I'm so scared."

"Of what?"

"Of what she'll think. I love Dixie. She's become a good friend. How am I supposed to tell her that all this time I could see her? I mean, that's like the ultimate invasion of privacy. It is going to make her feel vulnerable. Violated, for crying out loud."

Mick stood and moved next to Faith on the couch. "She has to know the truth. Friendship has to be based on truth."

"I know." Faith wiped at her tired eyes. "You taught me that." She shook her head. "It's just going to shock the daylights out of her."

"I think she'll be okay."

"I'm not even sure I can say it, Mick. I mean, how do I tell someone I've been lying to them all this time?"

"She'll understand."

"You don't know that for sure." Faith sighed. "She could hate my guts forever."

"You're doing the right thing by telling her. After that, it's up to Dixie."

Faith slowly closed her eyes, as if processing a plan. Then she looked at Mick. "So you're leaving today."

Mick nodded. "Reggie stayed with me at the hospital last night. He went to grab some breakfast before picking me up." Mick cleared his throat. "I wanted to spend a little time with you before I left."

She smiled at him and took his hand. "Thank you." Then she leaned forward. "Feel like taking a walk?"

Radiant and delicate sunlight offset by a cool, gentle breeze provided the perfect setting for their morning walk, which Faith said would take about twenty minutes. "I know Dixie didn't sleep a wink last night worrying about me," Faith said as they walked the lonely sidewalks of the town toward Dixie's house. "She'll be glad to know I'm okay." Faith's hand pushed her sunglasses up her nose, as if to remind herself they were still there, but now for a different purpose.

After a few moments of silence, Mick said, "You know, what happened last night was pretty crazy. Are you okay? It was a close call, and I want you to know that if you're still freaked out about it, that's normal. I'm here to talk if you need that."

She smiled at him. "Thank you. But I'm fine. More than fine. It's given me a tremendous sense of confidence."

"Really?"

"God protected me even when I didn't want His protection. That builds confidence, doesn't it?" She laughed.

Mick and Faith continued to walk, talking about the

future, their lives, their intentions to stay in touch. Mick wanted to tell Faith the feelings he had for her, but he didn't have to. In the way their arms brushed against each other as they walked, Mick knew that she knew. And maybe down the road there would be room in her life for another relationship.

Mick smiled at the thought of how the timing for love in his life had always missed the mark by mere inches. *One of these days,* he told himself, *you're going to hit the bull's-eye, my friend.*

Dixie's apartment was just two blocks away, and Mick found himself slowing his pace, just to get a little more time with Faith. But suddenly Faith stopped.

"You okay?" he asked.

Her smile was strained, but she nodded. She glanced toward Dixie's apartment complex. "I'm a little nervous. I don't know if I can do this."

Mick took her hands. "You can. I'll help you."

A heavy swallow contradicted the confident grin she'd mustered up. "What if she hates me?"

"Don't ask what if. Just do what you know is right. God will take care of the rest. He knows how to handle Dixie."

She nodded. "Mick?"

"Yeah?"

"Don't give up on love."

Mick cocked an eyebrow. "You think I would?"

She stared at the sidewalk at their feet. "You have a lot to offer." She looked at him, a bashful glow illuminating her cheeks. "You're going to make some woman really happy someday."

Mick laughed out his embarrassment. "Yes, well, hopefully before I'm eighty."

She grinned and squeezed his hands. "Whoever gets you is going to be one lucky lady. And I mean that."

Mick tore his gaze away from hers and nodded. "Thanks."

"Mick?"

"Yeah?"

"What was her name?"

"Whose name?"

"Your lost love. The woman who went off and married the 'better guy,' as you put it."

"Why do you want to know her name?"

Faith shrugged. "I don't know. I guess you've spoken of her, but I don't know her name."

Mick sighed. "I haven't said her name to another soul for years."

"Maybe it's time to say it then. Come on . . . what was her name?"

"Jenny."

Faith repeated him. "Jenny. That's a nice name. I've never met a Jenny I didn't like. She sounds really sweet. Like someone you'd want to watch a thunderstorm with."

"I've probably seen enough storms for a lifetime. But I know she married the better man."

"Sometimes it's easier for us to see the good in other people."

"Yeah, I guess so." A quiet moment let Mick shift topics. "Do you know what a splitting storm is?"

"No idea."

"It's a massive storm that splits in two. One part dies out and becomes nonthreatening. The other part, though, becomes this supercell. One part Juarez, one part Bledsoe." Mick shook his head. "Or maybe that's who Wallace is. One part was a gentle shower, but the other part became something terrible. Maybe we're all like a storm about to split in two."

Faith grinned. "You should've been a meteorologist. Everything comes back to the weather for you."

"And sit behind a desk pointing at a blank screen? No thanks. I'll take storm chasing any day of the week."

"Well," Faith said, stroking his fingers, "are you at least going to tell me why you're so freaked out by food?"

Mick laughed, then pointed to the apartment complex. "Now come on. Stop stalling. It's time to go see Dixie."

"You're not going to tell me?"

"It's a whole other story, my friend. You couldn't appreciate it without hearing it in its entirety. Besides, it happened over ten years ago."

"Maybe someday then."

"Definitely."

They walked up to the apartment complex. Faith dragged her feet as they approached Dixie's door.

"God help me," she mumbled.

"Faith!" Dixie's whole face lit up with a mixture of surprise and excitement as she pulled Faith into a gigantic hug. "Oh, I'm so sorry! Are you okay? Did I hurt you? You look fine. Are you all right?"

Faith smiled and tried to rebalance. She pushed her sunglasses back up her nose, reminding herself that these were going to need to come off very soon. But not yet. Her heart thumped its fearful protest.

"Where's Sissy? Is she okay?"

"She's fine," Faith assured her. "Can we come in?"

"Of course! I'm so sorry! Hi, Agent Kline. Goodness! Look at you! You look terrible!" Dixie shouted every word like a fan at a football game.

"Hi, Dixie," Mick said.

Faith stepped a few feet into the apartment and

stopped. Dixie turned around, as if wondering why Faith had stopped. But Faith didn't want to play the part anymore; she knew the time was now. Dixie was firing off a rapid succession of questions about last night with hardly a breath in between.

Finally Faith held up her hands. "Dixie, I'll explain everything that happened in a moment. But first, there's something very important I have to tell you." Shame and fear cavorted around her. Inside her head she thought of all the various reactions she might get from Dixie. Her imagination twisted Dixie's face into an angry scowl, yelling at her. Faith blinked away the image and looked at Dixie, who had a kind and expectant look on her face.

"Yes? What is it?" Dixie asked.

Faith bit her lip and took of her sunglasses. She stared directly into Dixie's eyes. Dixie gasped in astonishment, covering her mouth with her hand and blinking so rapidly Faith thought she might be on the verge of passing out.

All Faith could utter was, "Dixie, I can see." Faith waited, wondering what kind of harsh words were about to fill her ears. She deserved every one, so she braced herself for whatever Dixie was going to say.

"It's a miracle!" Dixie cried.

Faith glanced at Mick, who was grinning.

"It's a miracle from God! You can see! Faith can see!"

Faith put up a finger and stuttered out a protest. "B-but . . . wait . . . Dixie . . . you don't understand. . . . "

"It's a miracle! It's a miracle!" Dixie was jumping up and down around her living room, raising her hands and laughing.

"Dixie, wait! I need to explain!"

"Honey, the proof is in the picture! Here you are, looking at me like you've never missed a day of sight in your life! Praise the Lord!"

"But—"

"I have to go call Pastor! I'll be right back! Don't move!"

"Dixie, wait!"

But Dixie was singsonging herself to a back bedroom in a joyful saunter. Faith threw up her hands and turned to Mick. "Now what?"

Mick was chuckling heartily. "My brother's favorite baseball player was Tug McGraw. And you know what Tug used to say?"

Faith shook her head.

"You gotta believe." Mick shrugged and laughed. "Sometimes you just gotta believe."

acknowledgments

there are so many people who work behind the scenes to get a book out of the head of the writer and onto the shelves for the reader. The hardworking team at Tyndale made this process smooth and fun. I'd like to thank Jamie Cain and Jan Stob, my wonderful editors, for all their encouragement and dynamic suggestions to make this book the best it could be. Thanks also to Becky Nesbitt for her guidance of the team. Travis, Anne, Andrea, Linda—thanks for all you do and for being such fun to hang out with!

Thanks also to Janet Kobobel Grant, the most awesome agent in the whole world! I'm glad we're teammates.

Thanks to Terry Phelps and Amy Gutteridge for reading this book and helping to make it better than it was. Your suggestions and enthusiasm for the project were terrific!

Special thanks to the following: Ron Wheatley—you know this would not be possible without you. Thanks for your keen insight and your amazing research help. I'm indebted to you. Bill Engleking—thanks for reading the book, for your suggestions and research, and your amazing positive attitude, even during gut-wrenching trials in your life. Thanks to Richard Ray Jr. and Dr. Brad Fielding for helping me with specific research in this book.

Thank you to my prayer partners. You know all the reasons why. You've made a tremendous difference in my writing and my life.

And thanks to The Flock That Rocks, Pastor Paul, and all my friends and family for your unending support and encouragement. And thanks to all my writer friends, who continue to be a source of inspiration for me.

Sean, my dear husband, I could not do this without you. You never cease to amaze me with your love and support. I am the luckiest girl alive! John Caleb and Cate—I love you, dear ones.

And my Lord, every day I get to do this is a gift from You.